K.D. Richards is a native of th[...]
who now lives outside Toronto [...]
sons. You can find her at kdrichardsbooks.com

Beth Cornelison began working in public relations before
pursuing her love of writing romance. She has won
numerous honours for her work, including a nomination for
the RWA *RITA* Award for *The Christmas Stranger*. She
enjoys featuring her cats (or friends' pets) in her stories and
always has another book in the pipeline! She currently lives
in Louisiana with her husband, one son and three spoiled
cats. Contact her via her website, bethcornelison.com

DEATH BY DATA

K.D. RICHARDS

COLTON'S SECOND CHANCE

BETH CORNELISON

MILLS & BOON

First Published in Great Britain 2025
by Mills & Boon, an imprint of HarperCollins*Publishers* Ltd
1 London Bridge Street, London, SE1 9GF

www.harpercollins.co.uk

HarperCollins*Publishers*
Macken House, 39/40 Mayor Street Upper,
Dublin 1, D01 C9W8, Ireland

Special thanks and acknowledgment are given to Beth Cornelison
for her contribution to *The Coltons of Alaska* series.

ISBN: 978-0-263-39736-9

1125

MIX
Paper | Supporting
responsible forestry
FSC
www.fsc.org
FSC™ C007454

DEATH BY DATA

K.D. RICHARDS

To my mother, Delria.
Thank you for the unwavering support.

Chapter One

A sharp clatter jerked Lisa Elkins out of a shallow sleep. She never slept well when her sixteen-year-old daughter wasn't at home. It didn't matter that she was spending the summer with her father in Paris. The distance only put Lisa more on edge. She listened, trying to determine where the noise had come from.

Seconds stretched into minutes, but all she heard was the sound of rain beating on the roof. It had probably just been a possum or a squirrel getting into her neighbor's trash bin, but she was fully awake now with no chance of getting back to sleep. She glanced at the bedside clock. Four a.m., a full hour earlier than she usually woke, but she rose anyway and headed downstairs to the kitchen and to her morning coffee.

She'd been up late the night before, working on a proposal to update the online security for a law firm client of her cybersecurity business. She'd be forever grateful to her attorney ex-husband for many things, their daughter, Layla, first and foremost. But he'd always been the biggest champion of the small firm that she was a partner in. A good number of the clients she'd brought to the company were law firms referred by Charles. The downside of being in demand was long nights and little sleep, but she wasn't complaining.

Thunder boomed, and lightning crackled in the sky behind the kitchen window as her coffee brewed. She reached into the fridge to grab cream when a sound from the living room sent her heart rate spiking. She froze, the hair on the back of her neck rising.

She pulled a knife from the butcher block on the counter and slipped her phone from her pocket with the other hand to dial 911.

As a single woman, she'd mentally run through all the possible ways out of her house hundreds of times. To get to the back door, she'd have to go down the short hallway between the kitchen and living room. Right past the room that appeared to have an intruder. But the window in the laundry room was big enough for her to crawl out of.

"911, what is your emergency?"

"I think there's an intruder in my home," she said as she slid into the laundry room and closed the door.

"What is your address?"

She gave the operator her information, tucking the phone between her shoulder and chin while she pushed the ironing board against the door. It wasn't much, but the washer and dryer were too heavy to move.

"Ma'am, can you tell me your name?"

"Lisa Elkins."

"And where is the intruder?"

"In the living room, I think. I'm in my laundry room. I think I can get out of the window."

"Lisa, I want you to stay on the line with me. I have officers responding to your house now. They will be at your location in five minutes."

Five minutes.

She wasn't sure she had that much time. She just needed

to get out and to the safety of a neighbor's house. But the window had opened six inches and gotten stuck.

The doorknob rattled behind her. Her heartbeat raced as adrenaline surged through her body.

"He's at the door," she said into the phone, trying to keep panic at bay. There was no need to be quiet since the intruder obviously knew she was inside the room. She banged on the windowsill attempting to loosen the sash.

"Lisa…are you still there?" the 911 operator called out.

The laundry room door burst open.

Lisa turned, dropping the phone. She pulled the knife from her robe pocket, holding it out in front of her with trembling hands. "Stop right there. The cops are already on the way."

The man, clad in black and wearing a ski mask so only his dark green eyes showed through, ignored her. He lunged forward, slapping at her hands hard enough that she dropped the knife.

Pain vibrated through her body as her back collided with the wall. Her head spun, and stars danced across her vision.

"Where is the code?" he asked.

She pulled at the heavy arm that held her against the wall without moving it at all. "What code?"

"I know Scott gave it to you, and I want it. Now," the man growled.

Her mind fought to process the words. Scott. Could he mean Scott Donlea? She had no idea what he was talking about, but one thing was clear: this man was no ordinary burglar.

"Who are you?" she asked.

"That's not your concern," he said. "Give me the code."

Lisa fought back tears, her entire body trembling with fear. "I don't know what you're talking about."

He shook her. "I know you're lying."

She began to protest, but his beefy hands went to her throat, constricting her airway.

He slammed her hard against the wall again. Five minutes. Plenty of time to hurt or even kill her if he wanted to.

Lisa formed a fist with her right hand and swung, catching him on the side of his nose. The impact reverberated up her arm. His grip loosened, likely out of shock rather than any real damage, and the man stumbled backward. She sucked in a breath, knowing she didn't have a lot of time before he recovered.

She kicked and punched with all the fear and fury she felt. The chaotic pummeling was sufficient to get the man to shuffle away from the door. She gave him one more strong shove and raced from the laundry room.

It seemed like miles to her front door, but she finally burst outside just as a police cruiser turned the corner, its sirens blaring. She hopped off her porch and ran down the driveway toward it, with a glance over her shoulder.

A shadowy, black clad figure hovered at the door. His menacing green eyes locked on her.

The cruiser pulled to a stop in front of her house, and Lisa instinctively put her hands in the air.

The officer jumped from the car with his hand on the butt of his gun. "Ma'am, are you the 911 caller?"

"Yes. The intruder… He attacked me. He is still in the house." She turned back toward the door which still stood open, but the doorway was empty.

THE SUN HAD just started to peek through the darkness when Detective Isaiah Reeves ducked under the crime scene tape just after 7:00 a.m. The CSI unit and the first responding officers had already taped off the scene in the usually quiet park.

He had played in this park as a child, swinging on the swings and jumping off the metal sliding board. The slide was made of plastic now, and the swings were gone. The entire playground was far more colorful and a lot safer, but at least he could say that there had never been a body in the park when he was a kid.

He stepped over to the bench where his partner, Detective Connie Lui, was already examining their victim. They'd worked several cases together since he transferred from the Chicago Police Department. He found her to be focused and very good at what she did. Every case he and Connie had tackled together in his six months on the Washington, DC, force had run smoothly and by the book, and he knew it was because of her experience and finely honed instincts. She was highly regarded among their colleagues.

Connie stepped away from the body. "Glad you could make it, Isaiah."

"Sorry I'm late," Isaiah said. "Rush-hour traffic."

"I'm just poking at you." Connie retied the band holding her dark hair in a ponytail while she spoke. "I know how bad rush hour can be. And it's not like this guy's going anywhere."

Isaiah shifted his attention away from Connie to the body slumped over the picnic table. Appearing to be in his mid-thirties, the victim was wearing beige khakis and a white collared T-shirt. A gun lay in the grass inches from the man's right hand.

"The medical examiner isn't here yet, but there are no marks on him other than the gunshot wound to the head," Connie said.

"This seems like a strange place to commit suicide. Maybe the park held some significance for him?"

"Maybe. It would have been deserted at night. No one to see him or stop him. And he still had his wallet with his credit cards and some cash in it, along with his phone."

"So, we are not looking at a robbery. Who is he?"

Connie looked down at her notes. "According to his driver's license, his name is Scott Donlea. He's thirty-six years old and lives a few miles from here."

Isaiah glanced back toward the street. "Miles? How did he get here then?"

"We found his car parked a block away."

"So, he drives several miles from his home to a random park and kills himself?" Isaiah shook his head. The scenario didn't make sense. They were missing something. "Who found the body?"

"A city maintenance man when he came to mow the grass. He said he found him about an hour ago. When he realized the man was not just a homeless person trying to get some shut-eye, he called 911." Connie pointed across the lawn to a man in a green jumpsuit. "He says he didn't hear anything or see anyone. And from the looks of it, Mr. Donlea has been dead for a few hours. I doubt we'll find any witnesses. Certainly no one is willing to admit to being in the park in the middle of the night."

Technically the park closed after dark, although that had never stopped anyone from using it at night.

Isaiah turned back to the body. "So why would this guy come to this specific park in the middle of the night and shoot himself?"

"If he did," Connie responded.

Isaiah was relieved to hear that Connie was thinking

along the same lines as he was. Something about this wasn't right. "Did we find anything else helpful?"

"His phone was in his pocket, but we couldn't unlock it, of course. There was a business card in his wallet." Connie handed Isaiah the bagged card. "It's for a cybersecurity architect named Lisa Elkins."

"Lisa Elkins." A memory surfaced in Isaiah's head. "I know her."

Connie's brow rose. "How?"

Isaiah stomped his feet in an attempt to ward off the cold trying to settle there. "We were in graduate school together at Georgetown University. I was in law school with the guy she was dating, and we got to be friends."

Connie flashed him a look of surprise. "Isaiah, have you been holding out on me? I didn't know you went to law school."

He chuckled. "Well, I don't share that with just anyone. I graduated from Georgetown Law. I sat for the bar and everything before I realized I didn't want to prosecute the bad guys. I wanted to catch them."

"Well, I, for one, am glad you had that realization. So, tell me, this cybersecurity architect, were you and she…?"

"No," he responded quickly. "We were just friends."

"Right," Connie agreed. "Well, it looks like you'll be renewing old acquaintances." She glanced at the watch on her arm. "Why don't you go have a quick chat with the maintenance man before we release him? I'll try to get a hold of Lisa Elkins."

Isaiah gave her a small smile. "Sure thing."

Lisa Elkins. A memory washed over him. Lisa, with her lithe runner's build, hunched over a glowing computer screen in the campus library while he and his friend Charles struggled to understand the rule against perpetuities. Or the way her eyes lit up when she talked about the latest horror flick or some arcane coding language. He'd had a mad crush on her, but she'd been dating Charles, so it had been hands off.

He wasn't surprised to learn that she had a fancy-sounding job. She'd been whip-smart back then and one of the hardest workers he'd ever met.

He crossed the expansive lawn to where the maintenance worker stood still giving a statement to a uniformed officer. "Mr. Langford, I'm Detective Isaiah Reeves. I'm sorry to keep you waiting."

"No problem, but I would like to get out of here. Finding a dead body is not exactly part of my job description."

"I'm sure it was jarring. I won't hold you for long. I'd just like to get a good picture of what happened when you found the body."

"I gave a statement to the officer here and told him everything I know."

"Tell it one more time for me, please."

"It's simple. I came to cut the grass early before the parents bring their kids. I mow the lawn here every two weeks. That's the city's schedule."

"Did you hear anything when you arrived? Gunshots maybe?"

Langford shook his head. "No, I'm sorry. It was quiet. Just a regular day until…"

"Did you recognize the man?" Isaiah asked.

Another headshake. "No. I've never seen him in the park."

"And you didn't see anyone else around when you arrived?"

"Not today. Sometimes there are homeless people who sleep here, but there was no one here except me this morning."

And the dead guy, but Isaiah kept that thought to himself. He asked the maintenance worker a few more questions, but the man had nothing else that could help them. Isaiah was handing the worker his card when Connie strolled to his side.

"This case just got infinitely weirder," she said.

"Weirder? How?"

"Your friend Lisa Elkins? She called 911 early this morning to report an intruder in her home. By the time the first responding officers arrived at her house, she'd gotten away from the guy who also managed to evade capture. But the uniform said she was lucky. The assailant had banged her up pretty good." Connie's brows went up. "It looked like the intruder was trying to kill her."

Chapter Two

Lisa forced herself to draw in a slow, deep breath. The uniformed officers that responded to her 911 call had searched the neighborhood for the intruder, but they had not found the man. After they took her statement, they insisted she go to the hospital to be checked out. She'd spent a couple of hours in the emergency room, and although her throat was still sore, the doctor had given her a clean bill of health.

Now she stood in her own living room, having shooed away more than one of her neighbors. Her Takoma Park, Maryland, neighborhood was usually a sleepy community of professionals and families that wasn't used to crime. She'd already heard murmurings about starting a neighborhood watch.

She couldn't say she blamed people for wanting to organize. She wouldn't feel safe in her own home until the police caught the guy who had broken in.

The intruder had been looking for a code. A code he thought Scott had given her. She'd attempted to call Scott while she waited in the hospital, but the call had gone straight to voicemail.

Scott, what have you gotten me into?

The doorbell rang, and she let out a startled yelp.

"Miss Elkins? It's MPD. Are you okay?"

Lisa pressed her hand to her chest, willing her heartbeat to slow. After a moment, she went to the door. MPD. Shorthand for the DC Metropolitan Police Department. Probably following up on the break-in report. Still, she gingerly pushed aside the curtain on the window next to the door, assessing the two people standing on her porch.

An Asian woman in burgundy trench coat, black slacks, and low-heeled boots, and a Black man in a dark suit and white button-down shirt, and no coat. They both had the hard-eyed look of cops, but she wasn't taking any chances after what had happened earlier that morning.

"Could you hold your badges up, please?" Lisa said.

They did as she asked. The badges looked authentic, but they could have been fakes.

Stop it. She wouldn't let this intruder make her afraid in her own home. She took a deep breath and opened the door.

"Miss Elkins, I'm Detective Isaiah Reeves, and this is my partner, Detective Connie Lui."

Lisa felt her breath catch as the man from her past stepped into her present. "Isaiah Reeves? You graduated from Georgetown University, right?"

She focused on his face, seeing the younger guy she'd known years ago in the handsome man who stood before her now. He'd definitely retained the raw magnetism he'd had at twenty-five years old. His hair was cut shorter, and she could see the beginnings of gray peeking out around his temples. But his jawline was still sharp and defined as it had been when they'd been in school. His piercing brown eyes bore into hers, and she felt her heart skip a beat.

Isaiah's eyes crinkled, and his mouth curved up in a smile. "You have a good memory. It's good to see you again, Lisa, albeit under less-than-ideal circumstances."

"You're a cop?"

"Yeah, it turns out I was right about a career in law, just not exactly how I thought I'd do it," he answered.

"Wow. It's good to see you. Well, not really." She stopped and tried to collect her thoughts. "I just mean because you're the police, and I was attacked. Not that I'm unhappy to see you." She forced her mouth closed before she could put her fist any further inside.

Isaiah's smile spread, and he held up his hand. "I get it. Don't worry about it. You've been through a lot today."

Lisa stepped aside and let the detectives into the house before she closed the door. "So, you're with the burglary unit?"

He glanced at his partner. "Homicide, actually."

Her eyes narrowed, mind spinning, trying to make sense of the information she'd given her. "Why would homicide respond to a break-in?"

"Unfortunately, we think your break-in is related to a death that may have occurred either late last night or this morning."

"May have occurred?" She led them into her living room, but none of them took a seat.

"It's not clear what the manner of death is at the moment, but we are proceeding as if it's a suspicious death until we are sure," Detective Lui answered.

"That sounds awful, but I'm not sure how this death would have anything to do with my break-in."

"Do you know Scott Donlea?" Isaiah asked.

Lisa felt her heart sink. "Yes."

Isaiah and Detective Lui shared another look before Isaiah spoke again. "Lisa, I'm sorry to have to tell you this, but Mr. Donlea's body was found early this morning."

"He's dead?" Lisa felt her knees start to buckle. She sank onto her sofa.

"Can I get you some water?" Detective Lui asked.

Lisa waved her off. "No. No, I'll be fine. I'm just... I can't believe it. I saw him yesterday. We met for coffee."

Detective Lui kept her keen eyes trained on Lisa. "How did you know Scott?"

"Scott and I were in the same graduate school class for computer sciences. He emailed me out of the blue two days ago. He wanted to meet for coffee. We met yesterday around lunchtime at a coffee shop near my office."

Detective Lui held her pen poised over her notepad. "The name of the coffee shop?"

Lisa gave it to her.

"What did you and Scott talk about?" Isaiah asked gently.

Lisa's mind churned. Scott was dead. Scott was dead, and the police were in her living room questioning her. The voice of her ex-husband sounded in her head, warning her not to say another word without a lawyer. She had spoken to a man who was now dead under what appeared to be suspicious circumstances, if the two homicide detectives standing in her living room were any indication.

But if she could help them find out what happened to Scott, she was going to do it.

"He wanted to know if I had any contacts on the West Coast. Said he was thinking about moving out there and getting a fresh start now that he was divorced. I told him I hadn't heard of anyone specifically that was looking to hire, but that I'd reach out to a few people I knew in Seattle."

"How did Scott seem? Was he nervous? Did he appear depressed at all?" Isaiah asked.

"Well, as I mentioned, I hadn't seen him in years, so I don't really have a reference point, but he did seem a little off."

"Off how?" Isaiah pressed.

Lisa took a deep breath, then let it out slowly. "Like anxious. He kept glancing out the coffee shop's window. Like he was looking for someone. I didn't think much of it, though."

She closed her eyes, letting the memory of their coffee meetup just two days ago wash over her. The faint aroma of freshly brewed coffee wafted through the air and mingled with the faint scent of pastries. The busy chatter of other café patrons and the clinking of glasses. Scott had clearly been on edge. His fingers had tapped nervously on his cup the entire time they spoke, and he'd avoided making eye contact with her when she asked if he was okay.

A knot formed in her stomach, unease settling in her chest. She couldn't shake off the feeling that he wanted to tell her something important. She couldn't help wondering if there was something she could have done for him.

She relayed all this to Isaiah and Detective Lui. "After he asked me about contacts on the West Coast, we chatted a bit. We both have daughters, mine a teen and his a preteen, and we'd both been through divorces around the same time, so we commiserated about that. Maybe he was a little sad about the divorce." She shrugged. "Divorce is rarely a high point in one's life. We finished our coffee, and I had to get back to the office."

Detective Lui looked up from her notes. "We found your business card in his pocket."

"I gave him my business card, but he didn't give me his. Frankly, I got the impression that things weren't going so well for him professionally, hence the consideration he was giving to moving to the West Coast. The whole coffee date took maybe thirty minutes. Probably less. I had a meeting I needed to prepare for. I almost canceled, but since Scott reached out to me out of the blue, I figured whatever he wanted must be important to him. And truthfully, I was a bit curious."

"Okay." Detective Lui looked up from her notebook.

"Tell us about the man who broke into your home this morning," Isaiah said. "Do you have any idea who he was?"

Remnants of terror ran through her at the memory of the man's hands on her. "Not at all. And I couldn't give the officers a detailed description. He wore dark clothes and a ski mask. And he had green eyes."

"Do you know how the intruder got in?" Detective Lui sat on the arm of the sofa.

"One of the officers who responded said it looked like he got in by breaking the lock on the sliding glass door." Lisa pointed to the rear of the house.

Isaiah glanced at his notes. "Did the man say anything?"

She hesitated at the question, remembering his words. "He said he wanted the codes Scott had given me. But I have no idea what he's talking about."

"Like a code to an alarm system? Or a bank code?" Detective Lui asked.

"I don't think so. He said, 'I know Scott gave you the code.'"

Isiah frowned, looking at Lisa with a mix of caution and suspicion that made her uneasy. "Why would the intruder think Mr. Donlea gave you something?"

Lisa chewed her bottom lip, a habit she'd picked up as a child when she was nervous. She couldn't seem to shake it as an adult. "I don't know. He didn't. Give me anything, that is."

Isaiah and his partner asked several more questions and several of the same questions in slightly different ways.

When they asked, Lisa showed them the email she'd received from Scott and let them take a look at her phone log.

She shook her head. "I'm sorry. I wish I could help more."

"You've helped a lot." Isaiah rose, followed by Detective Lui.

Lisa followed them both to the door. "If there is anything else I can do to help, please let me know. It had been a while since I'd seen Scott, but he was a friend once upon a time. He didn't deserve to be killed, and I'd like to know that the guy who broke into my house is caught and prosecuted."

Isaiah put his hand over hers and squeezed. "I promise you we'll do our best to find justice for you and Mr. Donlea. You have my word on that."

THE CHAOTIC SYMPHONY of ringing phones, murmuring voices, and clacking keyboards swirled around Isaiah. He was barely aware of it, his gaze fixed on the blinking cursor on the screen in front of him.

His mind had wandered back to Lisa, not for the first time since he'd left her house earlier that day. The memories flooded his thoughts and distracted him from his job well into the early afternoon.

God, she was beautiful. Even more so now than when they were young. The years had only enhanced her allure, adding a depth and maturity to her already elegant features that made his heart race. He could still smell the faint scent of her perfume, a delicate blend of jasmine and vanilla. When their hands had briefly touched, he'd felt a surge of electricity, igniting every nerve ending.

He remembered too the fear he'd seen in her eyes when she described the break-in at her house. His jaw clenched, his fingers curling into fists on top of his keyboard.

"I've got to find that bastard," he muttered, refocusing on his screen with grim determination. A man that would terrorize a woman in her home, a man that might very well be involved in a murder, needed to be taken off the street as soon as possible.

Connie bounded through the door to their shared office space, waving a manila folder. "Got the background on Scott Donlea," she announced, dropping it onto his desk.

Isaiah leaned back, flipping open the file. "What've we got?"

Connie settled into her chair across from him. "Married, one daughter. Though he and the wife—Emily—are separated."

"Legally?" Isaiah asked, skimming the report.

"Yep. He's got a brother, Todd Donlea, a security guard at a small private airport in Fauquier County."

Isaiah's brow furrowed. "Interesting. We'll need to talk to both of them—Emily and Todd. Hopefully they can shed some light on what might have landed Scott dead on a park bench."

He cast a quick glance up at Connie, taking in the sharp intelligence that sparkled in her eyes. She was more than good, she was exceptional—one of the most skilled detectives he had ever worked with. Second only to Brand.

Isaiah's heart clenched, his mind drifting back to the hospital waiting room, the sterile white walls that seemed to close in on him with each passing moment. The overpowering smell of disinfectant and the underlying scent of fear and grief filled his nose. He could still see the doctor's face in his mind's eye, grim and sympathetic, delivering the devastating news.

Brand, Isaiah's partner and friend, was gone. In a matter of seconds, his entire world had been changed, and a sense of emptiness had consumed him. He had yet to shake off the loss.

The all-too-familiar ache bloomed in his chest, a dull and constant throb that wouldn't heal. Despite his best efforts to push them down, the memories flooded back, reminding him why he kept everyone at arm's length now. Never again would he allow himself to be so vulnerable, he vowed silently. His heart couldn't take another devastating blow.

He couldn't think about Brand now. He had a job to do.

He forced his attention back to the report in front of him. His finger tapped against a certain section. "Hold on," he muttered, his voice contemplative. With a flick of his wrist, he flipped to the next page, and his eyes quickly scanned over the contents. "This guy's résumé reads like a flipping Rolodex. He's hopped from one company to the next," he paused, raising an eyebrow in disbelief, "almost every other year for the last decade."

Connie leaned forward, intrigued. "You think there's something to that?"

"Could be," Isaiah mused, stroking his chin. "People don't usually job hop like that unless they're running from something—or towards something."

"We should probably talk to his current boss," Connie suggested, absently tapping her pen against the desk. "It might give us some insight into his work habits, especially any recent changes in behavior."

Isaiah nodded, a hint of a smile tugging at his lips. "At least we've got leads. It's a start."

Scott's phone was another lead, one that just might tell them why Scott was in the park in the dead of night. Isaiah picked up his desk phone and called the forensic technician assigned to the case.

Ornery was probably the most diplomatic way to describe Lorne Newemburger. The sixtysomething man had been with the MPD for more than twenty-five years. He'd spent the last five of those years talking about putting in his retirement papers, although he'd made no move to do so. No one, including Lorne, believed he'd ever retire. Lorne was a lifelong bachelor, no kids, married to his work.

Isaiah didn't bother with pleasantries when he answered, since nothing about Lorne was pleasant. "When will you have something for me on the phone in the Donlea case?"

"I just got the dang thing!" Lorne's voice boomed from the other end of the line.

"It's a homicide."

"It's always a homicide!"

Isaiah fought to keep his patience. "Lorne, I need to know what's on that phone."

"You'll know when I know," Lorne growled before hanging up.

Connie grimaced from her desk. "That didn't sound like it went well."

"It didn't," Isaiah answered.

He replaced the receiver with slightly more force than necessary. Waiting for Lorne to get around to breaking into the phone could take weeks. The image of Lisa's big brown eyes sparked in Isaiah's head. He should keep her out of this case as much as possible. On the other hand, the faster he got answers, the safer she'd be.

He pushed up from his chair. "I have an idea about how we can get into Donlea's phone. I need to run it by the lieutenant."

Connie's shrewd gaze bored into him. "I think I have an idea what your idea is. And that's why I'm letting you pitch it to Garfino alone. Let me know how it goes."

"Thanks a lot, partner," Isaiah said sarcastically, heading for the office door.

"Hey, I got your back," Connie called out. "Just way back this time."

He could hear her chuckle all the way down the hall. He took a deep breath before knocking on his boss's door.

"Come in," Lieutenant Nicolo Garfino's gruff voice called out as Isaiah rapped his knuckles on the office door.

He stepped inside, taking in the familiar sight of his rotund boss. Garfino's ill-fitting suit strained against his ample frame, the fabric puckering at odd angles. His green spectacles perched precariously on a slightly crooked nose, magnifying eyes that had seen far too much during his time on the force.

Isaiah and Connie had already briefed Garfino on what they'd learned at the crime scene and from their chat with Lisa. They were still waiting on the autopsy report, which probably wouldn't be ready until the next morning. The medical examiner had confirmed that Scott's gunshot wound was the cause of death, and it had come from too far away to be suicide. They were looking for a murderer.

"Lieutenant, you got a minute?" Isaiah asked, trying to keep his tone casual.

Garfino's eyes flicked up from the paperwork strewn across his desk. "Just."

Isaiah took a deep breath, stepping into the office and closing the door, steeling himself. "The phone we found in Scott Donlea's hotel room is with Forensics right now."

"Who's got it?" Garfino's bushy eyebrows furrowed.

"Lorne," Isaiah replied, wincing internally at the unhappy grunt that escaped Garfino's lips. "Yeah, I know," he hurried on, "but I think I have a solution." He paused, watching as Garfino peered at him over the rim of those round glasses. Garfino's silence was unnerving, but Isaiah pressed forward. "Lisa Elkins works with all things computers. She or someone at her firm could probably get us into the phone like that." He snapped his fingers.

Garfino's eyes narrowed, and Isaiah felt a twinge of anxiety. "Isn't she the woman who met with Scott Donlea the day before his death? You know her personally, right?"

Isaiah nodded, his mind racing. "Yes, it's the same woman. We were friends in grad school. That's all."

Another grunt from Garfino.

Isaiah couldn't tell if it was good or bad, but he plowed ahead. "I don't suspect her in the case. Ms. Elkins gave us access to her email and phone. There's only one email chain with Scott setting up the coffee date, no calls between them. She's been nothing but cooperative. I think she's telling the truth—whatever Scott was mixed up in spooked him enough to reach out to her as a colleague, but for whatever reason he couldn't pull the trigger on telling her what it was."

Garfino's expression remained unreadable, and Isaiah felt sweat beading on his forehead. He rushed on, determined to make his full case before Garfino shot it down.

"Ms. Elkin's firm has consulted with Metro PD and several federal agencies, including the FBI. They're qualified and can move much faster than our in-house team. And because Ms. Elkins knew Scott Donlea, we might even get a discount."

At the word *discount*, Garfino's eyebrows lifted slightly. "I like the sound of that. Budget's already ugly, and we're only halfway through the year."

Sensing he was close to convincing Garfino, Isaiah pressed his advantage. "The way I see it, if Lisa says yes, we get the phone unlocked faster than we ever could in-house. But it's also a test. If she refuses, I'd have to take a harder look at whether that coffee date was really a one-off thing like she claimed."

Garfino's face hardened again. "Lisa Elkins? Any relation to that FBI agent that was running around here a few months ago?"

Isaiah nodded, his heart racing. "His sister. And Logan Elkins married Detective Dora Madison out of the Third Precinct a couple of weeks ago."

"Madison," Garfino mused. "Heard good things about her."

"Like I said, I don't believe Ms. Elkins has anything to do with Scott Donlea's murder, but—"

"But you'd like to run your little test," Garfino finished, his lips quirking with a hint of a smile. "Okay, I can give you some leeway on this. Just make sure you're there when she unlocks the phone, and that's all she does. And make sure you inquire about that discount."

Isaiah grinned, relief washing over him. "Yes, sir."

He turned to leave before Garfino could change his mind. He closed the door behind him and let out a long breath. He'd won this round, but he knew the real challenge might still be yet to come.

Chapter Three

Lisa's phone buzzed with two separate incoming video calls, her brothers' concerned faces popping up on the screen one after another. She propped the device against her steaming coffee mug, but the once comforting aroma of hazelnut now seemed suffocating in the small kitchen.

As she looked at Logan's tanned features and Dora's bright smile appearing alongside him from their honeymoon in Greece, Lisa felt a pang of jealousy. They were living their dream while she was stuck here dealing with the aftermath of a break-in.

"Sis, are you okay?" Logan's voice was laced with worry as his brow furrowed, his protective instincts kicking in despite the thousands of miles between them. "We can be on the next flight home if you need us."

Landon chimed in from his hotel room in Vancouver, his square jaw tightening with concern. "Yeah, I can wrap up this story in no time. Just say the word, and I'm there."

She was grateful for her brothers' support, but there was no need for them to disrupt their lives for her. Even though they were all in their forties, her big brothers still saw her as the little sister they needed to protect.

"Guys, I appreciate the offer, but I've got this under

control. It was just a break-in, nothing was taken, and the police are already on it."

As she spoke, her eyes drifted to the window next to her, where she could see the sun peeking through the trees and casting patterns of light on the floor. She took a deep breath and continued, projecting an air of calm determination that she didn't quite feel. "Plus, my security system worked perfectly—thanks to Landon's expert installation skills."

But even as she said those words, doubt gnawed at her stomach. Was she really safe? Could something like this happen again?

Dora's face appeared next to Logan's, her new sister-in-law's eyes filled with genuine concern. "Are you sure, Lisa? We don't mind cutting the honeymoon short if you need us."

She shook her head, torn between wanting them by her side and not wanting to ruin their special time. "Absolutely not. You two enjoy Greece—you've been planning this trip for months. And Landon, that exposé you're working on is too important to abandon."

She leaned back in her chair, trying to project an air of confidence she didn't quite feel. "I'm a grown woman, remember? I can handle a little home security scare on my own."

Logan's broad shoulders slowly relaxed, but the permanent crease between his eyebrows remained. "If you're absolutely certain..."

"I am," she insisted.

Landon smiled. "Always independent," he said. "Just... please promise us you'll call if anything else happens, okay?"

She nodded, grateful for her brothers' concern even as she tried to reassure them. "I promise. Now go enjoy your own adventures and stop worrying about me."

She ended the call and let out a slow exhale, her facade

of strength wavering, leaving nagging doubt in the back of her mind. The memory of the mysterious code mentioned by the intruder flashed through her thoughts.

She hopped into the shower and let the hot water wash away some of the tension in her muscles. As she showered, she wrestled with questions about the code. Why would the intruder think she had it? She barely knew Scott Donlea, and he certainly hadn't given her any kind of code. And what even could *the code* possibly be?

Wrapping herself in a fluffy towel, she padded to her closet. As she slipped on a silk blouse, her thoughts drifted to Isaiah.

She'd been surprised to learn he'd joined the police force, but he seemed to be in his element. She could already tell he was a diligent detective that cared about the job. And that empathy made him all the more attractive.

"Stop it," she chided herself aloud. "He's just doing his job. And you shouldn't be thinking about him like that anyway."

She glanced at her watch and groaned. "Great, I've already missed most of the morning."

She grabbed her briefcase and reached for her keys on her side table near her front door. The nearly dozen key chains jingled, and their combined weight made her think it might be time to thin the herd a bit. She'd become somewhat of a collector of key chains, almost by accident, but she did enjoy finding unique ones to add to her collection. She locked her door and headed to her car, making a mental note to remove a few when she got home that evening.

But when she arrived at the office, she found herself still too distracted by the morning's events to get any work done. The words on her computer screen just blurred before her eyes. Her mind kept replaying the visit from Isaiah and Connie. Scott, murdered. The thought sent a chill down her spine.

A gentle knock startled her from her thoughts. Harry, her partner, stood in the doorway, concern etched on his face.

"Mind if I come in?" he asked, already stepping inside.

She nodded, straightening in her chair as Harry settled into the seat across from her desk.

A fifty-five-year-old bachelor, Harry Sonfeld had devoted his life to his job, building a well-respected cybersecurity firm and becoming one of the best system architects that Lisa knew. Harry's dark suit was expertly cut, the shirt underneath bearing his monogrammed initials at his wrists. But her partner had not always been on track to be the polished businessman standing before her.

In his youth, he'd been a computer prodigy without direction, his talents leading him down a dangerous path. At his elite private school, he'd built a thriving business hacking teacher emails and selling exam answers. His downfall came when he attempted to alter his own grades and had been arrested and expelled.

He'd been lucky enough to have been born with a silver spoon in his mouth. Harry's wealthy parents had hired top-notch lawyers who negotiated probation instead of jail time. One of those attorneys, recognizing Harry's potential, introduced him to a friend who was also computer savvy and who over time became Harry's mentor. Under his mentor's guidance, Harry had turned his life around, graduating from a new high school, excelling in college, and eventually founding the very cybersecurity company where he and Lisa were now partners.

Harry took a seat in one of the two chairs opposite Lisa's desk. "You seem distracted. Everything okay?"

She hesitated, then decided honesty was best. "Not really. My home was broken into this morning, and I received the news that an acquaintance may have been murdered."

Her statement appeared to have stunned Harry into silence. She took the opportunity to give him the short version of the morning's events.

Harry's eyebrows shot up. "Oh god, I'm so sorry. That's awful."

"Thanks," she said, her voice barely above a whisper. She cleared her throat. "We hadn't been close since graduate school, but I actually had coffee with Scott recently." Her fingers traced the edge of her keyboard. "He seemed upset about something. Asked if I knew of any job openings on the West Coast."

Why had Scott been so eager to leave town? What kind of trouble was he mixed up in? She shook her head slightly, trying to focus on Harry's sympathetic expression.

"That must be quite a shock," Harry said gently. "If you need to take some time off, just let me know."

She managed a weak smile. "Thanks, Harry. I appreciate that."

Harry stood and shuffled toward the door. He turned before opening it, his hand on the doorknob. "I mean it, Lisa. You know you're like family. If you need anything, don't hesitate to ask."

The genuine concern in his voice touched her.

She bit her bottom lip, her mind racing over the question she was hesitant to ask. She knew Harry's past connections could prove useful, but it wasn't fair to drag him into her mess. Still, if she could do something to help find Scott's killer, she had to try.

"Actually, Harry," she blurted out, causing him to pause. "I was wondering…do you still have any contacts in the black hat world?"

Harry's shoulders tensed visibly, his expression a mix of surprise and wariness. Lisa could almost see the memories flickering behind his eyes.

The silence stretched between them. She wondered if she'd made a mistake in asking. She opened her mouth to apologize and take the request back, but Harry spoke first, his voice low and tinged with concern.

"Lisa, what exactly are you thinking of doing?"

She hesitated, her fingers absently tracing the edge of her desk. "Nothing," she said softly, but her eyes betrayed her thoughts. "I just… I can't help wondering what Scott got himself into."

Harry's brow furrowed, his posture stiffening. "I strongly advise you to let the police handle this. It's their job, and it could be dangerous."

She leaned forward. "I'm not going to interfere with the investigation, Harry. But you know as well as I do that the kind of people we're talking about… They're far more likely to open up to someone in the industry than to the police."

Harry's fingers hovered over the doorknob. She held her breath, watching him mentally fight himself.

After a long moment, Harry's shoulders sagged in resignation. He shook his head sullenly and turned toward the office door. "I may know someone you could speak to."

A surge of triumph sent a bright smile breaking across her face. "Thank you, Harry. Really, thank you."

Harry opened the office door but again paused at the threshold, turning back to fix her with a stern look. "I'll get you a name. But, Lisa…don't make me regret this."

As Harry's footsteps faded down the hallway, her smile dimmed. She stared at the empty doorway, a mix of determination and apprehension swirling in her chest.

What am I getting myself into?

Scott's troubled face flashing in her mind, and she knew, whatever it was, she couldn't let it go. Not until she knew the truth.

LISA SPENT WHAT was left of the morning catching up on paperwork and then turned to testing an enhanced firewall she was designing for a client. Her fingers flew across the keyboard, her brow furrowed in concentration as she attempted to breach the security a junior on her team had designed. He'd done a good job. The firewall was giving her a run for her money. Three monitors glowed before her, lines of code scrolling rapidly.

A soft buzz from her desk phone broke her focus. She tapped the intercom. "Yes?"

"Ms. Elkins, a Detective Isaiah Reeves is here to see you," Tani, the office receptionist, said.

Lisa tried to ignore the little skip her heart gave. "Escort him back, please."

She took off her reading glasses and scrambled to pull a compact mirror from her purse, checking her reflection. She'd chewed off all her lipstick while she worked, a habit. She hastily reapplied, finishing just as footsteps approached from the hallway.

The glass doors of her office opened. Tani stood aside and let Isaiah pass by her into the office.

Lisa rose, extending her hand across the desk. "Isaiah, what a surprise."

His grip was firm, sending a jolt through her. Those piercing eyes, the stubble darkening his jaw—he looked exhausted, yet somehow even more handsome than he had earlier that morning.

Stop it, she admonished herself. *This isn't the time for fantasies.*

"Coffee? Water?" she offered, gesturing to the sideboard in the office.

Isaiah shook his head. "I'm fine, thanks."

"Tani, hold my calls please."

Tani nodded, retreating and closing the door behind her.

Lisa indicated the two chairs facing her desk. "Please, have a seat." She sank back into her own chair, suddenly hyperaware of her body. Where to put her hands? Folded on the desk felt too prim, like an old-fashioned schoolmarm, but she didn't know what else to do with them.

"It's good to see you again," she said. "Although, I wasn't expecting to so soon. Any developments on the break-in?"

Isaiah's expression tightened. "I'm afraid not. That's not why I'm here. It's about something related, though."

Disappointment and curiosity warred within her. "Oh? How can I help?" She leaned forward, her former awkwardness forgotten.

He shifted in his seat, crossing his legs, and she noticed how his jeans hugged his muscular thighs. She gave herself another mental shake. *Focus, Lisa.*

"We found a burner phone in Scott's hotel room," Isaiah explained. "Our tech team is backed up and knowing your expertise with computers and your previous work with law enforcement, I was hoping you might be willing to help us speed things along."

She cocked her head, a small smile playing on her lips. "I'm glad you asked. I'd be happy to help." She paused, then added, "Actually, I hope I already have."

Isaiah's brow furrowed, his gaze searching. "What do you mean?"

She took a deep breath, choosing her words carefully. "It seems obvious that the break-in at my house is connected to my meeting with Scott. And whatever Scott was involved in… Well, it couldn't have been good."

She gave him a chance to deny it, but he remained quiet, his eyes never leaving her face.

"Since Scott worked with computers," she continued, "I took an educated guess that his…activities were tech related. I'm not one to frequent the darker corners of the internet, but I know people who do." She hesitated, thinking of Harry. There was no need to implicate him directly. "I reached out to a friend who gave me a contact. Someone who might be able to point you in the right direction regarding Scott's activities."

She reached for the yellow Post-it note on her desk where she'd jotted down the contact info Harry had given her. She held it out to Isaiah, her heart pounding with a mix of anticipation and trepidation. "Here," she said. "This person might be able to help you."

He reached for the note, his fingers brushing against hers as he took it. Lisa felt that same electric awareness spark through her that she had earlier that morning when he'd touched her. She quickly pulled her hand back, folding her hands on the desktop again.

"Lisa," Isaiah said, his tone a mixture of concern and frustration, "you shouldn't be conducting your own investigation. We don't know the full extent of what Scott was involved in. You could be putting yourself in danger."

She pushed down the flare of annoyance that arose. "With all due respect, Detective. I was already put in danger when Scott asked me to coffee. Someone clearly thinks I know what this 'code' is, even though I don't have a clue." She paused, her thoughts drifting. "I'm just grateful Layla, my daughter, is in Paris with her father for the summer out of harm's way."

Isaiah leaned forward, his expression softening. "Maybe you should consider joining her. Take a vacation, get away from all this for a while."

She shook her head. "I have too much work here in DC to just run off to Paris," she said firmly. "And I'm not going to let anyone intimidate me out of my own home."

She could see the concern in Isaiah's eyes, and it both touched and frustrated her. Part of her wanted to reach out and smooth the worry lines from his forehead, but she pushed that thought aside.

"I don't know what this 'code' is," she continued, her voice softening slightly. "And I certainly don't have it. But I am worried, Isaiah. I'd be a fool not to be."

"Just be careful," Isaiah replied. He rose from his chair. "If at all possible, I'd like to head back to the station with you now to try to unlock the phone." His tone was tinged with urgency. "I would have brought it to you, but chain of custody will be easier if I bring you to the phone."

She stood as well, her mind racing with various potential ways she might get by the phone's security. "That's not a problem," she replied, then paused, a sly smile playing at her lips. "But I'll work on the device under one condition."

Isaiah's brow furrowed. "You already said you'd try to unlock it. It's too late for conditions."

She cocked her head, her smile widening. "Is the phone unlocked? No. Then it's not too late for conditions."

His glare returned, but this time his frustration only fueled her amusement. She could see the muscles in his jaw working as he fought to maintain his composure.

"My condition is this," she continued, her voice calm but firm. "When you set up a meeting with the contact I just gave you, I want to be there."

"No way." Isaiah shook his head emphatically.

"Why not?" she challenged. "I might actually be of help translating tech speak to English."

She watched as he pondered her words, fascinated by the play of emotions across his face. His facial expressions betrayed his internal struggle, but also realization that what she was proposing made sense. She held her breath as she waited for his response.

After what felt like an eternity, he let out a resigned sigh. "Okay," he conceded. "You have a point about the computer speak. I'll let you know if I'm able to set up a meeting with your contact."

Triumph surged through her as she walked around her desk. "If you have trouble, let me know. I'll take a stab at it," she offered, unable to keep the satisfaction from her voice. "Some of these guys don't care much for law enforcement."

The corners of Isaiah's lips twitched upward in the barest hint of a smile. "You're just all types of helpful today, aren't you?"

She grinned, basking in her small victory. "I aim to please," she quipped, heading for the office door. "Give me a minute to collect some hardware I might need for the phone. I'll be right back."

Chapter Four

Isaiah turned over everything he knew so far in his head as he drove back to his office with Lisa. It might be a long shot but hopefully Scott's phone would lead them to his killer and whoever had broken into Lisa's house.

"Despite the circumstances, it is really good to see you again," Isaiah said as he drove.

Lisa smiled back at him. "I agree. It's good to see you as well. How long have you been back in DC?"

"Just six months. I worked out of the Chicago office for fifteen years."

"Fifteen years. That's a long time. Why did you leave?"

He let a beat of silence pass. It was no secret among his colleagues that his partner in Chicago had been killed in a bar robbery gone wrong. He'd struggled with Brand's loss. So, looking for a fresh start, he'd gone back to the city where he'd last been happiest. But all of that seemed like a lot to lay on Lisa now.

"I was just ready for a change," he answered. Thankfully, she seemed content to leave it at that. "What about you? Did you marry…what was his name?"

"Charles, and yes." She flinched. "I married him. And five years ago, I divorced him."

"Oh, I'm sorry."

"No. It was a long time coming. And there's no big story. We just grew apart over time. Last year he married one of the attorneys in their Paris office and moved to France."

"Wow. Talk about a life change." He glanced over at her before pulling away from a stop sign.

"Yeah. Layla loves it. She immediately switched from Spanish to French at school. She's spending the holiday with her dad."

"Ah, and how do you feel about that?"

Lisa chuckled. "Charles and I have our issues, but we've always put Layla first. Charles was a crappy husband, but he has always been a good father."

"That's great. And hey, the upside is that you get time to focus on yourself."

"Yeah, that was the idea, although so far it has not been working out as I'd imagined." She touched her throat lightly.

Anger stabbed through him. The guy who attacked her had better hope he didn't catch him alone. Putting your hands on a woman was a line a man should never cross.

"I want you to know I'm going to do everything I can to find the guy that assaulted you and figure out if it's related to your client's death. You can trust me."

Lisa smiled at him. "I do trust you."

A heartbeat passed between them. One in which he saw the twenty-three-year-old woman she'd been the last time he'd seen her, and his heart thudded. If he was being honest, he'd always had a teeny crush on Lisa Elkins, and it seemed time and distance hadn't quenched it. Not that he'd have ever made a play for her when she'd been with Charles. But she was single now.

And involved in a crime he was investigating, which meant she was still off-limits.

He turned into the underground parking garage of the nondescript office building on Fourth Street that he and a several hundred other officers, detectives, and civilians worked out of. He parked, then led Lisa into the building.

They navigated the maze of corridors that made up the lower level of the imposing building. The walls were a scuffed white, and the overhead lights of the hall were dim. Lisa's heels tapped against the polished floors as they made their way down the hall.

"Just through here," he said, gesturing to a nondescript door. He swiped his keycard and ushered Lisa inside.

The forensics department was a stark contrast to the dark hallway, brightly lit and gleaming with stainless steel surfaces and high-tech equipment. In the center stood a wiry man with salt-and-pepper hair, hunched over a keyboard.

"Lorne." Isaiah stopped next to the man's cubicle. "I've got someone here I'd like you to meet. Lorne Newemburger, I'd like you to meet—"

Lorne looked up, his familiar scowl already fixed on his face. When his gaze settled on Lisa, the scowl melted away, replaced by something Isaiah had never seen on Lorne's face before. A smile.

"Lisa Elkins," Lorne exclaimed, standing so quickly he almost knocked over his chair. "I was at the WaCo Cybersecurity Conference two years ago where you and your partner spoke on a panel. You were brilliant. Both of you. Simply brilliant."

Isaiah had never seen the usually curmudgeonly Lorne so animated. It was like the man had become an entirely different person.

Lisa smiled graciously. "It's a pleasure to meet you, Mr. Newemburger. I'm so glad you enjoyed our talk."

"Oh please, call me Lorne," he insisted, vigorously pumping Lisa's hand.

"Then you must call me Lisa."

Lorne grinned, and Isaiah felt as if he'd stepped into the Twilight Zone. Lorne was speaking quickly now, complimenting Lisa on some program she'd developed.

Isaiah cleared his throat. "Well, if you two are all set, I'll head back upstairs to work on the case. I'll check in with you both in a bit."

Lorne barely seemed to register his words.

Lisa smiled. "We'll be fine."

Isaiah made his way back to the elevator, still astonished at the change Lisa had brought on in Lorne. A couple of minutes later, he strode into the office he shared with Connie and sank into his desk chair.

She looked up from her computer. "So? Will Lisa be able to help?"

"She's downstairs with Lorne as we speak," he replied. "And she has somehow managed to completely charm him. He practically fell all over himself when she walked in."

Connie's eyebrows shot up. "Lorne? Our Lorne? The original Mr. Get Off My Lawn himself?"

Isaiah laughed. "It was like watching a schoolboy with his first crush. I half expected him to start blushing and stuttering."

Connie leaned forward and rested her elbows on her desk. "You know, I almost want to go down there and see this for myself." Her eyes twinkled mischievously. "Although, I can't help but wonder…is it possible that Lorne isn't the only one a bit taken with Lisa Elkins?"

Isaiah felt his cheeks warm slightly, caught off guard by Connie's perceptiveness. "I don't know what you mean."

"Right," Connie scoffed.

"Look, I told you," he said, feeling cornered. "Lisa and I knew each other a bit in graduate school. That's the extent of our relationship." He met Connie's gaze, his voice firm. "It won't interfere with this investigation."

Connie held up her hands in mock surrender. "I never said it would."

He took a deep breath and forced himself to focus on the case. "Any word from the medical examiner?" he asked pointedly.

Connie nodded, reaching for a file on her desk. "He sent over the preliminary report a little while ago." She handed it to him. As he scanned the pages inside, Connie continued, "One gunshot to Scott's chest. It was the cause of death. They recovered the bullet, but…" She trailed off with a grimace.

Isaiah looked up, having jumped to the punch line in the report and read the bad news. "Too damaged to be useful."

"Unfortunately. I'm afraid that's not much to go on."

He leaned back in his chair, frustration etching lines across his forehead. "You can say that again," he muttered, his mind racing through the potential next steps. "And I'm guessing it doesn't get any better from there?"

Connie's resigned sigh was all the answer he needed.

Isaiah pinched the bridge of his nose, feeling the beginnings of a tension headache. "All right, what else do we have?"

"I called over to the management company for Scott's apartment complex. The one listed on his driver's license."

"And?"

"The manager said Scott asked to be let out of his rental contract and moved out a month ago," Connie said, her voice tinged with disappointment.

Isaiah's lips twisted into a wry smile. "And I bet he wasn't considerate enough to have left a forwarding address for us."

"You bet correctly," Connie confirmed.

Letting out a heavy sigh, he put his hands behind his head and leaned back in his chair. He stared up at the ceiling, his mind churning with frustration. "So, we don't have any idea where our victim has been living for the past month."

"No, and it's definitely something we'll need to ask Scott's estranged wife and brother when we speak to them."

Isaiah nodded absently, his thoughts already racing ahead to what else they could be doing to find Scott Donlea's killer. "What about the estranged wife? What do we know about her?"

Connie consulted her notes. "Her name's Emily. She lives in Fairfax, Virginia."

"All right," Isaiah said. "I'll add speaking to the wife and brother to our agenda. Did you find anything that might point to a motive on her part?"

"I couldn't find anything obvious. No custody disputes, no restraining orders. There's nothing that screams *motive to shoot my husband* to me."

"So, we've got a victim with no known address, a wife with no apparent motive, and a bullet that tells us nothing. Great." The frustration in his voice was palpable. He couldn't shake the feeling that they were missing something crucial, some vital piece of information. But what?

He drummed his fingers on the desk for a moment before

looking back at Connie. "Lisa gave me a name. Someone who might be able to give us some insight into the illicit hacker world."

Connie's eyebrows went up. "That sounds promising."

He nodded. "It could be, but it came with a condition."

Connie's lips puckered but she said nothing.

"She wants to be there when we talk with the contact."

He watched Connie's face, trying to gauge her reaction. Bringing Lisa along to speak with the contact wouldn't exactly be standard operating procedure.

To his surprise, Connie seemed to consider the idea for a moment before responding. "That might not be a bad idea," she said slowly. "Neither one of us knows much about that world. Lisa does."

Isaiah huffed, a wry smile tugging at the corner of his mouth. "That's what she said."

He reached for his phone, his fingers hovering over the screen. Part of him still felt uneasy about involving Lisa further, but they needed a break in this case. With a resigned sigh, he tapped out a quick message to the number Lisa had provided.

The response was almost immediate. Isaiah's eyebrows shot up as he read the reply.

"Well, that was fast," he muttered, more to himself than to Connie. "Our contact wants to meet at a coffee shop on M Street. In two hours."

The office fell into a focused silence as he and Connie dove into their respective tasks. He pored over the medical examiner's report first, his eyes flicking back and forth across the pages, searching for any small detail that might shed light on Scott's final weeks and hours. When that yielded nothing, he pulled up Scott's credit report and the scant financial records they'd been able to find and read through them.

"Anything standing out?" Connie asked, not looking away from her computer screen where she was pulling background records on Scott, his ex-wife, and his brother.

Isaiah shook his head, frustration thrumming through him. "I was hoping his credit report might give us a clue about where he's been living. But nothing so far."

Connie frowned.

A sudden knock at the door jolted Isaiah from his concentration. He looked up to see Lisa in the doorway, a smile on her face. "Are you done already?" he asked.

Lisa nodded. "Since there was no legal wrangling to deal with, Lorne and I didn't have to wait to get started. Scott's phone was also old, and it only had a four-digit passcode. That made it a lot easier for my program to run the possible combinations. Lorne is pulling the information now."

Isaiah felt a surge of hope. Maybe this would be the break they needed. "Well, we are thankful to you. We need something to go right in this case." He pushed himself up from his seat, stretching slightly as he stood. The weight of the investigation seemed to lift a little from his shoulders.

"I was just about to come downstairs to retrieve you," he continued, grabbing his jacket from the back of his chair. "I reached out to Arnold, the contact you gave me. He wants to meet in about half an hour."

Lisa's face lit up with a grin, her eyes sparkling with excitement. "I'm ready when you are."

"I'll stay here. Keep going through these background reports," Connie said. "And I'll reach out to the ex-wife and the brother about an interview."

"Sounds good," Isaiah responded. "Let's hope this Arnold character can shed some light on our victim's activities. The hacker world is like a black box to me."

He gestured for Lisa to lead the way out of the office, his mind already racing with questions for their upcoming meeting.

Chapter Five

The rich, inviting scent of freshly ground coffee beans and warm pastries greeted them as Isaiah held the door of the bustling café for Lisa. The cozy space hummed with activity—baristas calling out orders, the hiss of espresso machines, and the low murmur of conversations blending like a symphony of sounds. Despite the crowded atmosphere, Lisa felt a sense of comfort and familiarity wash over her.

Isaiah's hand rested protectively on the small of her back as they weaved through the maze of tables. She could feel tense energy radiating off him, his unease palpable even in the busy café. She gave his arm a reassuring squeeze before leading them to an empty table at the rear of the coffee shop.

Isaiah immediately positioned himself with his back to the wall, scanning the room with an eagle eye. Lisa admired his instinctive protective nature, even though she knew it was born out of fear for their safety.

A perky waitress approached their table, her pen poised over her notepad as she smiled warmly at them. "What can I get for you two?"

"Black coffee," Isaiah said curtly.

"I'll have a latte, please," Lisa added with a smile, trying to counteract Isaiah's brusqueness.

As the waitress walked away, Isaiah leaned in. "I really don't like this," he repeated, his jaw clenched.

She resisted the urge to roll her eyes. "You mentioned that," she said, keeping her voice low and calm.

The café door swung open, letting in a burst of street noise. She glanced over and spotted a short, muscular man with a thick mop of black hair. He couldn't have been more than five foot one, but his presence seemed to fill the room as he scanned the tables.

His gaze locked onto her, and nerves fluttered in her stomach. This had to be Arnold. She felt Isaiah tense in the chair next to her as probably-Arnold approached their table.

The man extended his hand, a boyish smile on his face. "You're Lisa Elkins. I recognize you from your company's website."

She stood, shaking his hand firmly. "That's right. You must be Arnold."

"The one and only," he replied with a wink. His eyes shifted to Isaiah, who had also risen to his feet. "And you must be the detective."

Isaiah's handshake was noticeably firmer as he introduced himself. "Detective Isaiah Reeves."

The waitress returned with Isaiah's black coffee and Lisa's latte. She set both drinks down on the table, then turned to Arnold. "What can I get you?"

"I'll have a green tea." Arnold tapped his chest, right over his heart. "It's better for the ticker than coffee."

Lisa offered Arnold a polite smile. "Thank you for meeting with us."

Arnold settled into his chair, his posture relaxed but his eyes sharp. "Yeah, well, I usually don't meet with cops."

"I'm not with the police," she offered quickly.

Arnold's lips quirked. "And that's why I'm here. That and because Harry said I should talk to you."

Isaiah's jaw tightened. "I appreciate it," he ground out, reaching for his phone. Lisa could see the tension in his shoulders as he pulled up a photo of Scott.

"Recognize this man?" Isaiah asked, his voice clipped.

Arnold leaned forward, squinting at the screen. "Yeah, that's Scott."

"Scott Donlea," Isaiah confirmed. "His body was found yesterday."

Lisa watched Arnold's face, searching for any flicker of genuine surprise or hidden knowledge.

The short man's eyebrows rose slightly. "Damn, that's a shame," Arnold said, leaning back.

Isaiah's fingers drummed once on the table. "Anyone you know who might have wanted to hurt Scott?"

Arnold shrugged. "Didn't know him that well. Just saw him around sometimes."

"Around where?" Isaiah pressed.

Before Arnold could answer, the waitress returned with his green tea. He thanked her with a charming smile, waiting until she was out of earshot before speaking again.

"Around here and there," Arnold said vaguely.

Lisa gripped the handle of her coffee mug. Arnold was annoying, but he was all they had to go on. "You said you'd help," she reminded him gently.

Arnold sighed, his shoulders slumping slightly. "Look, the guy's a computer geek, and so am I. We run in the same circles. I've seen him at this meetup I go to sometimes."

The scraping of chairs interrupted them as the quartet at the next table noisily got up to leave.

Lisa finished off her latte, watching Arnold sip at his

tea as the quartet finally gathered their things and headed for the door. Isaiah still hadn't touched his coffee.

"What kind of meetup?" Isaiah asked once the noise level had again dropped the usual hum.

"It's a social thing for computer geeks and gamers. Like a knitting club, but for nerds." Arnold took another sip of tea.

Memory flared in Lisa's mind. "Oh, I've heard of those. I even went to a few when I was in grad school."

Arnold's eyebrows shot up. "Really? I'd have definitely noticed if I'd seen you there."

Lisa offered a tentative smile. "It would have been years ago now."

"Are you a hacker?" Arnold asked Lisa, leaning forward with interest.

"I work with Harry, so sometimes it's part of the job," Lisa replied.

Arnold grimaced and leaned back in his chair as if trying now to put distance between them. "So, you hack for the good guys."

"Afraid so," Lisa said with a shrug.

"Too bad," Arnold said, his tone tinged with disappointment.

"Could we get back on track here?" Isaiah said, making it clear that his patience was wearing thin. "Arnold, when's the last time you saw Scott?"

Arnold lifted his green tea but stopped before he put the cup to his lips. "Like I said, I didn't really know the man. Maybe at a meeting last month?"

"Do you remember what the meeting was about?" Lisa asked.

Arnold took a sip before answering. "If you've been to a meeting, you know they aren't formal. Sometimes we

discuss new tech or big news, but mostly people just so-
cialize. Some stick to their cliques."

Lisa nodded. "Yeah, I remember they could be cliquish."

"Do you remember seeing Scott with anyone? Any
names?" Isaiah pressed.

Arnold hummed, gazing at the ceiling. "Well, I think
I saw him talking to a few people." He rattled off a couple of names, which Isaiah dutifully typed into his phone.

"Is there anything else you could tell us about Scott?"
Isaiah asked once the noise level had again dropped the
usual hum.

Arnold began to shake his head in the negative, then
stopped abruptly. His eyes widened as if he'd been suddenly struck by a memory. "Now that I'm thinking about
it," Arnold said slowly, "I'm sure I saw Scott talking to Big
Joe at the last meeting."

"Who's Big Joe?" Isaiah asked, his interest piqued.

Arnold shrugged. "Big Joe is Big Joe. People at these
meetings don't like using given names much. Most of 'em
are borderline conspiracy theorists."

Lisa wondered if Arnold counted himself among those
paranoid ranks but refrained from questioning him about
it. Isaiah added *Big Joe* to the growing list of names on
his phone.

"Do you know what Scott and Big Joe were talking
about?" Isaiah followed up.

Arnold hunched over his tea, suddenly finding the swirling liquid fascinating. There was clearly something Arnold
didn't want to share with them.

Lisa leaned forward, her voice soft but urgent. "Please.
A man has been murdered. Anything you know could be
important."

Arnold looked up, his gaze locking directly onto Isaiah. Lisa felt a chill run down her spine at the intensity in Arnold's eyes.

"I don't know what they were talking about," Arnold said slowly. "I was too far away to hear. But their body language? It wasn't friendly. Scott even poked Big Joe in the chest. For a second there, I thought Big Joe was going to deck him."

A sudden crash of silverware hitting the floor made Isaiah jump. A baby's wail pierced the air, momentarily drowning out the ambient chatter of the coffee shop.

Arnold leaned back in his chair, his expression grave. "Look, Big Joe might be into computers and tech stuff, but he's not the kind of guy you want to piss off. Built like a grizzly bear and about as friendly as one too."

This Big Joe was sounding more intriguing by the second, Lisa thought.

"When's the next meetup?" Isaiah asked.

A slow grin spread across Arnold's face. "You're in luck. I do believe there is one taking place tomorrow night."

Lisa's pulse quickened. Maybe Isaiah would be able to get answers quickly.

"But there's no way either of you could show up there asking questions." Arnold waved a hand from Lisa to Isaiah and back. "These guys, they're not keen on talking to women…" he nodded at Lisa "…and you…" he looked at Isaiah "…you reek of cop."

Isaiah held for a beat, thoughts clearly racing through his head. Lisa wished she still knew him well enough to know just where those thoughts were leading him.

After a moment, Isaiah leaned forward, lowering his voice. "How would you feel about doing a little undercover work, Arnold?"

Arnold's eyebrows shot up, his eyes widening. "Like a spy?" he asked, a hint of excitement creeping into his voice.

"More like someone who listens and reports back anything he hears or sees. An informant. That's all," Isaiah clarified.

Arnold's forehead scrunched as he considered the proposition.

Lisa tipped her head, her gaze darting below Arnold and Isaiah. She wasn't sure it was a good idea. Arnold seemed…eccentric. And despite the help he'd given them, she wasn't sure they could trust him.

After a long minute, a slow, mischievous grin finally spread across Arnold's face. "A spy. I like it. I'm in."

Isaiah wasn't sure how smart it was to trust Arnold, but he was the best lead they had at the moment. He called Connie and updated her on his and Lisa's meeting with Arnold.

Connie reluctantly agreed to the course of action and got the ball rolling on the equipment they'd need to wire Arnold, as well as pulling whatever background information they could find on Big Joe and his group.

After hanging up with Connie, Isaiah sent Arnold a quick text letting him know their plan was a go and that he'd need to meet them at their offices to get wired up before the meeting. Arnold replied with a thumbs-up emoji.

Now he and Lisa were on their way to speak with Scott Donlea's widow, Emily. The Donleas' modest single-story house stood quietly in the afternoon sun, its well-manicured lawn and freshly painted trim a stark contrast to the turmoil Isaiah knew waited inside. He hesitated for a moment before rapping his knuckles against the front door, stealing a glance at Lisa beside him.

She'd been quiet since their conversation with Arnold, and he considered what was going on in that beautiful head of hers.

The door creaked open, revealing a woman with puffy eyes and disheveled hair. Behind her, a young girl peered out, her wide eyes rimmed with red. Isaiah's heart clenched at the sight.

"Mrs. Emily Donlea?" he asked gently. At her nod, he continued, "I'm Detective Isaiah Reeves, and this is Lisa Elkins. We're here about Scott."

Emily's lip trembled, but she stepped back, gesturing them inside. "Please, come in."

As they entered the cozy living room, Isaiah noted the family photos lining the walls, Scott's smiling face, a painful reminder of why they were here. Emily fidgeted with her hands, clearly uncomfortable.

"Can I get you some water? Coffee?" she offered, her voice barely above a whisper.

Isaiah shook his head. "No, thank you. We're fine."

Emily nodded, then turned to her daughter. "Zoe, sweetie, why don't you go to your room while the adults talk?"

Zoe's eyes darted between her mother and the strangers, fear evident in her expression. Isaiah wondered what the poor child had been through in the past few days. After a moment's hesitation, she shuffled down the hallway, disappearing from view.

Emily sighed, gesturing toward the sofa. "Please, have a seat."

Isaiah and Lisa settled onto the worn leather couch while Emily lowered herself into an armchair across from them. The ticking of a nearby clock seemed to echo in the tense silence.

Isaiah leaned forward, keeping his voice soft. "Mrs. Donlea, I know this is hard, but we need to ask you some questions about Scott."

Emily clasped her hands tightly in her lap. "I understand. I'll do my best to help."

He cleared his throat, his eyes meeting Emily's. "I apologize for intruding at such a difficult time, but it's crucial we gather as much information as possible about Scott's... situation."

Emily's shoulders slumped slightly, but she nodded again. "I understand. Please, ask me anything. I'll answer what I can."

"Can you tell us why you and Scott separated?" Isaiah asked.

Emily's fingers twisted in her lap, her gaze darting around the room. "It...it started gradually. Scott began spending more and more time online. At first, I thought it was just work, but then..." She trailed off, swallowing hard.

Lisa's brow furrowed. "What happened, Emily?"

Emily's words trembled. "He started believing these... these wild theories. Anti-government conspiracies. It consumed him. He'd stay up all night, ranting about things that made no sense. I tried to reason with him, but..." She shook her head, tears welling in her eyes.

Isaiah watched Emily closely, noting the pain etched on her face. He wondered how a seemingly normal man like Scott could fall so far down such a dangerous rabbit hole.

Lisa's voice cut through the tension. "Emily, I... I actually knew Scott. We were in grad school together."

Emily's head snapped up, her eyes widening. Her shoulders visibly eased. "Oh! That must be why you look so familiar. I started dating Scott in his last year of school. I may have seen you on campus when I visited him."

Lisa smiled warmly. "That's entirely possible. I'm sorry we're meeting again under these circumstances."

Emily nodded, a ghost of a smile crossing her face. "Small world, isn't it?"

"There's something else you should know." Lisa hesitated, then continued, "Scott contacted me about a week ago. We met for coffee."

Emily's eyebrows shot up. "He did? Did he…did he say anything that would tell you…what happened to him?"

Lisa shook her head. "Not really. But he was clearly upset about something, although he didn't tell me what was wrong. Do you have any idea what might have been bothering him?"

Isaiah watched the interplay between the two women. Emily studied Lisa, and whatever she saw there seemed to soften Emily's resolve to hold on to Scott's secrets.

Emily exhaled heavily, her shoulders slumping. "I suppose I should tell you what I know," she said, her voice barely above a whisper. "Scott… He told me he'd stolen credit card numbers from his bank's customers."

Isaiah felt his stomach lurch. Finally, a motive for Scott's murder. He glanced at Lisa, who met his gaze with a mix of shock and dismay.

"There's more," Emily continued, her fingers twisting in her lap. "He said he'd fallen in with some online group. They were using the money from selling those credit card numbers to fund their activities."

Isaiah leaned forward, his mind racing. "Do you know the name of this group? Or what their mission is?"

Emily shook her head, her eyes downcast. "I'm sorry, I don't. Scott didn't tell me, and honestly… I didn't want to know. I was afraid of what I might hear."

Isaiah nodded, understanding her reluctance. He could

see the pain etched on Emily's face, the struggle between love for her husband and horror at his actions.

"Emily," he said gently, "is there anyone Scott might have confided in? Any friends who might know more?"

Emily was quiet for a moment, her brow furrowed in thought. Then her eyes lit up with sudden realization. "Todd," she said. "Scott's brother. If anyone knows what Scott's gotten himself into, it would be Todd. They've always been close, even when Scott started…changing."

Todd. The brother who was already on Isaiah's list of people to speak to. This could be the lead they needed. "Do you have contact information for Todd?" he asked, already reaching for his notepad.

As Emily nodded and began searching for Todd's number on her phone, Isaiah wondered what they might uncover. What dark secrets was Todd privy to? And how deep did this conspiracy truly run?

Chapter Six

A small prop plane descended gracefully overhead as Isaiah steered the sedan down the rural highway. The sight of the aircraft stirred a mix of anticipation and unease in his gut. His eyes followed the plane's trajectory as he turned the car off the road and onto a two-lane street.

His body buzzed with adrenaline. Emily Donlea had given them a solid lead to pursue. Scott was stealing credit card information. That was the kind of thing that could make a lot of people very angry. Maybe even angry enough to kill.

Isaiah had called Lieutenant Garfino and Connie on a three-way call after leaving the Donlea home. Garfino had been less than pleased. Theft from a bank meant that the FBI could decide to get involved. He knew that Garfino would fight to keep MPD on the case for as long as he could, but it might be out of his hands.

Until then, Isaiah and Connie would work the case like they worked every other homicide case that came across their desks. Connie had assigned herself the task of reaching out to the bank to see if they could get a sit-down with someone who'd be able to confirm Scott's theft. Then he and Lisa headed out to speak with Todd Donlea.

Scott's older brother worked as a security guard at a private airstrip in Fairfax, Virginia, and Emily thought they'd be able to catch him there.

"We're getting close," Isaiah said, breaking the comfortable silence that had settled between him and Lisa on the hour-and-a-half drive. "I didn't get much on Todd Donlea's background check. Guy seems to be a bit of a hermit."

Lisa tore her gaze from the window, where rolling fields stretched to the horizon. "Pretty rural out here. Must appeal to those seeking solitude."

Isaiah nodded, his brow furrowing as he recalled the scant details he'd uncovered. "Todd doesn't appear to have any social media footprint. Can't find any evidence that he goes anywhere regularly except work and home. He's divorced, just like Scott, but his ex-wife and kids moved back to the ex-wife's hometown in Kansas about six years back."

"Sounds lonely," Lisa mused, a hint of empathy in her voice.

As they approached their destination, a modest building came into view. The small private airport stood isolated amid the pastoral landscape, its weathered exterior a testament to years of service. A short runway stretched out behind it, disappearing into the distance.

Isaiah parked the car and took a deep breath, steeling himself for the conversation ahead. "Ready?" he asked Lisa, who nodded resolutely.

They entered the lobby, a compact space that smelled faintly of aviation fuel and stale coffee. A few plastic chairs lined the walls, and a flat screen television played soundlessly in the corner.

Just inside the door a young man sat behind a high countered-desk in a pewter-colored security uniform, the name Cal etched onto his shirt pocket.

Isaiah approached him, badge in hand. "I'm Detective Reeves. I need to speak with Todd Donlea."

Cal's posture stiffened, his eyes narrowing. "A DC cop? You've got no jurisdiction here."

Isaiah maintained his composure, though he felt a flicker of irritation. He'd anticipated this reaction, but it still grated on him. "You're absolutely right. If you prefer, we can involve the local police. Of course, that would mean questioning every employee here. Probably shut down operations for a day, maybe longer."

He watched Cal's expression darken, and hoped the guard believed the veiled threat. Bringing in the county cops would add more headache than he needed right now, but he'd do it if that was the only way to get answers. And he needed answers.

After a tense moment, Cal's shoulders sagged in defeat. He grabbed his walkie-talkie, his movements sharp with barely contained annoyance. "Todd, front desk. Now."

Hopefully, Todd would be more inclined to help than his colleague. A door at the rear of the airport opened, and a man bearing a striking resemblance to Scott Donlea emerged. Isaiah studied him closely as he approached, noting the thinning sandy hair streaked with gray and eyes a shade darker than Scott's. Todd's skin had a ruddier complexion, like he spent a lot of time in the great outdoors.

Todd stopped in front of them, his expression mildly curious.

Cal jerked his thumb toward Isaiah and Lisa. "These officers want to talk to you." His scowl deepened. "They're from Washington, DC." The way Cal said the city name made it sound like a swear.

Todd's eyebrows rose slightly, but he didn't seem particularly alarmed. "Been expecting you. I was just about to take my break." He gestured at the exit. "Shall we?"

As they stepped outside, Isaiah observed Todd's body language. The man seemed relaxed, almost nonchalant. It didn't look as if his brother's death was tearing him up much at all. But Isaiah knew looks could be deceiving and that a lot of people didn't let others know when they were in pain or grieving.

Todd pulled out a pack of cigarettes from the pocket of his jacket. Isaiah noted the tattoo of a snake, uncoiling and rearing up on the back of his right hand, and wondered how much it hurt to get a tattoo there.

Todd held out the pack of cigarettes, first to Lisa who declined, then to Isaiah. When he declined as well, Todd shrugged. "More for me then. Not supposed to smoke on airport property," he said as he lit up, "but the boss turns a blind eye. Hard to find good security folks these days, so those of us who've stuck around for a while get some perks."

Isaiah nodded. "I don't want to keep you from your job, but I have some questions."

"About my brother, I suppose," Todd said, exhaling a plume of smoke.

"Yes," Isaiah confirmed.

Todd's eyes narrowed slightly. "Some detective called me about Scott's death. Wasn't you, though."

"No, that was my partner, Detective Connie Lui."

Todd's gaze shifted to Lisa, who shook her head.

Isaiah quickly added, "Ms. Elkins is a civilian consultant working with the department."

Lisa's voice was soft as she said, "I knew Scott a little from grad school. I'm sorry for your loss."

Todd gave a brisk nod in acknowledgment but said nothing.

Isaiah decided to cut to the chase. "Todd, do you know of anyone who might have wanted to hurt your brother?"

Todd let out a short, sharp laugh that struck Isaiah as off-key with the situation. "Absolutely not. Scott was harmless, a computer nerd. Who'd want to hurt him?"

Isaiah's jaw clenched at Todd's dismissiveness. "Someone did hurt him, Todd. Someone murdered Scott."

The amusement drained from Todd's face, replaced by a furrowed brow and tightened lips. "I know, and I can't understand it. Scott would never hurt a fly."

Lisa chimed in, her voice gentle but probing. "We think Scott might have gotten involved with some bad people—criminals. They may have needed his computer skills for something."

Todd sighed heavily, letting the hand holding his cigarette fall to his side, his shoulders slumping. "I could see Scott falling in with the wrong crowd," he admitted, quickly adding, "not on purpose, mind you." He ran a hand through his thinning hair. "Scott's always been smart. Too smart, really. Where we come from, that can cause a person problems."

Isaiah raised an eyebrow, encouraging Todd to continue.

"Scott got picked on a lot growing up," Todd explained. "Of course, some of it he brought on himself. He didn't mind telling people how smart he was, and not everyone took too that good, if you know what I mean. If I hadn't been the star quarterback in high school, looking out for him... Well, he would've taken a lot more beatings."

A wistful chuckle escaped Todd's lips. "Scott always said he'd show everyone. Become some big shot computer wizard, make a ton of money. Fancied himself the next Bill Gates."

Lisa's eyes softened. "Childhood dreams can be powerful."

Todd shook his head, reaching for another cigarette. "Wouldn't know. Never thought past being the high school quarterback. And look where that got me." The hand with the cigarette swept out to encompass the airport and field beyond.

As Todd put the dwindling butt to his lips again, Isaiah felt a twinge of sympathy. The man before him seemed a far cry from the golden boy he was describing. He seemed worn down by life's disappointments. But Isaiah couldn't let empathy distract him from the task at hand. He needed answers about Scott's death, and Todd was their best lead.

Isaiah cleared his throat, steering the conversation back to the investigation. "Do you have any idea who Scott might have been working with recently? Outside of the bank, I mean."

Todd shook his head, exhaling a plume of smoke. "No clue. Scott wasn't exactly forthcoming about his work life."

"We understand Scott changed jobs quite frequently," Lisa said gently.

"Yeah." Todd nodded, a rueful smile playing on his lips. "That goes back to that youthful dreams thing."

A low rumble filled the air, growing steadily louder. As one, Isaiah, Todd, and Lisa tilted their heads skyward, watching a small prop plane take off, its engine drowning out all other sounds for a moment. Isaiah found himself wondering if Todd worked in an airport because he did have dreams, dreams of flying, of soaring above his troubles.

As the plane disappeared into the distance, Todd continued, his voice tinged with a mixture of pride and frustration, "Scott had trouble keeping a job because he always thought he was smarter than everyone else, including his bosses." He paused, taking another drag from his cigarette.

"Thing is, he usually was smarter. But you can't keep a job going around telling your boss he's an idiot."

Isaiah nodded silently, thinking to himself that it wasn't always the brightest people who rose to the top. More often than not, it was those who knew how to play the game.

Lisa leaned in slightly, her eyes intent. "Did Scott ever mention anything to you about a code? Or 'the code'?"

Todd's brow furrowed in confusion. "The code? The code for what?"

"That's what we're trying to find out," Isaiah replied, his tone carefully neutral.

Todd took a final puff of his cigarette before grinding it out under his heel. "Look, my brother was the computer whiz. I don't even have one. Just an old iPad and my phone."

Sensing they'd reached the end of what Todd could tell them, Isaiah pulled out a business card and handed it to him. "Thank you for your time, Mr. Donlea. If you think of anything else that might help us, please give me a call."

As Isaiah and Lisa turned to leave, Todd's voice called out, stopping them in their tracks. Isaiah was struck by the raw grief etched across Todd's face.

"You'll find my brother's killer, won't you?" Todd asked, his earlier bravado crumbling away to reveal the pain underneath.

Isaiah met Todd's gaze, feeling the weight of the man's sorrow. "I'll do my best," he promised, knowing it wasn't enough, but it was all he could offer.

Chapter Seven

It was dark by the time they started the drive back to DC. Lisa considered what they'd learned about Scott from Todd. It wasn't much. It didn't feel like they'd gotten any closer to finding out who had killed Scott or what this code was.

Her chest tightened with frustration even as her stomach growled loudly, breaking the comfortable silence that had settled between her and Isaiah in the car as they drove away from the airport. She felt her cheeks flush with embarrassment.

Isaiah glanced over, a small smile playing at the corners of his mouth. "You're hungry. We missed lunch earlier—how about we grab some dinner?"

Her heart skipped a beat. That sounded suspiciously like he was asking her on a date. She hesitated, conflicting emotions warring within her. On one hand, the idea of extending their time together was appealing. On the other, she wasn't sure she was ready to blur the lines of their newly rekindled friendship.

Before she could overthink it further, her stomach let out another rumble. She smiled, embarrassed. "I guess that settles it. Dinner sounds great."

Isaiah's smile widened as he merged onto the highway.

"Perfect. How do you feel about Chinese food? There's this great little place not far from your house—Golden Dragon?"

"Oh, I love Golden Dragon! It's one of Layla's and my favorite spots. Their dumplings are amazing."

"Great," Isaiah said, switching lanes to take the next exit. "Golden Dragon it is."

As they drove, Lisa found herself sneaking glances at his profile. The years had been kind to him—he was even more handsome now than he had been when they were in their twenties. She averted her gaze when he noticed her looking.

It wasn't long before he turned the car into the parking lot.

The complex where the restaurant was located was drenched in holiday decor. Snowmen banners hung off the lamp poles, illuminating the parking lot. Multicolored lights twinkled around the roof and windows of the stores.

Isaiah held open the door to the Golden Dragon for her to pass through. The familiar aroma of ginger and soy sauce wafted out into the night.

She felt a pang of nostalgia. She'd shared so many meals here with Layla, but it seemed like so much was changing.

"Lisa! Happy holidays," a cheerful voice called out. The hostess, a petite woman with a kind smile, approached them. "It's so good to see you again!"

Lisa returned the smile, genuinely pleased. "Hi, Mai. It's been a while."

Mai's eyes darted to Isaiah, then back to Lisa, a hint of curiosity in her expression. "Where's Layla tonight? I haven't seen her in ages."

"She's actually in Paris for the school break," Lisa explained, her voice carrying a mix of pride and wistfulness. "Spending time with her father."

Mai's face fell slightly. "Does that mean you'll be alone for the holidays?"

Lisa felt a twinge of embarrassment, acutely aware of Isaiah standing beside her. She rushed to reassure Mai, "Oh no, not at all. I'll be spending Christmas with my brother Landon and his wife, Dora. They're on their honeymoon now, but they'll be back next week."

As Lisa spoke, she wondered if Isaiah had plans for the holidays. The thought surprised her, and she pushed it away quickly.

Mai nodded, relief evident in her eyes. "That's wonderful, dear."

As she followed Mai through the bustling restaurant, Lisa found herself hyperaware of Isaiah's presence behind her. She could feel the warmth radiating from him, smell the faint scent of his cologne. It was…distracting.

Get a grip, she chided herself silently. *This isn't a date. It's just dinner with an old friend.*

The restaurant hummed with the chatter of diners and the clink of cutlery. Lisa settled into the plush booth, the rich aroma of spices wafting through the air. Isaiah sat across from her, his dark eyes warm in the soft glow of the table lamp.

A waitress appeared, her pen poised over a notepad. "Good evening! Can I start you off with some drinks?"

"I'll have a jasmine tea, please," Lisa said.

"Make that two," Isaiah added.

The waitress departed.

Isaiah leaned forward, his elbows on the table. "So, how are you really dealing with Layla being away for the holidays?"

Lisa set her menu aside. She and Layla frequented the restaurant enough that she had it memorized anyway. She rested her chin on her clasped hands. "I miss her," she admitted. "More than I thought I would, actually."

Isaiah nodded, encouraging her to continue.

"I mean, I understand why she wants to be in Paris. It must be beautiful this time of year. And Layla needs to spend time with Charles and his new family, but…"

She trailed off, leaving the thought unfinished. In her mind, she could see Layla laughing in the snow, illuminated by the twinkling lights of the Eiffel Tower. It was a bittersweet image—her daughter happy but so far away.

She blinked, realizing she'd been quiet for a moment too long. She forced a smile, meeting Isaiah's gaze. "It's just different, that's all. I'm sure I'll get used to it."

But even as Lisa spoke the words, she wasn't entirely convinced. Would she ever truly get used to her daughter growing up, to their lives diverging? The thought left an ache in her chest that not even the comforting atmosphere of her favorite restaurant could fully soothe.

Isaiah leaned forward, his dark eyes filled with understanding. "But you wish she was with you," he finished softly.

Lisa nodded, feeling a lump form in her throat. "Yes," she whispered.

The waitress returned with their drinks and took their orders. A moment of silence stretched between them, filled with the gentle clinking of cutlery and the low din of conversation from nearby tables. Lisa found herself studying Isaiah's face, noticing the faint lines at the corners of his eyes that hadn't been there in their younger days.

"I hope you don't mind me asking," Isaiah began, his voice hesitant, "but when you were in grad school and Charles and I were in law school, you guys seemed perfect for each other."

Lisa's eyebrows rose slightly. She hadn't expected the conversation to take this turn. "So, your question is what happened, right?" she asked, a wry smile tugging at her lips.

Isaiah gave her a sheepish look. "Well, yes," he admitted.

Lisa sighed, placing her hands in her lap. "It wasn't just one thing."

"It never is," he replied, his tone gentle and free of judgment.

She smiled, her fingers tracing the rim of her water glass. "You know, things *were* perfect between Charles and me, or at least I thought they were when our relationship began. But looking back now, with age and wisdom, I can see that we never really fit."

She paused, her gaze drifting to the window where the city lights twinkled like distant stars. "We were just too different," Lisa continued, turning back to Isaiah. "Charles was steady and reasonable to a fault. I mean, the man could plan out his entire week down to the minute." She chuckled softly, shaking her head. "And me? I was always too impulsive, too stubborn for him. I'd want to spontaneously book a weekend getaway, and he'd fret about rearranging his carefully crafted schedule."

Isaiah nodded, his eyes never leaving her face as she spoke.

"Eventually…" she sighed "…our differences just grated on each other. What once seemed charming became irritating. His stability felt stifling to me, and my spontaneity stressed him out." She took a sip of water, gathering her thoughts. "Luckily, we realized our marriage wasn't going to work before we got to the point where we hated each other. We both saw the writing on the wall, I suppose."

"So, the divorce was amicable then?" Isaiah asked, his voice gentle.

"As amicable as a divorce can be. Charles and I made a promise to each other once we decided to divorce that we would put Layla first. And we have." Despite the pain of their separation, she and Charles had managed to keep their daughter's well-being at the forefront. It wasn't always easy, but it was worth it.

Isaiah leaned back, a warm smile spreading across his face. "It sounds like you guys did a great job. Layla sounds like a wonderful young lady."

Lisa felt her chest swell with pride. "She is," she replied, her voice soft with affection.

The waitress approached their table, balancing two steaming plates. "Here we go," she announced cheerfully, setting down their meals. "Enjoy!"

The aroma of savory spices and sizzling vegetables filled the air. Lisa's stomach growled in anticipation as she picked up her fork. Across the table, Isaiah dug in with enthusiasm.

For a few minutes, they ate in comfortable silence. Lisa savored the familiar flavors, letting the warmth of the food chase away the lingering chill from their earlier walk. As her initial hunger subsided, her mind wandered back to their conversation.

Setting down her fork, Lisa took a sip of water and cleared her throat. "Since we're delving into the past," she began, her curiosity getting the better of her, "why did you and Charles lose touch?"

Isaiah's hand, which had been raising another forkful to his mouth, paused midair. He slowly lowered it back to his plate, his brow furrowing slightly. Lisa watched as he chewed his current bite deliberately, taking much longer than necessary.

The silence stretched between them, growing heavier with each passing second. She wondered if she'd overstepped, but just as she was about to apologize and tell him to forget it, Isaiah set his fork down with a soft clink against the plate. His eyes, usually warm and inviting, now held a hint of vulnerability that Lisa had never seen before.

"Part of it was just the usual," he began, "getting the job with the Chicago PD, moving there. You know, friends growing apart stuff." He paused.

She sensed there was more. She waited.

Isaiah met her gaze, something in his expression making her heart skip a beat. "But most of it was you," he confessed.

Lisa felt as if the air had been sucked from her lungs. "Me?"

He held her gaze. "Charles knew I had feelings for you. I never kept it from him, and he knew I'd never act on them. I would never have disrespected you or him that way."

Her heart pounded in her chest. A thousand questions batted through her head.

"But after you two married," he went on, "it just felt… wrong to stay in your lives. And I needed to move on."

The restaurant around them faded away. In that moment, it was just the two of them, separated by a table and years of unspoken feelings. Her mind whirled with the implications of his confession, wondering how different things might have been if she had known sooner.

Her mouth felt dry as she struggled to form a response. "I didn't know," she finally managed, her voice barely audible over the ambient chatter of the restaurant. But even as the words left her lips, a small voice in her head whispered, *Liar.*

Memories flooded back, unbidden. The easy laughter they'd shared. The way his eyes would linger on her when he thought she wasn't looking. The inexplicable flutter in her chest whenever their hands accidentally brushed.

There had always been a spark between them. A connection she'd stubbornly ignored because she loved Charles. And she had loved Charles, so it was easier and safer to pretend that her feelings for Isaiah didn't exist.

Her eyes drifted back to Isaiah's face. His deep brown eyes were perpetually sad, but he was still undeniably handsome, perhaps even more so now with the added maturity the years had given him. She wondered how many women had vied for his attention over the years.

"And did you?" she blurted out.

Isaiah looked up, a curious expression on his face. "Did I what?"

"Move on?" she asked, holding his gaze.

The intensity in Isaiah's eyes as he looked at her made her breath catch in her throat.

"I thought I had," he said at last, his voice low and filled with an emotion she couldn't quite name.

The weight of his confession hung in the air between them, heavy with unspoken possibility.

"I…" she began, then faltered. What could she say? Her thoughts drifted to her own attempts at moving on, a rueful smile tugging at her lips. "I only tried dating again last year, you know."

His eyebrows lifted in surprise. "Really? I would have thought…"

She shook her head. "No. It took Charles remarrying to push me back out there. I felt… I don't know, vulnerable? Like I needed to prove something to myself." She laughed softly, a tinge of self-deprecation in the sound. "It didn't last long. Just a couple of weeks. But I consider it a success, in a way. At least I tried, right?"

"And now?" he asked, his voice gentle. "Are you ready to try again?"

The question hung between them, laden with possibility. Lisa's heart raced as she considered her answer. Could she take that leap? Possibly with him?

She opened her mouth to respond, but instead, a massive yawn escaped her, causing her eyes to water. She covered her mouth, embarrassed by the sudden interruption.

He chuckled softly, his eyes crinkling at the corners. He drained the last of his drink and set the glass down with a decisive clink. "You're exhausted. I should get you home."

She felt a twinge of disappointment, even as her body agreed with his assessment. It had been a long day, and she hadn't realized just how tired she was until that moment. "I guess I am," she admitted, stifling another yawn.

He signaled for the check and dealt with the bill, while Lisa gathered their leftovers, carefully packing the containers into the bag the waitress left at the table.

As they made their way out of the restaurant, she found herself contemplating the possibility that the dinner, not a date, had just opened up. The possibility of something more with Isaiah both thrilled and terrified her.

ISAIAH GRIPPED THE steering wheel tightly as he navigated the quiet suburban streets. The short drive from the restaurant felt interminable, the only sound between them the low hum of the engine and the occasional turn of the blinker.

He had let his emotions get the best of him. Telling Lisa he'd had feelings for her was completely unprofessional. Not to mention awkward and embarrassing. And now here he was tongue-tied, barely able to make small talk, not exactly sure what to say to smooth things over.

He glanced over at her, her profile illuminated by the passing streetlights. She turned and caught his eye, offering a small smile that made his heart stutter. He quickly looked away, focusing on the road ahead. Great. Real smooth.

"Everything okay?" she asked, her voice soft and full of concern.

He cleared his throat, trying to push down the knot of anxiety in his stomach. "Yeah, just…thinking." He forced a chuckle. "Guess I'm not much for conversation after all that food."

Lisa laughed, a sound that eased some of the tension in his shoulders. "You were pretty chatty at dinner," she teased.

He couldn't think of a response that wasn't mortifying, so he remained silent. Moments later, he pulled up to her house and cut the engine, plunging them into silence broken only by the ticking of the cooling car.

"Well," Lisa said, unbuckling her seat belt. "Thanks for dinner. And the ride home."

"Of course," he replied with a smile that still felt forced. He got out of the car and quickly rounded the front to open her door.

They walked side by side up the short path to her front door, their arms occasionally brushing. Each touch sent a jolt through his body. *Get it together*, he scolded himself. *You're not some hormone-addled teenager.*

Lisa fumbled with her keys for a moment before sliding her key into the lock and opened the door with a creak. She stepped inside, setting her purse and the box of leftovers on a small table just inside the entryway. She turned to face him, her features softened by the dim sconce overhanging the porch.

He lingered just inside the threshold, unsure whether to follow or say good night. The air between them sizzled with electricity as they stood silently gazing at each other for a moment.

Lisa finally broke the silence. "Would you like to come in for a nightcap?" Her voice was barely above a whisper, but it stirred something deep within him.

His heart stuttered as she took a step closer, their bodies so close that he could feel her breath against his neck. He was dancing perilously close to a line here. He should leave. He should say good night and go home to his empty apartment. But his feet remained rooted to the spot as Lisa's gaze dropped to his lips.

The urge to pull her into his arms, to feel her mouth against his, was almost overwhelming.

But a small voice in the back of his mind whispered it was a terrible idea.

"Lisa, I'm not a good bet," he said, his words rough with barely contained emotion.

"Why? Isaiah, why are your eyes always so sad?" Her hazel eyes bore into his, as if searching for the answer.

The question hit him like a physical blow. He swallowed hard, averting his gaze. "I lost my partner. In Chicago," he admitted, the words tasting like ash in his mouth. "I should have been there, but I wasn't."

The admission hung heavy in the air between them, and a familiar ache started in his chest. His vision blurred, the present fading into the background as the memories came flooding back. Not for the first time he was back in Chicago on that fateful night.

"Brand, my partner, was going through a tough time. A nasty divorce."

Lisa made a soft, sympathetic sound, but he barely registered it.

He could see Brand as clearly in his mind as he'd been

those last months. Slumped over his desk most mornings, eyes bloodshot, tie askew. The faint smell of the mints he used to try to cover up the alcohol on his breath when he spoke.

"He started hitting the bars after work," Isaiah said, his voice tight. "It became a habit, you know? A way to numb his pain. One night, as the bar was closing, a thief came in and tried to rob the place. Brand intervened." He refocused on Lisa, seeing that she already knew what was coming. "He was shot and killed."

Lisa's eyes went soft with sympathy. "You couldn't have known that was going to happen."

He shook his head, a bitter laugh escaping his lips. "Maybe not, but I knew Brand was in a bad spot. That night, he called me, asked me to come out with him. But I was tired. I begged off."

Lisa touched her palm to his arm. "How many times didn't you beg off?"

He sighed internally, knowing where she was going with the question. A part of him understood he couldn't have known, wasn't responsible. But that knowledge didn't stop the guilt from eating away at him a little more each day. "Most of the time, I met him for a drink," he admitted. "I'd have a beer with him, make sure he didn't overdo it. Got him home safe."

"Isaiah, you can't blame yourself."

His jaw clenched. "I can, and I do," he said, his voice low and rough. "I'm not sure I have anything to offer anyone right now."

Lisa's expression softened a little more, and she placed her hand on his cheek. "When my divorce was finalized, I felt the same way. But I was wrong, and so are you. I know you have a lot to offer, Isaiah. More than you realize."

Her words hung in the air, a gentle challenge and invitation. He knew he should resist for a whole host of reasons, but he could feel his resolve wavering, the walls he'd so carefully constructed beginning to crumble. Maybe it was time to let go of the past and move toward something that he'd always wanted.

His heart raced as Lisa took a small step toward him, her eyes never leaving his.

"Lisa—" Isaiah began, but whatever else he was going to say died in his throat as she leaned in.

Time seemed to slow. He could see every detail of her face—the flecks of gold in her hazel eyes, the faint freckles across her nose, the soft curve of her lips as they parted slightly.

The kiss was gentle, tentative at first, a question more than a demand. For a moment, he stayed frozen, his mind racing. Then his hand came up to cup her cheek, his fingers threading through her hair.

He kissed her back, with growing intensity. It was like coming up for air after being underwater for too long.

When he finally stepped back, it was with a rush of emotion that left him dizzy. What was he doing? Lisa was a consultant on a case he was working on. He shouldn't be kissing her. But at that moment all he could think about was doing more than just kissing her.

Which was why it was time to go.

"You should get inside. It's cold." He forced himself to ignore the disappointment that swept across her face.

"Good night, Isaiah."

"Good night, Lisa."

Chapter Eight

Sunlight streamed through the window blinds as Lisa perched on the edge of her bed, phone pressed to her ear. A smile played on her lips as her daughter's excited voice poured from the other end of the phone line.

"Mom, you wouldn't believe how amazing Paris is!"

"I'm so happy you're having such a wonderful time, sweetheart," Lisa replied, excited on Layla's behalf. She pictured her daughter strolling along the Seine, beret perched jauntily on her head, and her smile grew.

"Oh, and yesterday I went to the Louvre! It was amazing, Mom. I've never seen anything like it."

An image flashed through Lisa's mind as Layla continued describing the masterpieces: Lisa and Isaiah, hand in hand, gazing up at the glass pyramid entrance of the museum.

The image shifted into a memory of the previous night, reliving the unexpected, electrifying kiss they'd shared. Isaiah's strong arms encircling her waist, drawing her close. The intoxicating scent of his sandalwood and citrus cologne. His lips on hers, soft and insistent, igniting a spark she'd thought long extinguished.

Her heart raced, a wave of desire washing over her.

"Oh, Mom, I hate to cut this short, but I've got to run," Layla said, her voice tinged with regret. "I'm meeting some new friends."

Lisa felt a pang of disappointment but pushed it aside. "Of course, sweetheart. Have a wonderful time."

"I love you, Mom," Layla chirped.

"I love you too, darling. Be safe." She set her phone down and padded into the bathroom, her mind still buzzing with thoughts of Isaiah.

"Get a grip," she muttered, but couldn't quite shake the buoyant feeling. It had been a long time since she'd been this attracted to a man.

A nagging voice in her head piped up as she was putting on her makeup. What did that kiss really mean? Was it just a moment of weakness, or something more? Did she want it to be something more?

She shook her head, pushing the questions aside. "Don't overanalyze. Just enjoy it," she told herself firmly as she made the drive to work.

The moment she stepped into the office reception area, thoughts of Isaiah fled. Files lay scattered across the carpet, a trail of paper leading down the hallway. Her heart began to race, this time with fear rather than excitement.

"Harry? Tani?" She got no response.

She moved down the hallway toward the offices, dread building with each step. Rounding the corner into Harry's office, she gasped.

The room was in chaos, drawers upended, furniture overturned. Amid the destruction, Harry lay on the floor.

"Oh god, Harry!" She rushed to his side. She dropped to her knees beside Harry's motionless form. His chest was barely moving, and his skin was an ashen color that made her blood run cold.

"Harry! Oh god, Harry, can you hear me?" She pressed two fingers against his wrist, desperately seeking a pulse. After several agonizing seconds, she felt a faint but present pulse. Relief flooded through her.

"Hold on, Harry. Hold on." She fumbled in her purse for her phone. She punched in 911, her eyes darting around the ransacked office. Papers and belongings were strewn everywhere. Whatever the intruder had been looking for, they'd torn the place apart to find it.

"911, what's your emergency?"

Lisa gave the operator the details of Harry's condition and rattled off the address. As soon as she finished with the operator, she dialed Isaiah's phone number.

"Isaiah, it's Harry," she started as soon as the call connected. "He's hurt. Someone broke into our office and they… He…"

"Lisa, slow down. Are you hurt?" Isaiah asked, concern lacing his words.

She worked to slow her pounding heart. "I'm fine. It's Harry. I found him in his office. He's hurt badly. The ambulance is on the way, but, Isaiah… I need you, can you come?"

"I'm on my way. Stay there, okay?"

She kept Harry's hand in her own the entire time she was on the phone, his faint pulse reassurance that he was still there with her. "Help is coming, Harry. Just stay with me."

The wait for the EMTs felt like it went on forever. Lisa alternated between watching Harry's shallow breathing and glancing anxiously at the door. When the EMTs finally hurried into the reception area, relief rushed through her.

They swarmed around Harry, their words a rapid-fire exchange of medical jargon.

She stepped back, watching and feeling helpless, as they worked to save her mentor and friend.

"Ma'am, can you tell us what happened?" A police officer that Lisa hadn't noticed until then approached, notepad in hand.

She tore her gaze from Harry's pale face. "I—I don't know. I just found him like this when I arrived."

She answered the officer's questions, guilt gnawing at her. This was her fault. This had to be the work of the guy who thought Scott had given her the code. They wanted her, but Harry was paying the price for whatever mess she'd gotten herself into.

The EMTs got Harry onto a gurney and began wheeling him out of his office. She trailed behind them.

As they approached the elevators, the doors slid open with a ding.

Her heart leaped into her throat when she saw Isaiah step out, his eyes wild with concern. He stepped out of the EMTs' way and moved quickly toward her.

"Lisa! Are you okay?" His eyes darted between her and Harry's prone form.

The EMTs maneuvered the gurney into the elevator. The doors shut with finality, leaving Lisa and Isaiah alone in the suddenly quiet hallway.

Another surge of guilt and fear washed over her. She couldn't hold back her tears anymore.

"They hurt Harry because of me," she choked out, her voice cracking with emotion.

Isaiah pulled her into his arms, his embrace firm yet gentle. His warmth enveloped her, a stark contrast to the cold dread in her chest.

"None of this is because of you," he murmured, his hand moving in soothing circles on her back.

She pulled away slightly. "It's because they think I have whatever they're looking for. But I don't, Isaiah. I don't even know what it is!" Her shoulders shook as a fresh wave of sobs racked her body. She hated crying, especially in front of someone. Hated feeling weak, but Harry, Harry was almost like a father to her.

Isaiah pulled her closer and let her cry into his chest. "It's okay, Lisa. We'll figure this out," he said softly, his hand now stroking her hair. After a few moments, he pulled back. "I'm going to go talk to the officers. Will you be all right for a minute?"

She nodded, wiping her eyes with the back of her hand. She needed a moment anyway to get herself together. She watched as Isaiah strode into the reception area of the office. Through the glass front wall, she could see him approach the two officers, his posture radiating authority.

Lisa wrapped her arms around herself, feeling suddenly cold and alone in the empty reception area. She couldn't hear what they were saying, but she could see Isaiah's face growing more serious with each passing moment.

She stood there, her eyes unfocused on the scene before her, trying to control the chaos of thoughts and feelings roiling inside her. No matter what Isaiah or anyone said, she couldn't shake the guilt clawing through her.

"Lisa? What's going on?" Tani called out.

Isaiah spun at the sound of the new voice, hand on his weapon. He pulled back his suit jacket to expose his badge. "Ma'am, I'm with the police. Who are you?"

"This is Tani Reyes. She's our office receptionist," Lisa answered for the woman who appeared to have been stunned temporarily mute by the scene before her.

"Sorry." Isaiah removed his hand from the butt of his

gun. "I'm Detective Isaiah Reeves. Do you know what happened here?"

"No." Tani shook her head. "I went out to grab coffee about a half hour ago, and I just got back."

They moved down the hall into Lisa's office, which was just as much a mess as the rest of the office.

"What about building security?" Isaiah asked.

"You have to sign in with security in the lobby," Lisa answered. "There are cameras in all the common areas, the elevators, and the stairwell."

Isaiah frowned. "There are no cameras inside your company office space?"

"Harry and I contemplated cameras in the office space, but frankly, they are a security risk. They can be stolen and hacked, and some of our clients demand strict confidentiality." Lisa shook her head. "No. The computers and equipment that stays here in the office is password protected with dual verification and encrypted. Harry and I have laptops, but we take them home with us each night, and they are also password protected."

"What do you keep in your desk?" Isaiah directed the question to Lisa while studying the contents of the open drawers without touching them.

"Nothing important," Lisa answered. "Just office supplies. Any hard copy client files get locked away in that file cabinet or in secure storage off-site if the case has been closed for more than a year. Everything else is on the computer, saved in secure cloud storage."

Isaiah examined the file cabinet. "Were these scratches always here?" He pointed at the scratches around the locking mechanism. They looked fresh.

Lisa stepped up next to him and examined the lock herself. "No."

"It looks like someone tried to get inside, though it doesn't seem like they succeeded."

"Thank goodness. This is unbelievable." Lisa pressed her hands together in front of her.

"Why would anyone do this?" Tani asked.

"They were looking for something," Lisa answered without thinking. Isaiah shot her a sharp look.

"Looking for what?" Tani asked.

Lisa caught the slight shake of Isaiah's head. "We don't know," she answered without glancing at the receptionist. "Tani, why don't you take the rest of the day off?"

"Are you sure?" Tani looked conflicted, as if she wanted to run but didn't want Lisa to know it.

"The office is a crime scene anyway. I can't let you back in until we are done," Isaiah interjected. "I'll need to get your statement, but then I'll have to ask you to leave."

Despite her prior hesitation, Tani looked relieved.

Isaiah took Tani's statement, but it shed no light on who could have ransacked the office.

Tani reiterated that she'd stepped out for her second cup of coffee, something she did most mornings. Harry was in his office working, and she'd buzzed him on the intercom to let him know that she was leaving and ask if he wanted anything. He hadn't, so she'd left. She admitted to lingering longer than usual, flirting with a cute barista.

Whoever had broken in had likely been watching, scoping the office out, and had seen an opportunity when Tani left. There was no way to know if the assailants hadn't known that Harry was still inside or if they simply hadn't cared. But given the time frame between Tani leaving and Lisa arriving at the office, the assailants had been fast and violent.

Isaiah let Tani go home, then did a thorough search of

the building. Lisa overheard him telling the uniformed officers to have the door leading from the underground garage
into the building dusted for prints. Apparently, the lock on
the door had been broken, and that was the suspected entry
point for the intruders.

Then he joined her where she waited for him in the reception area.

She looked up at him as he entered. "You know this is
connected to the break-in at my house, don't you?"

"We can't be certain yet, but yes. I don't believe in coincidences."

Lisa shook her head. "Then if it was the same guy, he
was looking for the code that he thinks Scott gave me."

"That's what I think."

"But I swear I don't have it."

"That you know of. Just because Mr. Donlea didn't give
it to you directly doesn't mean you don't have it."

She swept her hands out. "Then where is it?" She
dropped her head into her hands.

"Are you sure you're okay?" Isaiah stepped in close and
put a hand on her shoulder. The simple act shouldn't have
been as comforting as it was. Or as stirring. "You could be
in shock. Maybe I should take you to the hospital."

"I don't need a hospital. I just don't usually have my
life threatened and my office broken into all in one day."

"Hey," he said, sitting down next to her. "I'm not going
to let anything happen to you."

Several charged seconds passed between them.

After a moment, Isaiah cleared his throat. "Listen, why
don't I drive you to the hospital anyway?" He put his hands
up when she started to argue. "Not because you need it,
but I'm sure you want to be with Harry."

The fight went out of her in an instant. She nodded.

"Yes, you're right. I do need to be there for Harry when he wakes up."

The attack on Harry had to be about Scott and whatever those men thought he'd given her. Which meant it was her fault. She should have gotten tighter security at the office after the break-in at her house. Gotten those cameras or at least alerted security to be on guard. She hugged herself tighter. She'd been careless, thoughtless. Of course, Harry would have been a target if she was. They were partners, after all.

She opened her eyes and looked at Isaiah. "I'm going to find out who did this," she vowed, her voice steely with determination and anger. "Whatever it takes."

THE ANTISEPTIC SMELL assaulted Isaiah's nostrils as he paced the sterile hospital waiting room. Harsh lighting cast a sickly pallor on mint green walls. The news played on the TV mounted in the corner, the sound muted. A vending machine hummed, its glass front reflecting Isaiah's haggard face as he passed by.

He pulled out his phone, hit the speed dial for Connie, and pressed it to his ear. She picked up on the second ring. He'd called her on the way to the hospital, letting her know about the break-in at Lisa's office and the attack on Harry.

"Connie, it's Isaiah. Lisa and I are still waiting to talk to the doctor."

"Damn. I'm at the scene now supervising evidence collection. We're going over this place with a fine-tooth comb."

"Good." Isaiah's gaze drifted to Lisa whose face was gaunt and drawn. What the hell were these bastards after? Questions swirled in his mind, pieces of a puzzle he couldn't quite fit together.

"We'll figure this out, Isaiah," Connie said, as if reading his thoughts. "How's Lisa holding up?"

He glanced across the sterile waiting room again at Lisa's hunched form. Her head hung low, shoulders slumped in defeat. The shadows hid part of her face, accentuating the worry lines etched around her eyes. They were the only two people in the room, isolated islands of grief in a sea of uncomfortable, empty chairs.

His jaw clenched. "Not good," Isaiah replied, his voice barely above a whisper. "She's taking it hard. Blaming herself for all of this."

A sigh crackled through the phone. "She shouldn't. There's no way she could have known what was going to happen. Hell, we don't even know what these guys are after."

He pinched the bridge of his nose, feeling the weight of helplessness settle on his shoulders. "I know, Connie. But you know how it is. Guilt doesn't always follow logic." He knew that from personal experience all too well.

"True enough," Connie conceded. "Keep me posted on Sonfeld's condition," she said. "I'll call when I know more about the office."

Isaiah hung up and slipped the phone back in his pocket. His footsteps echoed in the quiet room as he made his way back to Lisa. He sank into the empty chair beside her, the cheap plastic creaking under his weight. For a moment, he just sat there, studying her profile, searching for the right words to break the heavy silence.

"Lisa," he began softly, leaning in slightly. "I know this is tough. Believe me, I understand." He paused, memories of his own loss threatening to surface. He pushed them back down. "But if you can walk me through what happened when you found Harry, it might help us track down whoever did this."

Lisa remained motionless, her gaze fixed on the scuffed linoleum floor for a long moment. Her hands were clasped tightly in her lap, knuckles white with tension.

Isaiah stopped fighting the urge to reach out and comfort her.

"Don't you see? This is all my fault. The person who broke into my house... It must be the same guy. Looking for this code or whatever. I'm the reason Harry is in there—" The rest of her words were swallowed up by a sob.

"Lisa, listen to me. This is not your fault," he said. "You couldn't have known what was going to happen."

Lisa shook her head, and he could tell she was unconvinced. They sat in silence for a moment before Lisa looked up at him.

She locked eyes with him, her jaw set. "I'm going to find out what they want," she declared. "And I swear, Isaiah, I will make them pay for what they did to Harry."

Isaiah held her gaze. "Lisa, I understand how you feel, but you need to leave this to me and Connie. Getting any more involved could be dangerous—"

"Dangerous?" Lisa cut him off, her voice sharp. "I'm already involved, Isaiah. They broke into my house. My office. Attacked my mentor. That's more than just involved. I'm going to get to the bottom of this, no matter what you say."

Isaiah opened his mouth to protest further, but the words died on his lips as the waiting room's sliding glass doors hissed open. He and Lisa both turned, the conversation momentarily forgotten as a doctor in rumpled blue scrubs stepped through. The man's weary gaze settled on them.

"Harry Sonfeld?" he asked, his voice carrying a weight that made Isaiah's stomach clench.

Lisa shot to her feet. "Yes."

Isaiah rose beside her, placing a supportive hand on her shoulder.

The doctor's gaze flicked between them, his brow furrowing. "Are you family?" he asked, directing the question at Lisa.

She swallowed hard, her hands twisting together. "Harry has no biological family still living," Lisa explained, her voice wavering. "But I'm… I'm like a daughter to him." The words caught in her throat, and Isaiah could see the tears threatening to spill from her eyes.

For a moment, the doctor hesitated, clearly weighing hospital policy against the raw emotion before him. Finally, he gave a small nod and took a deep breath. "Mr. Sonfeld was beaten quite severely," he began, his tone carefully measured.

Isaiah felt Lisa stiffen beside him, and he instinctively tightened his grip on her shoulder.

The doctor continued, "We've made the decision to place him in a medically induced coma. This will give his body the best chance to heal from the trauma."

Lisa's sharp intake of breath echoed in the quiet room.

Isaiah's mind worked frantically, trying to process the implications. A coma. It was serious, but it also meant Harry was still fighting.

"The next several days will be crucial," the doctor continued, his expression grave. "We'll be monitoring him closely, but I want you to understand the severity of his condition."

As the doctor's words sank in, Isaiah saw Lisa's composure finally crack. Her shoulders began to shake, and without thinking, he pulled her into a tight embrace. She buried her face against his chest, her sobs muffled but heart-wrenching.

Holding her, his jaw clenched with a mixture of sympathy and anger. Whoever had done this to Harry, whoever had caused this pain, he'd find them and bring them to justice. And despite his earlier protests, he knew now that keeping Lisa out of the investigation would be impossible. Which meant he'd have to figure out a way to keep her safe while she threw herself into the path of danger.

Chapter Nine

Isaiah's breath frosted in the air as he cranked the heater dial in the sedan's dashboard to its maximum setting. The old Crown Vic's engine wheezed in protest, barely mustering a tepid breeze from the vents. He squinted into the rearview mirror, searching for any sign of Connie's return with their coffee. The street was empty just as it was the last time he'd looked. What was taking so long for that coffee?

He adjusted his position in the driver seat. Contrary to what television and movies liked to portray, stakeouts were mostly miserable. Too hot in the summer and too cold in the winter. And of course he'd forgotten his gloves. He glared at the dashboard, willing warmth into existence.

They'd already been sitting in this frigid car for an hour watching people go into the meeting Arnold had put them onto.

He glanced over at Lisa. She sat motionless in the passenger seat, her gaze fixed on some unseen point beyond the frosted glass. The shadows caught the curve of her cheek.

He'd done his best to convince her to go home and get some rest to no avail. Harry's assault had made her insistent on doing everything she could to get to the bottom of whatever was going on. He considered outright banning her from the stakeout but hadn't been convinced she wouldn't simply show up at Arnold's meeting tonight no matter what he said. At least if she was with him and Connie, he'd be able to keep an eye on her and keep her safe.

The sweet fragrance of Lisa's floral perfume filled his senses and clouded his focus. Despite their professional partnership, Isaiah was distracted by her presence, thoughts racing through his mind that had no place in their current mission.

A small smile tugged at his lips despite the cold. Maybe this wasn't the absolute worst stakeout he'd ever endured. The company, at least, was a marked improvement over some of his previous partners. It might have been the coldest though, he thought, blowing on his freezing fingers, the warm air providing momentary relief before the chill crept back in. He rubbed his palms together vigorously, the friction offering a pitiful semblance of warmth.

Lisa turned in the passenger seat to look at him. "Cold?" she asked, a glimmer of amusement in her eyes. "Didn't you just move from Chicago?"

He blew on his hands again, his breath forming a small cloud in the frigid air. "I hated every minute of winter there too. The wind…" He shivered involuntarily at the memory, his shoulders hunching slightly.

She laughed again, the sound a light tinkle, a stark contrast to the winter chill surrounding them. Her laughter seemed to warm him more effectively than the sputtering heater, and he found himself thinking of ways to make her laugh again.

"A tough detective like yourself can't handle a little cold," she teased, a hint of the light that had gone out of her eyes in the hospital coming back now.

"Even tough detectives like me can freeze to death," he grumbled, his words forming little clouds that dissipated against the windshield.

She reached for her purse, her eyes still sparking, and began pulling out an assortment of items: a small notebook, her cell phone, and a well-worn paperback book.

"It's like watching you go on a treasure hunt," he quipped. "What else do you have in there?"

She paused, giving him a playful look. "Wouldn't you like to know?" she said, her tone suggesting a wealth of secrets hidden within the depths of her bag.

The sultriness in her voice sent a jolt of lust coursing through him.

She pulled a set of keys out of the mysterious bag.

The sheer number of key chains dangling from the ring made his eyes widen. "Whoa! You could hurt somebody with those. Why do you have so many key chains?"

Her laughter filled the car again and brought a smile to his face. "It's kind of my thing," she explained. "Some people collect paintings or tchotchkes. I like key chains."

He found himself leaning in slightly, taking in the various key chains.

"I started picking one up whenever I traveled or if I just saw an interesting or unique one that I liked," she continued. "Then other people saw that I collected them, and they began buying them for me." She shook the keys, creating a cheerful jingle. "And here we are. This is only a fraction of the collection. I couldn't possibly carry them all. I rotate them in and out of circulation."

He nodded, charmed by this glimpse into her life outside of work.

She turned back to her bag, rummaging once more. "Here it is," she announced triumphantly, pulling out a small square object that looked like a miniature beanbag. She held it out to Isaiah.

He took it, turning the plastic packet over. "What is it?" he asked, genuinely puzzled.

Her eyebrows shot up in disbelief. "I'm surprised you don't know, having lived in Chicago," she said. "It's a hand warmer. Crush it between your hands like an ice pack, and it will warm up. You're supposed to use it inside gloves, but it will work this way too."

He did as instructed. As the warmth spread through his palms, he let out an involuntary sigh of relief. "Oh, that's it right there. I could kiss you."

As soon as the words popped out of his mouth, he wished he could shove them back in. There was little need for the hand warmer now, his whole body was aflame with embarrassment. "I didn't mean…"

Her laugh was so loud now that it all but bounced around the inside of the car. "I know what you meant, and you're welcome."

He hoped the dimly lit interior masked most of his mortification. There was something about Lisa, always had been, that made him comfortable enough to say exactly what he was thinking at the moment. Which was not necessarily a good thing when he was on a case. Or trying to tamp down burgeoning feelings for the one that got away.

The tap-tap of footsteps had him glancing in the rearview mirror again. Finally! Connie was headed their way, carrying a to-go tray with three large, steaming cups.

He let the driver side window down so he could take his and Lisa's coffees before Connie got into the back seat.

"It is freezing out there." Connie slid her coffee cup into the cupholder in the back seat. "I got us treats as well." She held up a brown paper bag. "Couple chocolate chip cookies, a muffin, and a banana for those of us who might be more health conscious."

"I'll take a cookie," Lisa said.

Connie laughed, handing the bag between the front seats. "My kind of woman. I was hoping you wouldn't ask for the banana."

"Not a chance." Lisa's laughter joined Connie's as she plucked a cookie from the bag.

"The banana is for me," Isaiah said. Lisa gave him a questioning look but handed it over. "What? I like to watch my sugar intake."

Connie leaned into the space between the seats, looking at Lisa. "This talk of sugary treats has reminded me that I've been meaning to extend an invitation to my annual holiday party. It's the event of the season, if I do say so myself."

"Oh," Lisa said, clearly surprised. "Thank you, but I don't want to intrude."

"You can't intrude. I invite the whole office. All my husband's coworkers. Friends. Family. I've even browbeaten this guy into coming." She hooked her thumb at Isaiah. "Tell her she should come."

Connie's last comment was directed at Isaiah. "I was hoping I could be left out of this," he deadpanned.

Lisa glanced at him. "If you don't want me to go…"

"No," he responded quickly. "You should go, really. The entire office is talking about how great Connie's parties are."

"See?" Connie piped up again. "Come. I promise you'll have a great time. I'll text you the details. I'm sure Isaiah wouldn't mind giving you a ride."

He made a mental note to throttle his matchmaking partner the next time they were alone but didn't have to force a smile when he said, "Of course, I wouldn't mind."

"All right. Thank you for the invitation. I'll be there," Lisa said.

A moment later, Isaiah spotted Arnold making his way down the sidewalk and toward the front door of the building where the hackers were meeting. He sat up straighter in his seat. "Hey, there's Arnold."

Connie had met with Arnold while Isaiah and Lisa were at the hospital and fitted him with a wire, which was the size of a button, sewn into the inside of Arnold's shirt.

They heard Arnold greet a group of people not long after entering but almost immediately, the conversation crackled over the wire, fading in and out.

"Connie…" Isaiah said, anxious. This would all be for nothing if the wire didn't pick up the conversation.

"I'm working on it." Connie fidgeted with a small receiver, fine-tuning the audio feed from Arnold's wire. "Got it," she murmured, as a voice crackled through the speaker.

"…reason we invited you, Arnold. We're a man down since…"

Isaiah's grip tightened on the wheel. He glanced at Connie, seeing his own tension mirrored in her furrowed brow.

"I appreciate the opportunity," Arnold's voice came through, steady despite the circumstances. "What exactly do you need me for?"

There was a pause, and Isaiah found himself holding his breath. *Come on*, he thought. *Give us something*.

"Word is you've got skills," the unknown man continued. "We've got a program that's acting up. Need someone to take a look, figure out what's wrong with it."

What kind of program? What were these guys up to? Isaiah was bursting to run in there and demand answers, but he knew they needed more. They had to let this play out.

"I could definitely help with that," Arnold replied, a hint of eagerness in his tone that made Isaiah wince. *Don't overdo it*, he silently warned.

Lisa shifted in the back seat. "He's doing fine," she whispered, as if sensing his thoughts. "Just give him time."

Isaiah nodded, forcing himself to relax. She was right. Arnold was their best shot at infiltrating this group. They had to trust him.

"Now, now, Arnie," the voice replied, "let's not get ahead of ourselves. We don't know you well enough for specifics just yet."

Isaiah's stomach tightened. Arnold was walking a razor's edge, and he wasn't sure the man could keep his balance.

"This here's just a meet and greet," the voice continued. "We're feeling you out, seeing if you're a good fit."

"Got it. Makes sense," Arnold said.

"So, have you ever crossed paths with Big Joe before?"

"Not officially, no," Arnold replied.

There was a rustling sound, followed by muffled voices. Suddenly, the first voice returned, "Big Joe, I got someone here I want you to meet. This here is Arnold."

A new voice, deep and gravelly, filled the car. "Well, Arnie," it drawled, the nickname dripping with disdain, "Ryan here says I should meet you."

Isaiah's muscles tensed. He leaned closer to the speaker, determined to catch every word even though they were taping the conversation.

"I've heard good things about you," Arnold managed, nerves ringing through his tone.

"Oh yeah?" Big Joe's tone turned menacing. "What have you heard about me?"

Isaiah could almost picture Arnold's face, struggling to find the right words.

"N-nothing," Arnold stammered. "Just…you're the man."

In the driver seat, Isaiah groaned inwardly. "He's blowing it," he muttered. "They're on to him."

Connie leaned forward from the back seat, her voice calm but insistent. "Just give him a chance."

Isaiah took a deep breath, trying to quell his rising anxiety. Years of police work had honed his instincts, and right now, they were screaming danger.

The conversation continued, and Isaiah focused intently on every word. Big Joe's voice came through again. "We might be needing someone with good computer skills to help on a project."

"Yeah, Ryan mentioned that," Arnold replied, his eagerness palpable even through the tinny speaker. "What kind of project?"

Isaiah winced. "If he keeps that up, they're going to know something's up," he said, his hand instinctively moving toward the car door. "We should pull him out."

Connie's hand shot out, gripping his arm. "Just wait a minute," she urged, her eyes fixed on the speaker. "Let's see if he can get Big Joe to mention what the project is. At least give us a damn hint to work with."

Isaiah hesitated, torn between his instinct to protect their asset and the need for crucial information. He settled back into his seat, every muscle coiled and ready to spring into action at a moment's notice. He glanced at Lisa, who also seemed tense with expectation.

The tension in the car was palpable as Big Joe's gravelly voice crackled through the speaker again. "Slow your roll, little man. Tonight, we're just going to get to know each other. Our last guy grew a conscience. We don't have time to deal with that mess again, so I've got to make sure you're solid before I let you in."

"Solid, yeah, sure. I'm solid," Arnold stammered. "I just need to know what I'm getting into, you know?"

Isaiah clenched his jaw. He'd seen too many undercover operations go south, and Arnold's nervousness was becoming more apparent by the second.

A loud harrumph echoed through the microphone, followed by the clinking of glasses and indistinct chatter. Isaiah's eyes darted to the club's entrance, where people had started to trickle out.

"Connie," he whispered, nodding toward the departing attendees.

Without a word, Connie raised the camera on her lap, discreetly snapping photos of each person leaving the building.

Suddenly, Big Joe's voice cut through the ambient noise coming through the microphone. "Come on in the back. We can talk about the project more there."

Isaiah tensed, his hand instinctively moving to his holstered weapon. "I don't like this," he muttered, more to himself than the others.

A moment later, a loud crash reverberated through the speaker, followed by Arnold's panicked voice. "Hey, what was that for?"

"Who are you working for?" Big Joe's accusation was unmistakable.

"No one," Arnold protested weakly. But the sounds of a scuffle and pained grunts made it clear that Big Joe hadn't believed him.

"Damn, they made him," Connie hissed, already reaching for the door handle.

Isaiah whirled around to face Lisa. "You stay here. Do

not move." Without waiting for a response, he and Connie burst out of the car, weapons drawn, and raced across the street toward the club. He and Connie pushed past a couple coming out the front door and ran into the club.

There were only a few people still in the big space. Their heads swung, matching looks of surprise on their faces, as he and Connie burst into the club. Isaiah scanned the room but didn't see Arnold anywhere.

"They took him in the back," Connie yelled, already moving toward the door behind the bar.

He followed.

They pushed through the heavy swinging doors into an industrial kitchen. Massive ovens lined one wall, their surfaces gleaming even in the darkened kitchen. The air was thick with the smell of grease and cleaning products, a testament to the constant use and maintenance of this space.

"Clear," he muttered to Connie, keeping his gun at the ready.

A muffled thud and grunt echoed from beyond the kitchen, causing Isaiah's jaw to clench as he swiftly moved past a row of prep tables. He could feel his heart pounding in his chest as he approached the source of the noise.

"You hear that?" he whispered to Connie, who nodded grimly in response.

"An office, probably. Let's go." They made their way toward a closed door at the far end of the kitchen, both tense and alert.

Isaiah took a deep breath and placed his hand on the doorknob. In one fluid motion, he flung it open and shouted, "Freeze! Police!" Connie echoed his command beside him.

The scene before them was chaotic and violent. Arnold, his face bloodied and bruised, was locked in a struggle with two men.

One of them, a massive figure that could only be Big Joe, spun around at their abrupt entrance, surprise evident on his face. The smaller man also froze momentarily, giving Arnold the opportunity to land a well-aimed punch on his jaw. The man crumpled to his knees with a pained groan.

Arnold shook out his hand with a grimace. "Damn. I think I might have broken it." He shot an angry glare at the man on the ground. "But it was worth it."

In the moment of distraction, Big Joe seized his chance and bolted toward a second door in the office.

"I got him!" Isaiah yelled, already in pursuit. He exited the kitchen cautiously, unsure if Big Joe had a weapon on him. He didn't see one, but that didn't mean much.

His heart pounded as he burst through the door into the alley, gun gripped tightly in his hand. The cold night air hit his face, chilling him but not slowing him down.

Ahead, Big Joe's massive form raced down the narrow passageway, surprisingly agile for his size.

"Stop! Police!" Isaiah shouted, knowing it was futile.

Big Joe reached the end of the alley and veered right, away from the car where Lisa sat.

Thank God. But just because Lisa wasn't in immediate danger didn't mean others weren't.

Big Joe made another turn, this time onto a residential street lined with row houses. Isaiah sprinted after him.

Warm light spilled from the windows of homes decked out with holiday decorations. Luckily, the street was empty, the cold weather no doubt discouraging late night walks. But that didn't mean it would stay that way.

Big Joe's heavy footfalls echoed off the sidewalk as he thundered ahead.

Isaiah's training kicked in as he assessed the situation. No visible weapon on Big Joe, but he still couldn't risk firing a warning shot in a residential area. He'd have to take the man down physically. Which meant he'd have to catch him first.

A cacophony of barking erupted as he and Big Joe raced past house after house. A gruff voice called out from an upper window, "What the hell is going on out there?"

Isaiah gritted his teeth, pushing himself harder. He had to catch Big Joe before noisy neighbors started to get curious and come out of their homes to see what was going on. He couldn't let this turn into a bigger scene than it already was. He needed to get Big Joe into custody now.

Big Joe darted down a second street.

By the time Isaiah rounded the corner, the man had vanished.

"Dammit," Isaiah muttered, scanning the area. No way a guy Big Joe's size had just disappeared into thin air. Where was he?

Cars lined both sides of the dark street, perfect hiding spots. In his head, Isaiah picked through worst-case scenarios. If Big Joe got into one of the surrounding houses, it could turn ugly fast.

His hand instinctively went to his phone. He should call Connie for backup. But doing so would let Big Joe know where he was. The soft crunch of his shoes on the pavement seemed deafening in the quiet night.

He crept forward, peering around each vehicle, gun at the ready. His senses were on high alert, straining for any sign of Big Joe in the shadows. *Where are you?*

A sudden movement caught Isaiah's eye. A figure darted from behind a parked sedan and sprinted down the street.

He cursed, adrenaline surging as he gave chase again. His legs burned with exertion, but determination fueled him. He couldn't let Big Joe get away. The man was the only lead he had in Scott Donlea's murder.

Big Joe's labored breathing echoed in the night air. Despite his initial burst of speed, Isaiah could see the man was flagging.

"Give it up, Joe!" Isaiah shouted. "You're only making it worse for yourself!"

Panic flashed in Big Joe's eyes as he glanced back. He grabbed a trash can, hurling it behind him.

Isaiah leaped over the obstacle, his momentum barely breaking.

They were approaching a busier street, neon signs glowing in the distance. Even at this late hour, there'd be people around. Potential hostages. Potential collateral damage.

Isaiah put on more speed, his resolve hardening. He holstered his gun midstride, calculating the risk. He had one chance. He had to make it count.

With a final burst of speed, Isaiah launched himself forward, tackling Big Joe around the legs. They crashed to the pavement in a tangle of limbs.

"Get off me!" Big Joe roared, struggling to break free.

Isaiah grunted, using his training to quickly maneuver the larger man onto his stomach. "You're under arrest," he panted, snapping the cuffs into place.

Big Joe wheezed, his face pressed against the sidewalk. "I ain't…done…nothing," he gasped out.

Hauling the man to his feet, Isaiah fought to catch his breath. "Arnold's face would beg to differ. But I tell you what, let's go down to the station and sort it all out."

Chapter Ten

Isaiah left Big Joe, whose real name was Joseph Hickman, and Ryan to stew in a holding cell overnight. He and Connie had been working the case nonstop, and they both needed a good night's sleep before tackling the duo's interrogations.

Not that it appeared to be helping now. Isaiah had come into the station at 9:00 a.m. on a full night's sleep, ready to get answers from Joe and Ryan, but it appeared that had been a whole lot of wishful thinking on his part.

He massaged his temples, emerging from the interrogation room with Big Joe. Hours of questioning had left him drained and no closer to finding Scott's killer than when he walked in.

Connie straightened from where she'd been leaning against the wall, her sharp gaze scrutinizing him. "No luck, huh?"

He shook his head, running a hand over his chin. "Big Joe's not giving me anything. It's like trying to squeeze water from a stone."

He mentally reviewed every tactic he'd employed. Was there something he'd missed? Had he pushed too hard? Not hard enough? The case hinged on cracking either Big Joe or Ryan. And so far, they were coming up empty.

Connie's brow furrowed. "Has he lawyered up?"

"No," Isaiah replied. "But we could keep going at him till the cows come home, he's not going to crack. He knows the system too well. He knows as long as he and Ryan don't talk, we got nothing other than assault. He's not afraid of doing time for that."

He leaned against the wall, feeling the cold cinder blocks through the back of his shirt. The weight of the case pressed down on him, each dead end another stone on his shoulders.

Connie's eyes flickered to a second door farther down the hallway. She nodded toward it. "You want me to have a go with Ryan?"

Isaiah followed her line of sight, considering. Ryan was younger and therefore more likely to be the weak link, to break under pressure. But he got the sense that Ryan was only a lackey, so it was also possible he didn't know all that much. They had nothing now, so Isaiah had little choice.

Isaiah blew out a heavy sigh, his shoulders sagging under the weight of exhaustion and frustration. "Let me try first," he said, his voice gruff with determination.

Connie nodded, a flicker of understanding passing between them. She swept one hand toward the door, gesturing for Isaiah to proceed. With her other hand, she extended a manila folder.

He took the file, nodding his thanks, then strode past Connie, his footsteps echoing in the stark hallway. As he approached the second door, he took a deep breath, steeling himself for what lay ahead.

The door creaked open, revealing an interrogation room smaller than the one next door where Big Joe still sat.

Isaiah's eyes fell on Ryan, who was slumped over the metal table, one hand secured to a bar with a gleaming pair of handcuffs. The young man's posture spoke volumes about his current state—a mixture of boredom, frustration, and anxiety.

At the sound of the door opening, Ryan's head snapped up, his eyes wide with a flicker of hope. Isaiah noted the dark circles under the man's eyes and the nervous twitch of his free hand. "Finally," he blurted out, his voice cracking slightly. "Are you letting me out of here?"

Isaiah pulled out the chair opposite Ryan, saying nothing. The chair's metal legs scraped against the floor. He lowered himself into the seat, fixing Ryan with a hardened gaze.

"I'm afraid you're not getting out of here anytime soon, Ryan," Isaiah finally responded. He placed the file on the table between them, a silent reminder of the evidence they had—or at least, what Ryan might believe they had.

Ryan's face fell, the brief spark of hope extinguished. Isaiah watched as the reality of the situation settled over the young man like a heavy blanket.

He's scared, Isaiah thought. *Good. Maybe that fear will loosen his tongue.* He leaned forward, his voice low and deliberate. "In fact, you're going to wish you were in a room this big and nice where you're going."

Ryan's eyes darted around the sparse interrogation room, as if suddenly realizing the relative comfort of his current surroundings. His confidence faltered for a moment before he puffed out his chest, trying to appear tougher than he felt.

"Man, you ain't got nothing to hold me on," Ryan spat, but Isaiah could hear the uncertainty in his voice.

Isaiah allowed a small, humorless smile to cross his face. "Oh, but we do. Arnold is pressing charges. You're being held for assault."

The words hung in the air between them.

Ryan's facade crumbled, his shoulders slumping in defeat. His eyes dropped to the table, avoiding Isaiah's piercing gaze.

He's close to breaking. Just need to push a little more.

Isaiah waited, letting the silence stretch out and do the work for him. He could almost hear the gears turning in Ryan's head as the reality of his situation sank in.

Minutes passed before Isaiah spoke again, his voice softer this time. "There is a way out for you, though."

Ryan's head snapped up, hope glimmering in his eyes once more.

"You could cooperate with us. Maybe those assault charges could go a little easier on you."

Ryan scoffed, but Isaiah didn't miss the flicker of interest that crossed his face. Ryan was trying to play it cool, but his body language betrayed him. His free hand fidgeted with the edge of the table, and his eyes kept darting between Isaiah and the door.

Isaiah reached for the file Connie had handed him, flipping it open with practiced nonchalance. His eyes scanned the pages, absorbing the details of Ryan's checkered past. A low whistle escaped his lips, more for show than genuine surprise.

"So, this isn't your first rodeo." He met Ryan's eyes across the table. "Loitering. Petty theft. Ah, and look at this—an earlier pop for assault."

Ryan shifted uncomfortably in his seat, the metal of his handcuffs clinking. "I was a juvenile."

Isaiah tapped a finger on the file, the soft sound echoing in the quiet room. "You're not a juvenile now. But you see, Ryan, this is the kind of stuff that gets under a judge's skin during sentencing. A repeat offender is what they call you." He leaned forward, his voice dropping to a near whisper. "You may not be aware, but repeat offenders tend to get harsher sentences."

The color drained from Ryan's face as the gravity of his situation sank in. Isaiah could almost see the walls of bravado crumbling.

"Look, man," Ryan blurted out, his voice cracking, "I didn't even hit that guy. Big Joe did."

Isaiah's heart raced. He leaned in closer, careful to keep his face neutral despite his excitement. "And why did Big Joe feel the need to assault Arnold?"

Ryan's eyes flitted around the room, as if searching for an escape. "I don't know," he mumbled. "He thought the guy was too nosy, I guess."

A pang of guilt hit Isaiah as he thought of Arnold. He'd dragged the poor guy into this mess. But he couldn't dwell on that now. He had to press on, had to get more information. "Too nosy?" Isaiah prodded. "What was Arnold being nosy about?"

Ryan's eyes darted away, his fingers drumming nervously on the table.

Isaiah could see the internal struggle playing out across the young man's face. "Ryan," Isaiah said, his voice low and urgent. "This is one of those crossroads moments. You're at the crossroads right now. You help me now, or there's nothing I can do for you later. Understand?"

Isaiah leaned back, giving Ryan space to process. He watched as the kid's shoulders slumped, defeat etching itself into every line of his body. For a moment, the only sound in the room was the faint hum of the fluorescent lights overhead.

Finally, Ryan cursed under his breath. "Look," he said, his voice barely above a whisper, "I'm not involved in all the stuff Big Joe and his crew are into."

Isaiah's pulse quickened. He kept his face impassive, not wanting to spook Ryan now that he was finally opening up. "What stuff?" Isaiah asked, his tone carefully neutral.

Ryan shifted uncomfortably in his seat, the handcuff rattling against the metal bar. "Big Joe's been talking about hitting it big lately," he mumbled, refusing to meet Isaiah's eyes.

Isaiah's thoughts swirled, working to piece together the implications of Ryan's words.

Ryan chewed on his lower lip, still not meeting Isaiah's eyes. "I wasn't exactly sure what he meant at first," he continued, his voice growing quieter with each word. "But I know Big Joe and his crew, they've been stealing credit card information."

Isaiah leaned forward, his interest piqued. He kept his expression neutral, not wanting to show his excitement at this potential breakthrough.

Ryan's words tumbled out faster now, as if a dam had broken. "They're using the stolen info to buy stuff, you know? And taking cash advances on other people's cards."

Isaiah's mind whirred, processing this new information. It sounded like a significant operation, though he knew little about this kind of theft. He bet it was something that Lisa knew quite a bit about. He made a mental note to ask her about it.

"Big Joe doesn't seem like the type to come up with a criminal plan this sophisticated," Isaiah said. "Stealing credit cards, that strikes me as taking some computer know-how."

To Isaiah's surprise, Ryan let out a bitter laugh, the sound harsh in the stark interrogation room. "Well, you're right about that. Big Joe ain't what anyone would call smart. He wouldn't have cooked this up himself."

Isaiah raised an eyebrow, silently encouraging Ryan to continue.

Ryan leaned back in his chair, as far as the handcuff would allow. "If you ask me, Big Joe's like... I dunno, middle management, I guess." He paused, searching for the right words. "Really, he's more like the muscle. You know what I mean?"

Isaiah nodded. Though, if Big Joe was just the muscle, then who was really pulling the strings? He leaned forward, his eyes narrowing. "Muscle for who?" he asked.

Ryan shifted uncomfortably. "I don't know, man. I really don't." He licked his lips nervously. "But I've heard Big Joe talk about 'the boss' a few times. So, I know he ain't the one calling the shots."

The boss. Someone above Big Joe. That made more sense. "What else can you tell me about this boss?" Isaiah pressed.

Ryan shrugged, the movement limited by his restraint. "Nothing, really. Big Joe doesn't share much, and I ain't high enough up in the crew to be asking too many questions, you know what I mean?"

Isaiah leaned back, studying Ryan's face. He seemed to be telling the truth, but Isaiah couldn't shake the feeling that there might be more. He tried a different angle. "Has Big Joe ever mentioned meeting with this boss? Any locations? Times?"

Ryan shook his head. "Nah, man. Like I said, I don't know anything about that."

Isaiah sighed internally. He'd hit a wall. He stood up with the file. "All right, Ryan. I appreciate your cooperation."

Ryan tried to stand, forgetting about the handcuff. The metal clinked sharply as it caught, yanking him back into his seat. "Hey, wait!" Ryan called out, a note of desperation in his voice. "What about me? You gonna let me go now?"

Isaiah paused, his hand on the doorknob, and turned back to face Ryan. "That's not up to me, Ryan. It'll be up to a judge, provided you can make bail."

Ryan's face twisted in anger. "Hey, that ain't fair, man. Hey!"

Isaiah stepped out of the room, a stream of profanities following him as he closed the door.

The boss. At least they had someone to look for now.

He found more good news when he made it back to his desk. A voicemail from the assistant to the deputy vice president of operations at Third National Bank. When it came to speaking with the bank about their security system and Scott's possible fraud, the higher-ups had been stonewalling him. The VP had time to meet with him at one today.

He glanced at the clock on his monitor. That didn't give him a lot of time, but he could make it work. And he hoped that Lisa could too. He reached for his phone. If he was going to meet with the bank's big guns, he was going to do it with a big gun of his own.

Chapter Eleven

Lisa drove over the Fourteenth Street Bridge into Arlington, Virginia, sister city to Washington, DC, home of Reagan National Airport, the Pentagon, and the headquarters of the Third National Bank. It was just after 2:00 p.m., and traffic was still relatively light. She knew that wouldn't be the case in an hour or so. Flex-time schedules for federal employees meant rush hour started early in the DC metro area.

She turned into the bank's parking lot, parked and hurried toward the towering skyscraper. It looked like the bank's employees either didn't go out for lunch much or they'd all made it back before she arrived. She'd only been able to find an open parking space in the rear of the building's surface parking lot.

The wind whipped across the parking lot. Lisa's heels clicked against the asphalt as she approached the towering building, her eyes fixed on the figure leaning on a pillar near the entrance.

Isaiah's tall frame cut an impressive silhouette against the glass-and-chrome backdrop of the bank's headquarters.

Her breath caught in her throat as she drew closer. His dark overcoat billowed gently around his legs, and his head was bent, attention focused on the phone in his hand. There was something undeniably attractive about his casual stance, a quiet confidence that radiated from him even in stillness.

As if sensing her approach, he looked up, his eyes meeting hers. A smile spread across his face, and Lisa felt her heart stutter in her chest, the memory of their kiss fluttering through her mind. She silently chastised herself for her reaction. This was work, not a romantic rendezvous.

"Lisa," Isaiah greeted her, pushing off from the pillar. "Thanks for coming."

"Of course," she replied, willing her voice to remain steady. "I'll do whatever I can to help, you know that."

She'd visited Harry earlier that morning, but he was still in a coma. The nurse's expression when she'd asked whether that was usual had said it all. She couldn't lose Harry.

"I wanted you here in case we manage to convince the executives to let us take a look at their system." Isaiah's voice pulled her out of her thoughts. "If they give us access, we'll need to move quickly to search for Scott's program before they change their minds."

She nodded, her mind already racing through potential algorithms she could use to detect any hidden software. "No problem." She tapped the gym-size tote hanging from her shoulder along with her purse. It contained everything she'd need to assess the security. "I'm ready whenever they are. Has the bank been giving you trouble?"

He sighed, his frustration coming through loud and clear. "They are not exactly being cooperative. They claim there's nothing wrong with their system, or at least that's what they're saying."

"If Scott was as good as I think he was, the bank might

not notice anything amiss unless they were specifically looking for it. He'd have covered his tracks well."

Isaiah nodded, his expression grave. "I also have my doubts about whether they'd tell us if they had found an errant program. They definitely wouldn't want the news that one of their own employees was stealing from the bank's customers to come out. I could see them trying to cover it up. Deny, deny, deny." He paused, meeting Lisa's gaze. "But having that program might help us solve Scott's murder."

She'd dealt with similar clients in the past. More concerned with protecting the company's reputation than protecting their customers. But if there was even a chance that this could lead them to Scott's killer, they had to pursue it.

"Well," she said, squaring her shoulders, "let's go make our case then."

Isaiah reached for her bag, sliding it off her shoulder gently and onto his own before gesturing toward the building's entrance. "After you."

They entered the building, showing their identification to the security guard on duty, then took the elevator to the twenty-fourth floor. At a second reception desk there, they gave their names and announced that they had an appointment with Myra Ronstalio, the deputy vice president of operations for the bank. They were directed to a seating area with plush sofas and an assortment of magazines to wait.

Ten long minutes passed. Lisa's fingers drummed against the glossy pages of an outdated fashion magazine, her eyes unseeing as they skimmed over last season's trends. The plush leather chair beneath her did little to ease the tension coiling in her stomach. She glanced at Isaiah, his calm demeanor a stark contrast to her inner turmoil.

"You okay?" Isaiah asked, his voice low.

She forced a smile. "Just anxious. I know how hard you all worked to get this meeting."

Isaiah nodded, his eyes understanding. "We're here now. That's what matters."

The reception area was quiet, the only sound the soft whir of the air-conditioning and the occasional rustle as Lisa turned a page in the magazine. She couldn't shake the feeling that they were interlopers in this pristine financial fortress.

A door opened, the sudden sound making Lisa start. A young woman emerged, her blond hair twisted into an impeccable chignon. Her black suit was crisp and tailored to perfection.

"Mr. Reeves? Ms. Elkins?" The woman's voice was polite but brisk. "I'm Danielle, Ms. Ronstalio's assistant. She's ready to see you now."

Lisa stood, smoothing her own suit, suddenly self-conscious. As she followed Danielle, she caught Isaiah's reassuring smile. She took a deep breath, steeling herself. This was her element, after all. Computers, code, security—this was where she excelled.

The assistant's heels clicked sharply against the polished marble floor as she led them down a wide corridor. Lisa's eyes darted from side to side, taking in the expensive artwork and the air of quiet power that permeated the building.

Danielle led them down a hall stopping in front of a conference room behind a glass wall.

Inside the room, four people, all impeccably dressed, were seated around a polished cherrywood table. Their faces were serious, expectant.

"For people who didn't want to meet with us, there sure are a lot of them," she said, apprehension rising within her.

As if sensing her unease, Isaiah leaned in close, his

breath warm against her ear. "How many of them do you think are lawyers?" he whispered, a hint of wry amusement in his voice.

She shot him a sardonic look in response. Trust him to find humor in this situation. But his lighthearted comment did its job, easing some of the tension in her body. She'd lived with a shark of an attorney for more than a decade. There wasn't anything these lawyers could throw at her that she couldn't handle. She squared her shoulders. She was the expert here.

"Ready?" Isaiah asked quietly, his hand ghosting over the small of her back in a gesture of support.

She nodded, lifting her chin. "Let's do this."

The assistant pushed open the heavy glass door, and Lisa stepped into the conference room, the scent of leather and polished wood enveloping her. A statuesque woman with silver-streaked dark hair rose from her seat at the head of the table, her crisp navy suit exuding authority.

"Myra Ronstalio. Detective Isaiah Reeves and Lisa Elkins," Danielle announced, her voice carrying a hint of deference.

Myra Ronstalio extended her hand, her grip firm as she shook first Lisa's hand, then Isaiah's. "Welcome," she said, her tone cordial but guarded.

Lisa noted the slight tightness around her eyes, betraying an underlying tension.

"Allow me to introduce my colleagues," Ms. Ronstalio continued, gesturing to the three men seated at the table. "Curtis Senor, our IT director, and Jesse Cole and Frank Bach from our legal department."

Lisa's gaze swept over the men, lingering briefly on Curtis. She wondered how much he truly knew about the bank's systems. The heads of departments weren't always the ones who knew the most about the technical aspects of a system.

As they took their seats, Lisa felt the weight of their collective stares.

Ms. Ronstalio settled back into her chair, folding her hands on the table. "I understand the police believe a former employee has been…inappropriately accessing client accounts," she began, her voice measured, but with more than a hint of skepticism in her tone. "We appreciate your diligence in bringing this to our attention," she continued, her gaze flickering between Lisa and Isaiah. "However, I want to assure you that we've conducted a thorough internal audit. We've found no evidence to support these allegations."

Lisa felt a flicker of frustration. She leaned forward slightly, ready to counter Ms. Ronstalio's dismissal, but Isaiah's subtle shake of the head stopped her. Reluctantly, Lisa sat back, her mind racing with all the reasons why a standard audit might miss what they were looking for.

Isaiah's eyes narrowed, a hint of steel entering his tone. "And would the bank inform the authorities if you had found such evidence, Ms. Ronstalio?" he asked pointedly.

The question hung in the air. Ms. Ronstalio's face flushed, a deep crimson creeping up her neck. She opened her mouth, then closed it again, visibly struggling to maintain her composure.

Lisa seized the moment of discomfort, her voice calm but firm. "The employee you are referring to was intimately familiar with your systems. It was his job, after all." She leaned forward, her gaze steady on Ms. Ronstalio. "He would have created a program designed to operate invisibly, running in the background of your existing software." Lisa's fingers twitched, itching to get a look at the system.

"This kind of program would be incredibly difficult to detect, even if you knew exactly what you were looking for."

Ms. Ronstalio's eyes narrowed, her lips pursing as she regarded Lisa with barely concealed irritation. "And you think you'd be able to find what our computer technicians couldn't?" The challenge in her voice was unmistakable.

Lisa felt a surge of determination, her ego and pride prickling at Ms. Ronstalio's doubt. She took a deep breath, steadying herself. "Yes, I believe I can," she replied, her voice level but tinged with steel. "I know the creator of this program. I believe I understand how he thinks, how he operates."

She leaned forward slightly, her eyes never leaving Ms. Ronstalio's. "This isn't just a job for me, Ms. Ronstalio. It's my passion, my expertise. Every day, I put myself in the mindset of potential infiltrators. I anticipate their moves, their tricks. Then I devise ways to thwart them, to protect systems like yours from exactly this kind of threat."

"Look," Isaiah said after several moments of silence. His voice was tight. "The MPD can't force you to let Ms. Elkins examine your system."

Ms. Ronstalio's lips curved into a smug, self-satisfied smile. Lisa really didn't like this woman.

The lawyers flanking Ms. Ronstalio remained silent, their pens scratching against notepads. The sound grated on Lisa's nerves.

"What we can and will do is inform your bank regulators that we have credible evidence your system has been compromised." Isaiah paused, letting the weight of his words sink in.

Ms. Ronstalio's composed mask slipped for a moment, revealing a flicker of alarm before her features hardened into anger.

"Of course, those regulators would be compelled to launch a thorough, comprehensive investigation. The kind that tends to attract…media attention."

Lisa could almost hear the gears turning in Ms. Ronstalio's head as she processed the implicit threat. The lawyers had stopped writing, their pens frozen midstroke.

Ms. Ronstalio's voice was low and trembled when she finally spoke. "Detective Reeves, is that a threat?"

Lisa held her breath, acutely aware of the tension crackling in the air. She resisted the urge to glance at Isaiah, keeping her eyes fixed on Ms. Ronstalio's face.

"Not at all, Ms. Ronstalio," Isaiah replied smoothly. "It's simply a fact. Your institution is a federally regulated bank. I'm an officer of the law, and as such, I have a duty to report potential security breaches to the appropriate authorities."

Ms. Ronstalio's face contorted into a sour expression, her lips pursed as if she'd just bitten into a lemon. She inhaled sharply, her nostrils flaring. "If you'll excuse us for a moment. I need to confer with my colleagues."

Lisa watched as Ms. Ronstalio stood abruptly. The lawyers followed suit. The trio huddled in the far corner of the room, their backs to Lisa and Isaiah.

Though their voices were hushed, Lisa could hear the urgent whispers, catching fragments of the conversation— liability and damage control. She strained her ears, trying to piece together their conversation, but the low murmur was frustratingly indecipherable.

Their discussion seemed to stretch on for an eternity. Lisa studied the tense set of Ms. Ronstalio's shoulders, the agitated gestures of the lawyers. She could almost feel the waves of anxiety radiating from the group.

Finally, Ms. Ronstalio and the attorneys turned back toward the table. Their faces were masks of professional neutrality, but Lisa noticed the slight tremor in Ms. Ronstalio's hand as she approached.

Ms. Ronstalio remained standing, her fingers curled around the back of the chair she'd risen from. "Ms. Elkins," she began, her tone carefully modulated. "I took the liberty of investigating you and your company before this meeting. Your reputation is sterling." The word seemed to pain her. "In light of this, I've been authorized to hire your company to conduct a security audit of our system."

Her lips thinned as she added, "This audit will either prove or, more likely I believe, disprove…" she stressed the latter word, her eyes narrowing slightly "…the allegations you've brought forward."

"I appreciate your cooperation," Isaiah said.

Lisa nodded, her mind already racing with all that needed to be done before she could even get started.

"Danielle will show you to our technology department." Ms. Ronstalio touched a button on the telephone set on the table.

Danielle appeared and, following a flurry of handshakes, led them back out of the bank's conference room. Lisa and Isaiah followed the assistant down the hallway.

Lisa couldn't resist a quip as they made their way out. "She seems nice."

Isaiah glanced at her, a smile tugging at the corners of his mouth. "That actually went better than I thought it would. I'm just glad they're going to let us review their system."

"Us?" Lisa echoed, unable to keep the laughter from her voice. She raised an eyebrow at him.

Isaiah's grin widened. "Of course, I'm going to be there to supervise."

Chapter Twelve

The hum of multiple computer towers filled the cavernous room where the IT department employees usually worked. Rows of empty desks stretched before her now, their monitors dark and silent. The employees that usually worked in the room had been cleared out. Danielle had said to give her and Isaiah privacy. Lisa suspected it had more to do with Ms. Ronstalio wanting to keep a lid on the news that the bank's system may have been compromised.

As she worked, Lisa glanced at Isaiah, who stood by the door, his eyes darting between her and his phone.

"Any progress?" he asked, his voice tinged with impatience.

Lisa sighed. "Not yet. This isn't like finding a needle in a haystack. It's more like searching for a particular grain of sand on a beach."

She turned back to her screen, lines of code scrolling past. Her specialized program, a labor of love she'd crafted over months of painstaking work, was methodically combing through the bank's vast system. Pride swelled in her chest at its efficiency, even if Isaiah didn't realize what a time-saver it was.

If Scott had truly embedded his program as she suspected, it would be well hidden. The thought of it challenged her on a professional level. What he'd done was a crime, but the intellectual challenge of digging it out and figuring out how he'd accomplished it—well, she wouldn't be a computer nerd if it didn't excite her at least a little.

"How much longer do you think it'll take?" Isaiah's question broke through her reverie.

She bit her lip, biting back the first retort that came to mind. Honestly, he sounded like a toddler. Or a teenager. Both of which she had experience with.

"It could be hours still. Maybe even tomorrow." Or the next day, but she kept that to herself. His shoulders were already slumping. "If it's here, I'll find it. I promise you that. But it will take time."

She could feel the tension radiating off him from across the room.

"You really don't have to stay. I can call you when I find something," she said, glancing over her shoulder. It was the third time she'd made the offer in the past two hours, her voice tinged with a mix of concern and mild exasperation.

"No, I want to be here when you find it," he insisted. "Anyway, I don't feel comfortable leaving you here alone."

She swiveled her chair to face him fully. "You don't think that someone else who works for the bank is Scott's accomplice, do you?"

Isaiah's expression turned even more serious, his eyes meeting hers. "We're looking at every possibility. One of Scott's coworkers being his partner makes sense."

Lisa felt her nose scrunch up involuntarily as she processed this information. "That's true."

The corners of Isaiah's lips turned up in a small smile. "You still scrunch your nose up like you did when we were in school and you were thinking. It's still cute."

She blinked, caught off guard by the unexpected compliment. A mix of emotions fluttered in her chest—nostalgia, warmth, and a touch of something she wasn't quite ready to name. She opened her mouth to respond but found herself at a loss for words.

Lisa quirked an eyebrow, a retort forming on her lips, when a sudden beep from the computer shattered the moment.

Isaiah was at her back in an instant, his breath warm against her neck as he leaned over her shoulder to scrutinize information on the screen he couldn't possibly understand.

"My program's found something. But I still have to go over the code myself to see if it's what we're looking for. It's going to be a while still."

Isaiah muttered under his breath, frustration evident in his tone.

She ignored him, her focus narrowing to the lines of code scrolling before her eyes. She could feel the weight of his impatience, but experience had taught her the value of methodical analysis.

The shrill ring of Isaiah's phone cut through the tension. He answered quickly, his posture straightening as he listened to the person on the other end of the line.

"That's good news," Isaiah said finally. "Text me the address." He glanced at her, a mix of excitement and hesitation in his eyes. "I'll be there as soon as I can," he added into the phone before hanging up.

"Connie?" She took an educated guess.

Isaiah nodded. "Yeah, we've found the hotel where Scott was staying. Connie's headed over there with a warrant now to search."

Lisa waved a hand toward the door. "Go. I don't need

you hovering. It's not going to make this go any faster. I'll call you when I know something."

Isaiah hesitated for a moment. "Make sure you have a security guard walk you to your car."

She rolled her eyes, unable to suppress a hint of exasperation. "Okay, Dad," she quipped.

Isaiah's dark eyes locked onto hers with an intensity that made her breath catch. "Lisa, I'm serious," he said, his voice low and urgent. "We are dealing with some pretty nasty people, and I don't want you taking any chances."

A chill ran down her spine. The memories flooded her from the break-in at her house and how Harry looked when she'd found him on the floor of his office. She swallowed hard. "I promise. I'll have the security guard walk me to my car, and I'll go straight home. Don't worry about me. Now go."

Isaiah's eyes remained on her, heating her blood. Her gaze fell to his lips and her thoughts to their kiss. She wanted him to kiss her again. Now. She didn't care how inappropriate or unprofessional it was. But was that what he wanted? He'd been nothing but professional since their kiss. *I'm not a good bet.* Did that mean he wasn't interested?

She pulled her gaze away, turning to face her laptop again.

"Be careful," Isaiah said to her back. His footsteps faded down the hallway moments later.

Focus. Lisa pushed away the swirl of emotions Isaiah's concern had stirred up. She had work to do.

She donned her reading glasses and spent the next two hours working before finally packing up. It was already dark outside although it was just minutes past six.

There were only a few people still milling around the bank's offices, including Danielle. Lisa let her know that Detective Reeves would be contacting her boss and then hurried away from the young woman before she could ask any further questions. She wasn't sure how much information Isaiah wanted to tell the bank at the moment.

She'd found the program Scott had embedded in their system. There was more work to do as far as figuring out exactly how he'd done it, but now that she knew what he'd done and made a copy of the program, she could do the rest of the work back at her office.

At the guard's desk in the lobby, she requested an escort to her car and waited while the guard radioed for one of his colleagues to come to the front of the building.

A uniformed guard appeared at the front desk. His navy jacket looked thin, completely inadequate for the frigid December night.

Lisa clutched her purse tighter. "I'm sorry to pull you outside on a cold night."

"It's part of the job," the guard said, but he didn't look like it was no problem.

They pushed through the revolving doors, and a gust of icy wind slapped Lisa's face. She shivered, pulling her coat closer. The guard's shoulders hunched against the cold.

As they crossed the parking lot, Lisa turned to the guard. "I really appreciate you doing this. I know it's freezing out here."

"No problem at all," he replied, but his chattering teeth betrayed him. He blew into his bare hands, rubbing them together for warmth.

"My car's just at the back," she said, quickening her pace and wishing for both their sakes she had been able to find a parking space closer to the building when she'd arrived.

"There it is." She finally pointed to her Audi in the last row. "Thank you again," she said when they reached her car. "I really do appreciate it."

The guard was already backpedaling, a polite smile frozen on his face. "My pleasure," he managed through clenched teeth, his words forming small puffs in the frigid air. Before she could say anything more, he spun on his heel and took off at a brisk jog toward the building, his figure quickly swallowed by the darkness.

She aimed her key fob at the door, the familiar beep of the locks disengaging piercing the quiet night.

Suddenly, the hairs on the back of her neck stood up. Before she could fully process the sensation, a strong hand clamped down on her arm.

Whirling around, she found herself face-to-face with a masked figure. His eyes, startlingly green, bore into hers with cold intensity.

"Get in the car," he growled, his grip tightening.

"No way in hell," Lisa spat back, her heart racing but her voice steady.

The man's eyes narrowed. "Make this easy on yourself. Just do it, and you won't get hurt."

Logan's self-defense lessons flashed through her thoughts. As a big brother and an FBI agent, he'd taken his duty to protect seriously and had pulled no punches when teaching her how to defend herself over the years. She twisted her arm, trying to break her assailant's hold. "I don't plan to make anything easy for you, buddy."

She jabbed the alarm button on her key fob. The car's shrill wail cut through the night, momentarily startling both Lisa and her attacker. His grip loosened.

"Hey! Stop right there."

Lisa's gaze jerked toward the other end of the parking lot along with her assailant's. The guard who'd walked her to her car called out, already running back toward her.

Lisa seized the opportunity, bringing the heel of her

hand up in a vicious strike to the man's nose. There was a satisfying crunch, followed by a string of muffled curses. He stumbled back.

She bolted for her car, diving inside and slamming the lock button. Her hands shook as she scanned the side and rear mirrors, searching for her attacker.

Nothing. He had vanished as quickly as he'd appeared.

Her breath came in ragged gasps, her heart hammering against her ribs as she dug in the bottom of her purse for her cell. Pulling it from her bag, she glanced in the rearview mirror again. The parking lot seemed eerily still now, as if the entire encounter had been some surreal dream. But the throbbing in her hand and the lingering fear coursing through her veins told her it had been all too real.

Chapter Thirteen

Isaiah pulled his coat tighter, steeling himself against the cold as he bounded up the stairs leading to the second floor of the motel where Scott had been staying before his death. It wasn't quite 5:00 p.m. yet, but the sun had already dipped below the horizon, painting the sky above. The motel was located on Michigan Avenue near the DC and Maryland border and was the definition of run-down. He strode past rusted railings and peeling paint, his footsteps echoing in the desolate silence of the outdoor hallway.

Room 217. He paused, took a deep breath, and pushed open the door. The stench of mold and stale cigarettes assaulted his senses as he stepped inside.

Connie looked up from where she was crouched by the bed. The evidence technician, a wiry young man Isaiah didn't recognize, was methodically dusting the nightstand for prints.

"Hey," Isaiah said, his voice low. "Any luck?"

Connie shook her head, frustration evident in the set of her shoulders. "Depends on what you mean by luck. This place is disgusting. I don't know if it's ever been cleaned. We've got hairs and fibers from the '70s, I suspect. Unfortunately, nothing that screams the name of Scott's killer."

Isaiah pulled on a pair of latex gloves, the snap of rubber against skin oddly loud in the oppressive quiet of the room. He moved deliberately, cataloging every detail of the squalid room: the sagging mattress, the water-stained ceiling, the grimy windows that barely let in the weak afternoon light. Each element told a story of desperation and secrets.

He approached the low cabinet, its veneer chipped and peeling, and eased open the top drawer. A black binder sat inside. The label on the cover read FinNet Software. Did it connect to Scott's murder or had Scott just brought some work home with him?

Isaiah motioned to the evidence technician. "Can you get some shots of this?"

The tech nodded, her camera clicking rapidly as she captured the binder from various angles. After a few moments, she lowered the device. "I need to grab some supplies from the van. Back in a minute."

As the door clicked shut behind her, Isaiah carefully extracted the binder. The weight of it felt significant in his hands, like it held more than just paper. He flipped it open, brow furrowing as he scanned the pages.

"Ugh," he muttered, "might as well be hieroglyphics." He looked over at Connie, who had crossed the room to examine the binder beside him. "Does any of this make sense to you?"

Connie leaned in, her eyes narrowing as she turned the pages, studying them closely. "Not a lick. But I bet I know someone who could decipher it." She gave him a pointed look.

He nodded.

"Speaking of…" Connie's narrowed eyes stayed on him. "Tell me to mind my own business if you want, but I have to ask. What's going on between you and the lovely Ms. Elkins?"

Isaiah hesitated, weighing his response. Part of him wanted to shut down the conversation. But he knew his partner well enough to recognize that would only fuel her curiosity. He sighed, running a hand through his hair. "You know we were friends in grad school."

Even as the words left his mouth, Isaiah knew they rang hollow.

Connie's teeth clenched, her detective's instincts clearly kicking into high gear. "Ever more than friends?"

Isaiah felt a knot forming in his stomach. He swallowed hard, trying to keep his voice steady. "She was dating her now ex-husband back then."

He saw understanding dawn on Connie's face. Her eyebrows shot up, and a knowing look settled in her eyes. "Ah, but you wished she hadn't been. You had feelings for her then. And now."

He could feel a flush creeping up his neck. "You're a better detective than that. You're jumping to conclusions," he said, turning away from Connie.

She shook her head, her voice gentle but firm. "No, more like making observations. It's pretty clear you care for her."

He made a noncommittal noise, regretting entertaining the subject in the first place. He headed for the small, dingy bathroom, his footsteps echoing in the silence. "Has anyone searched in here yet?" he asked.

Connie smirked, clearly not fooled by his attempt at deflection. "No," she replied simply.

He was stopped by Connie's voice as he reached for the bathroom door. "If it matters to you at all, it's clear to this seasoned detective that she has feelings for you too."

He didn't turn around, didn't respond. He surveyed the grimy tiles and rusted fixtures, finding nothing of interest.

Isaiah dug his phone out of his pocket when it rang and saw Lisa's name on the screen. His heart leaped with anticipation. She'd found something on the bank's computers. Finally, a break.

"Lisa, what've you got?"

The moment he heard her voice, his blood ran cold.

"Isaiah, I'm okay, but…" Her words tumbled out in a panicked rush. "Someone just attacked me in the bank's parking lot."

He was moving before he even realized it, bursting out of the bathroom. "What? Where are you now? Are you hurt?"

Connie's head snapped up as he barreled across the motel room toward the door.

"I'm still at the bank's offices," Lisa replied, her voice shaky.

Connie fell in step behind him without a word.

"Stay where you are," he ordered. "Connie and I are on our way. We'll be there soon."

THE TIRES SCREECHED as Isaiah wrenched the steering wheel, sending the car careening into the bank's parking lot. He slammed the gear shift into Park and jumped out, running for the entrance.

"Lisa!" His eyes frantically scanned the lobby until he spotted her, standing with two uniformed officers and two security guards. Relief flooded through him as he enveloped her in his arms.

"Thank God you're all right," he murmured for her ears only. His pulse began to slow but only slightly. Anger was beginning to replace fear.

He gently guided her away from the cluster of officers

and guards, leaving Connie to get the incident report. He cupped her face, searching her eyes. "Are you sure you're okay? Did he hurt you?"

She managed a wan smile. "I'm fine, Isaiah. A bit shaken up, but I'm okay."

"What happened? Tell me everything."

"I had one of the guards walk me to my car, just like I promised you I would. He started to head back, and the other guy was just...there." Her voice faltered.

Isaiah's jaw clenched, imagining the terror she must have felt. He wanted to pull her close again, to shield her from the world, but he knew she needed to finish. "Go on," he urged softly.

"He was just...there. Like he'd materialized out of thin air." Lisa shuddered, wrapping her arms around herself. "He tried to force me into my car." Her hands trembled slightly as she recalled the moment.

Isaiah fought to keep his anger at her assailant in check. "What happened then?"

"That's when the security guard must have spotted what was going on. I hit the attacker. The guard started running back toward us. The attacker took off."

Isaiah glanced over his shoulder and fixed the security guards with a withering glare. The idiot guard should have waited until Lisa was safely in her car. He turned back to Lisa. "I should never have left you alone. I knew how dangerous these people are. I should have stayed with you at the bank."

He'd made a stupid mistake, and Lisa had nearly paid the price. The thought of what could have happened if the guard hadn't spotted Lisa's assailant made his stomach churn.

Lisa's eyes flashed with a mixture of exasperation and

determination. "Stop right there," she said firmly. "I told you to go because you weren't helping anyone pacing while I worked." He started to protest, but Lisa pressed on. "Listen to me. You can't be everywhere at once. You can't protect me from every possible danger, and frankly, I wouldn't want you to. I'm an adult, Isaiah. I am capable of taking care of myself."

His shoulders slumped almost imperceptibly. He knew she was right, but the thought of what could have happened to her gnawed at him. He dropped his voice to an intimate whisper so none of the others around them would hear him. "If anything happened to you—"

The words caught in his throat, the depth of his feelings for Lisa threatening to overwhelm him.

Before he could finish, Connie approached, her brisk stride carrying her swiftly to their side. "The uniforms are taking statements from the guards," Connie reported, her tone all business. "They're also pulling the security footage from the parking lot." She hesitated, a flicker of frustration crossing her face. "Unfortunately, the cameras don't cover the lot as far back as where Lisa was parked."

"It wouldn't matter anyway," Lisa said. "The guy had a ski mask on."

Isaiah cursed.

Connie's eyes darted between them. "Why don't you take Lisa home?" she said to Isaiah. "I'll finish up here."

Isaiah nodded, grateful for Connie's willingness to handle the grunt work. He turned to Lisa. "Can I have your keys? I'll drive."

She fished the heavy key chain from her purse. "Thank you," she murmured, handing the keys over. "I'm still a little shaken."

He felt a surge of protectiveness. Despite Lisa's earlier

words, he couldn't shake the need to keep her safe. He placed his hand lightly on the small of her back and guided her toward the exit.

LISA WAS LOST in her own thoughts, her body still trembling slightly as Isaiah drove her home. She'd told him she could take care of herself. But could she really? The memory of the assailant's rough hands pushing her toward her car, demanding she get in… She shuddered. Maybe she should take a refresher on those self-defense classes her brother Logan and sister-in-law Dora had been after her to sign up for. At the very least it couldn't hurt.

Thank God Layla was out of town. The idea of her daughter in danger made her stomach turn.

Isaiah's gaze flicked briefly to her, but he didn't seem to have the will to engage in a conversation. He pulled into her driveway and cut the engine. Neither of them made a move to get out.

"Thank you for driving me home," Lisa finally said.

Isaiah nodded. "Of course."

"How will you get home?" Lisa asked, suddenly realizing that driving her home in her car meant he didn't have transportation.

"I need to head back to the station." He reached for his phone. "I'll just call a ride share."

She watched as he tapped at the screen, quickly requesting a car. The glow from the phone illuminated the planes of his face, highlighting lines of worry and exhaustion etched there.

"Do you want to come inside and wait for your ride?"

He shook his head. "No. No, thanks. The app says my car will be here in two minutes. I'll just wait outside."

"Isaiah, don't do this," she said, her voice barely above a whisper.

He finally turned to look at her. "Do what?"

"Pull away," she replied. "What happened today was not your fault."

His jaw clenched. "I wasn't where I should have been." He paused. "Again."

"Do you hear yourself? You sound like you have a hero complex. No one can be everywhere all the time. Not even big, bad detectives. We're all just doing the best we can."

Isaiah's gaze drifted back to the windshield, his expression unreadable. He shook his head slowly, clearly not buying what she was saying.

Without thinking, she reached out, placing her hand on his jaw and gently turning his face toward her. His stubble was rough against her palm. "You are not responsible for every terrible thing that happens to someone you care about."

The air in the car was charged with unspoken emotions. Isaiah's dark eyes locked onto hers. She held her breath, acutely aware of how close they sat to each other in the car.

Lisa wasn't sure which of them moved first, but in an instant, their lips crashed together. The kiss was desperate, hungry, a release of pent-up emotions they'd been denying.

The windows began to fog up as their breathing grew ragged. Lisa's mind went blank, lost in the sensation of Isaiah, the taste of him, the solid warmth of his body. For a moment, the world outside ceased to exist.

This was exactly what she wanted. Needed.

Isaiah cradled the back of her head, angling her to deepen the kiss. She parted her lips eagerly, teasing her tongues along his with playful strokes that drew a groan from his throat. She loved having that power over him. It made her feel bold. She fisted the front of his coat, pulling him closer as desire flared into an inferno.

He tasted like cherries and mint, a combination she thought she could definitely get used to.

"Lisa." Isaiah attempted to pull back from the kiss, but Lisa leaned in farther. What she needed was him closer. Everywhere.

She scraped her teeth over his bottom lip, pulling another moan from his lips. His kiss became more insistent, his hand slipping around her waist and under her, lifting her nearly over the console separating them. She just needed to swing her leg over his body, and she'd be straddling him. In her driveway of her house. In front of anyone who happened to walk by. And she didn't care at all.

Isaiah's phone gave an insistent beep.

She and Isaiah broke apart, both of them panting heavily. Isaiah fumbled for his cell.

"My ride," he said, glancing down at the screen.

Lisa followed his gaze out of the window and spotted a car idling at the curb.

"I should go," Isaiah said, releasing his hold on her. He got out of the car, and a second later opened her door.

Lisa's mind whirled as he walked her to the door of her house. She sneaked a glance at Isaiah's profile, noting the tension in his jaw, the furrow of his brow. She could sense the weight of guilt he carried. She wished she could ease his mind.

"Isaiah," she began, once she had her door open. She hesitated, unsure what exactly she wanted to say. Whatever it was, it was too much for the moment anyway, so she settled for, "Please be careful."

He nodded, his eyes softening before he turned away.

She closed the door and flipped the lock into place, then

moved to the side window. She watched Isaiah climb into the waiting rideshare car. As it pulled away, she pressed her forehead against the glass, her thoughts a jumble of concern, longing, and uncertainty about what the future held for them.

Chapter Fourteen

Isaiah spent the next day bouncing between following up on the leads he already had in Scott's case and scouring the security videos of Third National Bank's parking lot. Unfortunately, the video was too grainy to make out any details about the man that had attacked Lisa or the car he'd taken off in.

It had occurred to Isaiah that he might be getting in too deep with Lisa. Potentially even jeopardizing his career. But that hadn't stopped him from wrapping up work precisely at 5:30 p.m. so he could get home and get ready for Connie's holiday party.

It had been a frustrating day with little progress made on the case. Big Joe still wasn't talking, but the judge at his arraignment hadn't granted him bail so at least he wasn't going anywhere. Unfortunately, Big Joe couldn't have been the man who had broken into Lisa's house. Isaiah had confirmed Big Joe had been at his job as a warehouse floor attendant. Ryan also had an alibi. He drove for a rideshare company in the wee hours of the morning to make extra money to pay for college classes. Which meant Isaiah was looking for several unknown suspects.

His frustration was palpable. But this was the job. It wasn't glamorous, but someone had to do it, and he loved it.

Still, he knew how important it was to take downtime. And he couldn't deny that he was anxious to see Lisa. Even though Connie had offered up his services as chauffeur, it very much felt like he was picking Lisa up for a real date.

Maybe that's because you want it to be a real date. He did. He really did. But he hadn't been lying when he told Lisa he wasn't a good bet.

I know you have a lot to offer, Isaiah. More than you realize. Lisa's words sounded in his head as he climbed the steps and rang her doorbell.

ISAIAH'S BREATH CAUGHT in his throat. Lisa stood framed in her front door, a vision in a black two-piece evening gown. His eyes traveled slowly from her strappy high heels up the tantalizing slit in her skirt, drinking in the curves accentuated by the formfitting dress. The sweetheart neckline drew his gaze to her elegant neck and flushed cheeks.

"Wow, you look amazing," he finally managed, his voice huskier than he'd intended.

"Thank you," she said, the flush in her cheeks deepening.

He stepped inside the house, hyperaware of how close Lisa was as she closed the door behind him. Close enough for the subtle scent of her perfume to tease his senses, close enough to reach out, pull her into his arms, and...

"I just need one more minute," she said, gesturing toward the kitchen. "Make yourself comfortable."

Isaiah nodded, watching as she disappeared around the corner. He heard the faint click of computer keys, then silence.

"Have you been working?" he called out, curiosity getting the better of him.

Lisa reappeared, a rueful smile on her face. "Guilty as charged. I've been trying to keep up with my workload and Harry's. We've got a big potential client, and if we land this contract to overhaul their security systems..." She trailed off, her eyes gleaming with excitement.

"That's impressive. The company would be a fool not to hire you."

"This client could be a game-changer for our firm." Her smile widened, and his heart nearly stopped. How could one woman be so damned gorgeous? And her drive and intelligence made her that much more attractive.

Her smile faded ever so slightly. "Any updates on the case?"

Isaiah shook his head, "Not yet, I'm afraid. I reviewed the security tapes from the bank, but there's no footage of the attack on you that could help us. The footage is too grainy."

"What about the program I found on the bank's system? Did the MPD's forensic techs make any headway?"

He nodded. At least there was some movement in the case. "They're still analyzing it."

"Scott may have been on the wrong side of the law, but he was undeniably talented. It's a shame he didn't put those skills to use for the good guys."

"Even with this program, we're no closer to solving Scott's murder. Whatever he was killed for, it wasn't this. The program was already active in the bank's system."

A mischievous glint appeared in Lisa's eyes. "How did Ms. Ronstalio react when you told her I'd found it?"

Isaiah couldn't suppress a wicked grin. "Not well," he chuckled. "Her face turned an impressive shade of red."

Lisa's answering smile made him chuckle for a moment, but his expression quickly grew serious again. "There is one more thing I wanted to ask you about. When we searched Scott's hotel room, we found a binder. It looked like some kind of instruction manual for something called FinNet Software. I've got a call in to the forensics guy assigned to the case, but he's swamped. Does FinNet ring any bells for you?"

"FinNet? Yeah, I know it. It's ATM software. I've actually worked with it before with banking clients that use it in their ATMs."

"Is there any reason you can think of that Scott would have had that in his room?"

"He might have been brushing up on it," she suggested. "Staying current on updates would have been part of his job."

Isaiah nodded slowly, but he couldn't shake the feeling that there was more to it, though he couldn't put his finger on why. He wasn't likely to solve the mystery that night, so he let it go. "Well, should we head out? I'd hate to keep you from showing off that dress." He offered Lisa his arm.

Lisa smiled again, sending his heart into a light canter as she linked her arm through his. The silky fabric of her dress brushed against his suit, and Isaiah felt a flutter in his stomach that had nothing to do with the case.

"Lead the way, Detective Reeves."

"If nothing else," he said, guiding her toward the door, "I think we're in for a memorable night. I've heard Connie's holiday parties are the event of the season."

Lisa laughed lightly. "Oh boy. I'm not sure I can handle it."

Isaiah's laughter mingled with hers as they stepped out into the cool night air. "I think we'll do just fine."

Chapter Fifteen

A minivan eased away from the curb on Connie's street. Isaiah glanced at Lisa with a wry smile. "Perfect timing," he said, gesturing toward the newly vacated parking spot. "I guess that's a sign we have to go to the party now."

Lisa's stomach fluttered with nerves. She smoothed her dress, trying to quell the anxiety bubbling up inside her. Parties had never been her thing, especially when she barely knew anyone. She much preferred the comfortable solitude of working away on her computer or a quiet night in with Layla. But Connie had insisted that she come, and Lisa had found it impossible to beg off. The petite detective was very persuasive.

"I guess so," she replied, hoping her voice didn't betray her hesitation.

Isaiah's gaze flicked to her face once more. He waited patiently as the other car pulled away, then skillfully maneuvered into the tight parking space with ease.

She watched his confident movements, admiring how calm he seemed. She wished she could borrow some of that self-assurance. As Isaiah parked, she took a deep breath, steeling herself for the social gauntlet ahead.

"You okay?" Isaiah asked softly, his dark eyes searching her face.

She nodded, forcing a smile. "Just a little nervous. I'm not great with crowds of strangers."

"You'll be fine," Isaiah assured her, his voice warm. "I'll be right there with you. And Connie's great at making people feel welcome."

His words helped calm her somewhat, but she still felt the flutter of butterflies in her stomach as they prepared to exit the car. She reminded herself that she had faced far more daunting challenges than a simple holiday party. She could handle a few hours of small talk and appetizers.

"Do you mind if I leave my coat in the car?" she asked as Isaiah cut the engine. "It'll be easier than trying to dig for it when we're ready to go."

His lips curved into an approving smile. "No, actually, that's a good idea." He shrugged out of his own wool overcoat, draping it carefully over the back seat.

Lisa slipped off her coat. She felt a subtle shift in the atmosphere within the car. The air seemed to thicken, charged with an unexpected tension. She smoothed down her dress, suddenly hyperaware of the way the fabric clung to her curves.

When she looked up, she caught his gaze fixed on her, his eyes dark and intense. The heat in his look sent a thrill through her, igniting a spark of desire she hadn't felt in years. Her cheeks warmed, but she didn't look away.

"You're stunning," he said, his voice low and husky.

Her heart raced. "Thank you," she murmured.

Her previous nervousness dimmed, replaced by anticipation. The prospect of spending the evening by Isaiah's side, suddenly seemed far more exciting than it had just a moment earlier.

She tore her gaze away from his, her pulse still thrumming rapidly. Despite the mild December night, the car felt warm. Hot even. She shifted in her seat, acutely aware of Isaiah's presence beside her.

He shrugged out of his suit jacket, the movement drawing Lisa's attention to his broad shoulders. "Here," he said, draping it around her. "Put this on until we get inside. Don't want you catching a chill."

"Thank you," she said, slipping her arms into the jacket. His subtle, masculine scent enveloped her.

"We should head in," he said, his voice an octave lower than usual.

Lisa took a moment to fan herself when he exited the car, trying to cool her flushed cheeks. She watched through the window as Isaiah rounded the vehicle, his stride purposeful and confident.

He opened her door, and she placed her hand in his, enjoying the warmth of his skin. She stood, suddenly very close to him in the narrow space between the car and the open door.

"Ready?" Isaiah asked softly, his breath warm against her ear.

She nodded, not trusting her voice. Together, they made their way toward the house, the promise of the evening ahead sending a thrill of anticipation through her.

They walked along a stone pathway toward a Tudor house with timber beams contrasting with the cream-colored stucco. The yellow door added a pop of color to the exterior.

The door swung open, revealing Connie's beaming face. "You made it!" she exclaimed, enveloping Lisa in a hug. "I'm so glad you came."

The buzz of conversation and laughter washed over Lisa as soon as she stepped inside. The party looked to be well attended with people standing in groups in both the living room, dining room, and the hallway between. None of whom she recognized. She felt a momentary flutter of anxiety in her chest.

Connie linked her arm through Lisa's. "Come on, let me introduce you to everyone!"

Lisa slipped out of Isaiah's jacket, handing it back to him as they wove through the crowd. Her head spun with the parade of faces and names. "This is Tom from Forensics... Sarah from Records... Oh, and here's Detective Martinez..."

Lisa smiled and nodded, knowing she'd never remember half the names. She glanced back, relieved to see Isaiah following close behind, his tall frame easy to spot.

He caught her eye and winked, sending a little jolt through her.

"I feel like I'm cramming for a test," Lisa whispered to Connie. "There's no way I'll keep all these names straight."

Connie laughed. "Don't worry about it. They probably won't remember meeting you either, especially as the night goes on." She made a drinking motion with her hand. "Oh! Here's someone you should definitely meet."

They approached a distinguished-looking man with salt-and-pepper hair. He wore a suit that was slightly too small and a look that was half grimace, half smile. Even if Connie hadn't steered her directly to him, Lisa would have guessed he was important from the way people deferred to him.

"Lieutenant Garfino," Connie said, "I'd like you to meet Lisa Elkins."

Garfino's handshake was firm, his eyes alert. "Ms. Elkins. It's a pleasure meeting you. Thank you for your assistance with the Donlea cell phone. It was invaluable to our investigation."

"It was no problem at all. I was happy I could help."

She was grateful for Isaiah's comforting warmth at her back while talking to his boss. Even though they were at a social function, the man was intimidating.

Garfino's smile tightened, his eyes becoming more serious. "While we appreciate your help, Ms. Elkins, I want you to know that we're also concerned about your safety. We're all going to do our best to keep you safe."

Garfino's message wasn't missed. *Stay in your lane and out of our investigation.*

Lisa felt Isaiah move even closer, his arm barely brushing hers. The gesture was subtle, protective.

"I understand," Lisa replied, her voice steady despite the fluttering in her stomach. "I want to stay safe too. You can count on me to be cautious."

She could see her message hadn't been missed either. She'd take precautions, but she wasn't going to sit on the sidelines while someone targeted her and the people she cared about.

Garfino nodded stiffly, his gaze flicking between Lisa and Isaiah. Without another word, he turned and melted into the crowd of partygoers.

Lisa let out a breath. She looked at Isaiah, her eyebrows raised. "Wow, he's intense."

Isaiah's lips quirked in a wry smile. "You don't know the half of it," he murmured, his eyes still tracking Garfino's path through the room.

Lisa found herself relaxing as the party continued. She mingled with various guests, making small talk about the weather, the holidays, and Connie's beautiful home. Connie hadn't been exaggerating about people letting loose as the night wore on.

Scanning the room, Lisa's gaze landed on Isaiah several feet away. He was deep in conversation with a man she'd been introduced to but whose name she couldn't recall. Isaiah's brow was furrowed, his posture tense. Work never stopped for him, did it?

As much as she was enjoying herself, the mass of people was a lot. Needing some air, she made her way to the French doors leading to the deck. They'd already been opened slightly. On her way, she snagged a flute of champagne from the end of the bar where the bartender kept a tray of full flutes at the ready.

The cool night air was a blessed relief as Lisa stepped outside. She took a deep breath, feeling some of the tension leave her shoulders. Leaning against the railing, she sipped her champagne and tried to sort through her swirling thoughts.

Lisa gazed up at the starry December sky. The stars seemed to mirror the festive atmosphere inside. Her eyes wandered over Connie's backyard, taking in the covered pool and dormant landscaping. Come spring, she imagined it would be a riot of color and life.

A smile played on her lips as she considered how much better this evening had turned out to be. Especially since her original plan had involved sitting at home alone on her sofa watching reruns of old sitcoms.

She wouldn't deny that she'd been a little at a loss since Layla had flown off to spend the holidays with her father and his new family. But an empty nest was something she was going to have to get used to, sooner rather than later. In two short years, Layla would be off to college. The thought of her daughter leaving still tugged at her heart, but she knew she needed to start planning for her own child-free future. What was she going to do with all that newfound free time? She swirled the champagne in her glass, musing over the possibilities.

The soft whine of the hinges on the French door caught her attention. She turned to see Isaiah stepping onto the deck, his tall frame silhouetted against the warm light from inside. Her pulse sped up as he approached, and she found herself admiring the way his suit jacket emphasized his broad shoulders.

"You okay out here?" he asked, his deep voice tinged with concern.

She nodded, offering a small smile. "I'm fine. I just needed some air."

Isaiah leaned against the railing, his arm brushing Lisa's. She felt a spark of electricity at the contact. Her head swam. It had been a very long time since she'd reacted this way to a man, but she liked it.

"I can understand that," he said. "I know most of the people in there, and it's still overwhelming for me sometimes."

She turned to face him, studying his profile in the moonlight. "Really? But all the people inside obviously respect you a lot. The way they look at you, it's clear you've made quite an impression."

"I've tried to put my best foot forward these last six months. Especially since I'm still the new guy, you know?"

"You shouldn't worry. You're a good detective. Anyone can see that."

The tension that had been simmering all evening suddenly crackled to life. Isaiah's eyes met hers, dark and intense. She found herself unable to look away.

Her heart pounded in her chest. She was acutely aware of how little distance there was between them.

Oh, what the hell, Lisa thought, her inhibitions lowered by the champagne and the romantic atmosphere of the starlit night. She set her glass down on the deck railing and stepped in close. Slowly, deliberately, she placed her hands on his chest, feeling the solid muscle beneath his shirt.

"Lisa," he breathed, his voice low and husky. His eyes searched hers, a mix of desire and uncertainty. "Do you… do you know what you're doing?"

She met his gaze unflinchingly. "Absolutely." She stretched up and pressed her lips to his in a kiss that started off soft and tentative.

But when Isaiah's arms wrapped around her waist, pulling her closer, she deepened the kiss. Her fingers curled into the fabric of his shirt as she lost herself in the sensation of his lips on hers.

She was dimly aware of Isaiah guiding her backward until her back met the cool stucco of the house. Shadows drowned them in darkness, shielding them from view of the partygoers inside. Her head swam, overwhelmed by the taste of him, the feel of his body against hers.

"We shouldn't…" Isaiah murmured against her lips, even as his hands tightened on her hips.

"Don't stop," she whispered back, arching into him. "Please, don't stop."

Isaiah pulled back slightly, his breath coming in short pants. His eyes, dark with desire, searched her face. "Lisa, we should stop. This is… It's too fast. We're both…we've been drinking."

Lisa's heart raced, her body thrumming with need. She cupped Isaiah's face in her hands, meeting his gaze steadily. "We can stop if you want to, but for the record, I don't want to. I know what I want, Isaiah, and right now, that's you."

A low groan escaped him, and then his mouth was on hers again. This time, there was no hesitation. His kiss was hungry, passionate, and she met him with equal fervor. Her fingers tangled in his hair as his hands roamed her back, pulling her closer.

After several heated moments, Isaiah broke away, his forehead resting against hers. "Do you want to get out of here?" he asked, his voice rough.

She couldn't stop the laugh that bubbled up, giddy with desire and champagne. "More than anything," she replied, her lips curving into a smile.

He chuckled, the sound sending a shiver down her spine. "My apartment isn't too far," he murmured, his fingers tracing patterns on her lower back.

She leaned in, kissing him hard and fast, reveling in the way his body responded to hers. "Let's get out of here," she breathed against his lips, her heart pounding with anticipation and a touch of nervousness.

As they pulled apart, Lisa felt a moment of doubt. Was this too impulsive? But looking at Isaiah, seeing the warmth and desire in his eyes, she pushed the thought aside. For once, she was going to follow her heart and see where it led.

Chapter Sixteen

Given the late hour, it didn't take long to make it the several blocks from Connie's house to Isaiah's apartment. Lisa didn't let herself think about the wisdom of what she was about to do. She focused instead on the feelings that had swelled inside of her while they'd been kissing on Connie's deck. How she wished there hadn't been several dozen other people on the other side of the wall. What they could be doing if they were alone. She was about to get her wish.

Isaiah turned off Connecticut Avenue onto a side street and then quickly into a parking lot behind a red brick building. They got out of the car, and he took her hand, leading her into the building through a back entrance that required an electronic passkey for entry. He led her into the elevator, punching the button for the third floor, before turning and catching her in a scorching kiss that relit the fire he'd ignited earlier on Connie's deck.

The elevator pinged, and the doors opened. Isaiah ended the kiss, with some hesitation it seemed, she thought with satisfaction. Or maybe it was just her that felt immense disappointment at the loss of his lips on hers.

He steered them toward a green door with a brass

knocker, halfway down the hallway. He pushed the door open and flipped a switch on the wall.

She stepped inside, taking in the space. The gray sectional sofa situated across from the large television mounted on the wall. The round dining table off to the left of the living area, big enough for at least four people although there were only two chairs.

She turned and found Isaiah standing in the foyer, his back against the door, staring at her. He pushed off the door and walked to her, stopping and lifting a hand to her face.

She tipped her head back, keeping her eyes open until his lips met hers. Then she let herself get lost in the taste of champagne and the feel of his stubble against her skin as he pulled her in close.

His hands slid over her sides, hips, and butt before starting the sequence over again. She wrapped her arms around his neck and drew him in ever closer, feeling the broad expanse of his chest flush against hers. This was what she'd wanted, what she'd been craving, since he'd walked into her home just hours after it had been violated.

She sank into him, pushing away the ugliness of the situation that had brought them together.

He rocked his hips against hers, drawing a low moan from deep inside her throat. She could feel how turned on he was, and she'd never felt more sensual or desired. He pushed the hem of her shirt up and skirted his fingers over her rib cage ever so gently. Up, up, slowly, almost unbearably slow until his hand settled over her right breast. She moaned a second time as his hand pushed the lace of her bra aside, and his thumb brushed, not at all gently this time, over her nipple.

"Isaiah." Her voice was rough, hoarse.

He dipped his head down and kissed her in answer, his

other hand now palming her left breast. Every nerve in her body pulsated.

She trailed kisses over his neck and focused on staying on her feet. When she was just at the point where she was sure her legs would give out, he turned her in his arms. His hands still sending delicious shivers down her spine, he guided her down a short hall and into his bedroom. Isaiah didn't bother with turning on the lights this time.

The king-size bed loomed large, and her skin began to tingle in anticipation of what was to come.

"Are you sure about this?" he asked once again, his voice barely above a whisper.

She'd never been more sure of anything.

She wrapped her arms around his neck and pulled him down into a kiss that showed him just how sure she was. His strong arms tightened around her, and she deepened the kiss. She wanted him, and he wanted her, and that was all she wanted either of them thinking about for the night.

The kiss went on and on. At some point, Isaiah eased her back against the wall, stripping off her top and tossing it away.

She felt the warm air on her skin for a moment before his mouth closed over her breast, and she let her head fall back against the wall, reveling in the sensations he sent coursing through her body. He pinned her in place with his weight on her as he lavished attention on one breast and then the other. He kept her until she was squirming with need. Then he leaned back, but only long enough to pull her right thigh up, resting it against his hip, so she could feel the full, hard length of him grinding into her as he attacked her mouth once again.

It was the most erotic and desired she'd ever felt. His fingers moved up and down her leg, alternating between gently and just rough enough to shoot sparks to all the right places.

"Isaiah, please." She wasn't sure what she was asking for. Just that this was too much and not enough all at the same time.

He let her leg down, then found the zipper on the back of her skirt and let it down as well. Her skirt fell to the floor in a puddle at her feet. She stood before him in nothing but her lace bra and panties and high heels.

"You are the most gorgeous thing I have ever laid eyes on."

Heat flooded her skin. She reached out and trailed a hand over the stubble on his chin before moving down to the buttons on his shirt. Somewhere along the way he'd lost his jacket, though she couldn't remember when he'd taken it off. Free of his shirt, she went for his pants next, undoing his belt and then the button to his trousers, letting them fall to the floor as he'd let her skirt fall.

His hands never left her body as she undressed him. He trailed his finger over her breast, her navel and rib cage, her neck and mouth and back again. His touch had her already heated skin burning with desire for more.

When they were both down to nothing other than their underwear, Isaiah took her hand and led her to the bed. She lay back on the bed and he came over her, leaning in for another kiss.

The intensity of this one was different from the others. Raw and demanding. Fierce as well as exploratory. She felt him unclasp her bra and shuck it aside. Then he worked his way down her with his hands, mouth, and tongue until she thought she just might explode. He slid her panties down and tossed them as well, and then his hand was between her legs, and she ignited. Her world spun, and she clung to him, basking in the sensations that he brought forth.

She was still panting, coming down off the exquisite high, when he reached across her to the nightstand, opening the drawer there. He sheathed himself, and then he was over her, the now familiar weight of him on top of her, igniting the spark of desire in her again.

He kissed her deeply, then stopped to gaze down at her. She stared up at him for a long moment, something profound and real passing between them before she smiled and shifted so he was seated right where she wanted him. With a sexy smile of his own, he pushed into her.

She gasped, clinging to him tightly. Neither of them moved.

Then he did, starting a slow rhythm that had every thought that wasn't about him and this moment fleeing her head. She drew him in deeper, drawing a groan from his lips. She held on as he increased his rhythm until he was pounding into her. Every inch of her was on fire, and she wanted more.

"Isaiah, please," she begged again. This time they both knew exactly what she wanted.

He sped up his pace, and she matched it, soaring toward a peak she was sure she'd never reached before. One, even in her halfway drunk with lust state, she knew she wanted to reach again. And again. And again.

She needed him…in that moment and beyond. That thought was enough to push her over the edge.

"Isaiah." Stars exploded behind her eyes.

She was vaguely aware of his muscles clenching, his body tightening and going rigid, as he drove himself into her one last time.

She clung to him as pleasure surged through her, loosening every muscle in her body until she felt absolutely boneless.

Isaiah shuddered, then rolled, pulling her with him so he was on his back, and she was sprawled over his chest. They lay like that, content and satiated, until she felt his heartbeat return to normal and her own breath slowed.

She fell asleep, tucked tightly into the side of a man she feared she was falling in love with.

LISA'S EYES SNAPPED OPEN, her heart racing as she stared at an unfamiliar ceiling. Sunlight streamed through curtains she didn't recognize, illuminating a room that wasn't hers. For one panicked moment, she couldn't remember where she was or how she'd gotten there.

Then she felt the warmth of another body beside her, and it all came rushing back. She turned her head slowly, taking in the sight of Isaiah's sleeping form next to her. The sheets were tangled around his legs, his muscular torso bare. She suddenly became acutely aware that she was wearing nothing but his T-shirt.

She lay still for several minutes more, gazing at the ceiling as memories of the night before washed over her. The way Isaiah's calloused hands had felt on her body, leaving trails of fire in their wake. His lips on her neck, her collarbone, moving lower…

She squeezed her eyes shut, willing the vivid images away. What had she been thinking? This wasn't like her at all. She didn't do casual hookups or one-night stands. And yet here she was, in Isaiah's bed after a night of passion she couldn't bring herself to regret.

She sneaked another glance at his sleeping face. He looked peaceful. Her heart clenched painfully as she recalled his words from a few nights ago. *I'm not a good bet.*

"Stupid," she chided herself silently. "You knew going in this wouldn't mean anything to him. Do not get attached."

But as she lay there, listening to his breaths, she knew it was already too late for that.

She slid carefully out of bed, wincing as the floorboards creaked beneath her feet. She paused, heart racing, but his breathing remained steady and deep. Grabbing her clothes from where they lay scattered on the floor, she tiptoed to the bathroom, shutting the door with a soft click.

I'll just call a car, she thought to herself as she dressed quickly in the bathroom. That was the polite thing to do in this situation, right? Be gone before the other person wakes up? No muss, no fuss. It was best that way.

She caught sight of herself in the mirror, hair tousled, lips still slightly swollen from Isaiah's kisses. A wave of embarrassment washed over her.

Fully clothed, she opened the bathroom door. The bedroom door remained closed, no sound coming from within. Relief and disappointment warred within her as she padded into the living room.

Her purse lay on the floor where she'd dropped it the night before. As she bent to retrieve it, memories flooded back—Isaiah's hands on her waist, his lips claiming hers hungrily.

"Stop it," she whispered to herself, shaking her head to clear the vivid recollections. "It was one night. That's all."

But even as she tried to convince herself, she couldn't shake the feeling that last night had changed something. At least for her, if not for Isaiah.

Her fingers trembled slightly as she fished her phone from her purse, then slung the bag over her shoulder. She scooped up her heels…

She headed for the apartment door, already pulling up the rideshare app on her phone.

"Where are you going?"

Isaiah's deep voice caught her off guard, and she started with surprise. She whirled around, her face flushing with embarrassment.

He leaned against the wall that separated the hallway from the living space, expression unreadable. Her eyes traveled over his sculpted chest, down to where his boxer briefs hung low on his hips. Something stirred deep within her, a primal response to him that she desperately tried to push away.

She took a breath, trying to compose herself. "I need to go," she said, her voice steadier than she felt. "I'm going to be late for work." She gestured vaguely with her phone. "I didn't want to wake you, so I was just going to order a car."

Isaiah's eyes never left hers as he said, "You're sneaking out." His jaw clenched, his eyes narrowing.

The accusation in his tone made her wince. She felt a surge of defensiveness, coupled with a twinge of guilt. "I'm not sneaking," she protested, though even to her own ears it sounded weak. She sighed, shoulders slumping. "I just... I haven't done this before," she admitted, her cheeks burning. "It seemed like the right thing to do was to leave before we had to go through a weird 'how do you take your coffee,' 'would you like some eggs' morning rigmarole."

Isaiah's expression shifted, a hint of amusement creeping into his eyes. "It did, did it?" he said, the edge of annoyance in his voice softening.

She felt some of the tension ease from her body, although her heart still raced.

"Rigmarole?" His lips twitched as he fought a smile. "That's quite a word choice for this early in the morning."

She sighed, her gaze dropping to the floor. "Look, I'm sorry. I don't know what the right thing to do here is."

He closed the distance between them, his bare feet padding softly on the hardwood floor. He placed his hands on her shoulders, the warmth of his touch sending a shiver through her. She looked up, meeting his intense gaze as he leaned down, pressing a soft kiss to her lips.

"There is no right or wrong thing to do," he murmured, his breath ghosting across her skin. "Just talk to me. Tell me how you're feeling this morning."

The gentleness in his voice made her heart constrict. She took a deep breath, steeling herself. "Vulnerable," she admitted, the word feeling raw and exposed as it left her lips. "Like I said, I don't do hookups." She rushed to add, "And I know, you've made it clear that you aren't ready for more than that."

His brow furrowed, his eyes narrowing. "When did I say that?" he interrupted.

Lisa felt a flash of exasperation mingle with her ongoing embarrassment. "The other night," she said, her voice rising slightly, "when you walked me to my door. You said you weren't a good bet."

"I'm not a good bet," he admitted, his eyes dancing with a mix of humor and something deeper. "There are probably a million men who would be a better choice for you than I am."

Her heart sank, but before she could respond, Isaiah's expression shifted.

He paused, his gaze becoming intense and heartfelt as it locked onto hers. "But that still doesn't stop me from hoping," he said softly.

Her breath caught in her throat as his fingers brushed gently over her cheek, leaving a trail of electricity in their wake. Her heart pounded so loudly she was sure he could hear it.

"Hoping for what?" she asked, her voice barely above a whisper and trembling slightly with anticipation.

The air between them crackled with tension as she waited for his answer. Isaiah's lips parted, and she leaned in unconsciously, desperate to hear his next words.

Suddenly, the shrill ring of her cell phone shattered the moment. She jumped, looking down at the device still clutched in her hand. Her eyes widened as she recognized the number.

"It's the hospital," she said, concern coloring her voice. With shaking fingers, she swiped to answer the call. "Hello?"

"Ms. Elkins, this is Holy Cross Hospital," a crisp voice responded. "I'm calling to let you know that Mr. Sonfeld is awake. And he's asking for you."

Chapter Seventeen

The hospital's automatic doors whooshed open, admitting a gust of cold air along with Isaiah as he and Lisa burst into the hospital. Lisa's breath came in short gasps as she scanned the crowded waiting area.

"Harry Sonfeld," she blurted out to the harried-looking receptionist. "Please, where is he?"

The woman's fingers typed on the keyboard. "He's been moved to a semiprivate room," she said, her voice clipped but not unkind. She pointed them in the right direction.

Though he was a good six inches taller than Lisa, Isaiah had to jog to keep up with her as she raced toward the curtained area where the receptionist had said Harry was.

Lisa's breath caught when she saw him. "Oh, Harry," she whispered, tears welling in her eyes.

The man on the bed looked frail and elderly. Nothing like the vibrant picture of the man on his and Lisa's company website. He looked small, diminished somehow, as if the attack had stolen years from him in a single act. A white bandage encircled Harry's head, stark against his wrinkled, ashen skin. Tubes snaked from his arm, connected to beeping machines. His right eye was swollen shut, a mottled purple-black bruise spreading across his cheekbone. His chest rose and fell with shallow breaths.

"I can't believe this happened," Lisa choked out, her voice barely above a whisper.

Isaiah placed a hand on her shoulder. "We'll find who did this," he murmured.

Lisa nodded, wiping at her eyes. She had to be strong now. Taking a deep breath, she moved to Harry's bedside, taking his hand in hers.

Harry's eyes fluttered open, his gaze unfocused at first. Then, with what seemed like tremendous effort, he reached out his other hand toward her. She leaned in, clasping it gently.

"Lisa." The sound of her name only made her cry harder. "Shh, no tears now," Harry whispered.

Lisa swallowed hard, forcing back a fresh wave of emotion. "I'm here, Harry. I'm right here."

Isaiah waited, giving the two a moment before stepping forward. "Mr. Sonfeld, I'm Detective Isaiah Reeves. I'm investigating the assault on you."

Harry acknowledged him with a slight nod, wincing at the movement.

"I'm so sorry, Harry," Lisa blurted out, her words tumbling over each other. "This is all my fault."

Harry's brow furrowed, confusion evident in his one open eye. "Sorry for what? None of this is your fault."

Lisa shook her head. "It is. If I had just—"

"No," Harry interrupted, his grip on her hand tightening slightly. "I don't know what those men were after, but I know this wasn't your fault." He paused, grimacing, his eyes closing.

Isaiah cleared his throat softly. "Mr. Sonfeld, if you feel

up to it, I'd like to ask you a few questions about what happened. Do you think you're strong enough for that?"

Harry's eyes fluttered open, a spark of determination cutting through the haze of pain. "Yes," he rasped, his voice stronger than before. "I want to help. Ask away, Detective."

Isaiah nodded, pulling out a small notebook. "All right, can you tell me everything you remember about the incident?"

Harry took a deep breath, wincing slightly. "I recall some of it," he began, his gaze losing focus as he reached back into his memory. "I came in for work like I usually do. Nothing seemed out of the ordinary. But when I unlocked the office door…" He paused, his brow furrowing. "I felt someone push me from behind, hard. Shoved me right into the office."

Isaiah saw Lisa's hand tighten around Harry's, her face a mask of anger.

"And before that, Mr. Sonfeld?" Isaiah said. "Do you recall anyone following you into the building?"

Harry's forehead creased in concentration, his good eye squinting as he struggled to remember. "I… I'm not sure," he admitted, frustration evident in his voice. "Everything after that shove is a bit of a blur. I was focused on getting to work, you know? I didn't pay much attention." Harry paused, then added. "I was alone in the elevator, I'm certain of that. But when I got to the office floor…they were just there. Two of them."

Isaiah's jaw tightened imperceptibly. Two assailants. Probably waiting in the stairwell. The revelation sent a chill down his spine. Waiting for who though? Harry? Lisa? Or whoever happened to show up at the office first that day? He glanced at Lisa, noting the way her shoulders tensed at Harry's words. A surge of protectiveness washed over him, mingling with a growing sense of unease.

If these men were willing to brutalize Harry, what might they do to Lisa if they got their hands on her? The thought of her in danger made his stomach churn and strengthened his resolve to make sure they got nowhere near her.

"They kept yelling about some kind of code," Harry went on. "Demanding I tell them where it was."

Lisa started, then looked at Isaiah.

This was proof that the break-in at her office and her home were connected. Probably the same men, or at least men working together. And whatever this code was, it was important for these men to commit two felonies. So, what the hell was it?

"Can you tell me anything else about the guys, Harry?" Isaiah asked, pushing down his worry to focus on the task at hand. He needed more information, something that could help him keep Lisa safe and bring these criminals to justice.

Harry nodded, wincing slightly as he shifted in the hospital bed. "They were dressed alike," he said, his words still raspy. "Black shirts, blue jeans. Ski masks over their faces and gloves on their hands." His eyes suddenly lit up. "I got a good look at one of them. When he started hitting me, I fought back. I managed to yank his mask off."

Lisa squeezed Harry's hand, her voice thick with emotion. "Good for you, Harry."

Isaiah nodded approvingly, more than a little impressed by the man's courage. "That was quick thinking, Harry. Can you describe your assailant?"

"White guy," Harry said. "Green eyes, brown hair. Younger than me, in his late twenties, early thirties. Somewhere in there."

Isaiah jotted down the description, his mind already con-

structing a mental image of the assailant. He didn't miss
that Harry's assailant had green eyes. The same color as
the man who'd broken into Lisa's house. "You did good,
Harry," he said.

Harry's brow furrowed, his eyes distant as he recalled
the harrowing events. "I kept telling them I didn't know
what they were talking about. But they wouldn't listen.
One of them started tearing apart my office, throwing papers everywhere, upending drawers. The other one…" He
paused, glancing at Lisa. "He went down the hall. I figured
he was heading for your office."

Lisa's face paled. Isaiah squeezed her shoulder gently,
silently reassuring her.

Harry continued, his voice growing stronger with in-
dignation. "When the guy in my office realized I didn't
have whatever code he was looking for, he just…he lost it."
Harry's fists clenched on the hospital blanket, bunching it.
"He started hitting me. Then the other one came back." He
shook his head, wincing at the movement. "After that," he
continued, "it's all a blur. Next thing I remember is waking up here." He gestured weakly at the room.

Isaiah noticed Harry's eyelids drooping, the adrenaline
of recounting his ordeal wearing off. The detective's keen
eyes took in Harry's pallor and the slight tremor in his
hands. He decided it was time to wrap things up.

"You've been incredibly helpful, Harry," Isaiah said,
his tone gentle. "I think we should let you rest now. When
you're feeling up to it, I'll send a police sketch artist over.
With your description, we should be able to get a good
likeness of the man you saw."

Harry nodded, fighting to keep his eyes open. "Anything
I can do to help," he murmured. "Just want to make sure
my girl is safe." He patted Lisa's hand in a fatherly gesture.

Isaiah glanced at Lisa, seeing tears welling in her eyes again.

Lisa leaned in and placed a soft kiss on Harry's cheek. "Get some rest. I'll be back to check on you soon," she whispered, her voice thick with emotion.

Isaiah led Lisa out of the room, pulling the curtain closed behind them.

As they walked down the sterile hallway, the fluorescent lights casting harsh shadows, he could feel the tension radiating from Lisa. Her steps were quick and purposeful, her fists clenched at her sides.

When they reached the elevator, Lisa suddenly turned to him, her eyes flashing with an intensity he hadn't seen before. "I've never considered myself a violent person," she said. "But right now, I want nothing more than to hurt the men who did this to Harry."

Isaiah studied her face, noting the mix of anger and fear in her expression. He understood her feelings all too well. "Lisa," he said softly, placing a reassuring hand on her shoulder, "I promise you, we're going to find who did this. They won't get away with it."

THE SHRILL RING of Lisa's phone woke her the next morning. She groaned, fumbling for it on the nightstand.

The screen was far too bright for her sleep-deprived eyes, but the number on it was familiar. Her office line. She'd forwarded it to her cell the previous afternoon while she'd been working from her home and forgotten to unforward. She'd worked well past midnight and felt as if she'd only just closed her eyes.

The clock in the corner of the screen read 7:34 a.m. She felt a surge of irritation at the phone's next trill. Who in the world would be calling this early?

"Hello?" she mumbled, still half asleep.

"Ms. Elkins? This is Mr. Blackwell's assistant," came a crisp male voice over the phone line. "Mr. Blackwell is in town and would like to meet regarding the security proposal. Are you available this morning?"

Lisa sat up, suddenly alert. But the timing couldn't be worse.

"This morning?" Lisa repeated, buying time as she frantically considered her options. She could practically feel the weight of opportunity pressing down on her shoulders. Blackwell Industries wasn't just any client. They were the golden goose, the kind of account that could propel their small firm into the big leagues. Harry would kill her if she lost the opportunity to win their business.

"Today would be a bit difficult. Perhaps we could arrange something for next week instead?" Lisa held her breath, but any hope she had was quickly dashed.

"Mr. Blackwell's schedule is quite full," the assistant replied with the tone of someone used to others bowing to their wishes. "Mr. Blackwell was hoping to finalize the details of the proposal during this trip."

Lisa's annoyance kicked up a notch, but she sighed silently before injecting a hint of cheeriness into her voice. "I... I suppose I can make that work," she said, rubbing her temples. "I can meet Mr. Blackwell at our offices at 10:00 a.m. if that works for him."

"That would be fine. Mr. Blackwell will see you then."

Lisa hung up and sighed. With Harry still recuperating, this fell squarely on her shoulders. She pulled on a robe and padded to the front door, squinting in the bright sunlight as she stepped onto the porch.

The uniformed officer straightened as she approached. "Everything all right, Ms. Elkins?"

"Yes, fine, but I've had something come up at work. I need to go into the office. I'll be ready in about fifteen minutes if that's okay with you."

He nodded. "No problem. I'll just be waiting for you in the car. Come on out whenever you are ready."

She hurried back inside and upstairs. Standing in front of her closet, she flipped through possible outfits, her mind running through the Blackwell proposal as she did. She yanked a silk blouse off its hanger. She hated unscheduled changes. This was the kind of stuff that Harry lived for. A pang of guilt stabbed her. Harry was in the hospital because of her. The least she could do was keep their business afloat while he recovered.

But she'd planned to reach out to Isaiah, maybe treat him to breakfast, and see if she could get an update from him on the case.

Heat rose in her cheeks as vivid memories of the night they'd spent together flashed through her mind. Isaiah's intense dark eyes, the feeling of his strong hands on her skin, the way he'd whispered her name in her ear. She paused, clutching a silk scarf. The night had been electric—but what did it mean? She wasn't sure. They weren't graduate students anymore. She didn't do hookups. Heck, she hadn't done hookups when she was a student.

She gave her head a vigorous shake. Now was not the time for this. She forced herself to focus on the task at hand. "Get it together, Lisa," she muttered. "You've got a company to keep on the tracks."

Dressed, she smoothed her blouse, studying her reflection. The woman staring back looked composed, professional. But inside, she felt anything but.

"Fake it till you make it," she said softly to herself not for the first time. She headed downstairs and grabbed her purse from where she'd left it on the coffee table in the living room.

She slung the strap across her body and snatched her laptop from the desk. After making sure the house was locked up tight, she slid into the back seat of the police cruiser, the weight of responsibility for the business settled heavily on her shoulders. She couldn't wait until Harry was back up and running. A sliver of guilt wound through her even though she knew everyone was right and that Harry being in the hospital wasn't her fault. It was the fault of Scott and Big Joe and whoever else was involved in the scheme with Scott.

"Thanks for the ride, Officer Brady," she said, flipping open her laptop. "I'm sorry to be rude, but I need to review some notes for this client meeting. I hope you don't mind if I'm antisocial."

The officer chuckled as he pulled out of the driveway. "No problem at all, Ms. Elkins. Just pretend I'm your chauffeur."

She managed a weak smile before immersing herself in the security proposal on her screen. She muttered softly to herself, rehearsing key points and jotting down notes. The familiar routine helped calm her nerves, pushing thoughts of Isaiah and the case to the back of her mind.

Minutes ticked by as suburban streets gave way to busier thoroughfares. She was deep in concentration when Officer Brady's sharp exclamation jarred her back to reality.

"What the hell?"

Her head snapped up. In the rearview mirror, she caught a glimpse of a massive black SUV bearing down on them at alarming speed. Before she could process what was happening, the impact of the SUV hitting the back of the cruiser slammed her forward, laptop clattering to the floor.

"Hang on!" Brady shouted, wrestling with the steering wheel.

Another brutal hit from the side sent Lisa careening against the door. Her seat belt dug painfully into her shoulder as she was tossed about like a rag doll. Her head connected with the window, hard, and stars exploded behind her eyes.

Tires squealed. Glass shattered. The world spun sickeningly as the cruiser jumped the curb.

Awareness came in disjoined snapshots. The cruiser's door wrenched open. Rough hands yanking her from the wreckage. The acrid smell of burnt rubber from the tires. Her own voice, weak and slurred, trying to protest, trying to fight back.

But it was to no avail. A burly man lifted her as if she weighed nothing. Her head lolled against his chest as she was carried from the cruiser. The world tilted again as she was unceremoniously tossed into the back of the waiting SUV, landing hard on the black leather back seats.

As unconsciousness closed in, one terrifying realization crystallized in Lisa's mind. She was being kidnapped.

Chapter Eighteen

Isaiah burst into the station's conference room, his heart nearly pounding as if it was ready to leap out of his chest. Connie followed him.

Lisa was gone.

"What the hell happened?" he demanded.

Garfino turned from the whiteboard where he'd already started pinning up photos of the accident scene. Isaiah flinched at the photo of the crumpled police cruiser that Lisa had been riding in.

"I've still got men interviewing witnesses, but two guys rammed the cruiser that was taking Lisa to her office. Two guys grabbed Lisa, pushed her into a black SUV, and tore out of there."

"Roadblocks." Isaiah could barely speak past the lump of fear clogging his throat.

Garfino's gaze was pitying. "Done, but so far nothing."

"What do you mean nothing?" Isaiah barked back. "You said there were witnesses."

"Like I said, they gave us two guys, but no one saw enough detail to be helpful. Most people were trying to avoid the accident. A couple of the witnesses swear the men had masks covering their faces. Several others gave us descriptions that would suggest they saw the men's faces. You know how it is with witnesses during an event like this. If we get twenty witnesses, we'll get thirty descriptions of what happened."

Isaiah bit back a scream. He knew the lieutenant was right. Eyewitness accounts were notoriously unreliable. The witnesses would be running on adrenaline, fear, even excitement, all of which would distort their perspectives.

"A kidnapping in downtown DC in the middle of the morning," Connie growled. "Someone must have seen something."

"We're working on it," Garfino growled back.

"What about video?"

"Working on that too."

Isaiah ran his hand over his head, looking down at the scratched tile floors. His brain was flooded with what the kidnappers might be doing to Lisa. He struggled to breathe past the images. He couldn't let the what-ifs keep him from doing everything he could to find her. He had to keep his cop brain turned on if he had any chance of getting Lisa back.

And when he got her back, he'd tell her how he felt about her. Tell her he wanted to find out if the feelings that existed between them could grow into more, something they'd both been looking for all their lives. But he had to get her back first.

The conference room door opened, and a breathless uniformed officer rushed in. She held a laptop computer in her hands. "Got that security video you requested, Lieutenant."

"Good. Cue it up."

The officer set the laptop on the conference room table and Isaiah, Connie, and Garfino gathered around.

"It's pretty clear footage. I got it from the Smithsonian Museum across the street from the accident site."

Garfino grunted, but Isaiah and Connie remained silent.

The video came up, the first fifteen seconds showing nothing more than traffic streaming by on the street adjacent to the museum. Then an MPD police cruiser came into the frame. A second later, a black SUV roared up behind it, ramming it. The cruiser spun, jumped the curb, and slammed into the side of the building opposite the museum. The front of the cruiser was out of the camera's frame, but they could still see the rear doors.

A man in a mask jumped out of the back of the SUV. In a matter of seconds, he'd pulled Lisa from the cruiser, thrown her into the SUV, and jumped back into the passenger seat.

They rewound the video and watched it again at half speed. And then they watched it again.

"Wait! Pause it there," Isaiah said after he'd watched Lisa be thrown in the car for the third time. "Can you zoom in on where he reaches for the passenger door?"

The officer zoomed in.

Connie and Garfino leaned toward the laptop screen.

"It looks like a tattoo of some sort." Connie's eyes narrowed in concentration. "A ring or some type of swirl."

Anger thumped through Isiah's veins. "It's a snake. And I know who kidnapped Lisa."

WHICH WAS WHY he found himself studying Emily Donlea through the two-way mirror an hour later. The small observation room felt claustrophobic. A wall-mounted monitor displayed a crisp feed of the interrogation room, and a bank of recording equipment captured every sound and movement within.

Isaiah studied Emily as she chewed her nails. "You know something, Emily," he muttered under his breath, his own fingers drumming an impatient rhythm on his thigh.

The snake tattoo on the arm of the man who'd kidnapped Lisa wasn't enough to convict Todd Donlea, but it was enough to bring him in for questioning. If they could find him, which they hadn't been able to yet. Isaiah was hoping that Emily might point them in the right direction.

Emily had barely spoken since he and Connie picked her up at her house. He replayed the scene in his mind— Emily's quiet efficiency as she arranged for Zoe's care, her wordless compliance as she slid into the back seat of their unmarked car. Not a single question about why they needed her at the station. It was as damning as any confession.

Nervousness radiated from her in waves.

"What are you hiding?" he wondered, leaning closer to the glass. "And how much time have we wasted because of it?"

The weight of Lisa's disappearance pressed down on him, each tick of the clock another moment she might be suffering. Isaiah's jaw clenched, his patience wearing thin. He knew they needed Emily to talk, to fill in the missing pieces of this puzzle. Whatever she knew, whatever she'd been keeping from them, he was going to get it out of her.

The door to the observation room opened. Connie's head and shoulders poked through the narrow opening.

"You ready?" Connie asked, her eyes searching his face.

Isaiah nodded. "Yeah," he replied, his voice low and determined.

He followed Connie into the interrogation room, the fluorescent lights harsh after the dimness of the observation area. As they entered, Emily's head swung toward the door, her eyes wide and apprehensive.

Isaiah studied her, noting the slight tremor in her hands as she pulled the sides of her powder blue cardigan together.

Emily crossed her arms tightly over her chest, as if trying to make herself smaller.

"How long is this going to take?" Her voice shook ever so slightly. "I don't want to leave Zoe for too long."

The mention of her daughter sparked a flicker of anger in Isaiah. He thought of Lisa, wondering if she'd ever see her family again. If he'd ever see her again.

Connie pulled out a chair, its metal legs scraping against the floor. Isaiah lowered himself into the seat beside his partner, his eyes never leaving Emily.

"Well, Ms. Donlea," Connie began, her tone measured, "it may take a while. It depends on you."

Emily's brow furrowed, and she gnawed at another fingernail. "On me?"

Connie leaned forward, her elbows resting on the table. "Yes, on how quickly you tell us everything you know about your former brother-in-law, his kidnapping of Lisa Elkins, and anything else you've been keeping from us."

They'd sent a squad car to the address on Todd's Virginia driver's license, but there had been no answer. And a call to his manager at work revealed that Todd hadn't reported for his shift since he'd spoken to Isaiah and Lisa.

The color drained from Emily's face. Her mouth fell open, working silently for a moment before she found her voice.

Isaiah watched her closely, his jaw clenching as he fought to control his rising anger.

"I don't know anything about a kidnapping, I swear," Emily finally managed.

The words hung in the air, and Isaiah felt a surge of frustration. Emily was lying. It was clear from the way she wouldn't meet his or Connie's eyes.

Isaiah's temper flared at Emily's continued evasiveness. The harsh fluorescent lights flickered, casting shadows across Emily's face. His patience snapped. The fear for Lisa's safety and anger at Emily's deception boiled over. He slammed his hand on the table, the sharp crack echoing in the cramped interrogation room.

Emily flinched.

Isaiah leaned forward, his voice low and intense. "Don't lie to us, Emily. We know you're holding something back. Every second you waste could be putting an innocent woman's life in danger."

He could feel Connie's eyes on him, silently urging caution. His heart raced, thoughts of Lisa alone and afraid consuming him.

He leaned in, his voice razor-sharp. "Let me tell you how this is going to go. You're going to tell us everything, and you're going to do it without a lot of hemming and hawing first. A woman's life might be on the line, and the way I see it we could already charge you with obstruction and aiding and abetting kidnapping." He paused, letting the weight of his words sink in.

Emily's lower lip trembled. Her fingers clutched at her cardigan, her knuckles white.

"And if anything happens to Lisa Elkins, that puts you on the hook for additional charges. Your daughter will have her own kids before you see her again. So, if you don't want that, you better start talking. Now."

The threat hung in the air, heavy and suffocating. His heart hammered in his chest, guilt warring with determination. He wasn't proud of using Emily's daughter as leverage, but Lisa's life was at stake.

Emily's face crumpled, and she burst into tears, her shoulders shaking as she sobbed. "I didn't have a choice," she choked out between gasps. "He threatened Zoe if I told you anything."

Connie leaned forward, her voice softening in stark contrast to his harsher tone. Playing good cop. "Told us what, Emily?"

Emily's sobs intensified, her words becoming unintelligible.

Connie reached into her suit pocket and pulled out a pack of travel-size tissues. She slid them across the table to Emily.

"Scott was working on some computer program for Todd. I don't know exactly what it was, but Scott was so excited about it for a while at least." Emily dabbed at her eyes. "He said it was going to make him a lot of money. When it did, he was going to take me and Zoe on a great adventure."

Isaiah noticed Emily's use of past tense. "You didn't believe him?"

She shook her head. "No. Scott was always making promises he didn't keep. But then he changed. He started saying he thought he'd made a mistake, but he didn't know how to fix it."

"A mistake? How?" Isaiah pressed, leaning forward.

Emily twisted the hem of her cardigan. "I think it had something to do with the computer program."

Isaiah's frustration mounted. They were getting nowhere fast. "Let's go back to Scott saying the program was going to make him a lot of money. Do you know what he meant by that?"

Emily hesitated, twisting the tissue in her hands. "Scott didn't tell me."

"That's not what I asked you," Isaiah said.

Emily took a deep breath. "I… I overheard Scott talking to Todd on the phone one day. It was when he dropped Zoe off after his visitation."

Isaiah's pulse quickened. Finally, they were getting somewhere.

"He said he thought he'd made a mistake," Emily said, her brow furrowing. "But he didn't know how to fix it. He was pacing back and forth, yelling at Todd on the phone. I'd never seen him like that."

Isaiah leaned in, his eyes intent on Emily's face. "What exactly did you hear?"

Emily's gaze darted nervously between Isaiah and Connie. She swallowed hard before continuing, "Scott was telling Todd that he didn't think what they were doing was right. He said…he said they couldn't go through with it. Innocent people would be hurt."

Isaiah exchanged a glance with Connie.

Connie leaned in, her voice more steel now that Emily was talking. "Go through with what? Hurt how?"

Emily dabbed at her eyes with the crumpled tissue, her hands trembling. "I don't know exactly. I could hear him yelling through the phone." Emily swallowed hard. "Todd said, 'They're all insured. Stop being a baby.'"

"Did Scott mention anything specific about who might get hurt?" Isaiah asked, struggling to keep the urgency out of his tone.

Emily shook her head, her eyes wide with fear. "No, he didn't. But the way he said it… I've never heard Scott sound so scared before. It was like he suddenly realized the consequences of whatever they were doing."

Isaiah felt his pulse quicken. The pieces were starting to fall into place. "Insured," he repeated, his mind racing. "And you thought this had something to do with the bank?"

Emily nodded, her eyes downcast. "I figured it must be

related to Todd's work. But I... I didn't want to know any more. I walked away."

Maybe Scott had already been stealing credit card information from his bank's customers. Maybe he grew a conscience? Or maybe Todd had been pressing him to up the ante. Maybe. Maybe. Maybe. He took a deep breath, reminding himself to stay focused on the present. Finding Lisa was the priority now.

"Emily," he said, leaning forward, his voice low and urgent. "Is there anywhere Todd might have taken Lisa? Any place he might consider safe or secluded?"

Emily shook her head, her eyes wide with what seemed like genuine confusion. "I'm sorry, but I really don't know. Even when I was married to Scott, Todd and I were never close. I've only been to his house a handful of times."

Isaiah pressed on, desperation creeping into his voice. "Think hard, Emily. Any vacation spots, family properties, anything?"

"I swear, I don't know of anywhere else," Emily insisted. "Beyond his house, I have no idea where Todd would go. I promise I'm not lying this time. Please, you have to believe me."

Isaiah leaned back in his chair. He believed her, but that didn't make their situation any less dire. Time was running out for Lisa, and they were still grasping at straws.

Chapter Nineteen

Lisa's head throbbed as she blinked awake, her vision swimming into focus on unfamiliar log walls. The musty scent of damp wood filled her nostrils. She was lying on a threadbare sofa, its scratchy fabric rough against her cheek. Disoriented, she pushed herself up on shaky arms, her heart pounding as she took in her surroundings.

A bearded stranger sat at a rustic wooden table across the small cabin, but it was the man beside him that made her breath catch in her throat. Todd Donlea. Scott's brother. What was he doing here?

"Todd?" Her voice came out as a croak. "What's going on?"

Todd's lips curled into a sneer as he leaned forward, eyes glinting with malice. "What's going on is that I'm done playing games with you. You're going to give me the code Scott gave you. Now."

A chill ran down her spine as the pieces clicked into place. The break-in at her house, the attack on Harry and on her in the parking lot. Todd had been behind it all.

"I've told you, I don't know what you're talking about," she stammered, her mind racing to find the right thing to say or do that wouldn't trigger Todd's temper any more than it already was. "Scott didn't—"

"Don't lie to me!" Todd roared, slamming his fist on the table. His sudden burst of anger sent her burrowing back in the sofa cushions, attempting to put as much distance between herself and the men she faced as possible.

"I'm not lying!" she insisted, fighting to keep her voice steady despite the fear coursing through her veins. "I swear, Todd. Scott never gave me any code."

Todd's eyes narrowed dangerously. "You expect me to believe that? I know you met with my brother the day he died."

"Yes, I saw him," she admitted cautiously. "But he only asked if I had any contacts on the West Coast. He said he was thinking about moving there."

As Todd glared at her, Lisa's mind frantically searched for a way out of this nightmare. But trapped in this isolated cabin with Todd and his menacing associate, she realized with growing dread that her options were terrifyingly limited. She didn't even know where she was.

Todd's piercing gaze bore into her for several long moments before he let out a string of curses. Finally, he said, "I just might believe you," he muttered, his tone a mix of frustration and resignation.

For a moment, she felt a flicker of hope. Maybe he'd realize this was all a mistake and let her go. But as quickly as it had appeared, that hope was extinguished. Todd's expression changed again, his features twisting into something even darker than before.

"But you know what?" He leaned forward, his voice dropping to a menacing growl. "Even if Scott didn't give you the code, you're still going to help me. You're a computer whiz just like my little bro was. You can figure out a way to make the program work without it."

Fear clawed its way back up her throat. "I... I don't even know what program you're referring to," she said. "And even if I did, work like that could take weeks or months. It's not something I can just do on the spot."

Todd's lips curled into a cruel smile. "You better hope you're wrong."

ISAIAH'S FISTS CLENCHED and unclenched as he stared at the grainy security footage, his eyes burning from the strain. The conference room buzzed with frantic energy.

"Anything yet?" he called out to Connie, his voice tight with the same underlying tension that filled the conference room.

Connie shook her head. "Nothing so far on properties owned by Todd, Scott or Emily. I even checked for properties in Zoe Donlea's name. Nothing. I'm expanding the search to relatives, known associates..."

Lisa's face flashed in his mind—her warm smile, the determined set of her jaw. He couldn't lose her. Not now, not like this. Isaiah forced himself to take a deep breath.

Garfino's voice cut through the din. "Yes, I need every available unit searching that area. Leave no stone unturned." He slammed the phone down, running a hand through his thinning hair. "Fairfax PD is all over Todd's place. Nothing there yet either."

Isaiah's stomach churned. Where the hell could Todd have taken her? He rewound the security footage again, looking desperately for any detail they might have missed.

"Wexler, Greer," Garfino barked. "Anything?"

Garfino had assigned the two junior detectives to go through everything on Scott's death with fresh eyes and a fine-tooth comb, hoping they might catch something that had been overlooked.

Wexler looked down at the table in front of him, blanching. Greer met Garfino's gaze, but his expression said it all. "Nothing yet, sir, but we are still looking."

Isaiah turned back to the video, muttering under his breath, "Come on, Lisa. Give me something to work with here."

They would find her. They had to. He'd be no use to anyone, much less Lisa, if he let himself think about the alternative.

He tried again to focus on the grainy security footage they'd gotten from the cameras outside an office building across the street from where Lisa had been kidnapped. But this time, his thoughts drifted to Emily Donlea's tearstained face during the interview he'd conducted with her an hour earlier. Emily hadn't known where Todd might take Lisa, but she'd justified her actions by claiming that Todd would have hurt Zoe if she hadn't stayed silent. Even with Zoe's life on the line, Emily had to have known the possible consequences for Lisa. She could have reached out to Isaiah, but she'd chosen her daughter's life over Lisa's. Isaiah couldn't excuse that.

He turned to the video playing on the laptop screen again. Lisa needed him focused on finding whatever small detail would lead them to where she was being held. There would be time enough to make sure everyone involved in Scott's death and her kidnapping were held accountable.

He watched the black SUV slam into the police cruiser and send it spinning. His heart clenched as he saw Lisa's limp form being pulled from the back seat of the wreckage and tossed unceremoniously into the back of the SUV.

"Come on, give me something," Isaiah growled low,

leaning in closer to the screen. But no matter how many times he replayed the footage, the license plate remained a blurry, indecipherable smudge.

His frustration threatening to boil over, he called out to the room, "Any word on additional video from the surrounding area?"

Detective Wexler looked up from his stack of files. "Still working on it, sir. We've got requests out to every business and traffic camera within a five-mile radius."

"Push harder. We need those tapes yesterday." Isaiah turned back to the endless loop of grainy footage on his laptop screen. Where would Todd take her? What was his endgame? The uncertainty and fear for Lisa's safety was eating him alive.

Isaiah rewound the security tape once more, his eyes burning from the constant strain. "There has to be something here," he muttered again.

"We'll find her," Connie said softly, appearing at his side.

He met his partner's eyes, seeing his own concern and determination mirrored there. He wanted to believe Connie, but fear gnawed at his resolve. He cleared his throat, recalling that Lisa wasn't the only victim of the ambush. "How is the officer…the one who was with Lisa?" He struggled to recall the name, his mind foggy with worry and exhaustion.

"Officer Jovie," Connie supplied. "He's in the hospital. Got a concussion and a couple of broken ribs, but he'll recover."

"Good. That's good," Isaiah responded absently, his attention already drifting back to the grainy footage.

As he leaned in, squinting at the screen, his phone suddenly buzzed in his pocket. His heart leaped, a fleeting hope that it might somehow be Lisa. He pulled his cell from his pocket, but saw Harry's name on the caller ID.

"Harry, it's not a good time," he answered, unable to keep the edge from his voice.

"The officer you sent to guard my room told me that Lisa has been kidnapped," Harry said as if Isaiah hadn't spoken.

Isaiah ran a hand through his hair, frustration mounting. "I know you want to help, but there's nothing you can do right now."

"Maybe there is," Harry countered, irritation marking his tone now as well.

A spark of hope ignited in Isaiah's chest. "What do you mean?"

"You know those key chains Lisa carries? One of them is a key fob locator."

"A key fob locator? What is that?"

"It's used to help locate your car if it's stolen," Harry said quickly. "Thieves know how to disable GPS now, so you have to outthink them. They can't disable the key fob if they want to use the car, and as long as the fob locator is discreet, a lot of them don't realize what it is."

Isaiah's heart pounded. "Connie!" he called out. "Lisa has a key fob locator on her key chain. We might be able to track her location!"

Connie's fingers were already flying across the keyboard. "What company?" she asked, opening a new browser tab.

Isaiah relayed the question to Harry, who responded quickly, "Track Smart. We pay for the tracking through the firm, so I have the account password."

Harry rattled off the password, and Isaiah called it out to Connie. The tension in the room was palpable as they all waited for the website to load, each second feeling like an eternity.

He stared at Connie's laptop screen, willing the computer to work faster. Time was of the essence, but he couldn't shake the nagging fear in his gut. What if he was too late? What if Todd had already...? No. He pushed the thought away, focusing on the task at hand.

The webpage finally loaded, and Connie's triumphant shout cut through the tense silence. "We got it!"

A bright red dot pulsed steadily on the map that filled the screen. Isaiah's heart leaped into his throat. This was it. This had to be where Todd was holding Lisa.

"Where is that?" he demanded.

Detective Wexler, ever efficient, was already pulling up another map on his computer. He input the coordinates from Connie's map. "It looks like a lot of farmland," he reported, zooming in on the area.

"There are always structures that are unpermitted or forgotten on farmland," Isaiah said. "Zoom in and switch to satellite view."

Wexler did as Isaiah demanded. It only took a second.

"There." Isaiah pointed at a screen. "That looks like it could be a hunting cabin or even a small home." He was already moving toward the conference room door. "We need to get out there."

"I'm with you," Connie called.

Hold on, Lisa. We're coming for you. Just hold on.

Chapter Twenty

The car's tires screeched as Connie took a sharp turn, her knuckles white on the steering wheel. Isaiah braced himself with a hand against the dashboard. The dense forest flew by in a blur of green and brown.

"SWAT's ten minutes behind us," Connie said, her voice taut. "We should wait for backup."

Isaiah shook his head, checking the magazine of his gun with practiced efficiency. The cold metal felt reassuring in his hands. "You can wait when we get there. I'm going in."

Connie shot him a glance that he ignored. "That's not a smart plan, Isaiah. It's too dangerous."

He didn't respond. He already knew rushing in wasn't protocol, but every second they delayed could mean the difference between life and death for Lisa. He wouldn't be able to live with himself if waiting for SWAT cost Lisa her life.

"You're being reckless," Connie argued, frustration evident in her tone. "We need to approach this the right way."

It was his turn to shoot a withering look at Connie. "This ends now."

As the car sped onward, Isaiah visualized the layout of the land, the position of the cabin at the end of the driveway just in front of a large lake, and planned his approach.

The weight of his Kevlar vest pressed against his chest, a grim reminder of Brand's loss and of the danger ahead. But he pushed the fear aside as he'd done many times before, focusing on the task at hand. Lisa needed him, and he wouldn't let her down.

The car rounded a bend, and suddenly the cabin came into view. Isaiah's heart rate spiked as he took in the scene—a sprawling wooden structure perched on the waterfront, surrounded by a high metal gate. Two armed men stood guard, their weapons glinting in the afternoon sun.

Connie swore, slamming on the brakes. The car skidded to a halt.

Gunfire erupted. Bullets pinged off the hood of the car, shattering the windshield. Isaiah instinctively ducked, glass shards raining down on him.

"Why is it never easy?" Connie growled, her face a mask of determination as she threw the car into Reverse.

They burst out of the vehicle in unison, crouching behind the open doors as bullets whizzed overhead.

Isaiah steadied his breathing, years of training kicking in. He peered around the door, squeezing off two precise shots.

One of the gunmen cried out, clutching his shoulder as he fell.

"Nice shot," Connie called out, returning fire and taking out the second man.

"Clear!" Isaiah shouted to Connie. "Let's move!"

They scrambled back into the car, adrenaline coursing through their veins. Connie gunned the engine, the tires spinning in the gravel as they surged forward.

"Hang on," she warned, a fierce glint in her eye.

The car smashed through the gate with a deafening crash of metal on metal. Isaiah gritted his teeth as they bounced violently, the suspension groaning in protest. But they were through, racing up the driveway toward the cabin.

The car jerked to a stop, kicking up a cloud of dust. Isaiah's eyes narrowed as he spotted three more armed men emerging from the building, their weapons raised.

"Connie, we've got company!" Isaiah shouted, his heart pounding. He flung open his door, diving out and rolling behind the vehicle for cover.

The sharp crack of gunfire filled the air.

Connie was right behind him, her pistol already drawn. "What's the plan?" she yelled over the cacophony.

Isaiah's mind raced through the possible tactical approaches. Lisa could be anywhere in that cabin. "Secure the back!" he called out to Connie. "I'll cover you!"

He popped up from behind the car, squeezing off several rapid shots. The gunmen ducked, giving Connie the opening she needed.

"On it!" she shouted, darting away in a crouch.

Isaiah provided suppressing fire, his hands steady despite the chaos. He watched Connie's progress out of the corner of his eye, willing her to make it safely.

A glint of metal caught his attention. Isaiah's blood ran cold as he spotted a fourth gunman on the roof, taking aim at Connie's exposed back.

"Connie, roof!" he bellowed, swinging his weapon upward.

Time seemed to slow. Isaiah exhaled, squeezing the trigger. The rooftop shooter jerked backward, but not before getting off a shot.

A pained cry pierced the air, and his stomach plummeted. He whipped around to see Connie on the ground, clutching her leg.

"Connie!" he shouted, his voice raw with fear. His heart

went into his throat. Images of Brand, lying cold on a morgue slab, slammed into him. *No, please no. Not again.* He sprinted toward Connie.

Skidding to a stop beside her, his hands hovered uncertainly. "How bad is it?"

Connie gritted her teeth, her face pale but determined. "Just a flesh wound," she grunted. "I'll live."

Relief washed over him. He glanced at the cabin, torn between his partner and Lisa.

As if reading his mind, Connie grabbed his arm. "Go," she insisted. "Get Lisa. I'll be fine."

Isaiah hesitated, at war with himself. "Are you sure?"

"Damn it, Isaiah," Connie hissed. "You're the one who said every second counted. Now go!"

Isaiah rose and sprinted toward the cabin. With the gunfire over, silence settled over the outside of the cabin. The bodies of the two men who'd been shooting at them were sprawled on the ground.

Kneeling beside the nearest man, he pressed two fingers to the man's neck. Nothing. He was dead.

He moved to the second man who couldn't have been more than twenty. A waste, he thought grimly. He was happy to find a faint flutter beneath his fingertips when he pressed them to the man's neck. Alive, but for how long? Hopefully, the young man could hold on until EMTs arrived.

He pulled out his cell phone, fingers flying over the keypad as he dialed for backup. "This is Detective Reeves," he whispered urgently. "I've got an officer injured and multiple suspects down." He gave the cabin's address and was assured that help was less than five minutes out.

Rising, he headed for the front door of the cabin. How many more inside? And where was Lisa? These men had been willing to shoot cops. That made them more than dangerous. It made them reckless. He had to be careful. He didn't want to accidentally put Lisa in the line of fire.

Heart pounding, he approached the cabin's entrance. The weathered door hung slightly ajar. He took a steadying breath, gun raised, and nudged it open with his foot.

The interior was dimly lit, a stark contrast to the bright sunlight outside. As his eyes adjusted, he scanned the sparse living room. A rickety table dominated the space, littered with half-eaten food and empty beer bottles. The air was heavy with the stench of stale alcohol and sweat.

A familiar crack split the air. Bullet. He dove behind a ratty sofa as splinters exploded from the doorframe where he'd been standing.

The gunman kept firing, his shots punching through the thin walls of the cabin. Isaiah pressed flat against the floor, breathing in the musty scent of the old sofa. He scanned the area as best he could without making himself a target, trying to get a feel for where the shooter was standing.

"Come out, cop!" the shooter yelled, his voice trembling with a mix of fear and adrenaline. "You're not getting out of here alive!"

Isaiah's jaw clenched. He'd heard this kind of posturing before, from cornered men who knew they were out of options. He waited, muscles coiled.

He heard a click and immediately knew what it was. The shooter had run out of bullets.

In one fluid motion, Isaiah rose from behind the sofa, his gun already aimed. He saw the shooter's eyes widen, and he fumbled with the gun.

Isaiah grabbed the man before he could get the weapon to work again and wasn't all that surprised when the man didn't put up a fight. He pulled a zip tie cuff from a pocket in his vest and slid them on the man's wrists. Then he pushed the man to the floor in a corner of the room. "Sit and don't move, or I will shoot you."

The man glared back at him, but he sat.

Isaiah made his way through the cabin, checking rooms as he went. The place reeked of cigarettes and fear. As he neared the back of the house, the sounds of a fight caught his ear.

"Lisa," he whispered, hope and dread mingling in his chest.

He moved forward quickly now, his fear for her overriding his training. He kicked the door open, charging through the door and into the room.

LISA STARED AT the laptop screen, its glow casting eerie shadows across the dimly lit room. Behind her, Todd's heavy footsteps paced relentlessly, each thud sending a jolt of fear up her spine. Her eyes darted to the small device perched on the windowsill, its blinking lights a stark reminder that Todd wasn't nearly as much of a technological dummy as he'd professed. A satellite internet device that allowed him to access the web even in the remotest of areas.

"Figure it out," Todd snarled, waving the gun dangerously close to her head. "I need that program to work, and I need it to work now."

Lisa's fingers hovered over the keyboard. There was no way to make the program work without the code. She took a deep breath, trying to steady her nerves.

"Todd, please," she pleaded, turning to face him. "What you're asking...it's nearly impossible. Without that code, it could take weeks to get this program to work."

Todd's eyes narrowed, his grip tightening on the gun. "You're lying. I know it."

"I swear, I'm not lying. Scott was a great programmer. He wouldn't have made it easy to get around his security. I can't just pull this code out of thin air."

Todd slammed his fist on the desk, making Lisa flinch. "You're supposed to be some hotshot computer whiz. Figure. It. Out."

Her fingers trembled as she typed, knowing full well that her efforts were futile. She just needed to keep Todd distracted, keep him believing she was trying. Hopefully it would buy her enough time for Isaiah and help to arrive before it was too late for her. How long would it take for Isaiah to even figure out where she was?

As she worked, her eyes drifted to her purse sitting open on the desk beside her. Todd had taken her phone, but he'd overlooked the rest of her belongings. Her gaze settled on her keys, glinting in the dim cabin light.

The shark key chain caught her attention, and a lump formed in her throat. Memories of her daughter's bright smile flooded Lisa's mind. What if she never saw that smile again? Never received another thoughtful trinket from her little girl.

"Focus!" Todd barked, noticing her distraction.

She blinked back tears, her fingers resuming their fruitless dance across the keys. "I'm trying, Todd. I'm doing my best."

But as she typed, her thoughts remained on Layla, on the possibility that she might never make it home. The weight of her situation crashed down upon her, and it took every ounce of willpower not to break down right there in front of her captor.

Her fingers suddenly stilled on the keyboard, her breath catching in her throat. A chilling thought struck her, freezing her in place. Her eyes locked on the little shark dangling from her keys. The key chain.

Todd was so sure Scott gave her the code. What if he had, but she just didn't know it? She'd assumed it was Layla who'd given her the little shark. Something to make her smile when she saw it and miss her baby just a little less over the summer. But what if she was wrong?

What if it was Scott?

She strained to remember when she'd first noticed the shark. She drew her mind back to several days ago, picturing her key ring, trying to recall if it had been there before her meeting with Scott. But no matter how hard she tried, she couldn't place it before her coffee date with Scott.

Could he have really managed to slip her the key to this whole mess right under her nose?

Again, she brought up the coffee date she'd had with Scott in her mind. Had she left her keys at the table? Yes! She had. She'd left them on the table with Scott when she went to pick up her coffee from the barista. He could have slipped the key chain on then.

She reached down in her purse and touched the shark key chain. Yes. It was the kind that just snapped on to the metal circle. It wouldn't have taken Scott more than a second to affix it.

But why would Scott have given the key chain to her? Because he didn't think Todd would ever think she had the decryption code. But he must have figured it out somehow. Maybe he'd been following his brother.

Her fingers trembled as she touched the shark key chain, her mind whirling with questions and possibilities. Could this silly little key chain really be the key to everything?

"What is it? Did you figure out how to make it work?" Todd snapped.

She jerked, her heart racing as she was abruptly pulled back to the terrifying reality of her situation. For a moment, she had forgotten where she was, lost in her thoughts about Scott and the key chain.

Now, Todd's menacing presence loomed over her, his impatience palpable in the stuffy room.

Before she could formulate a response, Todd's eyes narrowed, fixating on her hand still hovering near her purse. In a flash, he lunged forward, roughly grabbing the shark key chain from her bag.

"What is this?" he demanded, his voice low and dangerous.

She searched for a plausible explanation. She knew she had to tread carefully. One wrong word could set Todd off, and the gun in his hand was a constant reminder of the peril she faced.

"It's…it's nothing," she stammered, trying to keep her voice steady. "Just a gift from my daughter."

As soon as the words left her mouth, she knew she had made a mistake.

Todd's face hardened, his eyes glinting with suspicion. He clearly didn't believe her. His fingers traced the contours of the shark key chain, his brow furrowed in concentration.

She held her breath, her heart pounding so loudly she was sure Todd could hear it.

He pulled the shark's head off, revealing the flash drive underneath. His eyes widened, a mixture of triumph and fury etched across his face. He grabbed a fistful of her hair and yanked her head back violently. "What's on this?"

A scream of pain and terror tore from her throat, echoing off the cabin walls.

She could feel Todd's hot breath on her face as he snarled, "And don't lie to me!"

Tears stung her eyes, "I don't know! I swear. I'm not lying."

Her scalp burned from Todd's grip, but she fought the tears. She wouldn't give him the satisfaction of seeing her cry.

Todd's grip on her hair loosened, and she gasped with relief. He pushed the flash drive into her trembling hands. "Put it in the computer. Now."

She inserted the drive into the laptop. A window popped up on the screen. Lisa's heart sank as she recognized the stream of numbers, letters, and symbols as a decryption code.

Todd's maniacal grin widened, his eyes gleaming with triumph. "Didn't have the code, huh?" he sneered.

"I didn't know I had it," she gritted out, anger and fear warring within her.

His laugh was cold. "Well, now you know. Get up," he ordered, gesturing with the gun. "Sit in that chair over there." He gestured toward a chair beside the desk.

She obeyed. Her scalp still throbbed where Todd had yanked her hair, a reminder of the danger she was in. She lowered herself into the chair and watched Todd slide into the seat she had vacated, positioning himself in front of the computer.

He put the gun on the desktop. Without looking at Lisa, he growled, "Don't move a muscle. One twitch, and I'll shoot you where you sit."

Her breath caught in her throat. She forced herself to remain perfectly still, her eyes darting between Todd's face and the weapon.

"You know, Scott was always the computer whiz in the

family. But what most people don't realize is that I'm the one who got him started."

Despite her fear, curiosity stirred within her.

"Of course, my little brother surpassed my skills pretty quickly." He paused his typing, staring at the screen with a faraway look. "I wanted to design and create video games, you know. I once thought I'd be bigger than John Carmack." He let out a harsh, mirthless laugh that made Lisa flinch. "But I guess we all have our childhood dreams dashed at some point, don't we?" His eyes snapped to Lisa's face, his gaze intense and menacing. "Well, most of us."

She swallowed hard, her throat dry. The gun on the desk seemed to taunt her. So close yet impossibly out of reach. "What does that program do?" she asked, curiosity getting the better of her.

Todd's fingers stilled on the keyboard. A slow, unsettling smile spread across his face as he turned to face her.

"When Scott joined the bank, I saw an opportunity," he said, his eyes gleaming with a mix of greed and bitterness. "My dear little brother was so frustrated. He thought he should have achieved more in his career, would have achieved more if people not as smart as him hadn't worked to keep him down. I simply capitalized on that."

Her stomach churned. She'd known Scott was a little arrogant, but she never imagined it could lead to this.

Todd continued, his voice taking on a conspiratorial tone. "I convinced Scott to start small. Just a little credit card fraud here and there. Nothing that would raise too many alarms." He leaned back in his chair, looking smugly satisfied. "It was a trial run, really. I needed to see if Scott would actually do it. And when he did..." Todd's grin widened, sending a chill down her spine. "Well, that's when I knew I could up the ante."

Her muscles tensed. The cabin door seemed miles away, and Todd's gun glinted menacingly on the desk.

His fingers danced across the keyboard. "I asked Scott to design a program that would give me access to his bank's ATM system. The ATM network has to communicate with machines all across the country, making it uniquely vulnerable." He paused, a hint of pride creeping into his voice. "I thought it would take more convincing to get Scott on board. But you know what? I think part of him couldn't resist the challenge. He agreed faster than I expected, almost like he wanted to prove he could do it."

Lisa's mind whirled. She'd known Scott was brilliant, but this…this was beyond anything she'd imagined. A tiny part of her was impressed by the technical feat, even as she recoiled at its purpose.

But his conscience must have gotten to him in the end. It was a shame Todd didn't seem to have one of his own. The irony of brothers so different struck her, but she kept her thoughts to herself, afraid to provoke Todd's temper.

The excited gleam in his eyes hardened into something cold and mean. His jaw clenched as he spat out, "But then after the program was done, Scott said he couldn't do it. Said it would be 'wrong' to use it," he sneered, mimicking his brother's voice.

Before she could stop herself, the words tumbled out, laced with horror and disbelief. "So, you killed your own brother?"

Todd's fingers froze above the keyboard. For a moment, the only sound in the cabin was the quiet hum of the laptop. She watched as a series of emotions flickered across Todd's face—anger, pain, and something that looked unmistakably like grief.

She held her breath, hoping that she'd managed to reach some part of Todd that was still human.

His fingers twitched, then resumed their frantic typing. His eyes remained fixed on the screen, but his voice came out strained, almost defensive.

"It was an accident," he muttered. "I didn't mean to… Scott just wouldn't give up the damn program. I only wanted to scare him into talking."

Lisa's stomach churned as Todd continued, his words spilling out in a rush. "My temper got away from me. Hitting him wasn't working. He just kept refusing." Todd's face contorted, a mix of anger and anguish. "I only meant to shoot him in the kneecap. Just to show him I was serious."

Isaiah had told her that Scott had been shot in the chest. Either Todd was a terrible shot, or he was lying to her, or to himself more than likely. Despite his attempts at justification, she could see the weight of his actions pressing down on him, threatening to shatter the facade of control he so desperately clung to.

After several more minutes, Todd leaned back, a triumphant grin spreading across his face. "I'm about to be a very rich man," he declared. With a dramatic flourish, he pressed a button on the keyboard.

In that same instant, the relative quiet of the cabin was shattered. The crack of gunfire erupted from outside, followed by shouts and the sound of splintering wood.

Lisa screamed even as her heart leaped. Isaiah.

Todd rose, all his attention focused on the closed bedroom door. "What the hell?" he snarled, grabbing for the gun.

Isaiah wasn't going to make it in time. It was now or never. She launched herself at him.

Chapter Twenty-One

Lisa's knuckles turned white as she gripped the gun, her heart pounding in her ears. Todd's fingers dug into her wrist, his face contorted with rage as they grappled for control of the weapon.

"Let go!" Todd yelled, pulling on her arm.

She gritted her teeth, planting her feet. She wouldn't let go. If she did, he'd kill her, there was no doubt in her mind about that. She had to hold on, had to fight, even as her muscles screamed in protest.

But Todd was stronger. She felt her grip slipping. With a savage yank, he tore the gun from her hands. She stumbled backward, her heart thumping in terror as she stared down the barrel. *This is it. I'm going to die.*

Todd's lips curled into a vicious smile.

The door to the room burst open with a crash.

Todd reached out and grabbed her arm, yanking her toward him before spinning her and locking his arm around her throat. Cold metal pressed against her temple. She froze, her pulse racing.

"Let her go!" Isaiah's voice boomed as he stepped into the room, gun raised.

Her eyes locked onto Isaiah, a mixture of relief and terror coursing through her. His jaw was clenched, eyes blazing as he aimed at Todd.

"Back off!" Todd growled, his arm tightening around her neck.

She struggled to breathe, her hands instinctively pulling at Todd's forearm even as fear that any sudden movement might cause his finger to twitch on the trigger.

The stench of Todd's body odor filled her nostrils, making her stomach churn. She could feel his rapid heartbeat against her back, his labored breathing hot on her neck. He was on the edge and more than willing to take her over when he went.

"I said let her go," Isaiah repeated, his voice low and dangerous. "It's over, Todd."

The gun pressed harder at her temple, and Lisa bit back a whimper. She closed her eyes briefly, trying to center herself. *Stay calm. Don't panic.*

Todd shouted, "Back off! Get out or I'll kill her!"

Isaiah's eyes flickered to her face, then back to Todd. His voice was steady, controlled. "You know that's not going to happen, Todd. Let's talk this through."

"It's going to happen, or she's dead!" Todd screamed, spittle flying from his mouth.

Her heart hammered in her chest. This was it. She was going to die here, in this room, at the hands of a madman. A wave of regret washed over her. *I never got to figure out how I really feel about Isaiah. Now I'll never know.*

Isaiah took a small step forward, his free hand raised in a placating gesture. "Todd, listen to me. You're upset, I get it. But this isn't the way. Let Lisa go, and we can work this out."

Todd's breathing grew more erratic, and his grip on Lisa tightened painfully. "Work what out? There's nothing to work out! You're going to back off, and I'm going to walk out of here."

She could feel Todd unraveling, his body trembling against hers. Suddenly, he swung his arm out, aiming the gun at Isaiah.

No! Moving on instinct more than rational thought, she dropped her head and sank her teeth into the fleshy part of Todd's hand holding her. Todd's scream pierced the air, but he released her, shoving her away with surprising force.

She stumbled forward, her heart racing as she heard the deafening crack of a gunshot. A bullet splintered the wood paneling behind her.

"Lisa, get down!" Isaiah shouted, diving behind the heavy oak desk.

She scrambled after him, her palms scraping the rough carpet. Her breath came in ragged gasps as she pressed her back against the solid wood.

Isaiah's eyes locked onto hers, concern etched on his face. "Are you okay?"

Lisa nodded, struggling to find her voice. "Yes," she managed, her throat dry.

The room fell eerily silent for a moment, broken only by Todd's labored breathing from across the room. Then, a barrage of gunshots erupted, wood splinters raining down as bullets tore into the desk. She flinched with each thunderous report, her ears ringing.

Isaiah's arms wrapped around her, pulling her close. He curled his body protectively over her, the rough fabric of his bulletproof vest rubbing against her blouse as more shots rang out. She buried her face in his chest, inhaling his familiar scent, a mix of sandalwood and gunpowder.

The gunfire abruptly ceased, replaced by the sound of retreating footsteps and a slamming door.

The silence that followed was deafening. Isaiah's arms loosened their grip, and he slowly pulled away from her. His eyes, intense and searching, scanned her face and body for any sign of injury.

Her heart still pounded, but she managed to steady her voice. "I'm okay," she said, answering his unspoken question. "Go after him."

He hesitated, his brow furrowed with concern. "Stay here," he instructed, his tone leaving no room for argument.

Not that she had any plans to argue. But she couldn't help fearing for him. She nodded, but her hand reached out, grasping Isaiah's arm. She could feel the tension in his muscles. "Be careful," she said, her voice thick with emotion she hadn't yet put to words.

His expression softened for a moment. He leaned in and pressed a quick, fierce kiss to her lips. "I'll be back," he murmured against her mouth.

He rose to his feet and her heart leaped into her throat as she watched him move toward the door, his gun held at the ready. He quickly but cautiously stepped out into the hall.

She felt a surge of fear unlike anything she'd experienced before. "Please, please come back to me."

A sudden beep pierced the silence. Her eyes darted to the desk above her, where the laptop sat precariously close to the edge. She reached up and carefully pulled it down to her lap.

Lines of code scrolled by on the screen. Todd's program was still running, seeking out bank accounts of innocent people it could plunder.

She couldn't help Isaiah, but she might be able to help these people.

She began to type furiously, her eyes scanning the code

for weaknesses, the familiar rhythm of problem-solving helping to calm her frayed nerves.

"Come on, Lisa," she muttered to herself. "You've cracked tougher systems than this." Her fingers flew over the keyboard. "You're not getting away with this, Todd," she whispered fiercely. "Not if I have anything to say about it."

ISAIAH'S HEART POUNDED as he stepped out of the room and into the hallway. Time seemed to slow as Todd whirled, the gun barrel aligning with Isaiah's chest.

"Freeze!" Isaiah shouted, but his command was drowned out by the deafening crack of gunfire.

A searing pain grazed his arm. He flinched, expecting another shot, but heard only an empty click.

Todd's face contorted with rage. He hurled the useless weapon at Isaiah.

Isaiah ducked. As he straightened, Todd was already charging, a blur of desperation and fury.

Isaiah lifted the hand holding the gun. "Todd, freeze—" His words were cut short by a vicious right hook to his jaw. His gun went flying, skittering away down the hall he had just come from. He tasted blood from a split lip but had time to process little else. Todd rained down blows.

Isaiah blocked what he could, but Todd was desperate and furious which seemed to have given him more strength than he might normally have.

"You ruined everything!" Todd roared.

Isaiah grunted, absorbing a punch to his ribs. He needed to end this before Todd immobilized him and got a hold of a gun. He surged forward, tackling Todd around the waist.

They crashed into the kitchen counter, a tangle of limbs and rage.

"It's over, Todd," Isaiah gasped, struggling to pin Todd's arms at his sides. "Don't make this worse for yourself than it already is."

Todd's only response was a headbutt that had Isaiah seeing stars.

They grappled across the cabin's worn floorboards. The man that Isaiah had zip-tied seemed entranced by the fight but unwilling to throw himself into the fray. He scuttled backward on his butt when Todd and Isaiah headed his way.

Todd landed a solid punch to Isaiah's solar plexus that momentarily winded him despite his Kevlar vest. Todd grabbed one of the empty beer bottles from the kitchen table and lunged.

Pain exploded at Isaiah's temple as glass shattered. His vision swam, darkness threatening to engulf him. He swayed, struggling to stay upright.

Todd seized the advantage, driving his fist into Isaiah's stomach. Air rushed from his lungs. He doubled over, gasping. Through the haze of pain, Isaiah saw Todd's frantic search and realized the man was looking for his gun. He couldn't let him get to it.

Summoning every ounce of strength, Isaiah shook off the fog clouding his mind and launched himself at Todd, tackling him to the ground. The impact sent shockwaves through Isaiah's battered body, but adrenaline dulled the pain.

Todd bucked wildly, his fist connecting with Isaiah's jaw. "Get off me, you bastard!"

He wrenched Todd's arms behind his back and reached for another pair of the zip tie cuffs.

"It's over, Todd," Isaiah said, tightening the cuffs.

As the cabin door burst open. Connie limped in, her gun drawn, face etched with pain and determination.

"Took you long enough," Isaiah quipped, securing the cuffs around Todd's wrists.

Connie leaned heavily against the wall, her breath coming in short gasps. "Yeah, well, you try walking with a gunshot to the leg." Her weapon was trained on Todd. "Looks like you didn't need my help anyway. Backup is a minute out."

As if on cue, the wail of approaching sirens pierced the air. Isaiah felt a wave of relief wash over him. It was finally over.

He hauled Todd to his feet, noting the man's bruised and bloodied face with more than a little satisfaction. "Watch him," he instructed Connie, pushing Todd toward her. "I need to check on Lisa."

Isaiah sprinted back to the bedroom, his heart pounding. The sight of Lisa, still sitting on the floor but now hunched over the laptop, her fingers flying across the keyboard, made his breath catch. She was safe, thank God.

"Lisa," he gasped, dropping to his knees beside her. "What are you doing?"

Her eyes never left the screen, her face a mask of concentration. "Scott's program," she said, voice tight. "Todd told me it's designed to skim money from ATM transactions. Thousands of people could be affected."

"Can you stop it?"

"I'm trying," she muttered, brow furrowed. "But it's complex. Scott was a damn good programmer. Too bad he didn't use his skills for good."

"Todd's in custody," Isaiah said, watching her work with some awe. He didn't know squat about computers. Scott may have been a good programmer, but Lisa looked like she'd been born behind a keyboard. And he found it sexy as hell.

"Great," she replied absently, still focused intently on the screen.

Isaiah held his breath, feeling utterly helpless. With all his training, all he could do now was watch and wait.

"I almost got it," she whispered, more to herself than to him. Her fingers flew even faster, a blur of motion. The lines on the computer were reflected in the lenses of her glasses.

A sharp beep emanated from the laptop. Her hands stilled, and she sat back, exhaling deeply.

"I did it," she said, turning to him with a mix of exhaustion and triumph. "I shut it down." Her shoulders sagged, and tension visibly drained from her body as a satisfied grin blossomed across her face. It lit up her entire face. Her eyes sparkled as they met his. "It's over," she breathed.

He felt a surge of emotion—pride, relief, and an overwhelming sense of love. He reached out and pulled Lisa into a tight embrace.

She melted against him, her smaller frame fitting perfectly in his arms. He could feel her heartbeat, still racing from the adrenaline, begin to slow.

"Yes, baby, it is," he murmured into her hair. "It's over."

Isaiah closed his eyes, savoring the moment. He pressed a tender kiss to the top of her head, breathing in her familiar scent, hoping that she'd give him the chance to hold her like this always.

Chapter Twenty-Two

The rich aroma of simmering gumbo filled Lisa's kitchen, a tantalizing blend of spices and seafood that made her mouth water. But as delicious as it smelled, Lisa found her eyes drawn to an even more appetizing sight.

Isaiah stood at the stove, his muscular back stretching the fabric of his T-shirt as he stirred the bubbling pot. The apron tied snugly around his trim waist only accentuated his athletic build. The way his biceps flexed as he lifted the heavy wooden spoon. The little furrow of concentration between his brows. The hint of a smile playing at the corners of his full lips.

How did he make stirring a pot so sexy? Heat rose to her cheeks even as she tried to focus on her phone conversation with Layla.

"Mom? Are you still there?" Layla's voice snapped Lisa's attention back to the call.

"Yes, sweetie," she lied, guilt washing over her. "I'm sorry, what were you saying?"

Layla giggled. "That I need to go. Dad's waiting. He's taking me out for dinner. Just the two of us."

"Oh, that sounds like fun. Be safe. I can't wait until you're home."

"Me either. Love you, Mom."

"I love you too." She ended the call and set down her phone. As happy as she was, it was tinged with a little sadness over not having her daughter with her.

She rose from her seat, padding silently across the cool tile floor as she approached Isaiah from behind. Wrapping her arms around his waist and pressing her cheek against the solid warmth of his back, she inhaled deeply. The mingled scents of his cologne and the simmering gumbo sent her stomach into a flip-flop that she wasn't sure was due to the food or the man.

She shouldn't feel this giddy over a man, like some swooning teenager. But there was something about Isaiah that made her feel young and alive in a way she hadn't felt in quite a long time. But she deserved it, she and Isaiah both did, after all that they'd been through.

Todd had refused to speak to the authorities, but his compatriots couldn't seem to shut up, according to Isaiah. They were giving up all the details of Todd's plan to bilk people of their hard-earned money. And, of course, they were blaming the entire thing on Todd and Scott.

It didn't matter whether Todd or his friends talked though. The cops had them cold on her kidnapping. They'd traced the call that had supposedly come from Blackwell Industries to a burner phone they'd found in the cabin. Todd must have seen the client file for Blackwell when he and his goons broke into her offices. They'd used the information to lure her out of her house. Between her kidnapping and testimony, and all the evidence the authorities had found at the cabin, they were all going away for a long time.

Scott. It was still hard to believe Scott had gotten himself mixed up in this. Had gotten her mixed up in this, but Lisa couldn't bring herself to stay angry with him. In the end, Scott had tried to make things right. And he'd been killed by his own brother because of it.

She would never understand it. Or forgive Todd for hurting Harry, even though the old curmudgeon was on the mend and already howling to get back to work.

She had decided to take a little time off too. Her injuries had been minimal, but the psychological impact of everything that had happened had taken a toll.

She'd battled nightmares the first several nights after the kidnapping. Connie had given her the name of a good psychologist, and she had set up an appointment for later that week. But until then, she was planning on taking it easy and enjoying time with the smoking hot man currently cooking her dinner.

"Mmm," she hummed contentedly. "That smells absolutely divine."

Isaiah chuckled, the sound reverberating through his chest. "It's an old family recipe," he said, his voice a low rumble. "I could teach it to you sometime, if you'd like."

As soon as the words left his mouth, he stiffened. He set down the wooden spoon with a clatter and turned in her arms, his eyes wide. "I mean, uh…only if you want to learn it. I'm not trying to imply… I don't want you to think I'm rushing things or suggesting we're, you know, family or anything."

Her heart fluttered at his flustered expression. She'd never seen him so unsure of himself before. It was endearing, really, how careful he was being with her feelings.

She placed a gentle finger on Isaiah's lips, silencing his rambling. "I know exactly what you mean. And I don't want to rush anything either." She paused, gathering her courage. "But this thing between us… It feels real to me.

Like something special." Vulnerability crept in. "Does it feel that way to you too?"

His expression softened, his dark eyes warm with emotion. Lisa's breath caught as he lifted a hand, his fingers tenderly brushing a stray lock of hair from her face. The simple gesture sent a shiver down her spine.

"Lisa," he began, his voice deep and sincere, "I've known these feelings were real from the moment I first laid eyes on you." His thumb caressed her cheek, and she found herself leaning into his touch. "We'll take it slow, of course. For our sakes and for Layla's." A small smile played at the corners of his mouth. "But I know what I want to do with the rest of my life, and that's to spend it with you."

Her heart soared at his words, a warmth spreading through her chest.

Without another word, Isaiah dipped his head, capturing her lips in a tender kiss.

Her eyes fluttered closed as she melted into his embrace, savoring the feel of his strong arms around her. In that moment, wrapped in Isaiah's warmth, she knew she finally had everything she needed.

* * * * *

COLTON'S SECOND CHANCE

BETH CORNELISON

For Paul, since college and always.

Prologue

Thirty years ago
San Diego, California

Will Colton stood on his parents' front porch watching his five-year-old son restlessly shift his weight from foot to foot. "Why didn't you go potty before we left the house?"

Eli glanced up, his nose wrinkling as he answered, "I didn't have to go then." The boy frowned and stared at the door as if he could will it open. "What's takin' them so long to let us in?"

"I don't know. I told them last night we were coming over this morning. Someone should be up." In deference to his son's emergency, Will knocked again, calling, "Mom? Dad? It's us."

Still no answer. Before Eli had an accident, Will twisted the knob of his childhood home and pushed the door open. A niggle of alarm crawled through him that they'd not locked the front door. They may not take the threats of the guy bothering Caroline seriously, but that didn't mean they should be lax in general home security. Even a safe neighborhood held the potential for crime. "Hello? We're here."

Eli pushed past him and sprinted inside, making a bee-line for the bathroom.

Will chuckled and turned to close the door and hang up his jacket. "Caroline? Mom? Where is everybody?"

The house was still dark, and no scent of brewing coffee welcomed him, which was odd, considering his mother considered coffee first thing in the morning an unbendable rule of life.

"It's for your own good," she'd tease. "You don't want to deal with me uncaffeinated."

So maybe the family had overslept? Will ducked his head in the kitchen, confirming no one was there before heading down the hall toward his parents' bedroom. He was just about to call out again, when Eli barreled out of the hall bathroom, zipping his jeans and crashing into Will. "Whoa, partner! No running in the house. Remember?"

"Sorry," Eli muttered, though, due to his recently lost front tooth, it came out more like *thorry*.

"I don't think Grandma and Grandpa are out of bed yet. Why don't you go wait in the kitchen, and I'll check on them. Okay?" Will turned Eli with a firm hand on his shoulder and nudged him down the hall.

With a shrug, Eli complied. "When are we eating breakfast? I'm hungry."

"Soon. Be patient."

As he headed down the hall to the last bedroom on the right, Will glanced in his younger sister Caroline's bedroom. Her bed was made, and the room appeared to be vacant. Again, this seemed odd. At seventeen, his sister typically slept until noon on Saturdays. For her to be up and gone early on a weekend morning was unusual. Had Caroline been given a last-minute modeling job? When they made plans last night to have breakfast together this morning, his mother had not mentioned anything on their calendar or Caroline's.

His parents' bedroom door was closed, and for a moment, he wondered if they might be taking advantage of Caroline's absence for a bit of morning—

Will shuddered, and with a wry snort, he shook his head. *Nope.* His brain refused to go there. His parents didn't have sex. He, Ryan and Caroline were brought by the stork. End of story.

Just the same, he knocked and waited for a reply before opening the door. When he got no response, he cracked the door open a sliver and called in, "Yo! Everybody decent in there?"

No answer. A pulse of growing confusion and, okay, *concern* pulsed through him. What was going on? Where was everyone?

He pushed the door wider. "Mom? Dad?" He peeked around the door. "Eli says he's hungry, and—"

Ice slithered through him. Horror froze him for a beat as he stared in disbelief at his parents lying in bed... blood soaking their sheets. The number of stab wounds, the pale color of their skin and the fixed stare of their eyes left no doubt they were dead.

Will opened his mouth to wail in grief and shock, but the sound that rang in his ears was not his voice but Eli's.

His son was screaming in terror.

Jolted from his own trauma by the fear in Eli's cries, Will stumbled backward from the bedroom and raced down the hall toward the kitchen. "Eli!"

But his boy's screams were coming from the family room. Choking on the bile that rose in his throat, Will rushed to find Eli.

He found his son standing in the center of the room,

shaking and crying, his wide blue eyes fixed on two figures on the sofa. Dread pooled in Will's gut as he rounded the end of the couch and took in the macabre scene.

Caroline was sitting on the couch, wearing a skimpy black dress. She had scarlet smears and bruises around her neck and was propped by decorative pillows to lean against a man. The man, whom Will recognized from police reports as Jason Stevens, Caroline's stalker, had blood all over his clothes and face and hands.

The bloody butcher knife that had likely been used to kill Will's parents was on the coffee table. A red-smudged syringe lay discarded on the couch beside Stevens. He and Caroline were both clearly dead.

Eli's continued screams shook Will from this fresh wave of disbelief and deep sadness. He wrapped Eli in a firm hug, trying to shield his eyes from the gory and disturbing tableau. When he could muster his nerve, he peeked at his sister again. She'd obviously been posed, her right arm draped around Stevens's shoulders, her left hand resting on her chest over her heart. Blinking away tears, he squinted when he noticed something on his sister's hand, winking in the early morning sunlight that peeked through the curtains.

A diamond engagement ring.

But… Caroline wasn't engaged to anyone, so where—

The answer came to him, and nausea roiled in his gut. The sicko Stevens had put the ring there, part of his delusion that he and Caroline were an item.

A roar of fury that his parents hadn't taken Jason Stevens's threat more seriously erupted from him.

Eli stiffened, then sobbed harder. "Daddy, I'm scared! Did that man hurt Aunt Caroline?"

Will lifted his son into his arms and carried him out of

the house. "I'm afraid so, son. We… I have to call the police now, and…your mother to come get you."

"But I thought we were having breakfast with Grandma and Grandpa."

His son's innocence, his inability to grasp the magnitude of what had happened broke Will's heart. Because someday, Eli would realize what he'd seen. Someday the horror would reveal itself. And because he and Eli would never have breakfast with his parents or Caroline ever again.

Chapter One

Twenty-eight years later
Seattle, Washington

Noelle Harris jolted when her phone rang. She'd been so deeply involved with the data on her computer screen, so enthralled by the analysis of her client's intricate web of finances that she'd shut out everything else. Until the melodic jingle of her ring tone had sliced into her concentration.

With an irritated huff, she glanced at the screen. Her caller ID identified the origin of the call as Shelby, Alaska, and her pulse bumped for the second time.

She aimed her finger at the red disconnect button, fully intending to reject the call. She had no interest in talking to anyone in Alaska. As a Korean-American, she'd always felt like an outsider growing up in Anchorage. Especially within her own white adoptive family. When she'd left for college, she'd put Alaska and all of its bad memories and heartache behind her, thank you very much.

But some odd niggle, a spike of pure curiosity made her shift her finger to the answer icon instead. Her muscles tensed as if bracing for a blow as she reluctantly raised the phone to her ear. "Hello?"

The caller took a beat before saying, "Noelle?"

"Yes." A tingle of premonition, a familiarity she couldn't quite place chased down her back in the few seconds it took before the caller continued.

"It's Eli." He cleared his throat and added, "Eli Colton," as if she wouldn't instantly know who Eli was, wouldn't know the voice she'd longed—or maybe dreaded—hearing from again.

Her fingers tightened around her phone, and her heartbeat reverberated so loudly in her ears, she could barely hear herself reply, "Eli. What…what in the world do you want?"

Yeah, her tone was a tad steely. But she had to project a coolness to mask the deep ripple of emotion his call triggered. She couldn't cave to the well of heartache she'd taken years to quash. As she'd asked twelve—no, thirteen years ago—she and Eli had maintained complete radio silence. But now he'd called her? What the actual heck?

Her gut coiled, and her already tight muscles knotted even more. She should just hang up on him. She didn't want to revive all those bittersweet, painful memories or—

"I'm afraid I'm calling with bad news, Noelle."

Noelle sat back in her desk chair, startled by his announcement. "Bad news? What do you mean?" Her doorbell chimed at that moment, and she groaned. Talk about bad timing. Ignoring the door, she said, "What kind of bad news?"

"Did I hear your doorbell?"

"Yeah, but I don't—"

"You need to answer it." Something about his tone sent a chill through her.

"Why? How would you know who—"

"Just…please let them in."

Her mind spinning and heart thumping, she made her way from her home office to the front door. Two uniformed Seattle police officers were on her front stoop.

Bad news. Police officers. Noelle gripped the doorknob and silently waved the officers in.

They both introduced themselves in grim tones, and with legs trembling, she showed them into her living room and took a seat on the couch. "All right, Eli. The policemen are here. What's happened?"

He cleared his throat again, and she heard him take a deep breath. "There's no easy way to tell you this, but... your sister, Allison, has been killed."

Noelle replayed the words in her head, once...twice. Eli must have thought her silence meant she'd not heard or had hung up, because he repeated the stunning news.

"I heard you. I just... How? When? And why the hell are you calling to tell me instead of letting these officers you obviously sent deliver the news?"

"I'm with the Major Crimes Division of the Alaska Bureau of Investigation, and her murder is part of a bigger serial killer case I'm investigating. I thought I should be the one to break the news to you instead of a stranger, because of our history. But protocol calls for officers to be present in person, so..." He let his words trail off.

She angled a glance at the two Seattle officers who wore awkward expressions, as if expecting her to melt down any moment.

Except her brain felt numb. Overwhelmed. Eli... Allison... "I—d-does Aunt Jean know? I mean, she probably wouldn't call me even if she did, but—"

"No. I haven't informed your Aunt Jean yet. You are Allison's next of kin and—"

"Next of kin?" She barked a humorless laugh. "What a joke."

"I assure you this is no joke," Eli said. "Surely you don't think I'd do something that—"

"No. That's not what I meant. It's—" Noelle plowed one hand through her inky black hair, trying to process all the truth bombs Eli was dropping on her. Allison was dead. *Murdered.* He was an ABI agent. He was working a *serial killer* case.

She shoved off her sofa to pace. The explosion of adrenaline dumped into her system made her too restless to sit still. She felt the gazes of the officers following her. "Hang on. Back up. Allison was murdered by a *serial killer*?"

"I know. It's a lot to take in." Eli's voice was calm and soothing. Kind. Warm. Damn it, she remembered his dulcet baritone voice all too well and how whispered intimacies could make her burn for him.

She pinched the bridge of her nose. That was not where her thoughts needed to go at the moment. *Focus!*

"And you're in charge of the case to find the bastard who killed her?" She goggled as the pieces of the picture finally slotted into place.

"Me and my partner, Asher Rafferty, primarily. Although we have a large support team." He hesitated. "Why?"

She scoffed. "Well, because…you know. Of all the gin joints in all the world…"

He grunted. "Yeah. That was kinda what I thought when the victim's ID came across my desk."

"The victim?" An eerie chill sank into her bones as the reality of what Eli was telling her sharpened into focus. Her sister had been murdered by a serial killer. *Oh, Allison!* She and her sister hadn't been close for years, but no one deserved to be brutally killed—

"I'm sorry. I shouldn't be so clinical. Family notification isn't usually my job, but I wanted… I thought you should hear it from me first. I thought I owed you that much."

Her gut roiled. He hadn't said how her sister had been killed. Had it been quick? Had she been tortured? Acid climbed her throat as the questions mounted and the horrific possibilities spun out.

"Noelle? Are you still there?"

One of the officers stood and crossed to her. "Are you all right, ma'am? Would you like to sit down?" He touched her arm gently, but she shook her head and paced away.

"How did it happen?" she asked Eli, hearing her voice shake. "Wh-what did he do to her? Has her killer been caught?"

"No. He's still at large, and we're still working on the details surrounding the manner of death. Her autopsy results are pending."

"Eli, don't play games with me. I want the truth! I can take it. Did she suffer?"

"I'm being honest with you. I don't have definitive answers yet, and I don't want to speculate. In truth, I can't reveal details of the investigation even if I had them. I only called because you are next of kin, and the medical examiner should be able to release the body for burial next week." His sigh filtered through the connection. "So you can make funeral arrangements…"

"Funeral arrangements," she whispered numbly. The shock of talking to Eli, the weight of this tragic news and the ramifications of her sister's murder all hit her anew. Her knees buckled, and she slumped down on the closest chair.

One of the officers moved to sit close by, a look of compassion creasing his forehead.

"Noelle, I'm so sorry. You'll need to come to Shelby

to sign paperwork at the ME's office. If you need anything while you're here for the funeral...if I can help in any way..."

While she was *there* for the funeral?

Her chest squeezed. Oh hell! She had to go back to Alaska to make the arrangements for her sister's funeral. Back to the state she'd avoided for half her life. To the town where Eli, the man who'd broken her heart, lived.

Her lungs seized, and she could only take small, shallow breaths.

Would she have to see Eli, deal with him at the ABI in order to claim her sister's body? She prayed not.

"Ma'am?" the officer nearest her said, leaning closer as she sucked in rapid pants.

"No." She lifted a hand to the officer and shook her head, answering both Eli and the Seattle uniform at the same time.

Get a grip! Fighting for calm, she mustered a firmer tone along with some semblance of composure. "No, Eli. I don't need anything from you. I don't *want* anything from you. It's too late for that."

Eli scoffed. "Right. I got *that* message a long time ago."

She bristled at his angry tone. "What does that mean?"

"Never mind. I didn't call to rehash our history. Again, I'm sorry for your loss. I'll text you the details about claiming Allison's remains. The Seattle officers can take it from here. Goodbye, Noelle."

She was still swallowing the harsh grittiness of the term *remains* and all it implied when he hung up. Before she could say any more. Before she could ask any more questions. Before they could poke any more old wounds.

Probably for the best. Her past with Eli was better off left in the past.

Lowering her phone from her ear, she stared at the floor blankly while the conversation rewound in her mind.

Allison. Murdered. Serial killer.

"Ms. Harris?"

She jerked her head up, having almost forgotten the two policemen in her living room. "I—I'm fine."

"Would you like a glass of water?"

She shook her head and rose unsteadily. "I'd just like to be alone right now."

The two officers exchanged dubious looks.

"Really. I'll be fine. Thank you for coming, but… I just need time to process it all." She crossed to her front door, signaling her readiness for the men to leave.

Finally with stiff nods and expressions of their sympathy, the two officers left.

Noelle leaned back against the closed door and choked on the sob that rose in her throat.

Despite the years of silence, the teenage disagreements, the favoritism her parents showed Allison, Noelle loved her sister. Allison had been her only family since their parents' deaths—if you didn't count her cold and cruel Aunt Jean and Uncle Clyde, whom Noelle didn't. Her mother's sister and brother-in-law had never accepted Noelle's adoption, never considered her real family. Especially after Allison, a daughter by birth, had come along. Noelle, being Korean-American, had been ostracized by her mother's family, not just because of her race, but because they felt Noelle's parents had been too hasty in adopting, too eager to have a child and had settled for Noelle too easily.

Settled. Damn that word still stung. *Settled* reeked of second best, of last resort and not good enough.

Noelle wiped the silent tears that rolled down her face. She'd lived with the stigma of being the lesser daughter, her parents' bad decision, from the day Allison was born. From age ten until she'd left Alaska in her rearview mirror to attend college, Noelle had felt like an outsider in her own family. Or, as she'd overheard her parents call her one night when she was fourteen, *the mistake*.

So why was she going back to Alaska? Back to the hostile environment where she'd always felt so unwelcome and unwanted?

Noelle dragged herself back to the couch and flopped down on it. She leaned her head back and groaned. She was going back because it wasn't Allison's fault she'd been born. Allison might have been spoiled and held in higher esteem by the family, but she'd been an okay sister. Though Allison was not close in age or much of a friend, Noelle had loved her just the same.

And Noelle was going back to Alaska because it wasn't Allison's fault she'd been murdered. Allison deserved to have a proper burial and to have her only sister there to grieve her death.

More important, Allison deserved to have her killer caught and punished. Rising from the couch, Noelle firmed her resolve. Before she left Alaska again, she intended to see that Allison had justice.

Shelby, Alaska

AFTER DISCONNECTING THE call with Noelle, Eli sat in his ABI office, fingers steepled and tapping his chin. He replayed the call, the sound of her voice and what wasn't said but plainly heard in the silences. Her flat refusal of his offer to help, saying she didn't need him, had cut him deeply and salted old sores. But he shouldn't have lost his cool, shouldn't have snarled at her the way he had.

I got that message a long time ago.

Eli winced at the memory of his harsh tone. Not the professional presentation he'd intended when he started the call. Maybe if she'd had even a morsel of warmth in her voice, sounded even a little bit happy to hear from him—

Happy? When he was giving her tragic news about her sister? *Come on, Colton. Get real.* The message was as clear now as it had been thirteen years ago. He'd always cared more for her than she had for him. How else could she have walked away from their relationship and cut off contact without a backward glance? He'd never understood her reasons for the breakup, but he had been left without any recourse. When Noelle left him, she was just...gone. She never took his calls again, never replied to texts, never explained herself.

And he'd never gotten over her. His love had been deep and true, and her departure wounded him, heart and soul.

"What's with you?" His partner, Asher Rafferty, strolled into their shared office. Rafferty brought both the clinging chill of the November day on his clothes and a cup of steaming coffee in his hand. "You look like you just lost your best friend."

Eli straightened in his chair and lowered his hands to his desktop. "Close."

Asher did a double take. "Dang. I was kidding, but... what's going on?"

"I just talked to Allison Harris's sister. I let her know we identified Allison as one of the Fiancée Killer's victims." He picked up a pen and tapped it on the file open on his desk.

"You made the next of kin notification by phone?"

"I made sure someone from Seattle PD was there with her. But I needed to be the one to break the news to her."

"Why? You didn't do the notification for any of the other victims' families."

"Because I know her. I was…involved with her in college. I wanted to be the one… If she found out I'm working the case and hadn't… I thought I owed her…"

"Because it was an excuse to talk to her again?" Asher asked, proving he was too perceptive to be convinced otherwise.

Eli rubbed the back of his neck and arched a dark brown eyebrow. "Maybe so. But isn't it better she knows I'm working the case before she gets here? Can you imagine if we meet by chance in the hall at the coroner's office or she reads my name in a newspaper article regarding the case? I don't want her to think I'm avoiding her."

"So she's coming up here?"

Eli nodded. "To claim the body and make the funeral arrangements."

"And you plan to see her? Even seek her out?" Asher asked, propping his feet on his desk.

"I, uh, guess I'll leave that up to fate. I don't plan to avoid her. If we run into each other…" Eli waved a hand, not knowing how to finish that sentence. What would he do if he saw Noelle while she was in town? His heart squeezed at the prospect.

"Yeah?" Asher prompted.

Eli bent over the file in front of him and flipped through the pages of notes. "Well, I'll cross that bridge when I get to it."

Two days later, when Eli stepped into the lobby of the medical examiner's office from the parking lot, he reached that bridge.

Chapter Two

Noelle stood with her arms crossed over her chest, clearly embroiled in a disagreement with an older couple whose backs were to him.

"My adoption made me her family. The law recognizes me as her sister, and that makes *me* next of kin!" Noelle said, her shoulders squared and her jaw rigid.

"Well, *I* don't recognize you as anything but trouble," the gray-haired woman retorted. "You're not our blood, and you shouldn't have a say in anything regarding *my niece.*"

His hackles raised on Noelle's behalf, Eli moved closer, blatantly eavesdropping. His approach caught Noelle's attention, and she visibly shuddered when she spotted him. Her distraction lasted only seconds before she raised her chin a notch, and fire blazed from her dark brown eyes.

Her hair was shorter than it had been in college, he noted. Her thick black hair hung in a straight curtain to her shoulders, parted on the side and tucked behind her ears.

The older woman had aimed a finger at Noelle and was still railing at her in caustic tones. "If you think you're going to get your grubby paws on my sister's inheritance or anything else that belongs to my family, you can think again!"

"Is there a problem here, ladies?" Eli said as he stepped into the ring Noelle and the older couple made.

The gray-haired woman pursed her mouth. "It's personal business and none of yours."

Eli reached in the inner pocket of his heavy winter coat and pulled out the bifold wallet where he kept his badge. He flashed it at the older couple. "It's my business if I feel you're disturbing the peace with your shouting. Besides, I'm a friend of Noelle's, and I don't like to see her being publicly berated."

The woman narrowed her gaze on him and flicked a glance to the badge. "Colton? You're the one in charge of the case. You're the ABI agent investigating Allison's murder."

"I am. The same," he answered, even though it hadn't been phrased as a question.

Noelle gave him a hard look. "I'm fine, Eli. I don't need you to defend me."

"Agent Colton, you can help us!" the woman said, angling her body to face him.

"And you are?" he asked, although he already had a hunch.

The older man finally spoke, extending his hand for Eli to shake. "Clyde and Jean Gates. Jean is Allison Harris's maternal aunt. We've come in from Anchorage to claim the body from the medical examiner."

When Eli dropped the man's hand, he stuck it in his coat pocket and divided a glance among the three parties. "I see. From what I overheard as I came in just now, you have some issue with Noelle's claim as next of kin. Is that right?"

"Eli," Noelle said in a dark tone under her breath. "I said I don't need your—"

"Darn right!" Jean interrupted. "She should have *no say*

in what happens with Allison or my family's estate! We're Allison's blood relatives. She was just...*adopted*!" The bitter woman spit the word out with a timbre to her voice that said she considered Noelle no better than trash.

Noelle's mouth tightened, and she turned her head away. But not before Eli saw the sparkle of tears that puddled in her eyes.

His heart wrenched in sympathy for her while, in his pockets, his hands fisted in outrage for how her aunt was denigrating her.

"I understand that Allison's death is upsetting for you," he said with more composure than he felt. Years of serving the public and dealing with all manner of human emotion and irrationality served him well in that moment. "However, the law is clearly on Noelle's side. Because of her legal adoption, she *is* Allison's sister, and therefore her next of kin."

Jean Gates took a staggering step back as if pushed. She knitted her gray eyebrows in consternation. "What? You can't be serious! Blood always comes first!"

Eli shook his head. "No, ma'am. Noelle is legally—"

"Now see here, young man!" Clyde puffed out his chest as he faced off with Eli. "My wife is entitled to the money and heirlooms her family has collected over the years, and we're prepared to take the matter to court!"

Noelle pushed in between Clyde and Eli. She scowled at Eli first. "I said, I don't need your help!" Then facing her uncle, she growled, "I don't want any money or any of the family's dusty old furniture and ugly tchotchkes. But I will see that my sister receives a decent burial and not some gaudy display meant only to earn you sympathy and attention from your stuffy old friends."

"Gaudy?" Jean said, her lips pursed in offense. "And I

suppose you intend to just throw her in a pine box and be done with it? You couldn't be bothered with the family for the last seventeen years, and suddenly you know what's best for Allison?"

"And how many times since I left for college has anyone in the family other than Allison bothered to reach out to me? I had maybe three calls and one letter in seventeen years. That's it! That's all the communication from my family I had. That's all anyone cared about *me*." Noelle's voice broke, and she slammed her eyes shut before drawing a deep breath and cutting an embarrassed glance at Eli.

Eli's gut twisted. He could remember how little Noelle had mentioned her family when they'd dated, but he was seeing a new side of the situation now. Had she been rejected by her parents? Clearly there was no love lost with her aunt and uncle. This vulnerable side of Noelle, whom he'd always known to be a pillar of strength, courage and capability, shook him.

Jean gave a haughty sniff. "Why should we be in touch? You're the one who left, and I say good riddance. You were nothing but trouble for your mother and father as a teenager."

Noelle raised a trembling hand. "Stop. I have no desire to rehash ancient history with you. I'm only in town to claim Allison's body and see her properly buried in the family plot outside town. You may come to the funeral, but beyond that I don't want to hear from you or see you again." She turned to walk away, but Jean Gates pursued and snatched at Noelle's arm.

"Just a minute, you! Allison is coming with *us* to be buried with my parents and the babies my sister lost before Allison was born. She should be with her *real* siblings for eternity!"

Noelle's back stiffened, hurt blazing in her eyes.

Eli had had enough. Noelle wouldn't thank him for interfering, but the argument was becoming a sideshow in the medical examiner's public lobby. He wedged himself between Noelle and her aunt and took the older woman by the arm. "That's enough. You need to leave now. You're disturbing the peace and blocking traffic in a public facility."

Jean shook his hand off her elbow. "Unhand me! I have business here. I'm not leaving without claiming my niece for burial!"

"I'm afraid not," Eli said, his tone brooking no resistance. "Noelle will be given custody of the body, but only when the medical examiner and police investigators are finished gathering needed evidence. Which will not be today. Now please leave the premises before I arrest you for harassment and disturbing the peace."

"What?" Jean shrieked, her voice a full octave higher. "Arrest me?"

Clyde Gates, clearly not wanting to press the issue, shuffled up to his wife and placed a hand on her shoulder. "Let's go, Jean. We'll let the lawyers handle it."

"No! I—" Jean met the uncompromising glare from her husband and snapped her mouth shut. With a disgruntled huff, she shot Noelle a narrow look. "This matter is not closed." Turning on her heel, the woman tromped outside into the icy November day.

After the door swished closed behind the older couple, Eli faced Noelle. "Are you all right?"

She rolled her eyes at him. "I'm fine. But maybe you should get your hearing checked. I said I didn't want your help."

"I heard you." He took a step closer to her, wanting to draw her into his arms and hug her, hold her, kiss her again after so many years apart. Instead, he curled his fingers into his palms, squelching the desire to reach for her. Her body language—arms folded over her chest, her jaw clamped tight, her eyebrows lowered—said she wanted no part of this reunion. He sighed. *As if her ghosting you for the past thirteen years hasn't sent that message already.* "Maybe I didn't like the way they were treating you, not listening to the legal facts."

She grunted. "Nothing I haven't dealt with most of my life." She blinked rapidly and angled her head away, but not before he saw the bloom of her tears.

Compassion and longing shoved aside restraint, and he laid a hand near her shoulder. "I'm sorry, Noelle. I never knew you—"

"Of course you didn't know. I never told you. On purpose."

"If you want to go somewhere more private, maybe get lunch, we could talk about it. You could vent to me."

She started toward the coroner's office, effectively removing his hand from her upper back. "I never said anything to you because I wanted to leave it behind. So why would I talk about it now?" With one final glance at Eli, she strode briskly toward the inner sanctum of the medical examiner's office.

"Because you're upset, and sometimes it helps to let off steam?" he said, keeping pace with her. "Can we not be friends, even if you don't want a deeper relationship?"

"Can I help you?" the receptionist in the medical examiner's office asked as Noelle stepped up to her desk.

"Yes. I'm Noelle Harris. I'm Allison Harris's sister, and I'm here to—" Noelle fell silent.

Eli angled his head toward her, and his chest squeezed, seeing her face crumple and tears break free from her eyelashes. He edged closer to her, his voice low and sympathetic. "Noelle..."

She raised a hand, holding him off as she sniffed. "I'm here to c-claim her body."

The receptionist yanked a facial tissue from the box on her desk and handed it to Noelle. "Of course, dear. Let me gather the paperwork. I'll need to see two forms of identification, please." The woman turned to Eli. "Are you here with Ms. Harris, Agent Colton, or was there something I can do for you?"

"I, uh, originally came to speak to Scott Montgomery about the Fiancée Killer case, but I ran into Noelle—Ms. Harris—in the lobby. Is Scott around?"

Noelle blew her nose on the tissue and wiped her cheeks with her sleeve. "Fiancée Killer? Is that what you're calling the case? Is that who killed Allison?"

Eli took another tissue from the receptionist's box and handed it to her. "Well, that's what we're calling the case now. The local media coined the term, because all the victims so far are wearing a diamond ring. Or a fake diamond anyway, clearly meant to look like an engagement solitaire."

Something in Noelle's expression shifted. "Even Allison? She was wearing one of these rings?"

Eli hesitated. He could understand why Noelle had questions. Having been living in Seattle, she'd have only recently heard of the serial killer he and the rest of local law enforcement had been tracking. She'd have not been privy to the media coverage as each body had been found and the links in the case pieced together.

As Eli debated what and how much to tell Noelle, the receptionist said, "Let me just go get the forms for Ms.

Harris, and I'll see if the ME is available to speak to you, Agent Colton."

Eli nodded his thanks to the woman then pivoted back to Noelle. "I can't go into many of the details, but…yes. Allison was wearing a ring. That and…" he cleared his throat "…the way her body was posed when the searchers found her are why we consider her one of the Fiancée Killer's victims."

Noelle pressed a hand to her mouth, shaking her head. "Geez, that's…sick. Does that mean she…had a relationship with this creep? That she dated him or—" Her nose crinkled as if she couldn't stand to voice the other possibilities.

"We really don't know that yet. And even as a family member, you're not allowed to—" Eli stopped short, seeing the shift in her expression.

"Not allowed? Are you saying you won't tell me what's happening in the investigation to find *my sister's murderer*?"

"I'm sorry, Noelle. But there are rules and restrictions about how much information we can reveal to the public, including family members. Policies regarding how an investigation is handled are put in place to ensure the case isn't tainted or suspects tipped off or evidence jeopardized."

She opened her mouth as if to argue the point, but the receptionist returned at that moment. "Here we are. I'll need you to fill out all of these forms, sign and date them. May I see your two forms of ID now?"

Noelle dug in her purse and produced her driver's license and some other small card Eli couldn't read from where he stood. The receptionist glanced to Eli then. "Mr. Montgomery is in the middle of an autopsy at the moment, but if you'd like to schedule an appointment to meet with him tomorrow, I can see what time is available."

Eli sighed. He hated delays, especially now that the Fiancée Killer case was finally beginning to develop. "All right."

While Noelle carried a clipboard with forms to a chair in a corner of the reception area, Eli left a message for the forensic expert, Scott Montgomery, to come up to his office as soon as he was available.

His business finished, he had no real reason to hang around the medical examiner's office. But neither was he ready to leave when he had this chance to talk to Noelle. She was still dabbing at her eyes and blowing her nose with the crumpled tissue as she completed the documentation for the release of Allison's body.

She could deny it all she wanted, but she needed support today and an opportunity to blow off steam. Knowing Noelle was not from Shelby and hadn't been back to Anchorage in years, he doubted she still knew anyone in Alaska, other than her aunt and uncle. They obviously would not be a source of comfort and strength during Noelle's time of shock and grief.

Squaring his shoulders, Eli decided he'd wait in the lobby for Noelle. Whether she wanted his help or not, he would stand by her and give her all the support and friendship she would need for the coming days—because he knew burying her sister and hearing details about how Allison died would take its toll on Noelle.

Chapter Three

Noelle was emotionally drained after the confrontation with her aunt and uncle, signing the paperwork to claim Allison's body…and running into Eli. She had to have the worst luck imaginable to have timed her trip to the ME's office such that she ran into *both* her hateful relatives *and* the man she'd most wished to avoid while in Alaska.

Before leaving the medical examiner's office, she donned her knit hat and zipped her coat, bundling up before heading out in the cold Alaskan autumn. She had her head down, pulling on her gloves when she heard someone call her name.

Her heart lurched as she snapped her head up and spotted Eli crossing the lobby. Of course he'd waited for her. She'd been foolish to think he'd give up so quickly and leave her alone for the duration of her stay, now that the initial contact had been made.

She grabbed for her composure with both hands, squaring her shoulders and lifting her chin.

"Hi," he said as he approached, his head tipped to one side as he studied her expression. "I'm glad I caught you before you left."

"Isn't that why you're out here? You were waiting for me." She turned and stalked outside toward her rented car.

He didn't deny it. Instead, he bobbed a nod and caught her arm. "Wouldn't you rather talk inside, out of the cold?"

Noelle shook her head. "Just tell me what you want. Why did you wait for me?"

"Because we haven't talked in years. I'm interested in what you've been doing, *how* you've been doing. And… well, after that scene in the lobby with your aunt and uncle, I really thought you might want to vent to someone. Blow off steam. I can't drink on duty, but I know a place we can get lunch, and you can get a glass of wine or a Moscow mule if you want."

Her pulse thumped. *Moscow mule* was far too specific to be random. He'd remembered her favorite cocktail all these years. She didn't want to be impressed or, worse, *touched* that he remembered that detail about her. Yet the tug in her core was undeniable. For him to have held on to that tidbit meant he either had a great memory for details or she'd mattered enough to him that he'd tried to remember such things about her. She hoped it was the former. As a cop—or rather an agent with the Major Crimes Division of the Alaska Bureau of Investigation—he would need an eye and memory for detail. She'd go with that.

She opened her mouth to refuse his invitation, when a new thought occurred to her. *He's in charge of the murder investigation.* The serial killer investigation. If she was going to get details about what happened to Allison, who better to question than Eli? She could lean on their former relationship to beg the favor of inside information. Surely he wouldn't deny her the truth about her sister's case?

"Fine. We can get lunch. But I'll take my rental car and meet you." She aimed her thumb toward the small sedan she'd picked up at the airport after she'd landed last night.

Eli shrugged. "All right." He gave her the name and address of the sports bar and grill he had in mind, and once in her car, she plugged the information into the rental's GPS.

Ten minutes later, she and Eli were tucked in an intimate corner booth ordering drinks—coffee for him and a local beer for her. She'd have liked a Moscow mule, but she didn't want him to know how on the nose he'd been.

After the waiter left, Eli smiled broadly and exhaled. "I can't tell you how good it is to see you, Noelle." His brow dipped, and his expression sobered. "And also how sorry I am for the circumstances. When the report with the identification came through—" He dragged a hand over his mouth. "Well, it was a real shock for me, too. I can only imagine how hard this must be for you."

"Difficult, yes. But… Allison and I haven't been close in a long time. She's my sister and I love her, but—" Noelle heard what she'd said and hesitated. "She *was* my sister." She leaned back against the booth cushions with a sigh. "Dang. The reality is still settling in. It's so…unreal." Flattening both hands on the tabletop, she pinned a probing stare on Eli. "So…a serial killer? Seriously?"

"Looks that way."

He reached out, covering one of her hands with his. The warmth of his palm against her cold skin felt delicious. Reckless.

She slid her hand out from under his, scowling her disapproval at him. "Eli, this isn't—" She waved a hand between them, searching for the right word. A date? She didn't want to plant that idea if she had read him wrong. "We're not—I don't want—"

A weary look filled his eyes. "Yeah, I get that. But for old times' sake, can't we be civil? Maybe even be friends?"

She'd sound like a real witch if she denied him that much after all these years. Besides, if she wanted him to share information with her, it didn't serve her cause to be adversarial with him. Puffing her cheeks out, she exhaled her concession. "Okay. *Friends*."

She made sure the word carried weight, so that he got the message that was all she could be. All her heart could take. Telling him goodbye once had been the hardest thing she'd ever done. To foster false hope of a reunion and break with him again would destroy her.

The waiter brought their drinks, and Noelle took a few large gulps of her beer before lifting her gaze to Eli again. "Tell me about the case. For starters, why was Allison brought here to Shelby? Last I heard, she lived in Anchorage, and I'm guessing the ABI office there is bigger, better equipped."

He arched a dark brown eyebrow. "Our office is smaller, yes, but we have access to all the same resources. And our people are top-notch. As far as why she was brought to the ME here in Shelby…" he paused and laced his fingers as he rested his hands on the table "…because Asher and I are the ones working the case. We're based here. And she and the first body were found closer to Shelby than any of the other satellite offices."

Noelle's stomach flip-flopped. Between the penetrating and memory-evoking blue of his eyes and the unsettling facts she was grappling with, she wasn't sure how she would eat anything. "How…how many other victims have you found?"

Eli seemed to measure his response, taking a beat before saying, "Allison was the second victim found. We've found five bodies with similar traits linking them to the same killer so far."

"And what is the unifying link between victims? Do you have any leads on who the killer is yet? Where were the bodies found? Were they together, like in a mass grave? Is there reason to think Allison knew any of the other victims? Why would the killer have singled out Allison?" She rattled off one question after another. While she had him talking, she intended to get as much information as she could. "You mentioned a fake diamond ring earlier. Is that what ties the victims to each other?"

Eli frowned and glanced away. "Like I said before, I'm not allowed to divulge detailed information—"

She held up a hand to cut him off, her mouth firming in frustration. "Eli, I understand the police have their policies, but some information has already been reported in the press. And while I read what I could find online on my trip up from Seattle, I know there's got to be more. I'm just asking you to fill in a few gaps, give me a better understanding of the big picture."

Eli shook his head. "I understand why you have questions, but I really can't divulge much. It could jeopardize the case. You wouldn't want that, would you?"

Noelle twisted her mouth, keying in on one word. "Much? Then you can tell me something. Right?"

He glanced away, and she gripped his hand to drag his attention back to her. "Come on, Eli. You know I won't tell anyone. I mean, I want this guy caught as much as anyone. I won't do anything to hurt the case."

"Noelle..." he said, his tone skeptical.

"You can trust me to keep everything you say confidential." The look she gave him pleaded for his cooperation, for his trust.

Eli pinched the bridge of his nose. Finally, with a sigh, he said, "Here's what I can say. Based on forensics, the first victim was killed about three years ago, indicating this guy has been operating for a while."

"Three years? That long?" She goggled at him. "H-how long ago was Allison killed?"

He leaned forward, angling his head as he narrowed his gaze on her. "Actually, you can help us with that question. When's the last time you heard from her? Did she mention anyone new in her life, romantically or otherwise? Maybe someone who was stalking or harassing her?"

Noelle dropped her gaze to the tabletop and chortled. "I rarely talked to anyone in my family after I left when I was eighteen. Don't you remember that I stayed on campus for holidays and worked internships during the summer?"

He nodded. "I remember everything about you and our time together. Including the fact you rarely talked about your family and changed the subject when I asked questions. But things could have changed since college. And you mentioned earlier you'd had some limited contact with Allison."

For her sanity's sake, she ignored his comment about their time together and focused on the investigation, on Allison. "I only had a handful of phone calls from Allison. One on my nineteenth birthday, another when I graduated from UW, and one when Mom and Dad were killed in the plane crash three years ago."

His expression shifted, and something akin to sorrow crossed his face. "Your parents were killed in a plane crash? I'm so sorry. I knew they were deceased because of our search for Allison's next of kin, but not…" He cleared his throat. "I'm sorry. That's terrible."

She pursed her mouth and gave a dismissive shrug. "Yeah, well, it was harder on Allison than me. I'd already grieved the loss of my parents for all practical purposes long before their plane went down in the mountains."

"What do you mean, you'd already grieved their loss? What happened?"

She waved off his question. "Not important now. All you need to know is that the call three years ago about our parents was the last time I talked to Allison. So, no, I know nothing about her love life or friends or new people."

Eli grunted. "Another dead end. Damn." His gaze flicked up, embarrassment flushing his cheeks. "Sorry. Poor word choice."

"Whatever." She wasn't concerned with semantics or tiptoeing around each other based on false sensibilities. Gathering her thoughts, she tried a new line of inquiry. "You keep saying 'he.' You're sure the killer is a man?"

He sipped his coffee, then nodded slowly. "Based on what little DNA we've found on the victims, yes. He's careful, though, and leaves little trace evidence behind. Unfortunately, his DNA is not in CODIS, which is the US database, or in Canada's system, either, so we haven't got an ID on him yet."

Their waiter appeared at the table again and asked if they were ready to order. When Noelle hesitated and scrabbled for the menu, Eli ordered his "regular."

"Grilled salmon sandwich with fries," the waiter said, not bothering to write it down.

Even though she could get all the fresh salmon she wanted in Seattle, Noelle told the waiter, "I'll have the same."

The waiter left, and Noelle nibbled her bottom lip as she processed what she'd learned. "So…he's not in the system. Meaning he's never been arrested before?"

"Not every person arrested is swabbed for DNA, but he likely hasn't been arrested for a sex crime, violent crime or a number of other significant felonies."

She frowned and lifted her beer for a sip, ruminating. "So what leads do you have? What ties the cases together? The news reports dubbed this guy the Fiancée Killer because of the diamond ring the victims wore, right?"

He nodded. "That's right."

"And I read that they were all found wearing a black dress. Right?"

He only stared at her with those heart-stopping blue eyes.

She took another swig of beer and steeled her nerve to ask a harder question. "How did Allison die? Did she suffer?"

He gave her a dubious look. "Noelle, do you really want to know the gritty details? Don't torture yourself with that kind of information."

Her grip tightened on her beer mug. "I know it's not pleasant. And I don't want to dwell on it, but… I need to know."

"Why? What good does it do?" His voice was gentle, compassionate. His expression said he didn't want to see her hurt.

Something in her core longed to reach out to him, to curl in the comfort his arms could provide…and sob. But her brain shut that foolish impulse down. She'd done what she had to in college in order to protect herself from that sort of vulnerability. When she'd felt herself growing dependent on him, falling in love with him, putting her heart at risk for him, she'd broken things off, shut him out. She wouldn't unravel the years of work she'd put in, knitting together a protective cocoon, constructing a new life for herself that put him in the past.

She squared her shoulders, hoping to present herself as more determined and courageous than she felt. "Because I need closure."

His blue eyes filled with sympathy and understanding. He nodded and appeared ready to tell her what she wanted to know, when she blew it by adding, "And because I want to work with you on the case. I want to help you catch the man who killed my sister."

ELI SLOSHED THE coffee he'd lifted toward his mouth, so stunned by Noelle's pronouncement that he'd flinched. "What!"

"Before you get defensive—" she started, holding up her index finger.

He scoffed an incredulous laugh. "Not defensive. Just practical. And, well, following the *law*. You cannot be involved in this case. Period."

"Not even if I can be helpful? I can offer my services at no charge to the ABI, and I won't—"

"Your services?" His coffee splashed again as he thunked the ceramic mug onto the table harder than he intended. "Are you saying you're in law enforcement?"

She shifted her weight restlessly on the padded booth seat. "Uh, no. But—"

"Well, then that's an end to it. Case closed."

"Would you listen? I can be valuable to the investigation."

He lifted an eyebrow. "How so?"

Her jaw firmed, and she drilled him with a level, all-business stare. Despite the seriousness of her gaze, his belly jolted as he met her beautiful dark eyes, remembering…

"Analytics."

He frowned. "What?"

"Computer analytics. Statistics. Data mining. It's a way of looking at large amounts of information in new ways, looking for patterns and contrasts. Of maximizing data to reveal truths not readily apparent otherwise."

"I know what analytics means. I've heard of sports teams using computer statistics and so forth to find the best players and the best game strategies. How would you use analytics on the Fiancée Killer investigation?"

"I'd input everything you know about the—"

"Nope, nope, never mind." He waved both hands. "I shouldn't have asked. You can't be involved."

Her brow furrowed over her dark brown eyes, and her mouth pinched. "Not even if I can be useful? Are you so stuck on your blessed rules that you'd shut out an offer to make a difference in the case? To get a better perspective on the big picture? I might be able to help you get a clearer idea of the sort of person the killer is."

"That's what our profiler does. We're already compiling an outline of the killer's likely personality and physical traits."

The waiter arrived with their meals, and Eli hoped it would be enough to derail the conversation. But he should have known better.

"What has your profiler determined?" she asked, choosing a french fry from the stack on her plate.

He rolled his eyes. Noelle had always been stubborn. When she fixed her mind on an idea or plan of action, she could rarely be persuaded otherwise.

The most painful example of this was her notion that because of their differences—a term she never defined—they couldn't have a future together. After an intense and passionate two years together in college, she'd abruptly broken things off. He'd tried to convince her he cared far more about the ways they were the same and that his love was strong enough to overcome any challenges. But she'd been certain their differences would someday come back to bite them. She'd said only that experience had taught her that even the people you loved and trusted most could change their mind about you and push you aside.

"Like you're doing now to me?" he'd retorted hotly.

Her guilty expression had said his comment had hit its mark. "Well, I learned from the best." She'd turned then and walked away, never to answer another call or text from him. Until two days ago, when he'd notified her of Allison's death.

Rather than answer her question, Eli picked up his salmon sandwich and took a big bite. Two could play this game. And he had the policies of the ABI backing his stance not to involve her in the investigation.

When it became clear to her that he didn't intend to answer, she groaned her frustration. "Okay then. I'll guess." She fixed a keen gaze on him, ignoring her food. He swore he could see the gears in her sharp brain turning. Calculating, even without her spreadsheets or analytics software.

"If he's been operating for three years and killed five women that you know of without getting caught..." she propped her chin on her hand, her elbow on the table "... he's patient. And if he hasn't left any significant, useful evidence behind, then he's intelligent. Smart enough to think things through and be careful. So, he's a planner. Organized."

Eli took another bite of his sandwich and chewed, trying to keep his face impassive despite being impressed with her logic. And accuracy.

She tilted her head to one side. "Am I right so far?"

He reached for the ketchup and squirted a puddle onto his plate.

"I am, aren't I? Your silence says yes, even if you don't."

He scowled at her. "That makes no sense. Silence is

just silence. I'm not committing to anything one way or another."

When she continued to stare intently at him, clearly reading his expression, trying to catch him out, he dropped his gaze to his plate. He dipped a fry into the ketchup and grumbled when the sauce dripped on his shirt on the way to his mouth.

Noelle chuckled. "I am right. You would always get peevish and evasive when you knew you'd been outflanked. At chess or poker or in life."

That she'd remembered that detail about him, that she'd used it against him, only irritated him more. He huffed and pushed his plate away. "Fine. You're right about the killer's profile, but you haven't deducted anything our department hadn't figured out within the first few hours of gathering evidence from the first body."

She sat back with a smug smile on her face and lifted her beer for another long drink.

"But," he added before she tried to wheedle any more information from him, "I still can't tell you anything else about the case."

Her grin morphed to a disgruntled pout.

"Besides, I brought you here so you could release some steam regarding your aunt's nasty behavior." He waved a hand. "So vent away."

Noelle rolled her eyes. "What's the point? It's nothing I'm not used to."

Eli cocked his head to the side. "What do you mean?"

She gave him a withering look. "I mean not every family is as happy and loving as the Coltons are. You may have grown up with familial harmony and support, but not everyone's so lucky."

"So your aunt's always been like that?" he asked, a pang

of sympathy spearing him. He had been lucky in most family matters. He and his siblings were as close to his cousins as to each other. Holidays were joyful, celebratory events, and support was woven into the family motto, *Believe.*

Noelle lifted her sandwich rather than answering him. "Mmm. That's good fish. But isn't salmon fishing over this late in the year? It can't be wild caught, could it?"

"Depends on the weather. Some years, RTA takes groups out salmon fishing as late as October or early November. Mostly Coho this late in the season, though, if I remember right, but you'd have to ask my cousin, Spence. I don't get too involved in RTA business."

"RTA?" she asked.

"Rough Terrain Adventures."

She nodded. "Oh right. Your family's outdoor adventure tours company. I remember now."

He arched an eyebrow. "Now who's being evasive and stealthily changing the subject?"

She set down her sandwich and plucked up another fry. "We can go back to talking about the investigation if you like."

When she batted her eyelashes in feigned innocence, Eli laughed. "Oh, Noelle. I have missed you."

When her cheeks blanched and her eyes widened, he realized how his offhand remark had sounded. But he wouldn't take it back. Because he had missed Noelle. Terribly.

And now, with her back in town for a few days, he had his chance to repair the gulf between them. He had the chance to right whatever had gone wrong all those years ago.

Chapter Four

At her rented hotel room that night, Noelle stewed over Eli's dogged insistence not to share case information with her. She knew she had skills that could prove useful to the investigation if she could just convince Eli.

She meditated on what her next steps should be. She'd come all this way to Alaska and didn't want to waste her time here. She couldn't schedule the funeral for Allison until the medical examiner and forensic specialists had finished gathering all the information they could and released her remains. She'd cleared her work schedule before leaving Seattle, so she had a few days, maybe even as much as a couple weeks to devote her time to another project. She wanted that project to be finding Allison's killer.

She knew she wasn't magically going to come up with an answer that Eli and all the law enforcement professionals, with their training, databases and specialized equipment, hadn't found. But deep in her bones, she believed she could offer a fresh perspective on the information they'd gathered that might be of use to the investigators. Or...she hoped.

The killer had to be caught. Not just to save the lives of any potential new victims, but to give his previous victims justice.

Noelle punched her flat pillow in the too-soft bed and tried to get some sleep. The snippets she knew about the case taunted her. Fake engagement rings. Three years of killing. An intelligent and patient killer.

Intelligent and patient. Those words could be used to describe Eli. She'd admired his sharp mind when they were students together at the University of Washington. And when she'd seen the writing on the wall, when she'd begun to pull away from him, he'd been infinitely patient with her mercurial moods. Her swings between the deep passion she felt for him and the indifference she had to muster in order to leave him behind would have driven most men away. But Eli's devotion to her and patience with her hadn't faltered.

Noelle's heart, which she'd believed healed, stung. Seeing him today had been a blessing and a curse. While she'd been happy to see him doing so well, in a lead position in his chosen field, the intimate lunch had opened old wounds. Looking into his beautiful blue eyes, hearing the mellow baritone of his voice, feeling the warmth from his smile... Dang it. She'd had to fight not to tumble right back into his arms. She'd have to do a better job of steeling herself if she were to survive the next several days. She knew her quest to learn more about Allison's death and the investigation meant she'd run into Eli. Repeatedly.

The next morning, after a strong cup of coffee and thirty minutes of yoga to prepare herself, Noelle went to the ABI office and asked to speak to the forensic specialist in charge of the Fiancée Killer case. She was somewhat used to the winter darkness clinging to the night in Seattle, but here in Shelby, even at 8:15 in the morning, the sun had yet to rise. The lingering night added to her sense of disorientation and surrealism.

Allison was dead. Having not seen or spoken to her sister for so long, the loss was difficult to wrap her head around. Her absence wouldn't be significantly felt, yet the tragic nature of her death was unsettling.

When Noelle finally muddled her way into the state troopers' offices, the woman working the front desk seemed prepared to deny her request to meet with the forensic specialist or, at a minimum, grill her about her purpose for being there. But, as luck would have it, a tall, blond man was filling a mug at the coffeepot in the lobby and heard her request.

Grinning broadly, his green eyes bright, the handsome man strode over to Noelle and extended his hand. "I'm the ME on the Fiancée Killer case. Scott Montgomery at your service. How can I help, Ms.—?" He let the title draw out, asking her to fill in the blank with a lift of his brow.

She took his hand and gave it a firm shake. "Harris. Noelle Harris. And I'm interested in learning more about the case."

His expression grew skeptical, the way Eli's had yesterday, and her stomach sank. She braced herself for being turned away, mentally calculating the best argument to be allowed access.

"Are you a journalist, Ms. Harris?" Montgomery asked.

"No. I'm a family member of one of the victims. I'm just trying to get a better idea of what happened to my sister and where the case stands."

"Of course. I can understand that." Montgomery paused a moment, his expression belatedly shifting to one of sympathy. "And my condolences on your loss."

She smiled politely. "Thank you."

He offered her coffee, which she declined. "What exactly is it you wish to know about your sister?"

"Anything and everything you can tell me. Reports in the media have been—"

"Noelle?"

Her words died on her lips as she pivoted to find Eli and another woman standing just inside the front door.

The woman's gaze flicked to Scott, and a smile lit her face. "Good morning, Scott. Stealing the visitors' coffee again, I see."

The forensic specialist's face glowed as he greeted the woman. "Kansas! Hi." He lifted his mug to her in a sort of salute. "You have to admit, it's far better than the witch's brew back in the office."

Eli stepped forward, his attention fully focused on Noelle. "What's going on here?"

"This is Noelle Harris," Scott said, brandishing another handsome smile. "She's—"

"I know who she is," Eli said, not unkindly. His mouth twitched in a lopsided grin.

The woman Scott had called Kansas gasped. "You're Noelle? *The* Noelle?"

Noelle blinked and divided a look between Kansas and Eli. "I'm *a* Noelle. I'm not sure if that makes me *the* Noelle."

Eli cleared his throat and glanced at Kansas. "Yes, she's *the* Noelle." He sighed, adding, "And unfortunately, Allison Harris, the second body found, was her sister." He turned to Noelle. "What brings you by this morning?"

"She wanted to talk to me about the case, get some details," Montgomery said before Noelle could answer. "What do you mean, *the* Noelle? I'm missing something."

Eli shook his head and flicked a brief glance at his colleague. "Never mind. I'll explain later. Suffice to say, I've told her everything we can divulge on the case already.

So..." He spread his hands. "Your trip this morning was in vain."

Kansas scoffed. "Eli, don't be rude! It's not in vain as far as I'm concerned, because it meant I got to meet you—finally! I'm Eli's cousin, Kansas Colton. I've heard so much about you."

Noelle gave Eli a querying look. "You have? Recently?"

"Well, not so much recently, but we all knew about you, heard all the stories, back when you were dating." Kansas shot her cousin a side glance as if realizing how awkward this meeting, years later, must be for Eli. "Um..." She hitched a thumb over her shoulder. "I better get going. I'm with the search and rescue team, and I'm just checking up on a few things before...the task force meeting. And I have to...report..." She let her excuse trail off, her cheeks flushing. "Well, it was nice to meet you, despite the sad circumstances."

Scott's eyes followed Kansas as she disappeared down the corridor, his expression clearly saying he wished he could escape the awkwardness himself but knew Noelle's wish to speak to him pinned him down.

Shifting her attention back to Eli, Noelle angled her head in query. "You told your family about me?"

Her question seemed to startle him. "Of course, I did. We were—" His gaze flicked to Scott before returning to her. After the briefest hesitation where he seemed to be choosing his words, he said, "Dating. Didn't you tell your family about me?"

Noelle, unwilling to get into their personal history or her family dynamic, especially with Scott listening, dodged the subject with a shrug. "Well, I don't want to keep you. I came to see Mr. Montgomery."

Eli squared his shoulders and divided a look between

the two. "And I, as the lead on the Fiancée Killer case, am saying Scott is not at liberty to share any details I haven't already given you."

Noelle sputtered. "Wha—you haven't told me jack-did-dly!"

"Exactly. Because we don't want anything to jeopardize the case." Eli directed a loaded look to Scott. "Isn't that right, Scott?"

The forensic expert raised both hands. "I'm sorry. My hands are tied."

Noelle gritted her teeth. She'd been sure Scott was ready to spill more details to her if Eli hadn't shown up. "Thank you anyway, Mr. Montgomery."

"Scott, please. Any friend of Eli's need not stand on ceremony with me."

She gave him a half smile as he retreated into the office. Facing Eli, she propped her hands on her hips, her gaze clashing with his. "I can't believe you're being so stubborn about this! I'm not a threat to the investigation. I can add value! I have software that can give you a deeper analysis of your data. I have a vested interest in seeing the case solved. I am trustworthy and honest and—"

"All right! All right!" Eli raised a palm, signaling defeat. He took her by the arm and led her to a corner of the lobby, out of the path of pedestrian traffic and away from the listening ears of the receptionist. "I have a meeting with the task force in a little while and interviews set up for this afternoon, but I can meet with you this evening. Where are you staying while you're in town?"

Noelle hesitated. Did she want him coming to her room at the hostel? That felt too…intimate. Nothing romantic would happen between them, of course, private setting or not, because she wouldn't let it. Sending him away had hurt too much in college to ever go through that pain again. But why tempt fate? The low hum of attraction still vibrated in her core when she was around him, and his piercing blue eyes could still stir heat in her blood. She needed a more public venue where societal decorum would ensure a chaste atmosphere.

"Why don't we meet at a restaurant instead and get dinner? My treat," she said.

He rubbed his chin as he studied her. "Okay. Yes to the restaurant, but no to you paying. I can't accept anything that even smells like a bribe."

She had to smile. "You always were honorable to a fault."

"The same place as yesterday?" he asked.

"That place was good, but I enjoy a bit of variety."

"Okay, then…the Cove is a nice place by the water. I can pick you up around six?"

His picking her up made the dinner feel like a date. Which it wasn't. Just the idea of a date with Eli made her chest squeeze with longing. She shook her head resolutely. "I have Google Maps. I'll meet you there. Six then?"

He frowned and opened his mouth as if to object. But after a beat, he sighed and bobbed his head in agreement.

That evening at 5:55, when she arrived, Eli was already at the restaurant. He'd gotten them a table by the window with a view of the marina, lit with twinkling lights strung along the pier. She'd had a tedious day of making funeral arrangements for Allison with a local mortuary and speaking to a lawyer about the probate of Allison's estate, and she was more than ready for dinner and a glass of wine to unwind.

He stood and pulled out her chair, greeting her with a warm smile that made her stomach swoop. Mentally she checked herself. *This is only a business dinner. Nothing more.*

"You look beautiful," he said, his compliment catching her off guard.

Heat stung her cheeks, and she flashed a grin of appreciation. "Um, thank you. I wasn't sure these slacks were classy enough for this place, but since the only other dressy clothes I brought was a black dress for the funeral, I didn't have much choice."

He gave her an odd look, then a forced smile before returning to his chair.

"What?" she asked.

"*What* what?" he returned, lifting an eyebrow.

"That funny look you just gave me. Something I said bothered you. What and why?"

He sighed. "Your comment about bringing a black dress. It just…" He made a weary buzzing sound with his lips. "I've been immersed in crime scene photos this afternoon and—"

She gasped. "Oh, that's right! You said the victims were all dressed in black dresses."

His brow creased. "Did I tell you that?"

She put her napkin in her lap. "Didn't you? Or did I read that in a write-up online?" She seized the opening. "I know the coroner's report I received said Allison was in a black dress. But the other victims were wearing similar dresses, too, weren't they? Isn't that one of the details that links the victims?" She gave him a level stare. "Am I right?"

His hand was resting on the table, and he tapped an index finger, a clear indication of his agitation. Which meant she was right. She sat back in her chair and tried not to look self-satisfied that she had been correct.

"Yes," he said, his tone flat. "You're right."

"It seemed a logical assumption. If the killer went to the trouble of dressing Allison in a little black dress, and the press reported he's putting fake engagement rings on all of them, it wasn't a stretch to guess they'd be dressed similarly."

Eli only grunted in acknowledgment of her assertion.

The waiter arrived, delivering glasses of water and a basket of rolls, then asked for their drink order. Once the waiter left, Eli inquired about Noelle's day.

"It was depressing. But don't change the subject. We're supposed to be talking about the progress of investigation."

"Now, wait a minute. You can't tell me your day was depressing and expect me to brush over that. What happened?"

She rolled her eyes. "Funeral arrangements. Probate issues. My aunt and uncle have already filed a lawsuit to prevent me from inheriting anything, and I'm anticipating further interference with custody of her remains. So, nothing I want to talk about any further, because it will spoil my appetite."

"And discussing the details of a serial killer's modus operandi and forensic evidence won't?"

"Well, discussing the case over a meal wasn't my first choice." Noelle gave him a pointed look. "I wanted to talk in your office or Scott Montgomery's. Dinner was my backup plan."

"I'll give you that one." Eli's attention was fully focused on her, and he gave her a half smile. "You haven't changed a bit since college. You're just as beautiful, just as dogged, just as decisive as I remember."

Noelle blinked and gave an awkward chuckle. "If not for the beautiful part, I'm not sure I'd take that as a compliment."

"Definitely meant as a compliment. You knew your mind and were fiercely independent and self-assured, and

I see no evidence that's changed. I remember you taking on the administration regarding the distribution of leftovers from the dining hall to food banks and the homeless. You didn't give up until changes were made. I was so proud of you fighting for a cause you believed in."

She shrugged. "If you give up easily, is it really a core belief or just a passing fancy?"

"You're right. And I remember how glad I was that the administration finally listened to your concerns, because I did not want to see you chain yourself to the dining hall doors and risk arrest. How would it have looked for me, pursuing a career in law enforcement, to have been dating someone arrested for trespassing and disturbing the peace?"

She frowned. "Would that have mattered to you? Was I supposed to abandon my cause to keep from embarrassing you?"

He shook his head, his smile fading. "Not at all. I was teasing. I never wanted you to change anything about yourself for me." His expression grew more serious. "Which is why I never understood why you ended things with me. All you ever said was that you could never be what I needed or wanted. That we were too different. But I never asked you to be anyone but yourself."

Noelle's heart tripped, and her palms grew clammy. "Please, let's not rehash our breakup. That's hardly pleasant dinner conversation, either."

"Don't I deserve to understand why you cut me out of your life? We had something good. No, something *great*. And then it was just…gone in an instant."

Noelle took a moment, staring down at the starched white tablecloth. "You do deserve to understand. So I will try to explain it before I leave town."

"Good."

"But not now, not tonight. I just can't…" Her voice broke, and she had to catch her breath and shove her runaway emotions back in a box before she could meet his gaze again. "I'm sorry."

ELI SAW THE sparkle of tears filling Noelle's eyes, and pain cleaved his chest. He reached for her hand and pressed it between his. "Not now, then. We'll find something happier to discuss."

She pulled her hand from his and used her napkin to dab at her eyes. "I'm sorry. I think my emotions are just raw tonight because of the unpleasantness of my day. And I didn't sleep well."

"Don't apologize. You've been dealt a number of emotional blows lately." *Not the least of which being me showing up in your life again.* He let the obvious go unstated. "You're allowed to be on edge." He paused as their drinks arrived, and he searched for a topic he knew would comfort her. "I saw a cat in a bookstore window the other day that reminded me of your old neighbor Mrs. Hooper's cranky old cat. What was its name? Whiffles or something."

Noelle's expression brightened, and her nose wrinkled as she thought. "It started with a P. Puffy… Puffles—"

"Puffin!"

She snapped her fingers and pointed at him. "Yes. Puffin. It was black and white, and Mrs. Hooper thought it looked like a puffin when she found it on the shoreline." She chuckled. "And it wasn't cranky toward me. I think she just didn't like men."

"Who? Mrs. Hooper or her cat?" he teased. "Because Mrs. Hooper always gave me the stink eye when I came home with you, too."

"She was just protective of me. She didn't want some Lothario taking advantage of me."

Eli barked a laugh. "She didn't know you well, then. You were way too confident and smart for anyone to take advantage of you."

"I appreciated her concern, just the same." She dropped her gaze, and her voice softened. "It's nice for someone to care."

He detected an odd note of despondency in her tone, but rather than quiz her about it, he lifted his glass. "To Mrs. Hooper and Puffin."

Noelle joined him in the toast, clinking her wineglass to his. "Where is this bookstore? I wasn't sure how long I'd be in town or how much free time I'd have. I may want to pick up some reading material if the ME delays the funeral much longer."

"I'll be sure to point it out on the way home. It's near your hostel."

After a short, awkward lull in the conversation, Eli asked Noelle about her life. Did she live near the UW campus? No. She lived in Bellevue now. Was she still in touch with any of her old professors or friends? A few. She still met her mentor, Professor Norris, for coffee from time to time.

"Do you remember Kathleen Block and her boyfriend Tim Allscert?" Noelle asked.

"Sure. We went to the Lady Gaga concert with them. Had weekend barbeques and very competitive volleyball games. Why?"

"I've stayed friends with them. They married and had two kids. I went to their daughter's baptism last month. They…asked about you."

"Oh." He smiled and nodded. "What did you say?"

"That we'd lost touch. They'll be interested to hear we ran into each other this way and caught up."

He selected a roll from the basket. "I liked them. Tim had a great sense of humor."

"He still does."

"That Gaga concert was something else, wasn't it?"

Noelle smiled and nodded. "The woman has some pipes on her, huh?"

"I particularly liked what we did after the concert." He peered at her over his glass as he sipped water, wondering if she'd recall that part of the date.

She paused in the middle of buttering a roll, angled her gaze to his. "The first night I slept with you."

"Mmm-hmm."

An endearing flush rose in her cheeks, and a sultry smile tugged her mouth. "That part was nice."

He cocked his head, feigning insult. "Just nice?"

Noelle rolled her eyes. "Very nice. Superb. Best I've ever had." She grew somber then and whispered, "Our lovemaking was never the problem between us."

His chest clenched at the abrupt shift in the conversation back to the raw topic. "I thought you said we weren't going to talk about our breakup."

Noelle turned to stare out the window at the marina lights. "I know. I—"

"But if we don't talk now, when will we talk about it? You're leaving town again in a few days. When am I going to have another chance to see you, get answers?"

She stiffened. "Was that why you agreed to dinner, if you didn't plan to answer my questions about the investigation? So you could corner me into talking about our breakup?"

He sighed. "No. I agreed to come because I've missed

you. I wanted to be with you. Maybe I even hoped we could…reconnect."

Noelle's dark brown eyes widened, bright with what he could only call alarm. She shook her head vehemently. "I can't go down that path again. It was hard enough getting over you the first time. If I let myself feel anything for you again—"

Eli fisted his hands in his lap. "It just…makes no sense to me, Noelle. If it was hard to get over me, if we had passion and shared interests and great sex, why would you throw that away? Why did you push me out? Was it something I did?"

She was silent for so long, her eyes misted with tears, he'd almost decided she was not going to answer. But finally, after several heartbreaking moments, she bit her bottom lip and raised her gaze to his. "No. You did nothing to deserve the pain I caused you. It was my family that did everything wrong."

Chapter Five

Eli opened his mouth and closed it again, clearly swallowing the burning questions that had to be bubbling inside him like magma, ready to erupt. Noelle respected his willpower, his ability to shove down the queries. But he was a man of integrity. He'd promised to let the topic rest during their dinner, and he would honor his promise.

"How about this?" she asked, reaching across the table to lay her hand on his. "Tomorrow or the next day, we can make a trade. You have questions about our breakup, and I have questions about my sister's murder. We'll meet somewhere quiet and swap information."

His brow dipped in consternation. "You're going to hold personal information about our relationship hostage if I don't give you classified intelligence on an active investigation? That's apples and oranges, Noelle. Not an even trade."

A pulse of heat spiked in her core. "When you put it that way, it sounds bad. I only meant we both want information…"

"I can't barter case information, Noelle."

She nodded, guilt plucking at her. "Of course not. Forget I asked."

"But…" His cheek dented, telling her he was biting the inside of his mouth.

She remembered from college this habit of his that told her he was deep in thought. Images of him from those earlier days flashed in her brain. Her chest knotted with bittersweet agony, and she sucked in a sharp breath.

"You mentioned before that you think your work in analytics could help us get a better overview of the case." Eli took a slow sip of his water. "How would that work?"

Noelle straightened in her chair, the first whispers of encouragement stirring in her since she'd arrived in Alaska. "It's really not as complicated as it sounds." She filled her tone with the enthusiasm for her job and the hope that she could offer something to the investigation. "I'll feed case data into the programs, at which point I can then break the information down statistically or create databases to search for commonalities or use for cross-reference. Tell me what would be most helpful, and I'll do my best to get the program to run that analysis for you."

He snorted and gave her a wry grin. "Any chance it can look at the case as a whole and spit out the name and address of the perpetrator? 'Cause that's what I need it to do."

Returning an enigmatic smile, she lifted her chin. "You never know until you try."

AFTER FINISHING THEIR MEAL, Eli had asked for a demonstration of Noelle's analytic programs. "I'm not promising anything regarding the Fiancée Killer case, but I am intrigued to see what you do for a living."

Noelle vacillated briefly. While she still wanted to avoid an overly intimate setting, she couldn't miss this opportunity to prove the value she could add to the investigation.

In the end, she had him follow her back to the hostel. As she set up her laptop, she tried not to think about the bed just feet away and how she'd tossed and turned the night before, her body aching for Eli and her mind replaying sensual encounters from their past. Summertime skinny-dipping. All-nighter studying that eventually evolved into sex at dawn. Dinners that turned into frisky food fights and creative uses for vanilla pudding and sugar sprinkles.

When the software was up and running, she cast a sly side glance at him. "The best way to show you the program's usefulness to you would be to input information from the case and let it run a simple algorithm."

He arched a dark eyebrow and gave a soft laugh. "You're right, of course." Turning up his palms, he stalked back toward the front door. "Fine. You've worn me down. I'll call you a hired consultant on the case, which means you're sworn to protect the information I share with you and keep the details confidential."

She lifted her chin, relieved to finally be getting what she wanted but also a tad hurt he'd felt the need to couch the access as he had. "You don't need to call me a consultant before you confide in me with the case information. Do you really not have any more faith in me than that?"

He sighed heavily, dipping his head as he stared at the floor. "Of course I trust you, but this satisfies the department's protocols."

"So why didn't you call me a consultant the first time I asked?"

His head came up, and the muscles in his jaw flexed and bunched. "Because your potential contribution to the case wasn't evident then. I can't grant every family member and inquisitive citizen special status on a whim." He flipped up his palm in query. "Why are you being prickly about this? You got what you wanted."

Why, indeed? She needed to rein in her turbulent emotions. She was already walking a thin line between professionalism and heartbreak with Eli. The only way she would survive this trip with her soul intact was to detach her emotions from her business. She only had to keep it together a few days, a couple weeks, and she could find closure with both Allison and Eli.

She exhaled a cleansing breath, sobered by the promise of putting the past firmly behind her at last. "You're right. I'm sorry. You're doing me a favor, and I'm being difficult. Forgive me."

He took a step nearer her and brushed a wisp of her hair back from her face. The tips of his fingers skimmed her cheek, and her pulse skittered. "Forgiven."

He lingered a moment too long. His gaze, the same startling blue of an Alaskan glacier, held hers, making her heart thump and a hum of longing stir deep inside her.

"Let me get my case files from the Jeep," he said at last. His timbre held a husky rasp that fanned the heat in her belly. "Be right back."

"So much for emotional distance," she muttered to herself as she returned to her laptop and opened the software. But then her body had a mind of its own, it seemed, when it came to Eli. How did she quash an attraction so strong that a simple touch or lingering look could turn her on so powerfully?

"Why couldn't the lead on the case have been some wrinkled, smelly, old man? Or a brash, icy woman?"

"What's that?" Eli asked, returning from his vehicle.

She chuckled awkwardly. "Just talking to myself. So what do you have?" She gestured to an empty spot where he could set his files as she slid her chair over to make room for him to pull another up beside her.

They huddled over the laptop, choosing bits of information that could be processed and organized in ways that might reveal patterns. The ages and physical description of the victims. Their level of education. Line of work. Home address. Frequently visited restaurants, stores, offices. Hobbies.

Noelle studied the data her program spit out, hoping some telling pattern or salient characteristic stood out.

"Hmm." Though thoughtful instead of sexual, Eli's low hum vibrated in her like a plucked guitar string.

Swallowing hard, she glanced at him and studied the furrow in his brow. "Do you see something new?"

"Not exactly, but it's interesting to look at things from a different angle, so to speak."

She found herself staring at the cut of his jaw and savoring the light scent of his aftershave. *Focus, Noelle. You're supposed to be helping. Show him the value you can offer the investigation.*

Turning back to the computer, she tapped a few keys. "We can analyze the raw data for a number of factors, even though our sample size is small." She hit Enter on the keyboard, and after a moment, the program displayed a number of graphs and charts. "Voilà!"

He nodded. "Impressive."

She studied the displayed information and pointed to the screen. "That's curious."

He leaned closer, squinting at the laptop. "Huh. All of the victims had dark brown hair and blue eyes."

"That's not a common combination." She pointed to the statistic the program had produced. "Most dark brunettes have brown or green eyes, statistically speaking. I don't remember the exact percentage, but my parents used to comment on how special Allison's blue eyes made her." She forcefully quelled the spike of envy that reared its head. "Here…" She clicked the mouse and called up new data. "We can cross-reference and get the exact—wow. According to this, fewer than ten percent of people with black hair have blue eyes."

Eli gave a wry grunt. "Guess that makes my family the exception to the rule. Most of us have dark brown or black hair and blue eyes."

A tingle raced through her as she met the blue eyes in question. "Really? The whole family? That's exceptionally rare."

"That's genetics," he said with a grin. "My parents both have blue eyes. And my uncle Ryan."

"So does this mean anything to you?" She waved a hand at the laptop screen, indicating the new statistical data.

"Well… I don't believe in coincidence. Clearly this connects the victims in a new way we hadn't recognized. I'll take this to the team in the morning, but in the meantime…" He pivoted on his chair to fully face her. "You've made your point. Your analytics could prove very useful in breaking the case. Well done."

Pleasure poured through Noelle, disproportionate to the small admission from Eli. Having his approval, knowing she had something to add to the case, seeing the light that came into his eyes, directed at her, soothed an ancient ache. The hurt predated Eli by many years but had contributed to their breakup and a different sort of pain in the years since college.

She'd found ways to compensate for her childhood wounds, had built a life and a career and a self-confidence to match the one she projected to the world, but…

Returning to Alaska, seeing Eli and dealing with her aunt had all contributed to unearthing the vulnerabilities of her past. Raw places she'd thought healed were scraped and bleeding again.

"Noelle? Are you okay?"

She shook herself from her morose tangent and forced a smile. "Just thinking about the case."

Eli looked unconvinced but clapped both hands on his thighs as he pushed his chair back and rose. "So, I'm going to provide you a copy of my whole case file and see what your magic little computer comes up with."

She cast him a side glance as she shut down the computer program. "It's not magic. It's math. Science. Facts rearranged and viewed in new light."

He took her hand and pulled her to her feet. In the close quarters of the chairs and desk, she ended up pressed against his body. "Call it what you will, but I want more."

She inhaled his pine scent and savored the hard planes and sculpted sinew of his body. The warmth he radiated both from his skin and his smile. *I want more, too.*

"Can you stop by the ABI office in the morning to pick up the files? Give me until at least ten. There's a lot of copying to do, even if that's just sending it all to a jump drive for you."

"Sure. That gives me time to do my yoga and go by that bookstore before I come in."

He drew back slightly and lifted an eyebrow. "You practice yoga?"

"Yeah. Have for some years. I love it."

"My brother Mitchell is dating a—what would you call her—a yogini?" He flapped a dismissive hand. "Anyway, Dove has a yoga studio in town. I'll give you the address if you want to take a class with her."

She shrugged. "Why not?"

Because the last thing you need is to become more entangled with Eli and his family before you leave town. Connecting with his family will only serve to remind you what you never had, with the chance that died with Allison.

Noelle curled her fingers into her palms. She really needed to find that pesky naysaying voice in her head a hobby. Maybe it could take up crochet?

"All righty then," Eli said, stretching his back and angling his chair to face her. "I did as I promised. Now it's your turn."

Noelle's pulse jumped. "What do you mean?"

"You promised you'd tell me what happened in college that changed your feelings about me."

ELI DRILLED NOELLE with an even stare, determined to get answers from her. He'd lived with questions and an aching heart for all these years, and he wasn't going to let this chance to find the truth get away.

Noelle dropped her gaze to her hands. "I told you, you were never the problem."

"Then what *was* the problem? You never gave me an answer better than you couldn't be with me." He tried, and likely failed, to keep his hurt and residual frustration out of his tone. "You said that we were too different, and it was better to end things as friends than drag out the inevitable bad ending."

She chewed her bottom lip and continued to avoid his eyes. "I know I was vague, but… I couldn't verbalize my reasons well. It was a gut feeling, a growing sense of doom."

"Doom? Isn't that a bit melodramatic? What differences did you think spelled disaster for us? I thought we were great together. We had a lot in common."

"Not the right things, though."

Eli sat again and folded his arms over his chest with a grunt. "We had the same tastes in music, books, food, movies. We shared the same politics and aspirations, the same quirky sense of humor, the same love of animals. I enjoyed being in nature and taking risks more than you did because of my family's business, but I never forced you to go paragliding or snowmobiling or fishing—"

"I know!" Her chest rose and fell in quick short breaths, a sure indicator of her distress. "I guess I thought you were too good to be true. The love you gave me was so new to me, so unexpected. I didn't know whether I could trust it. Whether I could depend on it."

"And what did I ever do to make you think you couldn't trust me or my feelings for you?"

The jangling notes of an incoming call on Eli's cell phone interrupted. Reluctantly, he checked the caller ID. Asher. Which meant it could be important. He sighed. "Sorry, I need to take this. Asher, what's up?"

"Potential new victim of the Fiancée Killer. Uniform on his regular beat found the body of a woman around the same age as our victims in an alley. I'm headed out now. Can you meet me there?"

Eli took down the address and promised he was on his way. As he shoved his phone back into his pocket, he looked over to Noelle. "I have to go, but…we're not through with this conversation."

She opened her mouth as if to argue, then closed it again. "I'm still coming to your office in the morning?"

"Yeah. I'll have the files ready." He headed to the front door but paused before crossing the floor back to her and capturing her face between his hands. He dropped a lingering kiss on her lips before backing away. "I enjoyed dinner,

Noelle. And for the record, I'm glad you're here. I'm sorry about Allison, but this reunion is many years overdue."

Noelle's heart was in her eyes as he backed toward the door. Longing, sorrow, and some undefined pain that he was determined to get to the root of before she left. Whatever ghosts haunted Noelle, he would find a way to vanquish them, if only to save her from the pain that clearly plagued her life.

Chapter Six

The next morning, Noelle found Dove St. James's yoga studio and joined a class. Dove, a tall woman with long auburn hair, welcomed her warmly. A prick of something Noelle refused to call jealousy needled her as she prepared for the class and watched Dove greet the other participants. Eli's brother had found a lovely girlfriend—the sort of woman the Colton family likely wanted Eli to find.

"You're from out of town, you said?" Dove asked, returning to her after finishing with the other ladies. "How did you find the studio?"

"My hostel is just down the way a bit." Noelle chose not to mention her connection to Eli. She didn't want to answer the inevitable questions.

We're not through with this conversation.

Noelle shoved aside the unfinished business with Eli and tried to clear her mind as she worked through a few warm-up stretches. She had to admit, the soothing scent of diffused essential oils and tranquil music Dove played during the class helped her relax more than if she'd gone through the motions by herself at the hostel.

She thanked Dove at the end of the class, promised she'd

be back, then went into the dressing room to change before heading to the ABI offices.

When she arrived at the ABI building an hour later, something big clearly had the staff busy and buzzing. The receptionist was on a phone call and held up a finger asking Noelle to wait. After a few minutes, Noelle called Eli directly from her cell phone.

"I'll be down in a moment. I'm wrapping up a meeting," he said.

She wandered across the lobby to the coffee pot, remembering that Scott Montgomery had claimed the lobby coffee was better than what was brewed in the offices. She'd just finished doctoring her java with creamer and sugar when Eli arrived from the stairs.

"Sorry for the wait. A patrol officer found a woman in an alley last night, and my team needed to look at the evidence in case she was a new victim of the Fiancée Killer."

Noelle gripped her coffee tighter, her stomach swirling. "And was she a new victim?"

Eli rubbed the back of his neck. "Probably not, it turns out, but we have to go over all the evidence." He hitched his head toward the stairs. "Come on. I have everything you need upstairs."

She followed him, casting her gaze around the office, knowing this space, these rooms, these people were a huge part of Eli's world now. She drank it in, wanting to fill in as many blanks about his life as she could. "How do you know this woman's not a new victim?"

He seemed ready to answer, then held up a finger. "Let's get in my office before we talk."

He led her through a door at the end of a long corridor and closed the door behind them. A man with light brown hair, beard and mustache glanced up from the desk across from Eli's. With a wag of his finger, Eli introduced Noelle to his partner, Asher Rafferty, and vice versa.

Asher rocked his swivel chair back and linked his hands behind his head. "I hear you're joining the investigation. You must have really dazzled Eli with your analytics skills."

"I'm not sure *dazzled* is the word," Eli said, "but I saw the merit of a fresh set of eyes and applying the unbiased perspective of latest technology to the case."

"I just want to help any way I can," Noelle said. Turning to Eli again, she said, "You were going to tell me about the woman found last night."

Eli motioned to the chair beside his desk, and she sat. "Right. Her age was what caught the patrol officer's attention. She was young and pretty like the other victims, but we think she died of a drug overdose. No sign of strangulation."

"No little black dress, no pose with her hand up, no diamond ring," Asher added.

The office door opened, and a familiar handsome face appeared. "I'm headed down to the morgue now to start the postmortem on—" Scott Montgomery spotted Noelle and stopped midsentence. "Oh sorry. I didn't know you had a visitor."

Eli waved the forensic specialist in. "It's okay. We're reading her in on the investigation as a consultant."

A curious wrinkle in his brow, Scott stepped into the office and closed the door behind him. "What kind of consultant?"

"Analytics," Noelle volunteered. "I use specialized computer software and statistics to look at data from any number of angles."

Scott sat on the corner of Asher's desk and folded his arms as he focused on her. "Interesting. What sort of things can your program tell us?"

Asher coughed in his hand. "Geek."

Noelle cast Eli's partner a glance. "What?"

Scott waved a dismissive hand. "Ignore him. He's just ragging on me because I love all kinds of science. Biology, computers, forensics… It all fascinates me. So you were saying about your program…?"

"Don't you have a body waiting in the morgue?" Eli cut in. "If Noelle's program comes up with anything relevant to your area of the investigation, we'll let you know."

"Yeah, vamoose!" Asher waved a file folder, swatting at the hip Scott had propped on Asher's desk. "City desk is waiting on your report on last night's Jane Doe."

Scott snorted and slid off the desk. "Spoilsports. It was just getting interesting in here." He nodded to Noelle. "Nice to see you again. Maybe we can get coffee and discuss your program some other time?"

She gave him a stiff smile. "Maybe."

Once Scott was gone, she turned back to Eli, who was frowning. "What?"

"He was flirting with you."

She wrinkled her nose. "No, he wasn't."

Asher scoffed. "He flirts all the time with Kansas, too. Drives me nuts."

"Why would that bother you?" Eli asked.

His partner shrugged. "No reason. Forget I said anything." Lifting a notepad, he deftly changed the subject. "We were talking about our latest Jane Doe."

Noelle sat taller, her interest engaged. "You were saying she doesn't fit the profile of the Fiancée Killer's other victims."

"Right. So just focus on what's here—" Eli unplugged a flash drive from his desktop and handed it to her "—and here." After rummaging through a stack of papers, he extracted a thick file. "Everything we've compiled on the case is in your hands now. Protect it. It's confidential for a reason."

She bobbed a nod. "Understood."

"How long do you think it will take your program to analyze all that material?" Asher asked.

"Not long, once I get it all fed in. It's transferring the data that will take a while." She stood. "Well, I'll let you get back to work." She hefted the massive paper file. "I have a full day ahead of myself, it seems."

Eli rose from his desk and escorted her back to the lobby. "Don't wait until you've gone through everything to report back. If you spot anything irregular or telling, call me immediately. Last night's Jane Doe may not have been one of the Fiancée Killer's victims, but he's still out there, and there's no telling when he might kill again."

BACK AT HER HOSTEL, Noelle set up a workstation on the tiny café table in the kitchenette. After brewing herself a cup of tea, she got to work, entering and double-checking the information in the files.

Though the input of data was tedious, she knew a sense of purpose. She was finally doing something useful while she waited for Allison's remains to be released. The notion that she could even help narrow the scope of the investigation and bring the killer to justice fueled her when her muscles grew achy from sitting in the hard chair. After hours of staring at the laptop screen, her sight blurred.

Deciding she needed a break and a meal, Noelle ventured out from her hostel around four that afternoon. Darkness was already gathering as she strolled the sidewalk down the quaint town street. Before long, she found the bookshop Eli must have been referring to at their dinner earlier in the week.

When she stepped inside, a tiny bell tinkled over the door, and a voice called from the back of the shop. "Hello! Please have a look around. I'll be right with you."

Noelle headed for the fiction shelves, admiring the stationery display and greeting cards as she passed them. Stopping at the end of the first shelf of novels, she was engrossed in the selection of books when she felt something brush her leg. Startled, she gasped as she glanced down to find a cat rubbing against her shin. "Well, hello, kitty."

She squatted to pat the feline, remembering that the cat was how the subject of the bookstore came up at dinner.

"Is Igor bothering you? I can put him in the backroom."

She stood, shaking loose fur from her fingers, to greet the woman who approached from the back of the shop. "Not at all. I love cats, but my current landlord doesn't allow pets. Igor was just convincing me it was time I moved to a more pet-friendly building."

"Well then, good job, Igor." The shop clerk smiled. "Can I help you find anything?"

"No, thanks. Just browsing."

The bell jangled again, and both the clerk and Noelle glanced toward the door. If Noelle hadn't already recognized the attractive brunette woman who breezed in, the store clerk's greeting confirmed the new arrival's identity.

"Hi there, Kansas! How can I help you? Are you ready for the next book in the *Outlander* series now?"

"Soon. I haven't had a lot of time to read lately, but I have some time coming around Christmas to curl up by the fire and dive in. I'm actually here for a birthday card.

The family is having a big dinner this weekend for Aunt Sasha's birthday, and I need a card to go with the scarf I got her." Kansas spotted Noelle, and her expression brightened. "Oh hi! Noelle, isn't it?"

Noelle returned a smile. "That's right. Good memory."

Kansas turned her attention to the card rack but said, "I hear you and Eli have been spending a good bit of time together since you got to town. In fact, a little bird at the ABI office says you're consulting on the investigation. Is that true?"

Noelle hesitated. How much did she want to divulge? Of course, Kansas was at least tangentially involved in the case as a member of the search and rescue team that had recovered the victims' bodies. "I'm running some data analysis for Eli, yes."

Kansas inhaled sharply, her expression saying she'd just had an inspiring thought. "Has Eli mentioned the family dinner this Sunday? It's Aunt Sasha's birthday, and the whole family is getting together. You should come! We'd love for you to join us as Eli's plus-one."

"Oh, uh…" Noelle squatted to pat the cat again as a means to stall. "He hasn't said anything, and I probably shouldn't impose—"

"Nonsense! When you have a hoard as big as the Coltons, what's one more? Come as my plus-one if not Eli's. It will be a great chance to meet the whole family at last!"

Noelle's heart stuck in her throat, and her voice fled. Her whole life, she'd wanted to be part of a big, happy, loving family like the Coltons, but she had no right to horn in on this gathering. She and Eli weren't an item, and she wasn't staying in Shelby more than a few days. She didn't want to give Kansas or any of the Coltons the wrong idea about her relationship with Eli. Especially not Eli.

When she didn't answer, Kansas flapped a hand toward her. "Don't worry. I'll talk to Eli about it and let Uncle Will know to count on one more. It'll be fine." She pulled a card from the rack, read it and walked to the counter to pay. "I'll take this one."

Noelle sighed and whispered to Igor the cat, "What have I gotten myself into?"

Chapter Seven

"I saw Noelle yesterday at Tattered Pages," Kansas said the next morning.

Eli looked up from his computer monitor to find his cousin leaning against the doorframe to his and Asher's office. "You did?"

"Mmm-hmm. I invited her to Aunt Sasha's party on Sunday. Honestly, I'm surprised you hadn't already." Though she didn't verbalize the question, the *why not?* hung in her tone and lifted eyebrow.

"Don't meddle," he said. "I know you're trying to play matchmaker and get us back together, but our history is… complicated. Even I don't understand all the factors that went into our breakup, and if you push her, you might scare her off."

Kansas frowned. "Okay. I hear you. But…how can you not know what happened in your own relationship? She had to have given you a reason for dumping you."

"You'd think, but what little she said doesn't hold water. I'm hoping to get to the truth while she's in town, but I won't if she starts feeling pressured and withdraws."

"But she's working on the case with you," Kansas said. "Doesn't that count for anything?"

"Who's doing what with who?" Scott Montgomery said, appearing behind Kansas in the corridor.

"The analytics lady you met earlier," Asher volunteered from his desk, his mouth pressed into a scowl. "You need something, Montgomery?"

"I was just bringing Kansas a cup of coffee," Scott returned tartly, then softening his tone, he handed Kansas the paper cup. "Just the way you like it."

"I think Kansas can get her own coffee if she wants it," Asher said with a growl in his tone.

"And I think I can speak for myself, Asher." Kansas turned from Asher and smiled awkwardly. "Oh, uh, thanks, Scott, but I've already had all I plan to drink this morning. Any more, and I'll be too jittery."

Scott tightened his jaw, clearly disappointed in Kansas's response, but he gave her a small smile as he turned to leave.

Eli followed the exchange, conscious that there was a growing tension in the office involving the trio. But just as he'd asked Kansas not to meddle in his affairs, he'd stay out of her work relationships. If the strain between his co-workers and Kansas interfered with the business of the office, he'd step in. But until that time, he'd let the three of them handle it their own way.

"Well, I better scoot. Things to do, you know?" Kansas said, giving Asher an odd lingering look as she left the office.

"Speaking of Noelle," Asher said.

"Were we?"

"Have you heard from her this morning? Wasn't she going to run her analysis yesterday?" Asher's chair squeaked as he turned the seat to face Eli.

"She started yesterday, yes. But she said it could take

some time to enter all the information and get all the different angles covered." Eli drummed his fingers on his desktop.

He was restless, eager to not only see what Noelle's analysis found but anticipating their next chance to see each other.

Kansas had poked a sore spot with him. He was frustrated by Noelle's dodging of his questions about their relationship, and he longed for the day when he could invite her to family events without any doubts or reservations of how she'd react.

"It's just that with the media coverage of the investigation, and the recent steady discovery of body after body, I'm concerned that our killer is going to either flee and move to another state to continue his killing…" Asher steepled his fingers and propped his elbows on the arms of his chair "…or he'll ramp up his spree, and we'll have more murdered women on our hands before we find this creep. It's been months. Why can't we break this case?"

"I'm as anxious to wrap this case up as you are, but we don't need to get sloppy in our haste."

"I hear you. I get it. And I know cases like this can take years to solve sometimes, but…" Asher sighed. "I just have this pit in my gut when I think about the women of the community who could be his next victims. I mean, how would you feel if your sister or Kansas were the guy's next victim?"

Eli's hand balled into a fist, and nausea sawed in his gut. "I'd want to eviscerate the guy, but that doesn't change the fact that we have to be methodical and precise in our investigation. We have to get every step right, so that when we catch him—*when*, not if—the court doesn't have any reason to throw the case out. We have to get things absolutely right."

SOMETHING WAS WRONG.

Noelle stared at the spreadsheet on her screen and double-checked that she'd entered all the variables correctly. She'd spent hours with the case files and documentation of forensic evidence, and her program was churning out consistently different results than Eli and his team came up with in key aspects of the investigation. She had to be missing something. She must have forgotten some piece of data, not accounted for some element of the forensic process or overlooked some detail of investigative case handling that would account for the discrepancies.

She sighed and gritted her teeth. She'd wanted to give Eli her findings today, but her eyes were so tired, they were virtually crossing. Fatigue didn't lend itself to careful and accurate work. Maybe she could just take a short nap. She'd been up late last night inputting data, then was back at the laptop early. She didn't function well on three hours of sleep.

Rubbing the kinks in her neck, she strolled to her kitchenette and fixed herself another cup of tea. Spotting an unopened yogurt on the counter, she realized she'd gotten so distracted by the case files this morning, she'd never eaten breakfast, either. Tossing the probably-now-spoiled yogurt in the trash, she grabbed the last banana from the small fruit basket she'd stocked earlier in the week and made a mental note to go shopping again. When she'd gotten groceries before, she hadn't thought she'd still be in town this long. Now it seemed it could be several more days before Allison's funeral happened and Noelle's part in helping Eli with the case was resolved. She refused to return to Seattle before she had closure on both matters.

And what about her past with Eli? Would she be able to find closure there? *All he wants is the truth. He deserves that.*

If only the truth weren't so painful, so…shameful. So humiliating.

Her cell phone rang, shaking her from her personal pity party, and she tensed. Expecting the call to be Eli, wanting an update, she checked the caller ID reluctantly. Instead, the funeral home's number glowed from her screen, and she answered, praying this meant the funeral could proceed.

"Ms. Harris, I just wanted to confirm the changes you've requested regarding the service for your sister." The man sounded rattled, distressed even.

Confused, Noelle rubbed her dry and tired eyes. "Changes? What changes?"

But it clicked, just as the funeral director began his explanation, "The change in burial site and memorial service location."

Anger flashed hot in her blood. "Were these changes, by any chance, requested by Clyde or Jean Gates?"

She heard the rustle of paper, a murmur of voices.

"Why, yes. Mrs. Jean Gates of Anchorage. She's here now, asking for these changes." The man's voice quavered with stress. Aunt Jean did that to people.

Noelle took a breath, striving for calm. "Please put all of my original plans back in force. Jean Gates is not authorized to make any alterations to the funeral. She's a disgruntled family member who has no legal authority in this matter."

"Oh I, uh…apologize. I wasn't aware." He cleared his throat. "Unfortunately, Mrs. Gates ripped up the contract you signed with us. In order to reinstate your funeral arrangements, we need you to come by the office and sign a new contract."

Despite her irritation with Aunt Jean, Noelle felt sorry

for the funeral home owner. She could hear her aunt in the background, arguing vociferously.

"Can't you email me a link to sign electronically?" Noelle asked, realizing almost as soon as the words left her mouth what the answer would be. When she'd been at the family-run funeral home last week making the initial arrangements, the owner, an elderly gentleman, had handwritten everything in their meeting, and the only computer she remembered seeing was a clunky desktop with a huge monitor that looked like it had been on the office desk since the 1990s. She wondered if they even had an internet connection.

When the funeral director confirmed her suspicion that she would, in fact, have to drive out to the funeral home again, she saved the work she was doing on her laptop and promised to be there before he closed the office that afternoon. She grumbled to herself as she gathered her coat, purse and gloves and swapped her comfy slippers for boots.

The winter sun was already low in the sky as she climbed in her rental car and backed out of her hostel's parking spot. She set the car's GPS navigator with the funeral home's address, letting her thoughts drift as she drove.

While she'd known returning to Alaska would bring a harsh reminder of all she'd escaped when she left for college, she hated having to deal with Aunt Jean on top of the painful reunion with Eli. Going back to her lonely apartment in Seattle and her routine fact-crunching job was starting to sound pretty good—if not for the tiny detail of how much she'd miss Eli.

Eli.

When Noelle returned from her errand, she'd have to notify Eli of the perplexing inconsistencies she was finding with her analysis. How would he take the news that she'd found glaring problems with the case data?

She sighed as she pulled onto the two-lane highway that bypassed the busiest parts of Shelby and was far more scenic. She turned on her headlights as she entered a stretch of road that was shaded on both sides by tall pines. The road grew curvier as it passed through the foothills of the nearby mountain range, and she tapped her brakes to slow the car before navigating an especially tight turn.

The brake pedal felt mushy to her, giving little resistance, and the car didn't slow nearly as much as it should have. Her pulse spiked as the rental car took the curve too fast, and she drifted into the oncoming traffic lane. Trembling with the rush of adrenaline, Noelle stepped on the brakes again, heard a squealing sound from under the hood. She gasped as the pedal went all the way to the floor without the car slowing.

Noelle's breath came in short, shallow pants as she grasped the danger she was in, speeding around mountainous curves and down hills without any way to stop or slow the car. Her hands sweated inside her gloves as she squeezed the steering wheel tighter. She continued to stomp the brakes, despite the lack of response. The twin beams of her headlamps lit only a few dozen feet in front of her, giving her little warning of what turns or obstacles lay ahead.

Could she use her parking brake to slow the car? Grasping the stick lever of the emergency brake, she pulled it up slowly. Her efforts earned her a grinding noise and a hot smell, but the rental car did seem to be slowing. She'd just released a sigh of relief when an elk doe stepped into the road from the shadowy shoulder.

With a shriek of surprise and dread, Noelle cut the wheel hard to the right, and the rental car bumped off the road.

In quick succession, the headlights illuminated dirty snow drifts, weeds and a thatch of seedlings before a large pine trunk loomed before her. Instinctively, she braced her arms against the steering wheel. The airbag exploded, dousing her with powder as it smacked her in the face and chest.

For several seconds, Noelle only sat in stunned silence. She took a slow and careful inventory of her physical condition, her unexpected situation and her isolated location. She coughed as her frantic breathing led her to choke on the fine dust from the airbag. In her ears, she heard the thumping of her heartbeat. Her nose ached, but when she felt the length of it, she didn't think it was broken. She'd bitten her tongue, though, she realized, tasting the metallic flavor of blood.

The rental car was going nowhere without a tow truck, and she gritted her teeth in anger for the rental company having loaned her a faulty vehicle. She added Aunt Jean to the list for her grievances. If Jean hadn't messed with her funeral plans, she wouldn't have been out on this dark road in the first place. While she was at it, she grumbled mentally over the Luddite funeral home that didn't have the means to sign paperwork electronically.

Then tears pricked her eyes, and she wallowed for a moment in pity. She felt so alone. Why had she bothered to come to Alaska at all? Did she really think that Allison would have gone to this much trouble had their situations been reversed? If Noelle had been murdered, Allison likely wouldn't have even attended her sister's funeral. The relationship had always been lopsided that way. Noelle had tried to love her sister, but only received lukewarm sentiment in return.

Only Eli had ever matched her depth of emotion…

A stinging pang slashed through her chest, and she

quickly shut down that line of thought. Wiping her face with trembling hands, she reached for her purse, which had landed on the floor of the passenger side. She fumbled out her cell phone, praying she had reception here. And groaned when she found she didn't.

Fortunately, another car came along ten minutes later and picked her up. She rode with the middle-aged woman and her three children back into the business district of town where, after Noelle refused to go to the ER as a precaution, the woman dropped her off at the car rental office.

The car rental company was in the process of closing for the day, but when they learned what happened to Noelle, the manager stayed late to help her. He set her up with an upgraded replacement vehicle at no charge and dispatched a tow truck to recover the wrecked sedan, all while repeatedly apologizing and asking after her health. The rental manager was so obsequious, Noelle grew awkward with his fawning.

"I can't imagine how this happened," he said, handing her the paperwork for the new vehicle. "We are meticulous in inspecting every vehicle and staying up to date on all maintenance. Our mechanic checks all of the cars routinely. He's not sloppy. I just don't understand. I'm so sorry! Can I get you anything else? Some water or coffee?"

"Just the replacement car, please. I'm not injured. Only rattled, and I want to get home and soak in a hot bath." Her muscles would be plenty stiff tomorrow she was sure, hot soak or not.

"Of course." He took the keys from a hook on the wall and handed them to her. "The white Chrysler out front."

Noelle accepted the keys and headed for the door, pausing when a thought came to her. "When your mechanic has the wrecked car back and has determined why the brakes failed, will you call me with his diagnosis?"

The manager hesitated a moment before nodding. "Yes, ma'am. I will."

Noelle sat in the front seat of the new vehicle, familiarizing herself with all the knobs, screens and switches to operate the car. She pulled out her phone to call the funeral home and tell the director she would not be able to make it tonight but would try again first thing in the morning.

She debated calling Eli to tell him what had happened but discarded the idea. He was already loaded with responsibilities and worries due to the serial killer case. Since she was, except for a sore nose and some muscle aches, no worse for the wear, she would spare him the news. As it was, she had to tell him about the strange inconsistencies she was uncovering in his case files. One bad news bomb was enough.

Once she'd driven back to the hostel, she filled her bathtub with the hottest water she could stand and climbed in to soak. She tried to relax, to regroup, but the terrifying moments before the car crashed left her edgy. The knowledge her aunt was undermining her with Allison's final arrangements and the disturbing results of her initial analysis of the Fiancée Killer files paraded through her brain, leaving her more tense and achy than before the bath.

She found much the same that night when, even after taking an over-the-counter pain medicine for her body aches, she lay awake and restless for hours. Finally, fed up with her insomnia, Noelle got up and crept back to the makeshift desk where she'd left her laptop. If she was awake, she might as well work. Maybe she'd figure out why her results were so skewed. Before she alerted Eli to the strange results she'd gotten in her first run of the data, she wanted to double-check her work, try new calculations and confirm everything.

If she was going to turn his investigation upside down, she darn well wanted to be sure of her facts.

TWO DAYS LATER, Eli was deep in the weeds of record-keeping and witness reports when his cell phone rang. He rubbed both eyes with the heel of his hands, attempting to ease the fatigue of tedium before he answered. His pulse jumped when he saw Noelle's number.

"Have you got something for me?" he asked without preamble.

After a beat of silence that felt heavy, Noelle said, "Do you think I could come by your house for a while?"

He detected a strange quality to her voice. Was this a booty call? His blood heated at the thought, and he had to consciously calm himself. "I can't right now, Noelle. I'm at work until at least five."

"I'm aware. But this is…important. *Very important.*"

The emphasis she put on the words rang alarm bells. He started saving files on his computer and closing up things at his desk for the day. "All right then. I'll meet you there as soon as I can."

He was already shoving back his desk chair by the time he disconnected. "I'm going out," he called to Asher. "Not sure if I'll be back tonight."

"What's up? Should I come with you?" Asher asked.

Eli waved him off. "No. I don't think so, but I'll ring if it turns out I need backup."

"Backup?" Scott asked, strolling in with a cup of coffee in one hand and a file in his other. "What's happened? Another body?"

Eli brushed past the forensics specialist and shook his head. "No. Personal business."

As he pulled on his coat and hurried out of the office, he heard Scott ask, "What sort of personal business requires your backup?"

"I don't know," Asher said, "and mind your own."

A weak winter sun peeked through the clouds as Eli rushed to his Jeep. At 3:30 in the afternoon, the sun was already low in the sky, approaching sunset. The long nights and cold winds from the bay added a gloom to the season that wouldn't release its hold until spring.

Traffic was light, and he made his way home in record time. His mind taunted him with all manner of disaster as he drove—from plumbing backups at her hostel to a hostile visit from her aunt to the Fiancée Killer having detected her work on the case and tracked her down.

By the time he arrived at his house, she was already in his driveway. His heart drummed double time as he climbed out and rushed to her. Taking her by both arms, he drew her against his chest, thankful she seemed physically unharmed. She grunted as he hugged her, and he tried not to let her odd response to his embrace bug him. Was all physical contact between them off the table? He'd thought they were reconnecting at least as friends.

A large messenger bag slid from her shoulder, and she backed away from him and grabbed the strap before the bag could hit the ground.

"Thanks for coming so quickly," she said, avoiding his eyes. She seemed unhurried, stiff as they moved inside.

"Of course I came. You said there was an emergency."

Noelle wrinkled her nose, and he noticed dark smudges like bruises under her eyes. "No, I didn't. I said it was important."

"But you sounded—" He rubbed his temple and tried again. "Just…tell me what's wrong."

"I'd rather show you." She crooked a finger and strolled to his kitchen table. She opened the messenger bag and pulled out her laptop and a few paper files. He offered her a drink while she set up her makeshift desk, but she declined. She woke her laptop and clicked through a series of screens with charts, maps, spreadsheets and graphs. "I've spent the last three days inputting all the information in the files you gave me on the Fiancée Killer crime scenes and the condition of the women's bodies."

"Okay. And?"

"And it doesn't add up."

He flashed a wry grin. "I could have told you that. If it added up, we'd have found our killer and arrested him by now."

She shook her head and angled a stern look at him. "What I mean is, the information in the files is…wrong."

Chapter Eight

Irritation plucked at Eli as he absorbed Noelle's assessment. "Oh really? And you're basing this on all of your personal experience in criminal investigations."

She lifted a calming hand. "Don't get testy."

"Those files are based on expert witness testimony, missing person reports, the latest investigative technology and—"

"Eli! Listen to me." She scowled and grabbed his sleeve to quiet him. "I'm not questioning your expertise or skills as an investigator. But somewhere along the way, some data got…" She hesitated, clearly looking for a word that wouldn't set him off.

"Got what?"

She groaned. "Let me just show you." She opened a spreadsheet and pointed to the screen. "This is the file where I input all the data from your case files. You can double-check it, but I've gone over it three times to make sure I didn't input anything incorrectly." She closed that screen and opened another program. "In this file, I have all the data Scott Montgomery included. His report details information on the relevant parameters and contributing conditions that factored into his determination of how, where and when the victims were killed. His determinations were based on degree of decomposition, evidence of insect, bacteria and wildlife damage, temperature, environmental conditions such as sun or shade at the crime scene, soil or rock, moisture—"

"Yeah, I'm familiar with the things that go into his forensic analysis."

"Right. Well, so that is all here..." she pointed to the screen "...as well as dates and locations gathered through interviews with the victims' families about when they went missing, where they were last seen..." She glanced up at him, and his face must have reflected impatience, because she waved a hand, saying, "Et cetera."

Eli saw that her explanation could take a while, so he dragged a chair over to sit beside her. She scooted aside, so he had a better view of her screen. "I researched how forensic data is compiled and the rates of decomposition. There are calculators for that sort of thing available online and through professional journals. Did you know that?"

"Are you saying the average layman could do the job we're paying Scott Montgomery to do?" Eli asked wryly.

"No. I'm not. In fact, I called experts in Seattle, both at our alma mater and the Seattle medical examiner's office, for explanations of some of the process. I also asked them to look at the data and results I got to see if my conclusions were sound."

Eli shifted uneasily on the hard chair. "And what conclusions did you come to?"

She took a breath, nibbling her bottom lip nervously. "Well, I wanted to be absolutely sure I had the data that could be easily verified correct first."

Her extensive preamble told him she was building up to a bombshell and wanted to buoy the veracity of her findings. Eli could feel his body drawing tighter, coiling as if bracing for an attack.

"I used official weather bureau historical records regarding daily temperature, humidity and rainfall and compared it to what your guy used to make his calculations." She paused and gave him a disconcerted glance. "Eli, when I ran the numbers, Scott Montgomery's data was consistently off by more than ten percent."

"What?" Eli shot her a dubious look. "You're sure?"

"I'm sure. You understand that amount of variation will throw off calculations significantly, right?"

"I do. But Scott's usually so precise. I don't get it."

Her expression darkened further. "The experts I consulted also found discrepancies in other areas relevant to determining when the women were killed. I can show you the details of the science if you want, but when I input the new information from the forensic specialists in Seattle, my analysis program and the Seattle experts' both came up with far different results than Scott did. His estimations concerning the length of time since death for all of the bodies was off across the board."

"But that makes no sense. Scott knows what he's doing. He's never been wrong before." Eli leaned closer to stare at the jumble of data that could have been in German for all the sense the statistics and detailed charts made for him.

"And..."

Eli's gut clenched. "And? You mean there's more?"

She nodded. "The experts asked why critical information from the more recently killed victims didn't contain more detailed information about fingernail scrapings or inconsistent hairs or carpet fibers found on the victims, the sorts of things that can help identify the perpetrator were missing or incomplete."

Eli ran a hand over his mouth, dredging up conversations in task force meetings and how Scott had explained his findings. "When we asked him about that, Scott said he hadn't found any such evidence. We wrote it off as the killer knowing what he was doing and taking pains to leave a clean crime scene."

"Well, that may be true. But the experts found it suspicious." Noelle's returned frown echoed his concern. Fueled his suspicions. "Anyway, I knew this was big. That's why I had my contacts in Seattle double-check everything in my work, and they agreed. Scott's work is significantly flawed. But also *uniformly* flawed. The incorrect data was consistently off by a specific measure. Possibly to make the discrepancy harder to spot than a single outlier."

Eli flopped back in the wooden chair and scrubbed both hands on his face. "Were any of Scott's analyses *right*? Have we been on a complete goose chase? Did the experts you talked to—and I'm going to need their phone numbers, so I can interview them myself," he added, wiggling a finger in her direction, "did they agree with strangulation as the cause of death, for example?"

"Yes. Mechanical asphyxia is the term they used, but you can see here..." she pulled up a document and pointed to the laptop screen "...they mention strangulation when they refer to the damage to the hyoid bone."

"Well, that's something anyway." Eli shoved out of the chair and stalked the room like a caged tiger. "If we accuse Scott of negligence or, worse, malfeasance, every case he ever worked for us would suddenly be subject to review. It's a huge can of worms to be opening, Noelle."

"I get that. But there's another issue I don't think you've grasped yet."

Eli swung back to face her. "Go on."

"What I found wasn't one careless error. It was a systematic misrepresentation of easily verifiable data. The glaring omissions all fell under the same category. The pattern of errors indicates he did it on purpose. The question we should be asking is why?"

A chill ran through Eli. "You think he was intentionally throwing off the investigation?"

Noelle raised her hands, her expression regretful. "From my outside perspective, that's how it looks. Dr. Chou in Seattle suggested as much as well and threatened to call the FBI. I asked him to hold off until I spoke to you. I knew you weren't party to any fraud or malfeasance, so…" Noelle sighed heavily. "I asked him to give you and the ABI a chance to sort it out, for the sake of your ongoing investigation and the department's reputation."

Gratitude poured through him that she'd asked for a reprieve, for time for his office to sort this mess out. In the bigger picture of Scott's miscalculations, Eli didn't miss her statement of faith in his own integrity as a law enforcement officer. Was that belief in him enough to build a foundation for their future? He filed away the gift she'd given him, unwilling to let the ugliness of Scott's apparent errors—perhaps even corruption—defile the sweetness of her professed trust.

"I need to talk to Asher, but not at work. I need him to come here. I don't want to risk anyone overhearing this discussion at the office. We have to proceed carefully." The weight of her discovery settled on his shoulders and in his gut like sacks of sand.

Was it possible Montgomery had tampered with the investigation? To what end? Was he covering for someone? Could he have simply made a consistent error throughout his calculations? The notion of his colleague being so sloppy with his work was disheartening. But the idea that Scott misrepresented his work intentionally was…sickening. Infuriating.

Eli stumbled into his living room and dropped heavily onto the couch, growling his frustration.

Noelle crossed the room to sit next to him. "I'm sorry, Eli. I know this is upsetting to you, and that was the last thing I wanted when I offered to help. I wanted to ameliorate the stress you were under, not add to it. I thought my analysis would pinpoint answers or support evidence. Instead, I've all but torn the case apart."

"Don't apologize." He angled his body to face her, sliding a hand beneath her hair to cup her cheek. "If you're right—and I'm not questioning your work. I'm just saying I want to look into it more myself before we do anything drastic that we can't undo," he amended quickly when he felt her tense beneath his fingers, "then you've shined a light on a truth that needed to be exposed. Our priority is finding the truth, no matter where it leads, bringing the killer to justice and giving the victims' families closure."

"That's what I want, too. I just wish my efforts didn't hurt you in the process."

He stroked her jawline with his thumb. "Thanks for that. And for all your hard work. It sounds like you've spent hours on this."

She pulled a half grin. "I've spent a few late nights and missed a few lunches working on it. But I don't regret it. Not if it proves useful."

Focusing again on the dark smudges under her eyes, Eli touched them lightly with one finger. "Are these…bruises?"

Her eyes closed as she winced. "Probably."

He sat up straighter. "What happened?"

"I…had an accident." She lifted a dismissive shrug. "Hit my nose. I'll be fine."

His phone rang before he could question her further about her injury, and he reluctantly leaned back from her to take the call. Seeing Asher's name on his screen, he answered with, "I was just about to call you. What's up?"

"Nothing really. But before I headed home and got in the shower, I wanted to make sure you don't need me. You mentioned backup before…"

"Right. Well, it turned out to be a different sort of emergency. Get your shower and a meal, then come by my place later to talk."

"It won't keep until morning at the office?" Asher asked.

"No. It won't. Let's say eight? I have a few other calls to make before we talk."

"You going to tell me what this mysterious heart-to-heart is about?"

Eli exhaled his frustration. "The investigation. But I'd rather not say more until we meet."

Once Eli disconnected the call, he turned back to Noelle. "You better give me a detailed rundown on your analysis." He checked the time. "But first I want to try to catch your experts in the office. You have their phone numbers handy?"

Chapter Nine

Three hours later, after speaking to both forensic experts in Seattle and taking a deeper dive into the statistics and charts Noelle pulled up for him, Eli was convinced the pattern of incorrect information throughout Montgomery's work was no accident. He kneaded the tense muscles in his neck as he leaned back in his chair.

Noelle, who'd been milling about the kitchen, making them sandwiches for dinner and randomly tidying to keep busy while he perused her data, stepped up behind him and bumped his hands out of the way. She rubbed his shoulders and neck and applied direct pressure to spots that were especially knotted with tension.

The warmth of her hands and relaxing massage worked magic on him. He felt a catharsis and release of the stress he'd been harboring while at the same time growing keenly aroused by the erotic manipulation of her hands. Shoving the files aside, he turned in the kitchen chair and drew her into his lap.

Noelle gave a feeble protest which he quieted with a kiss.

"I made us a little dinner. Are you hungry?" she asked, her voice breathless enough that the question sounded like a sexy invitation.

"Not for food," he said, capturing the back of her head and kissing her again.

Noelle draped her arms around his neck, twisting her lips into a lusty grin. "I think I have what you need."

Eli groaned his pleasure as he rose from the chair with Noelle in his arms and carried her to the nearest flat surface. Laying her down on the couch, he covered her body with his own and plundered her mouth. His tongue dueled with hers, and his hands tugged at her clothes. Years of pent-up desire and longing were unleashed as they touched and nibbled and explored each other.

"I want to make love to you, Noelle. But not unless you're sure it's what you want, too." He levered up on one arm to peer directly into her soulful brown eyes. "I moved on with my life after college, but I never stopped wanting you."

NOELLE'S BREATH STUCK in her lungs. Desire had her body humming and left her mind a muddle. She still clung to enough of her senses to realize Eli had said he'd wanted her, not that he'd loved her. For a moment, she knew the sting of disappointment. A too-familiar pain swelled in her chest.

Unloved. A complication. A burden.

A mistake.

The word she'd heard her mother use echoed hollowly inside her.

When Eli brushed his fingers through her hair and narrowed an inquiring look on her, she realized she'd never answered him. "Oh. I, uh…"

This works well for you, a part of her brain justified. *You can satisfy your hunger for him, perhaps even work him out of your system for good and leave town again without entanglements. If he doesn't love you, you won't break his heart again when you go.*

Noelle forcibly dismissed the whisper that argued, *And what about breaking your own heart?*

Fisting her fingers in his hair, she drew greedily on his mouth, then whispered, "I'm a big girl, Eli. I know what I want and can take care of myself."

A frown flickered across his face, but she didn't let herself think too hard about the reason behind it. After toeing off her shoes, she stroked her foot down his jean-clad leg, before encouraging him to continue by raising her hips to meet his.

His shirt came off, then hers. Hands stroked, lips searched and sampled, and the heat rose quickly in her blood.

Eli had just unhooked her bra when a loud knock sounded on his front door. They both froze like high school kids discovered necking in a parent's car.

"Are you expecting someone?" she whispered.

"No. I told Asher to come at eight. If that's him pushing things earlier, I swear I'll…" He didn't finish the threat as another knock pounded on his door.

Scrambling to right his clothes, Eli headed for the door, hesitating only long enough for her to restore her bra and shirt as well.

An attractive young couple, their arms around each other, waited on Eli's front porch when he opened the door.

"Took you long enough," the man with shaggy brown hair said, pushing past Eli without a verbal invitation to enter. His gaze took in Eli's rumpled hair and clothes as he ushered the blonde with him inside. "Were you asleep?"

"Um, no. Why—?"

The couple pulled up short when they spotted Noelle

sitting on the couch, finger combing her hair. She knew her lips were swollen and that she'd missed a button when fastening her blouse. *Busted.*

"Oh hello." The blonde glanced from Noelle to Eli to her partner. "We didn't know you had company. I'm sorry."

Eli dismissed the woman's concerns with a flick of his hand. "You're not interrupting anything. I was just, uh, discussing the Fiancée Killer case with Noelle. Her sister was one of the victims, and she, um, wanted a briefing."

"A briefing? Is that what the kids are calling it these days?" The shaggy-haired man's eyes twinkled with mischief.

Eli rolled his eyes and punched the guy's arm lightly. "Don't be crude, man." Motioning with his hand, Eli introduced the couple, his younger brother Parker and Parker's girlfriend, Genna. "So, you had a reason for stopping by I assume?"

Instead of answering his brother's question, Parker sent Noelle a curious look, much like the one Kansas had given her when they met earlier in the week. Noelle braced herself for the connection and suppositions. For subsequent necessary explanations. For judgments.

When Parker remained silent for several seconds, Genna answered, "We're taking a quick trip up north to check conditions before a group from Boston arrives to go snowmobiling and cross-country skiing. We want to go now so we don't miss your mom's party this weekend." She divided a glance between Parker and Noelle, her brow creasing as she elbowed Parker. Returning her attention to Eli, Genna said, "Anyway, I left my snowshoes in Hetty's plane, and she's out on a trip at the moment, so I was hoping I could borrow yours?"

"Um, yeah. I'll go dig them out of my closet." Eli started

to leave but noticed his brother still staring at Noelle. "Parker? If you have something to say, just say it."

Parker slanted a sly grin at his brother. "No. Nothing. But I am glad you took my advice."

"Advice?" Genna sent Parker a querying look.

"Likewise, brother," Eli said before turning to Genna. "A couple months back Parker and I had a conversation about…not missing opportunities."

Genna glanced at Noelle. "Do you have any idea what they're talking about?"

Noelle lifted her shoulders. "None."

Parker motioned for Eli to hurry. "You were getting the snowshoes? We have a few more errands to run and have to arrange a plane that can leave at first light tomorrow." He smirked. "And we want to let you get back to what you were doing."

Noelle felt the heat that stung her cheeks, and she self-consciously smoothed a hand over her misbuttoned blouse.

Eli sent his brother a withering look as he headed down the hall to his bedroom.

"So…your sister was one of the women killed by the creep Eli is looking for?" Parker asked, his tone sympathetic. "I'm so sorry. I hate that we're meeting under these circumstances, but I'm glad to finally make your acquaintance."

Genna blinked and glanced at Noelle. "What am I missing?"

"Noelle and Eli dated in college. They were pretty serious to hear Eli tell it. But the family never got the chance to meet her before they went their separate ways after graduation."

"Oh," Genna said, then, "Oh!" as if suddenly remembering who Noelle was. A pink flush rose in her cheeks as she flashed an embarrassed grin and schooled her reaction. "Yes, it's nice to meet you, Noelle. I hope we'll be seeing more of you in the future." Genna's tone put a period at the end of the sentence, but a lift of her eyebrows made it a question.

"I don't know. I only plan to be in town until my sister's funeral, but that's on hold until the medical examiner releases her body."

Parker and Genna exchanged a look Noelle couldn't interpret, and she fumbled for a way to change the topic.

"Has Eli asked you to our mom's party?" Parker asked.

"Um, no. Kansas has, but I don't think—"

Parker snorted. "What is wrong with my brother? Of course you're invited. I'll talk to him."

"You don't have to—I mean, I appreciate the invitation, but…" Desperate for a way to change the subject, Noelle started to ask why they weren't driving to their destination, then caught herself. Had she really been gone from Alaska that long? The sheer size of the state and vast wilderness without any roads meant getting to remote areas required small planes, often seaplanes that landed in lakes or on rivers. What few roads there were often required long roundabout trips around mountain ranges to get from point A to point B.

Fortunately, Eli returned a moment later, carrying his snowshoes with him. "Glad someone can get some use out of them. Until I wrap up this case, I don't see myself getting away anywhere for recreation."

"Except Sasha's party, you mean?" Genna asked. "We've invited Noelle to come, so you two work out the details, okay?"

Parker leaned close to his brother and muttered something like "finishing what he started" under his breath, his grin wickedly teasing.

Eli sighed and opened the front door. "Don't you have to be going now?"

Parker laughed and gave his big brother a hug on the way out. Genna, too, stopped for an embrace and a cheek kiss. "Thank you, Eli. We'll bring them back in a couple days." Turning to Noelle, she waved and called, "Nice to meet you, Noelle."

Noelle returned a wave as the door closed behind the couple.

Eli faced her and groaned. "Sorry about that. I hope they didn't put you on the spot while I was out of the room."

"You mean any more than we already did looking like this?" She waved a hand to her buttons and ran her fingers through her hair.

Eli skewed his face with mortification. "I haven't heard the end of this. Parker will pull this out to embarrass me at family dinners for years to come."

Noelle noticed he didn't mention the upcoming party, and her chest squeezed. Was there a reason he hadn't invited her before now? And since the subject had come up with Parker and Genna, why wasn't he asking her now? Noelle had to battle down a swell of hurt. Was her relationship with Eli amusing to the family? She wanted to believe he meant the fact that Parker had interrupted their interlude, but old demons whispered that she might be the source of the awkwardness.

Did his family have a problem with Eli dating a woman of Korean descent? Was there another reason Eli seemed reluctant to introduce her to the whole family?

She swung away from him, struggling to keep her composure. How many times had she fretted over these questions in college? Eli's family was so important to him, such a big part of his life. How could she ever fit in? Even if race weren't a part of the equation, she didn't have warm familial experiences as any sort of reference. She was terrified that once the Coltons met her, she'd prove a disappointment somehow. That she'd embarrass Eli or cause dissension in the family in some way, because that was all she knew of family life. Rejection. Regret. Isolation.

Eli moved up behind her and wrapped his arms around her, kissing the side of her neck. "Now where were we?"

She wiggled free and buttoned her blouse correctly, tucking the tail in her slacks. "Maybe it's a good thing Parker and Genna stopped by when he did. They saved us from making a mistake we'd regret."

"A mistake?" He sounded truly stunned by her assessment, and she pivoted to face him, frowning.

"Yes, a mistake. I'm only in town for a few days, and sex between us would be fraught with all kinds of emotional baggage. We'd be foolish to open old wounds like that."

He lowered himself slowly to the couch. "Emotional baggage," he mumbled and bit the inside of his cheek. Then glancing up at her, he firmed his jaw. "The night we went to the Cove for dinner, you agreed to answer my questions about why you shut me out after college if I shared case information with you."

Her gut swooped, and her mouth dried.

"I found a way to legitimately include you in the investigation. I've given you access to confidential files in the name of finding the killer. Now it's your turn to make good on our deal."

Noelle rubbed her hands on her slacks and moved across the room. If only the physical distance were enough to re-establish the emotional distance she'd once created.

Or had she? Seeing Eli again, the speed with which she'd fallen back under the spell of his blue eyes, his intoxicating kisses, his magnetism would say she'd never gotten over him the way she pretended. Maybe all she'd ever done was bury her feelings, hide from the truth, fool her heart into believing she could find happiness without him.

But had she been happy these past many years?

Content, maybe. But she'd had no interest in dating anyone else. She'd not wanted second best. She'd searched for ways to fill the hole in her life by reading romances, learning yoga, working overtime. All of her attempts helped, in their own way, yet the empty ache remained.

"Is it smart to start this conversation when Asher is due here in a little while? Maybe we should wait until—"

"Noelle." Eli's tone stopped her. "I deserve answers, and I want them. Now."

Chapter Ten

Noelle took a deep breath as if fortifying herself for a giant task. Her unease with this conversation pooled anxiety in Eli's gut as well. Did he want the truth? Was there some dark story? Another man? A life-threatening illness?

He fisted his hands, bracing for what was coming, expecting a sucker punch and tensing his abs to receive the blow.

"You're right," she said, her chin bowed to her chest, her fingers tangling nervously. "Like I said before, it was never your fault. Truly. I just…" She turned to stare out his window at the November darkness. "I was scared."

"Of what?"

"More of what I already knew."

"What does that mean? Wasn't I good to you?"

"Not you. My family."

Eli huffed in frustration. "Noelle, come sit by me. I don't want to talk to your back."

She turned, and when he saw the glimmer of tears on her cheeks, his heartbeat stilled. Softening his tone, he patted the cushion next to him and murmured, "Please, sweetheart. Come here."

Her shoulders slumped, but she finally joined him on

the sofa. He placed a hand on her knee and nodded once. "Okay, go on."

"Geez, where to start?" She wiped her cheeks and lifted her gaze to his. "You saw how hostile my aunt was toward me. She doesn't want me to inherit, doesn't want me to have a say in Allison's burial, because she doesn't accept me as real family."

"Because you were adopted?" he ventured.

"Right. Thing is, my mother and father tried for years to have a child. When they couldn't, they adopted me. I was six years old, not the baby they wanted, but I was the first child that came available through the agency they were using."

"What happened to your biological parents? Where did you live before you were adopted?"

She lifted one shoulder and pulled a tissue from her pocket to blow her nose. "I never knew my real parents. I was told I lived with my biological grandmother for a couple years, but I was too much for her to handle apparently. She turned me over to the orphanage. My earliest memory is of crying and clinging to an older woman, who turned her back and walked away, leaving me with a stern lady at the children's home."

"Oh, Noelle. I'm sorry."

"So…anyway, my dad was eager to finish the adoption process, and he pushed Mom to accept me rather than wait for a baby. Apparently, my parents had a few strikes against them that made them less than sterling potential parents. Lower income, some minor reservations from the social worker… Nothing to stop the adoption, but Dad didn't want to risk being knocked off the list, I guess. Mom was never one hundred percent on board, but they took me in just the same so they would have the child they wanted."

Eli scowled. "How do you know all this? You were only six."

"Oh, they told me. More than once. It was held over my head when I acted out. 'Be grateful you have a home at all. You weren't our first choice.'"

Eli's jaw dropped, and he gaped at her. "Are you serious? That's awful!"

"I took it to heart, too. I did everything I could think of to earn their love and make them glad I was their child. I lived in fear of them sending me away if I didn't behave just right or proved unworthy in some way."

He continued to goggle at her, nausea churning inside him as he imagined the stress and emotional pain she grew up with. "That's a terrible thing for them to have put on you! Good grief, Noelle…"

She raised a hand. "There's more." She took a beat to gather her thoughts, and Eli edged closer, wrapping her hand in his. "I was the only Korean student in my school in Anchorage. We had a few Black students and a large Inuit population along with white people, but I was…the only Asian. I stuck out—or at least I felt like I stuck out. I had a friend or two, but kids are fickle, and they would abandon me for other friends when I got teased."

Eli's chest hurt. He could only imagine how Noelle had struggled and ached as a child. He wanted to scoop that young girl into his arms and hug her and tell her she was valued and loved. Instead, he drew grown-up Noelle into his arms and pressed her head to his shoulder. "I'm so sorry, sweetheart. That's horrible. I never knew."

"Because I didn't want you to know. I never wanted you to know anything about my family or my past. I wanted to leave my past behind me. I knew how golden your childhood was and how you treasured your big family, and I had nothing that remotely resembled that."

He opened his mouth to say something, anything to soothe her pain, but she must have anticipated what he intended, because she cut him off, adding, "And I especially didn't want your pity. I still don't. Back then, I wanted anything you felt for me to be genuine, to be mine because you really cared and not because you felt sorry for me."

"Can't I feel sorry for how you were treated and still care about you for who you are?" He stroked her hair and felt the tremble that raced through her. He tightened his hold on her, wanting to pour himself into her and chase out all the ugly memories, all the hurtful words and unfair shame her parents put on her.

"Maybe. I don't know. I didn't think so for a lot of years." She exhaled, and her warm breath on his neck stirred something tender deep in his core. "Allison was born when I was ten. Just like that, my parents had the baby, the biological child, they'd dreamed of. They pampered and coddled and spoiled her. She could do no wrong, whereas I was just in the way."

"And you're sure this wasn't just your youthful jealousy of the new baby talking? Couldn't some of your memories be skewed by immaturity? I know I had a hard time sharing my parents' attention when my brothers came along."

"You have to *have* your parents love and attention to be jealous of losing it." Her voice cracked, and she paused and cleared her throat. "No, I knew I was in the way, that they didn't want me around, because I overheard my mother tell my aunt—"

Her phone rang, interrupting her, and Eli grimaced. He hated for her story, her explanation to be left hanging at such a crucial point.

"Don't answer it. Finish what you were saying."

But when she glanced at her phone, she held up a finger. "I should take this. It'll only be a minute."

He leaned back on the sofa cushions and watched as she carried her phone across the room to take the call.

"Yes? And what did he find?" Noelle's face creased with what appeared to be confusion. "Are you sure? But I didn't have a problem before—" Her face grew pale, her expression stark.

Eli sat forward, alarmed by Noelle's reaction to her call.

"I see. Yes, of course. Thank you for calling." She disconnected, then stood with the phone in her hand, staring blankly at the floor.

He shoved to his feet and crossed to her. "What was that about?"

Noelle jerked her head up as if startled to find him there. "I, um…" She shook her head, then took a deep breath. "Do you remember earlier I said I'd had an accident, hit my nose?"

He lifted a finger to the purple smudges still coloring her face. "Which gave you these souvenirs."

She nodded. "It was a car accident."

Eli stiffened. "What? When?"

"A few nights ago. I was driving over the mountain ridge to redo the paperwork on Allison's funeral—that's another story—and my rental car's brakes failed. I left the road and hit a tree. Airbag did this. Otherwise, I'm fine. Sore muscles, but fine."

"Okay," he said, his tone anything but okay. "So who was that call?"

"The rental company. Their mechanic examined the brakes to determine why they failed."

"And?" he asked, his gut tightening as if bracing for a blow.

"The brake fluid had drained out. It was fine the first several days I drove it, but…within a few hours of when I wrecked, the brake line had been cut."

"Cut?" Eli repeated, stunned. Chilled.

Noelle lifted a shaking hand to her mouth. "The mechanic said it was a clean slice, not a tear."

"Then it was intentional. Someone wanted you to wreck."

She raised wide frightened eyes to his. "It seems so."

Chapter Eleven

Asher arrived a few minutes later and strode into the living room, dividing an all-business look between Noelle and Eli. "All right, what's going on? Have you made a break in the case?"

After a perfunctory greeting, Noelle turned her back and found a tissue to blow her nose and wipe her face. Asher sent Eli a curious look that silently asked about Noelle's emotional state.

Eli debated telling his partner about Noelle's accident and the cause, but until he figured out if and how it fit in with the Fiancée Killer case, he wouldn't distract his partner with it. Eli would keep a close eye on Noelle himself, while Asher focused on the new twists to the murder investigation.

He led Asher to the kitchen table where Noelle's laptop and paperwork were still spread out, and he walked Asher through her findings. Eli covered what he'd learned after speaking to the experts in Seattle and the incriminating evidence that Scott's work was significantly skewed.

Throughout Eli's explanation to his partner, Noelle hovered close by, nodding her confirmation whenever Asher looked to her in stunned disbelief.

When Eli finished spelling everything out, Asher's expression reflected the same shock and righteous anger that had racked Eli since he'd learned the news. Asher huffed his exasperation and slapped a palm on the tabletop.

"That son of a—" Asher cut his eyes to Noelle and swallowed the rest of the epithet. Taking a moment, his jaw tight, Asher asked, "Have you confronted Montgomery yet?"

"No. I wanted you to be in the loop first. And we need to proceed carefully. This is volatile stuff. Until we get an explanation from him, we can't fly off the handle, or—"

"Or punch him in his geeky, coffee-guzzling face?"

Eli chuffed a humorless laugh. "I know how you feel, but before we blow this case up, we need to be sure we're reading this right and not making false assumptions. We should build our case before we confront him. This—" he waved his hand at the laptop "—may have a legitimate explanation."

Asher arched an eyebrow. "Really? I think there are only two possible explanations. He's covering for the killer, or he's incompetent in his job. Both are pretty damning for Montgomery."

Noelle moved from the counter where she'd been leaning, listening, and said quietly, "It could be worse than that."

Both men lifted their eyes to her.

She wet her lips. "I think you should consider the possibility that Scott *is* the Fiancée Killer."

NOELLE WATCHED THE color drain from Eli's face, then, in the next moment, his blue eyes turned flinty. "You're right. All options have to be on the table."

Asher balled and flexed his fist on the tabletop, clearly

struggling with a fresh wave of rage. "Right under our noses," he muttered before rising from the table to stalk the floor.

"So what is our next move?" Eli asked.

"Call him on it." Asher braced his hands on his hips, and his nostrils flared as he stared back at his partner. "We show up at his house tonight with a warrant to search his place for evidence."

"Is what we have here, the discrepancies in his work, enough for a judge to issue a warrant?" Noelle asked. "I offered the worst scenario only to keep all the possibilities open. But we can't dismiss the possibility he just made some uniform errors or something threw off his calculations or—" She raised her shoulders and shook her head.

"So we gather more evidence against him," Asher said flatly. "Where do we start?"

"Well," Noelle said, moving to her laptop and scrolling through the open files and charts. She bit her fingernail as she mulled over what they knew and turned it to look at different angles in her mind. "The thrust of the misinformation has to do with the time of death, the amount of time the bodies had been left to decompose. Why would he focus on that?"

Eli drew a slow breath as he scrubbed hands over his face. "Alibi."

Noelle cut a sharp look at him. "What?"

"The time of death helps us in several ways, but a key factor in regard to eliminating suspects is whether they can provide an alibi for the time the crime was committed."

She considered this, a niggling sense they were on the verge of breakthrough teasing her brain, dancing just out of reach. "But we don't have precise times for the women's deaths," Noelle said. "Just estimates, give or take *days*. Even *weeks* for the first victims."

Asher joined them at the small kitchen table again, his eyes bright with determination. "*Does* Montgomery have an alibi? Where was he for the days or weeks when we believe the women were killed, based on the adjusted estimates the Seattle experts derived?"

Eli shook his head slowly, his frown dark and troubled. "I don't know, but we need to figure that out."

"How?" Noelle asked. If her own gut was twisting in knots and adrenaline spiking her pulse, she couldn't imagine how Eli and Asher felt.

Frustrated? Edgy? Betrayed? Guilt pinched her for having dumped this seismic information on them. But if it was the break they needed, if it led them to catching Allison's killer, if it meant other women's lives were spared, she couldn't regret it.

Squaring her shoulders, she asked, "In order to get to the remote areas where the bodies were found and commit the murders without leaving any evidence that connected him to the crime, the killer would need more than a few hours. That takes planning and time for execution." She grimaced. "Sorry poor word choice. I mean, time to commit the murder without leaving key evidence behind."

The men exchanged a look, and Eli nodded. "She's right."

"So who at your office would have a record of when Scott took leaves of absence from work or called in sick? He'd have to have an excuse for being gone for several days at a time without raising questions. Wouldn't he?"

Eli's face brightened. "He would." He checked his phone. "It's pretty late. Do you think we can get Joetta from HR down to the office now to show us Scott's personnel file?"

"Not without a court order," Asher replied.

"Well, then, let's get busy. Wake a judge or two."

THREE HOURS LATER, the groggy and disgruntled human resources manager handed Eli the file with Scott Montgomery's personnel information. "Can I ask what this is about?"

"You can ask, but I can't answer."

The HR manager rolled her eyes. "I don't see why it couldn't have waited until morning."

"Sorry to have disturbed your sleep, Joetta, but this is urgent," Asher said, looking over Eli's shoulder as Eli thumbed through the file. The men thanked her again and took the file upstairs to their office where Noelle was waiting.

"Well?" Noelle asked.

Eli waved the file and took a seat behind his desk to spread the pages out for examination. "Let's see. Vacation time requests... Here we go." Eli read out the dates of Scott's past vacation days while Asher cross-checked the times with the new information about the murders Noelle's work had derived. One after another, the dates synced with the newly adjusted timeline for the women's murders.

"So every time one of the Fiancée Killer victims was murdered, Scott was on leave from work." Noelle's expression hardened. "That sounds pretty incriminating to me."

Eli ground his back teeth. "Yeah, but it's also circumstantial. I'm just not ready yet to make such a drastic accusation without hard evidence tying him to the crimes." He glanced at Asher. "We need to talk to him, clear this up. I'll call him and ask for a meeting first thing tomorrow."

"WHAT'D HE SAY?" Asher asked the next morning, long before anyone else in the ABI had made it into the office.

Unable to sleep with this new information ping-ponging in his brain, Eli had come to work, only to find Asher already there.

"He was understandably curious and concerned why we wanted to talk to him, and when I told him it was a personal matter, he suggested we come to his house rather than discuss it at the office. I agreed."

"His house?" Asher grunted. "As long as we're going, should we get a search warrant for his house and car?"

Eli nodded. "Can't hurt. Let's send it to Matthews again since he just granted the one for Scott's personnel records and is familiar with the case."

"Right," Asher said, turning his chair to get started on the legal forms to request the search warrant.

Eli, meantime, called Noelle and updated her. "We're meeting with Montgomery at his house later this morning. Do me a favor and don't go anywhere alone until we figure out who cut your brakes and why."

She was silent for a moment but finally agreed. "Call me as soon as you get back from Scott's?"

"I will."

"And you be careful, too. I guess I don't have to tell you if he is the killer, and he realizes you've picked up his scent, he's likely to be dangerous."

"I'm trained for this stuff, Noelle. But…thank you for your concern." He gave a half grin she couldn't see, but he poured gentleness into his tone. "It's nice to know you care."

She was quiet again, then said softly, "Of course I care. That's never been the issue for us." He heard her sigh. "But we'll finish that talk later. Today you need to concentrate on handling Scott and solving this case. There'll be time for our personal problems later."

"I'm going to hold you to that."

Across the room, Asher stood and grabbed his coat. "We're on. Judge Matthews will see us in his chambers in fifteen minutes. Let's ride."

WHEN ELI AND Asher had the search warrant for Scott's home and car secured, they headed to the street address listed in his personnel file, using a GPS map application as a guide.

"You've never been to his house before, either?" Asher asked as Eli drove. "Do you not find that odd?"

"No. There are plenty of folks at the office whose homes I haven't been to. I got along with him well enough at the office or if he joined the group for a drink after hours, but I never considered him a close enough friend to drop by his house."

Asher scowled.

"Look, this should go without saying," Eli said, "but since I know you're both interested in Kansas—"

"What!"

Eli raised a hand to stave off argument. "Dude, I have eyes. I'm not stupid. You both stare at her like she hung the moon when she's not looking. All I was going to say is, keep an open mind. We have to keep our personal feelings about Montgomery and the possibility he's duped us all these years in check. Be professional."

Asher gave a nod and pressed his splayed hands on his thighs. "I know. I'm cool."

The voice on Eli's GPS directed him to turn, and as he did, he asked, "What's the house number again?"

"Two twenty. That'd be it," Asher said, bending forward for a better view through the front windshield. "I'm beginning to see why he never had us over for beers after work. That's one of the smallest houses I've ever seen."

"Don't judge. He's a bachelor, and a little house is all he needs. Besides, it may be bigger on the inside than it looks." Eli parked on the street in front of the small house.

"You're sure he's expecting us? The windows look dark." Asher opened the passenger door and climbed out.

"He picked the time, so he knew we were coming." Eli got out and joined Asher on the sidewalk to the front door. The lawn was winter-dead, and the deciduous trees appeared skeletal without their leaves, but Scott's yard was neat and trimmed, showing it had been cared for through the summer. "If he's not here, then we let ourselves in. We have the warrant, so we're covered."

Eli reached the door first and knocked firmly.

Asher tucked his hands in his pockets and scanned the yard. "This is a nice area. Not a lot of neighbors, but if you like privacy, that's a plus."

When Scott didn't answer the door after a minute or so, Asher knocked again louder, calling, "Scott? Are you there? Open up! It's Eli and Asher."

Eli moved his gaze over the doorframe, looking for a Ring or similar app-synced camera. No buzzer, but he did locate a small camera over the door. He looked right into the camera and waved. "Scott? You there? Can you let us in?"

Asher tested the doorknob, and when it turned, he pushed the door open. "Scott? Hey, Montgomery, are you here?"

They both stepped inside, and Eli led the way deeper into the house. Lights appeared to be off throughout the residence.

"I'll check the bedroom," Asher said as he moved down the short hall to the next room.

Eli swept the living room with an attentive gaze. The

room was sparsely decorated and had only basic furniture—a couch, a side table with a lamp, a flat screen TV on the wall. The only wall art was a modern piece in dark tones and slashing lines that gave Eli a creepy sensation.

Turning from the disturbing art, he spotted a piece of paper taped to the bottom of the TV screen. His name had been printed on the folded sheet in block letters. He pulled the paper down and opened it. The note read simply, *Surprise!*

As he puzzled over the note, the blink of a green light caught his attention from the corner of his eye, and he turned to look for the source. What he found under the side table chilled him to the marrow. The wires, tubes and countdown timer attached to an initiator left no doubt.

Scott had rigged his house with a bomb. Eli and Asher had likely triggered the timer when they'd entered the house.

The timer screen read 00:12.

00:11

00:10

Eli's feet started running before his brain could fully form his next thought.

"Asher, run! Bomb!" he yelled as he fled the living room.

Chapter Twelve

Eli tore through the front door and down the sidewalk toward his Jeep. He dove behind his Renegade for protection. From behind his vehicle and with a mental clock counting *four*, *three*, *two*, he rose only enough to see if Asher was behind him.

Asher appeared in the front door just as Eli's mental clock hit one.

Ducking low again and raising his arms around his head, Eli braced, prayed.

The explosion shook the ground, thundered in his ears and echoed in his chest. Bits of building material rained down on him as the small house was blown to bits.

When his ears quit ringing, the sound that reached Eli first was a guttural cry of anguish.

Asher.

Pulse racing, Eli ran back toward the house and found his partner lying among the blasted debris and burning detritus of Scott's house. "Asher!"

He knelt beside his friend, who, while in one piece, had clearly caught a considerable amount of the building-supply shrapnel. Glass shards, splintered wood, bent metal and tattered roofing tiles lay in a mosaic of destruction, with Asher in the middle. Bleeding. Groaning. But alive.

"Where were you hit worst?" Eli asked, hearing the note of panic in his voice. *Stay calm. You can't freak out. Manage the situation.*

"Hard to say," Asher rasped, his face pinched in pain.

Eli did a quick survey of Asher's limbs, head and torso, checking for any critical injuries. He yanked off his coat and draped it over Asher, hoping to stave off shock. Next he stripped down to his undershirt, pulling the T-shirt off to soak up blood as he applied pressure to his partner's injured leg. "Can you hold this while I call for an ambulance and some uniforms to secure the scene?"

After pulling his top shirt back on, Eli called for help, his gaze taking in the rubble.

Clearly Scott had no intention of returning, was in full fugitive mode now. If there had been any evidence in the house to support or refute Scott's involvement in the Fiancée Killer case, it was now either burning or scattered, shredded and tossed to the four winds.

Eli gritted his teeth, frustration and adrenaline tap dancing along his nerves. He hated that Scott's duplicity had been right under his nose, and he'd missed it. He refused to let the bastard win. Whatever his part in the Fiancée Killer murders, whether perpetrator or accomplice, Eli swore that he would make Scott Montgomery pay.

NOELLE READ THE data that her latest calculations had spit out and frowned. She'd spent the entire night and morning gathering information, statistics and expert opinions from both forensic specialists and data analysts to double-and triple-check her results.

But the more information she got, the more certain she was that Scott Montgomery was either the sloppiest scientist and most negligent medical examiner in history or one of the smartest to have so neatly altered the crime scene data and forensic data to yield the results that served him best. And gotten away with it. Until now.

She didn't want to believe Scott was guilty of anything nefarious, largely for Eli's sake. Being betrayed by someone he worked with and trusted had to be a painful blow. *Like the sucker punch you dealt him when you walked away.*

She shook her head and shoved the guilty thought aside. She could reexamine her past with Eli once the pressing issues related to this murder investigation were resolved.

She was scanning the table integrating meteorologic history, entomological findings, environmental conditions and decomposition studies with everything the investigation had yielded when her phone rang.

Her pulse skipped seeing Eli's number on her screen. "Hi, did you talk to Scott? What did you learn?"

"No and a lot. In a sense. I—" He sounded odd. His voice quavered a bit, which was highly unusual for the man with the courage and constitution to investigate gruesome serial murders and manage the roughest of criminals.

"Eli? What's wrong?"

"I'm at the hospital."

"What!" she cried, not caring how much her reaction gave away about her feelings for him.

"I'm fine. But Asher's pretty banged up." She heard him exhale heavily. Wearily. "We're both lucky to be alive. Montgomery had rigged his place with a bomb that was triggered when we entered his house. Clearly he had something to hide and wanted to both destroy the evidence and take out the people who were onto him. He accomplished one of the two goals."

Noelle sank onto a nearby chair. Her mind spun as she

rattled off questions. "How bad are Asher's injuries? Is there anything I can do? Where is Scott?"

"Asher will live, but he's going to be in the hospital for a few days, recovering. He's in radiology now for CT scans, checking for internal injuries."

"But how—" She cut herself off. "Never mind. I'll get the whole story when I get there. Which hospital?"

"The only one in town." He forced a note of humor to his tone. "We're lucky we weren't farther out in the mountains. He was bleeding pretty heavily."

"And you promise you're all right?" she asked, a lump knotting her throat at the idea of anything happening to Eli.

"Minor cuts and scrapes. I'll be fine. You really don't have to come to the hospital."

"Of course I'm coming," she said, already gathering her purse and coat and keys to the replacement rental car. "Your partner was injured, and I want to be there for you."

And my findings are the reason you were at Scott's house to begin with. She clenched her jaw as guilt tripped through her.

Eli didn't reply, and for a moment she thought she'd lost her connection.

"Hello? Eli?"

"Thanks, Noelle," he said, his voice thick. "I'd appreciate the company. I'm in the ER waiting room at the moment, but they'll be moving Asher to a room soon."

She paused at the hostel door, glancing back at her laptop and the files spread out. On an impulse, she went back inside and packed her laptop into her messenger bag.

Noelle made it to the hospital in record time, but when she arrived, Asher was already settled in a private room.

Eli sat in a chair by the side of Asher's bed, but Noelle's focus was entirely on Eli, until she'd assured herself he was as whole and unharmed as he claimed. She gave him a fierce hug and clung to him for several long moments, betraying the depth of her concern and relief that he was safe. Her fingers combed through his hair, and he kissed the top of her head.

"What's this?" Asher said from the bed, his voice slurring slightly, likely because of pain medication. "Judging from…that steamy hug, she's more than…just a consultant." His lips twitched in a groggy grin.

They were spared from replying when the sound of quick footsteps preceded Kansas's appearance at the door. Her face was pale, her expression distressed, and her gaze flew to the bed immediately.

"Asher! Oh my God! What… Are you…?" Her boots clattered on the linoleum floor as she crossed to the side of Asher's bed and took in his battered and bandaged appearance. "Are you okay? Really?" When Kansas's gaze flew to Eli, a note of reproach hovered in her glare. "How did this happen?"

"Long story." Eli motioned for Noelle to take his seat, then returned a wry look to his cousin. "I'm fine, by the way. Thanks for asking."

His cousin's eyes widened. "You were there, too? At the explosion site?"

"I was. We both very nearly bought the farm. I only spotted the bomb with a few seconds to spare. Scott clearly wanted to take us out along with any evidence in his house."

Both of Kansas's hands flew up, palms toward Eli. "Hold on. Back up. Scott who? Not our Scott?"

"Our Scott," Asher said, though his eyes were closed, "isn't our Scott, after all."

"What?" Kansas said, dividing a stunned look between her cousin and Asher.

Eli moved to the corner of the room to drag another chair close to Asher's bedside. "Have a seat. I'll give you the lowdown after I get another chair from the hall."

Noelle gave Kansas a quick smile of greeting when the confused woman glanced at her.

"Noelle, hi." Kansas blinked as if surprised to see her there. "Were you with them, too?"

"No. I'm just here…for support."

Clearly Kansas heard the hesitation in her voice, since she gave Noelle a curious look.

"And why are *you* here?" Eli asked his cousin when he stepped back into the room with another chair. "You and Rafferty are always sniping at each other. I wouldn't have thought after you knew he survived that you'd be so worried about his sorry hide."

Kansas sat taller in the chair and cast an inscrutable look to Asher before glancing back at her oldest cousin. "Let's just say things aren't always what they seem."

Eli's brow snapped into a deep V. "What?"

Kansas ignored her cousin's confused frown. "Answer my question first. What did you mean about Scott? How is he connected to the explosion?"

"His house," Asher said.

Kansas gasped. "Was Scott hurt? Was he—"

"He wasn't there," Eli said quickly. "He's likely the one who set the bomb, with the intention of killing me and anyone who came with me to his house."

Kansas was clearly having a hard time taking in the truths Eli was laying out. Recognizing this, Noelle stepped in with more background.

"I volunteered to help Eli analyze the case with some data software I work with," she explained, "and it turned up inconsistencies with the forensic data. Based on the patterns of irregular information the program revealed, we think Scott Montgomery has been deliberately sabotaging the Fiancée Killer investigation."

Kansas glanced to her cousin, then to Asher for confirmation.

Eli nodded, and Noelle expounded on the information from the files she'd input, the resources she'd used as backup, the cross-references, the charts she'd double-checked and the patterns of misinformation her analysis had uncovered.

"I called Scott early this morning, after Noelle showed us what she'd found. He agreed to meet with me. He asked that we meet at his house for privacy." Eli took a beat, and his expression darkened. Noelle saw guilt in his eyes when he glanced at his injured partner. "I asked Asher to come with me as backup."

"Wasn't there. Rigged a bomb for us," Asher mumbled, clearly fuzzy from his painkiller.

"He left a note," Eli said, pulling a crumped sheet from his pocket. "Just says *surprise*. I'd say that's evidence the bomb was intentional."

"Surprise… I'd say so." Asher chuckled dryly, then groaned in pain.

Noelle frowned as she mulled the situation. "Are you saying he had time to rig a bomb and make his getaway in the couple of hours between your call this morning and when you arrived? That's hard to fathom."

Eli shot her a startled look. "I hadn't thought about that before now, but you're right. He had to have had the materials at his house already and known what he was doing to rig the explosive that quickly."

Asher grunted. "Or already made. In case we found out."

Noelle gasped. "So he could have been waiting for you

to make the connection between him and the Fiancée Killer and set the trap days or weeks ago?"

"And only set the trigger at the door when he knew we were coming for him," Eli said in a dark tone of dawning understanding. "Damn it."

"But I don't..." Kansas began, her expression saying she was struggling to take in this turn of events. "You're saying you think Scott Montgomery is the Fiancée Killer? That's...crazy. I mean, Scott has always been so...nice." She furrowed her brow and slumped in her chair, her hurt and confusion plain in her expression. "A bit of a geek, yes. But he's never seemed like the sort who could kill anyone. Much less *five* women. Or his coworkers!"

"Serial killers are good at hiding their deviant tendencies," Eli said, then shook his head. "It burns me up that we missed what was right under our noses, though."

"The bastard..." Asher said, sounding even more groggy.

"Maybe we should relocate to the waiting room and let the patient have peace to sleep?" Noelle suggested.

"No," Asher muttered, "I'm fine." The word was barely out of his mouth before his breathing shifted to a deep, slumberous cadence.

Kansas leaned forward and gently touched his cheek, whispering, "Oh, Asher. I'm sorry I've been so awful to you. Please get better." When Kansas glanced up, her gaze narrowed on her cousin's puzzled look. "What? Can't I be worried about a colleague?"

"Did I say anything?" Eli asked, his grin teasing.

"So, Scott's on the run?" Noelle asked, in summary more than for information. "Now what happens with the investigation?"

Eli's blue eyes were icy with purpose when he faced her. "We find him."

THE AFTERNOON STRETCHED OUT, with Asher's three visitors finding ways to pass the time and grapple in their own ways with the twist the investigation had taken. Neither Eli nor Kansas was willing to leave Asher's bedside for more than a few minutes to get coffee or use the restroom.

When the doctor checked on Asher, he said that CT scans showed Asher had a concussion. While the doctor was also concerned about possible infection in his numerous open wounds, antibiotics and a few days of rest would get him over the hump.

"When can he return to work?" Eli asked, knowing that he needed Asher's help to bring Scott in. The sooner, the better. Sure, he could read in ABI agents from other offices in the state, but Asher had been with the investigation from the beginning and shared the personal interest in bringing Montgomery to justice.

"Let's not rush things," the doctor said. "He'll need a couple days here before he's released, then a week or more bed rest at home. After he's released, someone will need to stay with him and monitor him for side effects. Seizures, trouble walking, signs of memory or sensory loss. Head trauma is serious business, and healing takes time. And he'll need clean bandages every day until the wounds are past the worst."

After the doctor left, Noelle could see Kansas's stress levels were off the charts. Clearly she was fretting over Asher's condition in light of the doctor's caution. Deciding she could help Kansas by distracting her from her worry, Noelle searched for a conversation topic they hadn't already covered that afternoon. "Tell me more about your role with the ABI, Kansas."

Eli's cousin smiled weakly at Noelle, though concern

for Asher still filled her eyes. "I'm not specifically with the ABI. I'm with the state troopers in search and rescue."

"That's right." Noelle said, remembering that from when she'd been introduced to Kansas last week. "That's got to be difficult work. Stressful."

Kansas nodded distractedly. "But satisfying. Recently, I've helped with a few cases of missing persons that the ABI was involved with. In fact, we've had more cases than usual for such a small town recently, because—"

Eli's cousin stopped herself. Shivered. "I just can't get over the idea that Scott could be responsible for..." Her blue eyes found Eli's again. "I worked with Scott on the Whitlaw case a couple months ago, and he was so friendly toward me. He even apologized for not being more helpful with what his DNA tests revealed." Her nose wrinkled. "It makes my skin crawl, thinking he could be involved with the murders of those women!"

Eli nodded. "I know. We don't have more than circumstantial evidence against him now, but it certainly looks bad for him."

"I don't know how you two deal with so much tragedy and evil every day and not lose all faith in humanity," Noelle said, again trying to steer the conversation away from Scott, at least for a while. "My computers and numbers are dry and boring sometimes, but comfortably emotionless and drama-free."

"Oh, not all of my searches have sad outcomes." Kansas tugged up a corner of her mouth. "In fact, much of the time we're witnesses to happy endings."

"I love a happy ending," Noelle said.

"Don't we all?" Kansas grinned, then continued. "For example, a few months ago, we saved a couple of lost hikers at the Muskee Glacier Pass. They'd gotten dehydrated and confused and were wandering aimlessly until a bush pilot spotted them from the air. Then last summer, we found a runaway teenager from Shelby on the Two Bears River Trail north of town. His mother was so relieved to have her boy back safely, she hugged us as hard as she hugged him."

"I can imagine," Noelle said, though her heart stung, knowing her parents had never loved her that deeply.

"Probably the sweetest rescue was when we brought an elderly fisherman home after he got stranded. We reunited him with his wife on their forty-fifth wedding anniversary. She cried and said we'd given her the best anniversary present of all."

When Eli grunted, Noelle glanced his way, expecting to see him grinning over Kansas's stories. Instead, his frown was deeper than earlier. He stared at the floor, clearly lost in thought.

"Eli, what's wrong?" Noelle asked.

"Where was the fisherman found?" he asked, his dark gaze lifting to Kansas. "Was it Lake Chahoogee?"

Kansas tipped her head and blinked. "Um, no. He was on Byers Lake. But..." she wrinkled her brow in thought "...we did have a medical evac from Chahoogee a couple years ago. After a few years, you get calls from all over the state. Why do you ask?"

Eli dragged a hand down his face as he mumbled a curse under his breath.

"What is it, Eli?" Noelle asked, his behavior stirring a jittery feeling in her belly. Lake Chahoogee rang a discordant bell with her, as well, though she couldn't determine why. It unsettled her to think Eli had struck on something disconcerting as well.

He rose from his chair and split a look between Noelle and his cousin. "I don't want to say anything yet. It's probably nothing, but—" He flexed and balled his hands at his sides, and his mouth tightened. "I want to run an errand and check something. I'll be back soon."

Noelle stood as well. "I'll come with you."

His gaze shifted to his partner in the hospital bed. "I don't want to leave Asher—"

"Go," Kansas said. "Do what you need to. I'll stay with Asher."

Eli lifted one eyebrow. "If you're sure?"

"I am." Kansas waved him out of the room. "Both of you go. Do your thing. I'm fine."

Noelle followed Eli out of the room, having to take two steps for every one he took to keep up with his brisk strides. "Want to tell me what's going on?"

"Not yet. I don't want to alarm anyone if I'm wrong."

"Wrong about what?"

"Let's just say I don't believe in coincidence, and I've just realized something important about the Fiancée Killer investigation."

"Can I help?" Noelle asked. "Maybe run some new data through the algorithms? I have my laptop." She patted the messenger bag that hung from her shoulder.

"Not yet. First I want to talk to my father."

Not the answer she expected. Noelle ran a few steps to get ahead of Eli and stood in front of him to stop him. "Your father? What does he have to do with any of this?"

"Hopefully nothing." He took her hand and towed her forward with him as he plowed through the hospital door and into the parking lot. "But I'm afraid he can shed an important light on a disturbing angle of the Fiancée Killer investigation."

Chapter Thirteen

Eli was largely silent and brooding on the drive to his parents' house. Noelle didn't pester him about his disturbing hunch and questions for his father. If he wanted her to know, he'd have told her what he suspected. Besides, she had her own preoccupying thoughts swirling in her brain.

Eli's parents. She was about to meet Eli's parents. Not in the way that a couple announced their serious intentions toward each other, of course, but she was nervous just the same. They were Eli's parents, after all.

Despite him asking many times in college for her to accompany him home, she'd always put him off. Healthy family dynamics were not her forte, and she'd feared that after meeting her, his family would disapprove of their relationship. If her own birth mother and adoptive family could all shun her, what other family could ever want her part of their ranks?

Eli parked at the side of his parents' house, a beautiful home outside town with views of the Chugach Mountains from their front porch and tall trees in the backyard.

Noelle took a deep breath of the pine-scented air as she climbed from the passenger seat. "You grew up here? In this house?"

"After about age six. We moved here from California, and my father and uncle opened the outdoor adventures business the younger Coltons still operate." Eli hitched his head toward a building behind the main house. "Let's try back here first. Dad's probably hanging out with Mom while she works."

"While she works? Visitors don't distract her?" Noelle asked. She couldn't imagine having people around, talking and bothering her while she tried to concentrate.

"On the contrary, she claims people give her more creative energy. She loves having Dad's company."

"Creative energy? What does she do?"

"Come see." Eli took her hand and led her to the door of the building. He paused and stuck his head inside, calling, "Hello? Anybody home?"

Noelle heard joyful voices reply, "Eli! What a treat."

"Come in!"

Eli tugged her forward, and Noelle shuffled into the brightly lit space that was nothing she'd expected. Muddy-looking tables and shelves were filled with earthenware in varying states of completion. The works in progress cramped one end of the large room, while a pottery wheel and large kiln took up most of the far side of the room. The mingled scents of clay, paint and the herbal scent from an essential oil diffuser perfumed the air, while classic rock played from the speakers mounted on the walls.

A petite woman, with a face much younger than her silver hair would imply, rose from behind the pottery wheel, wiping her hands on a towel as she crossed the room. Her long hair was twisted into a messy bun, and her blue eyes were so like Eli's as to identify her as his mother even without context. She wrapped Eli in a tight embrace and kissed his cheek. "It's so good to see you, sweetheart!" The smile on his mother's face faltered as her eyes dropped to Eli's hip, where he wore his service weapon. "Oh, son. You know I don't like you wearing that thing when you're here."

"Sorry, Mom. But I'm on duty." With a wave of his hand, he gestured for Noelle to step forward. "Mom, Dad, this is Noelle Harris. She's a friend from my college days, and she's helping me with my current case." He motioned from Noelle to his mother, then to a man with salt-and-pepper hair, who moved out from behind a table in the corner of the room. "Noelle, my parents, Will and Sasha Colton."

Sasha's eyes glittered warmly as she drew close, smiling broadly. "Noelle! So nice to finally meet you!" Both of the older woman's hands stretched toward Noelle, but when Noelle raised her right hand to shake Sasha's, Eli's mother drew her into a firm hug instead. "We've heard so much about you!"

Noelle blinked. "You have?"

Sasha backed away to arm's length, still holding Noelle's shoulders and grinning. "Of course. You were the love of our oldest boy's life for years. He spoke of little else when he came home on holidays. I'm so glad you two have been able to renew your friendship."

"We, uh—"

Will tugged his wife's arm. "No hogging the guest, honey." He stuck his hand out, and Noelle took it in hers. Will pumped her hand heartily and offered his welcome.

Sasha faced her son then and gasped. "Eli, dear! What on earth happened to you?" His mother reached to touch the bandage on his forehead and scanned the other cuts on his face and hands.

"I was involved in an incident earlier today."

"An incident?" his father echoed, his tone saying he wasn't buying Eli's euphemism.

"I'm fine, but… Asher is in the hospital." Eli frowned, before continuing, "A house we were visiting as part of our investigation was rigged with a bomb. I saw it in time to warn Asher, and we both got out alive."

"How badly was Asher hurt?" Sasha asked, her face gone pale with worry.

"No broken bones, just a concussion. Mostly he's cut up and had a few bits of shrapnel removed from his legs and torso. He'll be fine with a few days of rest."

"Gracious!" Sasha put her hand to her chest and sank down on a nearby stool. "Days like this do not help me sleep at night, Eli. I worry enough about you taking on criminals without knowing you're nearly blown up by bombs!"

Eli stepped over to hug his mother again. "I know you worry, and I'm sorry. But I swear I'm as careful as I can be."

Noelle shifted her weight from one foot to the other. Sasha's maternal concern was touching but also foreign to Noelle. And it left her off-balance. She faltered, feeling both hollow for what she'd been deprived of as a child and a tad jealous of Eli's good fortune and strong bond with his mother.

Sasha shook her head and pasted on another smile. "Where are my manners? Noelle, can I get you something warm to drink? Coffee or hot tea?"

"No, thank you."

"Whiskey or gin?" Will asked with a wink. "It's five o'clock somewhere."

Noelle gave a polite chuckle. "I'm fine."

"How about you, son?" Will asked.

Eli refused a drink, as well. "On duty. I came because I need to talk to you about something important, Dad."

Will's gray-flecked eyebrows lifted. "Oh my. Well, sure. We can go in the house if you want privacy."

Eli nodded. "Noelle, do you mind chatting with Mom until I get back?"

Noelle's stomach flip-flopped. What if his mother drilled her about her past relationship with Eli? Or their current status? Or her family? Or—

Sasha hooked her arm with Noelle's and led her toward one of the cleaner tables and chairs. "You boys go on. Noelle and I will be getting to know each other."

Once the men exited, Sasha gave Noelle a warm but serious look. "Well, I feel like I already know you, thanks to everything Eli said about you when you were dating."

"That's what others have told me," Noelle said and flashed an awkward smile.

"What I don't know is what changed. Eli went from top of the world to a living hell. And forgive me for being blunt, dear, but I surely don't want to see him hurt again. If we can figure out what went wrong before, maybe we can put things right now." Sasha tipped her head as she invited Noelle to reply with a bob of her head.

"It's a long story. A complicated one for me to explain." Noelle chewed her bottom lip. How on earth did she give Eli's mother any kind of understanding or resolution when she was struggling for the strength and courage to give Eli the whole picture?

Sasha remained silent, patiently waiting for Noelle to say more, to find some words. Finally, Noelle swallowed hard and offered, "I guess it boils down to…fear. I loved him, but—"

"Stop." Sasha's blue eyes flashed hot as she pinned a hard gaze on Noelle and raised a hand. "My dear, do not ever use *I love you* and *but* in the same sentence. Nor

should you use *trust* and *but* together. Love and trust have to be unconditional. If you could not commit to Eli fully and unconditionally, then perhaps what you felt wasn't love at all."

Noelle flinched, the harsh assessment like a slap to her. Yet at the same time, Sasha's words seeped into the cracks and pits that had riddled Noelle since she broke up with Eli. She *had* let fear win. If she could do that, put fear over Eli, maybe she hadn't loved him enough.

She curled her fingers into fists and drew a restorative breath. "So how do I fix it? How do I get past the things that scare me so that I can love and trust Eli unconditionally?"

Sasha smiled broadly and pulled her into a firm hug. "Oh, Noelle, darling girl, you've just taken the first step. Wanting to change things is the first step."

"What's up?" Will asked as he took a seat in his favorite recliner. "And what are you leaving out about the bombed house you visited this morning?"

Eli settled on the couch across from his father and sighed. "I've said all I can for now. It's related to the serial murder case I'm working."

Will scowled, then bobbed a nod. "Then what is it you want to discuss?"

Eli drew a deep breath. "Caroline."

His father's chin jerked up. "What?"

"I know you don't like to talk about your sister, but I need to know a few details about her murder."

Will shook his head, a dark scowl drawing down the corners of his mouth. "Son, that case has been closed for decades. Our family has gone to great lengths to put that evil behind us."

Eli scooted to the edge of the cushion, leaning toward his father as he pressed on. "I know that. But I need to look at it again, and I only remember fragments of that day, the crime scene we stumbled upon. I need clarification. Confirmation. Details filled in that my child's mind may have warped or blocked."

His father dragged a hand down his face. "Eli, please don't go there. We moved to Shelby to put our loss, the media attention and notoriety behind us. Your mother and I made the decision long ago not to discuss her death with you any further after you finished the counseling sessions your doctor recommended. We felt it was better for you to put it behind you and build a new life, with happy memories here in Alaska. For *all of us* to make a fresh start."

"I understand your reasons and can appreciate what you did, but I need information."

His father sighed and tipped his head back against his chair. "All right. I don't like it, but if you say you need answers, I believe you."

Believe. His family's motto filtered through Eli's mind. As he had many times growing up, he appreciated his family's determination to have an open mind and trust each other. To support each other in all circumstances.

Eli studied the grim tension in his father's face. Revisiting his family's brutal murders, the disturbing crime scene he'd stumbled upon, had to be difficult for Will. "I'm sorry, Dad. I wouldn't dig this up if it weren't important."

His jaw tight and eyes bleak, Will raised one hand from his lap. "Ask your questions."

"I'm primarily interested in how Aunt Caroline's killer—"

"Jason Stevens." His father spat the name out in a low growl, like a foul word. "I don't like giving him the anonymity of a tag like *Caroline's killer*. He should bear the guilt and be recognized for the evil man he was."

"Stevens then." Eli paused to gather his thoughts. "I remember that Caroline and Stevens were both sitting on the couch in the living room when I found them. At first I thought they were asleep, but I realized soon after that that Aunt Caroline looked…odd. The color of her skin… Her eyes bulging—" He stopped short, knowing a more graphic description of his aunt's body was unneeded.

"Yes. You've told us this. The scene frightened you as a child, gave you nightmares for weeks until your counselor helped you manage your fears and memories."

"Maybe too well." Eli rubbed his hands on his jeans. "Some of the details are fuzzy. What was Aunt Caroline wearing? Her nightgown?"

"Wh—" His father blinked rapidly. "Why?"

"I hope it's nothing, but tell me. Please."

Will's hands fisted, and he swallowed hard. "Stevens had put her in a little black dress and stuck a diamond ring on her finger, playing out his fantasy that they were a couple."

Eli's gut clenched, and bile rose in his throat.

"After he drugged her and strangled her to death," his father continued, "he posed her with her left hand over her heart, so we didn't miss the ring, and her right arm around him as if they were cuddling." His father gave his head a small shake as if shuddering at the vile memory.

"Go on. What else did the investigators conclude?"

"Stevens had initially injected Caroline with a sedative. Once he'd killed her and posed her, he injected himself with a lethal dose of the same sedative and died beside her. A far more peaceful demise than he deserved, the bastard."

Eli dropped his gaze to the floor, his brain processing

this information with a growing unrest in his soul. Black dress. Diamond ring. Posed.

"Is that what you needed to know?" his father asked.

Scrubbing a hand over his chin, he sighed. "I'm afraid so."

"Can you tell me now why you needed to resurrect this dark period from our family history?"

Eli hesitated. Could he divulge what he suspected? It wasn't confirmed yet. His hunch was just that—a hunch. But what his father had shared was too similar to the current investigation to be coincidence. *I don't believe in coincidence*, he'd told Noelle earlier.

He cleared his throat and gave his father a grim stare. "When the victims of the Fiancée Killer were found, they were all wearing a diamond ring. Even the older more skeletal remains still had a ring on the left hand."

Will nodded. "So the news reports have said. That's how the case got that name, right?"

Eli gave a nod. "They're also wearing short black dresses, and the cause of death has been pinned as strangulation." For all that Montgomery had tainted the forensic records, at least that much could be confirmed.

"Like Caroline," his father said darkly.

"Very like Caroline. The victims we've found before scavengers got to the bodies have been posed with the ring hand up."

"Also like Caroline," his father rasped, his blue eyes widening. "Are you saying the current killer is copying Caroline's murder?"

"Maybe. I need to run more checks and verify—"

"But why? Caroline was killed twenty-eight years ago! In southern California! What's the link?" His father stiffened. "Do you think that whoever is doing this could harm our family? Is he doing it to taunt us or—?"

Eli raised both hands. "I don't know anything for certain yet. I can't make assumptions without facts." He raked fingers through his hair and expelled a frustrated breath. He refused to believe that his assignment as the lead in this case and having been the first to find Aunt Caroline murdered was a coincidence. Was *he* the link? "Just in case, keep a close eye on Mom. Don't let her go anywhere alone."

His father's grim expression said he clearly read between the lines. "I'll tell her not to—"

"No." Eli lifted a hand in apology for his abruptness, then took a beat before adding, "You can't tell her or anyone else anything yet. This is confidential information related to my case. Besides, I don't want her frightened. Just… stay alert." Eli shoved to his feet. "I'll let you know what I learn after I look at this angle more closely."

His father stood, as well. "Eli, I—I'm sorry if we failed you back then, after Caroline and your grandparents' murders. That had to be a traumatizing thing for you to walk into."

Eli shrugged one shoulder. "You got me counseling."

"Some. But was it enough? Were we right to move you away from your friends and the only home you knew? To make such a drastic change when you were grappling with such horrible memories? Maybe it was a mistake for us to stop talking about it and shut it out like it never happened." His father raised a shaky hand to his mouth. "We thought we were doing what was best, but if we made it harder on you…"

Eli stepped over to his father and placed a hand on his shoulder. "I know you did your best with what you knew at the time."

"Were we wrong? Could you forget?"

"Clearly I shut out some of it," he said. "That's why I needed your help today. But... I did have nightmares of losing family. Finding my siblings and cousins dead or running from a monster who wanted to kill me. I still do on occasion."

Will's face reflected pain and sympathy. "Oh, son. I'm sorry. If we could do it over, your mother and I would do so many things differently."

Eli squeezed his father's shoulder. "Hey, don't dwell on it. We all do the best we can with the information and life experience we have at the time." He gave a soft, wry chuckle. "And I turned out all right, didn't I?"

His father's eyes grew moist, and he clamped both hands on Eli's upper arms. "You turned out better than all right. I am so very proud of you, Eli. Your work, your ethics, your support of our family... You're an inspiration, my boy." He drew Eli into a firm hug and pounded his back. "I just wish—well, never mind."

Eli backed out of the embrace and tilted his head. "No, say it. What do you wish?"

Will snorted and glanced away before drilling him with a look that was warm despite the ice blue of his father's eyes. The same eyes Eli saw every morning in the mirror. "Your mother and I have been so happy together. We fulfill each other and take strength from each other. She makes me so incredibly grateful."

Eli smiled. "It's obvious to anyone who knows you."

"I want that same happiness for you, dear boy. I wish you could find someone who brings you joy, someone you can settle down with and make a family. I don't want you to be alone, Eli. Not when marriage has been so good to me and your mother."

Eli's heart kicked. Images from a few nights earlier, the passionate kisses and whispered intimacies he'd shared with Noelle, flickered in his mind's eye. "I want that, too. I have for a long time, but…the woman I want to settle down with keeps pushing me away. I believe she loves me, but she's scared for some reason. She's been hurt before, and she hasn't trusted me enough yet to open up about what frightens her about our relationship."

"May I assume you're talking about the young lady out in the pottery studio with your mother right now?"

"Noelle. Yes."

"She's the one who broke your heart in college, isn't she?" his father asked.

"How do you know about that?" Eli asked. He thought he'd kept his personal affairs and heartache more private than that.

"To be honest, your mother picked up on it first. You went from talking about Noelle frequently when you were home on holiday to saying nothing at all after graduation. And you were far more subdued, even glum at times. Your mother put two and two together and shared her theory with me."

"Of course she did," Eli said and flashed a half grin. "She doesn't miss much. I never could get away with any shenanigans growing up."

His father chuckled. "That's as likely because you're a terrible liar. You have more tells than a novice poker player."

Eli's eyebrows shot up. "I do? Like what?"

His father hitched his head toward the door, and Eli followed him out toward his mother's studio. "I'm not telling you. How would I ever beat you at poker again?"

Eli groaned. "I may never play poker again."

Giving him a clap on the back, Will sobered. "Just as long as you don't give up on Noelle. If you love her, fight for her. Be her safe place, and with patience and encouragement, she's bound to come around." Will's expression perked. "Say, why don't you bring her on Sunday to the family party?"

"It's been suggested, but she doesn't seem keen to meet the whole boisterous brood of us."

"Pssh." His father waved a dismissive hand. "I'll invite her and let her know we're nothing to fear. No vipers among us. No one bites. Teddy bears all."

Before Eli could mount a counterargument, his father headed out to the pottery shed.

Eli hurried to catch up to him. If his father came on too strong, would he scare Noelle away? He recalled what she'd said about her cold family, her isolation as a child and her discomfort with the dynamics of a large family.

When they reached his mother's studio, Noelle's expression was stark, her cheeks tearstained. His mother sat close beside her, an arm around Noelle's shoulders and clay-crusted fingers dabbing moisture from Noelle's face, leaving dirty smudges in her wake.

Eli's gut lurched. What the heck had happened? What had his mother said to Noelle?

He rushed to Noelle's side and crouched by her chair. "Sweetheart, what's wrong?" He shot his mother a quick, scolding look.

Sasha lifted her chin. "Don't glare at me in that tone of voice. I did nothing wrong."

Eli grinned at his mother's familiar catachresis.

Noelle sucked in a deep breath and blew her nose on a questionable-looking rag from his mother's pottery cleanup supplies. "I'm all right. Really. And your mother has been nothing but kind."

Eli angled his head, trying to meet her eyes. "If you're sure…" Placing a hand on Noelle's knee, he asked, "Are you ready to go? I have what I need from my dad."

Noelle sniffled again and nodded. She led the way out of the pottery studio, clearly eager to leave.

Before following her, Eli hugged his mother and gave her a searching look. "What happened?" he mouthed.

"Talk to her," his mother whispered back.

Eli nodded. He planned to do exactly that.

Chapter Fourteen

"You want to tell me what upset you when you were with my mother?" Eli asked when they were back in his Jeep headed to Shelby. "We have some time now to talk. Alone. No distractions."

"Yeah. Okay, but I want to know from you what this trip was about, too. You were very mysterious concerning what your father could contribute to the investigation."

"Sorry," he said, "I wasn't trying to be mysterious. I just didn't want to say anything until I was sure about my suspicion."

"And now you are sure?" she asked.

Eli cut a glance from the road to Noelle and nodded. "I am. I'm just not sure what to do with it."

"So spill. What did you learn?"

Eli drew a fortifying breath. "In college, did I ever tell you I had an aunt who was murdered when I was five years old?"

He heard her low gasp. "What!" Then a beat later, she said, "Wait. I think you did, just in passing. You didn't want to talk about it, so I let it drop. I mean, I had my touchy subjects that were taboo, so…" Noelle shifted on her seat. "What about your aunt?"

"The details of the murder scene, how she was killed, how she was dressed and posed, even the engagement ring her killer put on her hand and made sure we saw are almost identical to the Fiancée Killer. My aunt's killer left her in my grandparents' living room, not out in the wilderness, and he killed himself beside her. But there are too many similarities to disregard."

Noelle said nothing for a moment, and when he glanced her way, her expression said she was deep in thought, digesting this new information in light of what they knew.

"Maybe it's just a coincidence?" she said, though her tone said she didn't believe that theory any more than he did.

"I've told you my belief about coincidence, especially in police work."

"But if Scott is behind all this, like we think, and he's recreating the scene of your aunt's murder—"

"Which I was the first to come across when it happened."

Noelle inhaled sharply. "Eli! You never told me that! At five, you saw your murdered aunt?"

He confirmed this with a bob of his head. "And here I am investigating the new murders."

"How can you sound so casual about this? He set a bomb to try to kill you when you sniffed out his guilt!" Noelle raised both hands to her face and groaned. "Eli, has this all been about some grudge Scott has against you? I mean, we determined earlier that the victims all have dark hair and blue eyes like the Coltons, like *you*! But when he started killing women, how could Scott have known you'd get the case instead of some other ABI agent? And what in the world did you do to set him off like this?"

Eli scrubbed a hand over his chin. "Hell if I know. Scott's

never really registered on my radar before now. He was just this geeky guy from forensics I saw around the office from time to time. I may have teased him at some point, but nothing vicious. Just the kind of good-natured ribbing all men do with each other."

"So, what does this mean? If this has something to do with a vendetta against you, where does it go now that Scott knows you're onto him and his first attempt to kill you failed?"

"Well, for one thing, I want you out."

"What? No!"

"Noelle, I want you far away from this case for your own safety. And we have to make sure anyone who knows you were working on the case with me says nothing about it. I don't want him coming after you to get to me."

She touched his arm, drawing his attention away from the road. Her face was grim. "He already knows."

"Huh? How?"

"That morning I came by ABI headquarters to get your files on the case, he stopped by. You told him you were including me on the investigation as a consultant."

Eli's gut swooped. "I did?"

"You did."

When the day in question replayed in his brain, Eli slapped the steering wheel and muttered a bad word.

"What's more, someone has already come after me. Someone cut my brake line, remember?"

The heat of anger rose in his blood and climbed to his cheeks. His temples pounded as he mulled the truth from a new perspective. Someone had targeted Noelle. Scott knew of her involvement helping with the case. Fresh resolve hardened inside him. "Well, then, here's the new plan. I want you to stay close to me until we figure out where he is and what he's planning. I know that puts you in the line of fire, so to speak, but I can protect you better if I'm with you than if I'm not."

"You really think I—"

"Or..." Eli squeezed the steering wheel as another option occurred to him. "Maybe you should go back to Seattle now. Handle your sister's funeral from there. I can see that your directions for her remains are handled the way you want."

"Go home?" Her voice was soft and flat. "Is that really what you want?"

"No. But I want you safe, and you'll be safer far away from Shelby."

"What if I'm willing to take the risk in order to see this case through? To see my responsibilities to Allison through? I'm not a quitter, Eli."

He jerked a sharp look her way and clenched his jaw. "Well, you were once."

Her despondent sigh reached him. "Oh. That. Right."

When he glanced at her, she was staring out the side window, her brow puckered.

"I guess it's my turn to spill." She angled her gaze to him again. "I was crying at your parents because your mom was so sweet to me, so interested in me and my life, so... caring..." She sniffed, then opened her purse to pull out a tissue and wipe her eyes, her nose. "It just drilled home to me all the more what I'd missed not having a mother who valued me."

Eli frowned his sympathy. "I hate that you felt unloved, Noelle. But are you sure you're not remembering it through a dark lens? Maybe the fact that they favored your sister means you were a little jealous and saw things in a dimmer light than reality. I mean, they adopted you. Parents who want a child enough to adopt don't—"

"I know what I lived, Eli." She huffed her frustration, and he was jabbed with self-recrimination. The Coltons had pledged to live by the credo *believe*, yet the first time Noelle presented him with truths about her life that he found hard to swallow, he'd doubted her. Was that why she'd broken up with him years ago? Had he unwittingly given her the perception he didn't believe her? Had he diminished her truths and discounted her reality without knowing? Guilt kicked him at the notion he could have broken the family's core value with the person he wanted to form his own family with.

"I'm sorry. You're right." He reached for her leg and gave it a quick squeeze of apology. "Only you can know what you experienced and how it shaped you. Please go on."

She blinked at him as if his confession caught her off guard. "Thank you for that. I—" She cleared her throat. "The thing is, after a point, I got what I asked for. I gave them reason not to want me, not to love me. I became belligerent and acted out. I pushed the limits and rebelled after I heard—"

When she fell abruptly silent, he cut a side glance to her. "Heard what?" Eli held his breath. He didn't want to know the awful thing she'd heard that had clearly caused a deep rift and a lasting pain.

"I heard my mother and aunt talking in the kitchen one day when I was about fourteen. After years of trying to be perfect for them and a model student and daughter, I heard my mother say it had been a *mistake* to adopt me. A mistake she regretted every day."

Eli muttered a curse and reached for her knee. "Lord, Noelle, I am so sorry. What a terrible thing for her to say!"

"Yeah. Well, that was the truth I lived with. Once I knew she didn't care about me, I saw no reason to behave or try to earn her love any more. I was angry and hurt, and I saw no reason not to be as difficult and unlovable as they seemed to believe I was. I couldn't leave home soon enough. The animosity grew between us throughout high school. After I left for college, I never went back to Anchorage. Never really even spoke to my parents and only talked to Allison occasionally."

Eli pulled the car to the side of the road. Once the Jeep was stopped, he turned on his emergency blinkers and the dome light. Facing Noelle, he cupped her cheek and held her gaze. She was telling him the deepest hurts of her life, and he owed her his undivided attention, his undiluted care and comfort. "Noelle, I—I wish I could do something…"

"You can't, though. Nothing can change the past." She squared her shoulders, then raised her chin. "I'm all right now. I've learned to move forward. I have my career, friends, and I've built a new life without my family."

"I hate to think of you not having the kind of family support I've had," he said. "I can't imagine how lonely you must have felt growing up. Why didn't you tell me all this in college?"

"I told you earlier. I didn't want your pity. We had something special, and I didn't want to tarnish it by dumping my miserable history on you. When I heard how you talked about your family and how important they were to you, I just couldn't tell you how terribly my own family didn't measure up to yours."

"We *did* have something special, Noelle." Eli framed her face between his palms, his gaze probing hers, his heart breaking all over again. "And having heard all this about how heartless and cold your family was toward you,

I have to wonder all the more why you would give up what we had."

"It's hard to explain. I'm not even sure I understand all the reasons. Fear can be complicat—"

Eli's phone rang, making Noelle start and fall abruptly quiet. "Ignore it," he said. "Finish what you were saying. This conversation is more important to me than whatever the person on the other end of that call has to say."

Noelle's expression softened, and her eyes reflected an appreciation and affection that made Eli's chest ache all the more. His precious Noelle had been deprived of love, undervalued for so many years. Yet knowing the strong, intelligent and capable woman she'd become despite her circumstances made him appreciate her even more.

The phone quit ringing, and he gave her an encouraging nod. "There. All gone. Now finish."

"I was only saying I'm still figuring out for myself what—"

Again his phone rang, and Eli growled his frustration.

"Answer it," Noelle said, pushing his hands from her face. "Your partner is in the hospital, and a colleague suspected of mass murder is on the run. Odds are it's *very* important."

A quiver chased to his core at the reminder of the chaos he'd left behind in Shelby for this side venture. "True enough."

He took the call, and without a greeting, Kansas said, "Thank goodness! I was starting to worry! How could you take off on some mysterious errand and not be in touch for hours when we know Scott tried to kill you this morning?"

"Sorry if I worried you. Noelle and I are headed back now."

"You missed Asher's neurologist, the one who'll be treating his concussion. He stressed the importance of Asher resting, no screens, no reading print, no activity for several days. His brain needs time to heal."

"Damn. Bad time for him to be out of commission, too," Eli grumbled. "This case just burst wide open, and our prime suspect is on the lam."

He heard Kansas grunt. "I'm sure he'd much rather be helping you hunt down that bastard than be lying in the hospital with a cracked head."

Eli pinched the bridge of his nose. "You're right. That was insensitive of me."

"No." Kansas groaned. "I'm sorry, Eli. I'm just edgy and out of sorts because of everything that's happened."

"We all are. Look, I'll check by the hospital when we get back in town, but then I have to go to the office and start putting these new puzzle pieces in place."

He disconnected with Kansas, and after putting his phone away, he faced Noelle again. "Okay. No more interruptions, I promise. Please…finish what you were saying. I want to hear everything."

"You have the gist of it, I think. What's important now is finding Scott, whether or not he turns out to be the Fiancée Killer."

"He's the key to solving the case, at a minimum." Eli nodded. "All right. Let's go home." After turning off the dome light, he pulled back onto the dark highway.

"We," Noelle said.

Head buzzing with too many thoughts, Eli blinked at her. "What?"

"You told Kansas *you* would be working on the new puzzle the case has presented. But I'm going to be working on it with you. You just said you're shorthanded since

Asher is in the hospital. So *we* are going to figure this out together."

Warmth filled Eli's chest. He liked the sound of that. Sparing a glance from the road, he smiled at her and repeated, "We."

IN ORDER TO have the space to spread out and the privacy to talk openly about their suspicions without someone in the ABI office overhearing, Eli and Noelle decided to work at his house.

"I'd like to stop by the hostel and pick up a few things if this is going to be an all-nighter, as I suspect—" Noelle caught the intrigued lift of Eli's eyebrow as he cut a lustful glance her way. She returned a dry look. "A *working* all-nighter, Colton. We're trying to catch a killer, remember."

He shrugged. "First we work, then we play."

Noelle snorted indelicately but gave no other reply. She turned her gaze out the passenger window, studying the lights of the town and harbor as they approached her hostel. Was *play* how he viewed any intimacies between them at this point? Noelle had never considered their lovemaking anything but the most private and intentional connection between them. Nothing about it had been casual. Playful at times, but never casual or intended as cheap thrills.

But if that was how Eli now thought of potential sex between them—an itch to be scratched, a fun distraction or stress reliever—perhaps it would do her well to rethink her position.

She angled her head back toward Eli, studying the masculine cut of his cheeks and jaw, made all the sharper and more defined in the dim glow from his Renegade's dashboard lights. His lips were pressed in a grim line at the moment, a sure indication his thoughts had reverted to his case. Scott's deception and vicious attack or some other stressor from a long litany clearly haunted him. She let her attention linger on his mouth, remembering all the sensations those lips had stirred in her in past years, all the private places on her body they'd grazed, tasted and wakened with tender manipulation.

A tingling flush raced over her skin, and she felt her breath hitch, as if Eli were kissing her now.

The crunch of gravel under tires roused her as Eli pulled onto the drive of her hostel and parked. She sobered quickly and retrieved her keys from the front pocket of her messenger bag. Seeing the empty place where her rental should be parked reminded her she'd left it in the hospital lot.

"We should probably pick up my car from the hospital parking lot on the way to your place," she said as she climbed out of his Jeep.

"Good idea," he said, waiting at his front bumper for her to precede him up the walkway to her door.

Hostel key in hand, Noelle approached the small concrete landing and aimed the key for the knob—and noticed the door stood ajar.

The wood around the latch plate was freshly scarred and splintered.

She gasped, and a chill washed through her.

Eli seized her arm. He tugged her backward, dragging her behind him with one hand while his other unsnapped the holster of his service weapon. "Stay here."

"But it's—"

His blue eyes glinted with steel. *"Stay here."*

Crossing her arms over her chest to ward off both the cold of the Alaskan night and the foreboding of what could be inside, Noelle waited. Her breath clouded around her, the white puffs lit by the pinkish glow of the security lamp at the edge of the street. After a couple of minutes, she drew a breath, prepared to call to Eli for a progress report but stopped, the words in her throat. If someone was inside with Eli, she couldn't alert the prowler to Eli's presence.

Then she remembered what had happened the last time Eli had investigated suspicious circumstances at a house. *Rigged with a bomb...triggered when we entered...*

His hoarse voice from earlier in the day echoed in her brain, and her blood flashed hot, then icy. "Eli, no! Get out! There could be another bomb!"

He appeared at the door, his face grim but calm. "It's all good. I checked for a trigger as I walked in, but when I saw the condition of the place, I realized a bomb wasn't the intruder's goal."

She frowned. "Condition of the place?"

He pulled the door open wider and waved a hand for her to enter.

Noelle looked past him, wary. "No bombs? You're sure?"

"I gave the place a pretty thorough search. No sign of anything remotely resembling an explosive device or components."

She hesitated another few seconds, working up her courage, until Eli sent her a look that asked, *Don't you trust me?*

She did trust Eli. With her life. But was she ready to trust him with her heart?

Another problem for another time.

He took her hand and led her inside the dark studio apartment. He flipped the light switch by the door and lit the room.

Noelle squawked her shock at the upheaval that greeted her. The furniture had been upended, cushions flung about and ripped open. Her suitcase was dumped on the floor. Her possessions had been ransacked, broken, scattered.

Loose paper was spread everywhere, and books unshelved. Drawers were open and carelessly emptied on the counter-top. The scene was pure chaos. Pure destruction.

A sense of rage and vulnerability swamped her. The invasion of her privacy, the mistreatment of her belongings, the calculated disregard and intrusion…

She swayed on her feet, and Eli caught her elbow. Clinging to his coat sleeve, she wobbled to the kitchen chair that he righted for her.

"You should see if anything is missing and report the break-in to the landlord."

She nodded, numb and shaking. "Who would do this?" she muttered. "Why?"

Noelle covered her face with her hands and allowed a frustrated and rather frightened growl to roll from her throat. "I haven't even been here for two weeks! Hardly anyone even knows I'm here besides you, and my aunt and unc—" She snapped her head toward Eli, her hands balling in rage. "My aunt and uncle! I've already had to sign a second contract with the funeral home because of their meddling. Do you suppose…is their grudge against me, their disdain for me so great that they'd—" She stopped short.

Eli was shaking his head slowly, the anger and clarity in his gaze unnerving.

"Then who?" As soon as she spoke, an echo reverberated in her head. She'd asked the same question when she'd learned her brake line had been sabotaged.

"You're right that very few people know you're in town. But Scott is one of them, and he knows we had a relationship once, knows we've been spending time together since you arrived. If this is about me, as I'm starting to suspect, he could have lured you here to taunt me. He could have targeted Allison to get you here because of our past. The

Fiancée Killer has already dug up my aunt's murder and copied it. Based on everything else we're learning, I'd say he's striking out at me through you."

If she hadn't already been sitting, Noelle might have slumped to the floor. As it was, her body shuddered, and her head spun. "You really think he killed Allison to lure me here? So that he could get at you… How? By hurting me?"

Or killing me. Ice rippled through her.

When Eli squatted beside her, she met his gentle eyes. "Noelle, think about it. Your brakes were cut. Intentionally." His voice was calm and soothing despite his frightening message. "I'd say Scott has already tried to hurt you. Or worse."

Scott…

Noelle sucked in a sharp breath as her gaze cut to the table where she'd been working. It was empty. A sensation like electricity raced through her veins. "Oh no," she rasped.

"What?" Eli whipped his head around to look across the room where she stared in horror.

"The paper files. All the sheets I'd printed off and the hard copies of information you gave me on the case." She swallowed hard, regret churning in her gut. "I—I had them on that table when I left."

Eli's eyes widened, and he mumbled a curse. Surging to his feet, he moved to look among the detritus scattered around the base of the empty table, then scanned the room slowly, as she did, for any evidence of the files. But they were gone.

"I'm sorry," she whispered, guilt filling her. "You trusted me with those files and—"

He touched a finger to her lips to silence her. "No.

You've done nothing wrong. The files were locked in a room where you had every expectation they would be safe."

Her heart tripped, doubting she deserved the grace he offered her. She should have kept the paper case files as secure as she'd kept her computer. Scott—because she, too, felt in her bones the forensic specialist was behind the break-in—now knew the details of what they'd uncovered about his tampering with the case.

"So, now what happens?" She hated the tremor in her voice, but this turn of events, piled on top of so much other emotional upheaval in recent days left her off-balance.

"Well, I'll call the locals to come take pictures and dust for prints, but you can bet he was wearing gloves if it really was Scott."

"I meant now that he has your files."

Eli scratched his chin. "If Montgomery is the one who broke in here and took the files, then all he's really gained is confirmation we're onto him. He was already privy to most of the casework already."

She pressed a hand to her mouth and sighed. "And we know he's still close, somewhere in town. Or was here within the last few hours, anyway."

Eli nodded, stroking her cheek to brush her hair back. "Another thing I know is you're not staying here at the hostel any longer. When you notify the landlord about the break-in, tell him you're checking out."

She jolted, more surprised and hurt by his suggestion than she wanted to admit. "You're sending me back to Seattle?"

He blinked. Frowned. "No. I'm moving you to my house. I'm keeping you near me until—" His expression shifted, softened with sorrow and acceptance. "Although it's true. You might be safer in Seattle…if that's where you'd rather go."

Here was her chance to walk away if she chose. No one could blame her if she left before Allison's funeral. She'd already made the funeral arrangements and signed the paperwork at the coroner's office. Did she really want to stay for the service?

Someone had tried to kill her. Her lodgings had been ransacked. And the longer she stayed near Eli, the harder it would be to avoid breaking his heart and her own again when they parted. Staying would be foolish, wouldn't it?

Yet another part of her refused to leave before Allison's killer had been caught or before Scott Montgomery was brought in for attempting to kill Asher and Eli or before she'd done everything she could to help Eli resolve the Fiancée Killer case for the sake of the victims' families.

Drawing a deep breath, she found her resolve and squared her shoulders as she angled her body toward Eli. "No. I'm not going anywhere yet. We have work to do, and I won't leave until Allison and the others have justice."

ELI SWALLOWED AGAINST the lump that swelled in his throat. He couldn't be sure whether the rise of emotion choking him was rooted in relief that Noelle was staying or pride in her conviction to see the case through. Either way, he leaned in to give her a quick kiss.

He cleared his throat as he rose to his feet and held a hand out to her. "All right, let's get the police out here to take a report. Once they take pictures and process the scene, you can pack a bag, and we'll get you settled at my house."

The local police worked for close to an hour before they allowed Noelle to organize and pack her possessions. While the police were processing the scene, Noelle and Eli stopped in the landlord's office to turn in her key and report the crime. Eli asked the hostel owner about security cameras for the property, both for his own knowledge and to speed the process for the local uniforms.

"Not inside the rental, but there's one that covers the front door and one for the backyard," the landlord said.

"I want a copy of the footage. Tonight." When the owner started shaking his head, Eli pulled out his badge and narrowed a hard look on the man. When the man sighed and jerked a nod, Eli added a tight, "Thank you."

He told the landlord that the local police were already on-site, collecting evidence, and to make an additional copy of the video for them. After handing the man his business card with the email to send the video footage, Eli escorted Noelle to his car.

When he took her to pick up her car in the hospital parking lot, they dropped in to check on Asher briefly. He was asleep, but a nurse informed them Asher was doing fine and not showing any adverse symptoms. Kansas, the nurse added, had left to get a meal and some rest only a few minutes before they'd arrived.

In the parking lot, Eli searched Noelle's rental car for sabotage before she got in to follow him to his house.

The idea that someone, probably Montgomery, had targeted Noelle, likely because of her association with him, sat like glacial ice in Eli's gut. Now that he was aware of the danger his coworker posed to her, Eli swore Scott would have to come through him to get near Noelle again.

Noelle set her bags in a corner of Eli's living room, and he, eager to get back to work on catching Scott Montgomery, cleared a spot on his kitchen table again to be their workspace. He booted up his home laptop to check his email and found the security video from the hostel had already arrived.

Noelle looked over his shoulder as he played the footage from the relevant hours of that day. They saw Noelle leaving, hurrying to the hospital following his call, a moose that wandered through the backyard, but nothing else.

"Damn. I was sure we'd have Scott dead to rights on camera." Eli groaned and laced his fingers behind his head as he leaned his chair up on the two back legs.

Noelle returned to her seat with a sigh. "He's no fool. He'd know to be wary of security cameras and not to be caught. He could have gone in a window at the side or out of frame at the back."

"True enough." Eli closed the lid of his laptop and faced her. "Where were we on your analysis?"

"I've run everything we had before this morning, but until we have more quantifiable evidence to add to the algorithm, I don't know how I can help with building your case against Scott."

Her phrasing hit him in the gut like a fist. Eli pressed his mouth in a hard line and held up a hand. "Hang on. Stop there. I know the evidence we've got now all points to Scott, but my job, the job of the ABI is not to build a case against anyone. That's the DA's job after he's arrested and formally charged. Our job is to collect evidence and follow the case wherever the evidence leads. I can't make the mistake of letting my personal bias or fears dictate a particular spin on the findings. When we have enough evidence to support an arrest, we make the arrest. But we can't fall in the trap of making assumptions about a person's guilt and risk getting tunnel vision, missing the bigger picture and wasting time going down the wrong path."

"But don't you have enough evidence against Scott to arrest him now?" Noelle asked, sounding as frustrated as he felt.

Eli twisted his mouth, skeptical. "Evidence he tried to kill me and Asher with the bomb at his house? Maybe. Indications that he tampered with the evidence and sabotaged our investigation? Yes. Proof that he's the Fiancée Killer? Not as much. We need physical evidence, eyewitnesses, a confession…something solid that connects him specifically with the women's deaths. Right now all we really have is a lot of incriminating circumstantial evidence. And we don't have any solid proof he's the one targeting you. Just hunches and gut feelings."

"So where should we focus tonight? I can help you look at the big picture."

Eli nodded. "Yeah. The big picture is likely where we'll find his motive, for trying to blow me and Asher up if nothing else. From there, we follow the evidence." He drilled his finger on the tabletop as he made his point. Scowling, he pulled out his cell phone. "Speaking of evidence, let me see what the forensic crew with the Shelby PD found in the rubble of Scott's house and if anything there helps our case."

While Eli talked to the Shelby PD, he watched Noelle doodle on a notepad, drawing boxes, connecting lines and sketching Venn diagrams. Her expression was one of intense concentration, a look he remembered well from college and studying together. His fingers itched to soothe the tiny line that creased her forehead between her eyebrows, and his lips tingled at the notion of kissing the taut line of her mouth.

He was so involved in her every move and subtle facial shift that he almost missed the Shelby police detective's comment when he finally came on the line.

"We're still combing through the debris and cataloging what's found. The fire department wouldn't let us get at it until they were sure there were no more explosive materials or smoldering embers that could reignite."

Smoldering... Yeah, Eli could use that word to describe Noelle as she nibbled her bottom lip and angled her head so that her long hair brushed her cheek.

Eli pressed the pads of his fingers into his closed eyes, trying to redirect his thoughts. "All right. Just...please be sure your officers know that there could be critical evidence related to a serial murder case at the site. Call me immediately if anything related to the Fiancée Killer victims, the crime scene locations...or my family comes up."

Noelle looked up, a degree of surprise lifting her eyebrows.

"Your family?" the police detective asked, echoing what was written on Noelle's face.

"Long story. And that link is both unconfirmed and confidential. Do you understand, Detective?" Eli thanked the local detective and disconnected. "Nothing useful from Scott's house yet. They're still processing it."

"You're pretty sure this is about you or your family then? Is that the bigger picture we need to look at?" Noelle said, her pen tapping her notepad restlessly.

"Since a significant number of those lines—" he pointed to her sketches "—have me at the center, it's something we need to explore." Eli paused, then leaning toward Noelle, he shot her a quizzical look. "Right?"

She blinked. "You're asking me?"

He spread his hands and stated in a serious tone, "I just want to be sure I'm not being...egocentric or biased in some way. Those connections..." he tapped her pad again where she'd graphically linked him to Scott and the murders "...can't be coincidence, can they?"

"You don't believe in coincidence. Or so you keep telling me."

"But am I right?"

A tender expression lit Noelle's face. "You are an intelligent man and an excellent lawman. I've always known you to have good instincts. Trust them. If your gut's telling you to pursue this path, there's something there to be discovered. And for what it's worth, that's what my gut is telling me, too."

He smiled his appreciation for her reassurances and leaned in to give her a kiss. "Then let's get to work."

Chapter Fifteen

Five hours later, Eli threw his pen down on his coffee table with a frustrated huff. "This is getting us nowhere. Meanwhile, Montgomery is who knows where, doing who knows what. Maybe the *why* isn't as important right now as just catching him and making sure he can't kill anyone else."

Sitting beside him on his living room couch, Noelle reached over to massage Eli's shoulder. Tension radiated from him like heat waves off pavement in summer. They'd been looking for an incident or other link between Eli and Scott Montgomery that would explain why Scott was targeting women who looked like Eli's murdered aunt, why he was copying the MO of Caroline's murder. Did Scott have a grudge against Eli or the family as a whole? Had Eli somehow cost Scott a promotion? Embarrassed him personally or professionally? Had Scott used the Colton family's adventure company and formed a grievance as a result?

But every avenue they pursued appeared to be a dead end, and their previous convictions about Montgomery's motives and Eli's links to the case wobbled.

Eli rolled his shoulders as she kneaded the muscles in his neck, and the groan that purred from his throat was far more sensual than frustrated. The sexy sound of the rumble from his chest instantly shifted Noelle's thoughts away from crime fighting and to the attractive man sitting beside her.

Despite the serious nature of the work they were undertaking, Noelle had been battling distracting thoughts about Eli all evening. She'd keyed in on how intimate it was to be sitting close to Eli on his couch, where days before they'd given in to the pulsing need that lay just beneath the surface for them both.

The fire in his fireplace and the scent of his aftershave filling her senses only added to the romantic ambience. More than once she'd had to remind herself that they had important work to do and to stop staring at the way his long fingers held his pen as he scribbled notes or the way the muscles in his square jaw bunched as he clenched his teeth in concentration. Her mind kept drifting to the evening they'd tangled limbs on this very couch and might have made love had his brother not stopped by.

Make love to him once and get it out of your system, she'd reasoned that evening. She'd held her feelings for Eli at bay for thirteen years. She'd gotten good at it. With all this practice, surely she could enjoy a night of physical enjoyment without losing her heart. Couldn't she?

She glanced at his mantel clock. It was after midnight. Surely no one from his family would be dropping in to visit at this late hour. If things grew steamy between them now, nothing stood in the way of finishing what they started.

"Noelle? What do you think?"

Her pulse jumped, afraid of what he might have read in her moony-eyed gaze. What had he asked earlier? New angles? "Um, you're right. Maybe we do need to step back and look at this differently."

Noelle quashed the hum of desire that touching him had

awakened. Dropping her hands to her lap, she pushed aside the distracting feel of Eli's strong neck and broad shoulders, trying to refocus the random information they had about Scott Montgomery and the string of murders he'd apparently committed. *Apparently* being the key word. They had to find proof.

"I know the fact that he altered the case files is highly incriminating, but what if he's just in league with the person killing the women? He could be getting blackmailed by the real killer and altering the information to avoid being outed for something in his past. Or he could be covering for friend or family member."

Eli's only answer was a dispirited sigh.

Noelle pushed off the sofa and moved to the table where they'd set up her laptop. "This link to your aunt's murder could point to someone that was associated with her killer. A family member of Caroline's stalker wanting revenge? Could someone who worked on the old case have contacted Scott?"

Eli curled his fingers into his hair, growling, "Holy hell, I'm so tired of going in circles on this case! Every time I think we're a step closer, a hundred new questions and possibilities come up."

Noelle gripped his wrist. "Forget my last questions, then. Maybe I'm muddying the water, and we ought to stick with Occam's razor. The simplest and most obvious solution is what we need to focus on."

"Me being the common factor," Eli said darkly.

Without directly answering him, Noelle mulled how to use her analysis software to help with this new twist in the case. "If we factor in everything we know about Scott's contact with your family and add that to the analyses we've already run, maybe something new will pop."

"How do you quantify his contact with my family?" Eli asked. "And how do we reconstruct every family member who has stopped by the office to see me and run into Montgomery?"

"Maybe we can't."

Eli twisted his mouth in thought. "But we can have Parker or Lakin pull records at the family's business to see if Scott used RTA in the past. That's a start."

"Okay," she said, making a note. "We'll do that first thing in the morning."

He dragged both hands over his face as he sighed. "I still feel like this has to be about me somehow. I was the one who went with my dad to my grandparents' house that day twenty-eight years ago and found Caroline's and her stalker's bodies. I work with Scott, and I'm the one who got assigned to solve this case. Now we have reason to believe he's tried to kill me and my partner, and he's gone after you, my ex-girlfriend. But why? I just don't see the reason behind it. What is his grudge?"

He stood up to pace, and Noelle moved to block his path and lay her hands on his chest. "Does he have to have a reason? Can't it just be a matter of something sick and twisted inside him? If he learned about your aunt's murder and already had psychopathic tendencies, he could just be killing these women and getting a thrill that you haven't made the connection to your aunt yet. Maybe now that you've figured it out, he'll stop killing and—"

Eli shook his head. "Serial killers don't stop. They may lie low for a while or move to another state, but the *whatever it is* that drives them to kill doesn't go away. We have to bring him in, sooner rather than later."

Noelle stepped closer and pulled him into a hug. "Okay. Try this on for size. You should put a pin in all this for now and get some sleep. We seem to be going in circles without making any progress at this point."

Eli's expression dimmed. "How am I supposed to sleep knowing Montgomery could be stalking his next victim or *killing her* while we dither around trying to figure out the connection to me?"

"I wouldn't say we're dithering, exactly. And the state and local police have issued an APB for him, right? We'll look at it again in the morning with fresh eyes. Okay?"

He scowled, clearly unconvinced.

Stroking his cheek, she tried a new tact. "Sometimes, when I'm trying to fall asleep…" she took his hand and led him toward his bedroom "…or early in the morning, when I'm not fully awake, my subconscious speaks to me, and I see situations I've been debating in a whole new light."

His eyebrow quirked. "That's happened for me before." He stumbled tiredly in her wake, and his head lolled in concession. "Fine. I'll get some sleep…" he pulled her up short and wrapped her in his embrace again "…if you'll join me. It's late. Come to bed with me."

His voice held a husky rasp, and heat rushed through her. Did he mean his request the way it sounded?

"To sleep?" she asked, her head tipped flirtatiously.

"At some point, probably." He tugged his cheek up, flashing a devilish grin. "But…" he speared his fingers into her hair, combing it back from her face "…anything else that happens is up to you. I won't press you for anything you're not comfortable with."

A sweet mellowness weighted her core. This sort of kindness and understanding had made her fall in love with Eli in college. Having evidence of that same noble character again was both a potent reminder of what they'd once shared and a warning that, by making love to Eli, she could easily get ensnared in levels of emotion and attachment that were unhealthy for her heart. Yet she wanted just a sip from the cup of passion he offered…

He held her in his blue gaze, his desire and tenderness as clear as the bright Alaskan moon.

Rising on her tiptoes, she pressed a kiss to his lips. "All right. Lead the way. We have unfinished business, you and I."

Chapter Sixteen

Walking backward as he kissed her, Eli drew Noelle into his bedroom. When his legs hit the edge of his bed, he toed off his shoes and pulled her shirt from the waist of her slacks without breaking the contact of their lips. His body was aflame, wound tight with a hunger he'd suppressed for years.

He'd been with other women since Noelle, but none had meant a fraction of what his intimacies with her had meant, and he'd quickly lost interest in pointless sex. When you've had something as rich and powerful as making love to your soulmate, anything else felt empty, even like a betrayal.

To have her in his arms again, to be able to touch her, kiss her, savor the sweet connection that two could share with their bodies and hearts joined was paradise to him. Maybe he could show her physically the truth that his words had not yet been able to convey. She belonged with him. There was no challenge or difference or past heartache they couldn't overcome together.

"I've missed you, missed this, sweetheart," he murmured as he dropped tiny kisses along the curve of her throat. Her breath caught, and the sexy sigh that followed stirred the ache in his core to feverish new heights.

Patience. Savor this. Make it count.

He knew he might not get another chance to set things right with her, and he wanted everything about this night to reawaken the feelings she'd once had for him.

He took his time, nibbling the sensitive spot below her ear, massaging her nape with his thumbs, tracing the shape of her lips with one fingertip. He felt her muscles slowly relax, her body tremble in response to his caresses. He tested all the spots that had once been her favorite places to be kissed, and he grinned when he won gasps of delight and pleasure from her.

She slipped her hands beneath his shirt and dug her fingers into his back, encouraging him by canting her hips and sliding her body against the length of his.

Patience. Savor this, he told himself again, even as his breathing grew rough and choppy, his libido firing and hungry.

One item of clothing followed another, while they stared into each other's eyes. Her shirt, then his. Her slacks, his jeans. Her lacy underwear and bra, a wonder to behold both on her and then off.

When they were both naked, he lifted her, and she wrapped her legs around his hips. Turning, he tumbled them to his bed and quickly wrapped them in the warmth of his blankets.

Burrowed deep in a snug cocoon of blankets, he let his hands roam, his mouth taste and his gaze worship her. As his passion rose, so too did the tender ache in his marrow that could only be called love. "It's only ever been you for me, Noelle. In college, now, forever. Only you."

In the dark of their blanket nest, he heard a hiccupping sob, felt the dampness on her cheeks, and he dried the tears with his kisses. "Only you, Noelle. Only you for me."

NOELLE LET ELI'S words sink into her soul and nudge aside the pain that had resided deep inside her for so long. Rejection from her birth mother. Rejection from her adoptive family. Rejection from classmates who saw only her differences in her youth.

The scars created when she was young. The longing in her soul for love and acceptance had shaped so many of her choices in life. Perhaps the most difficult choice had been to break up with Eli in order to protect herself from what she'd believed to be inevitable pain in the long term. No one had ever loved her long term. No one had ever kept promises, kept faith, kept her close.

Except Eli.

And she'd pushed him away anyhow.

The stinging truth of that realization, seen afresh some thirteen years later, slashed her with needlelike tines. A sob broke from her throat, and Eli lifted his head from kissing her breast.

"Noelle? What's wrong? Do you want to stop?"

She curled her fingers in his hair and shook her head. "No. I only… I was thinking how much I'd missed this. Missed you."

"Ah, love, me too." Pulling back a corner of the blanket and letting in the dim light from his bedside clock, he continued to stare at her, his eyes intense. "Are you sure that's all that's wrong?"

She gave a wry half laugh. "You know me too well, huh?"

He leaned on one elbow, studying her face while he drew lazy circles on her skin with his finger. "I used to, but I'm not sure I do anymore. Tell me what's bothering you."

"Now? In the middle of—" she waved a hand between them "—and break the mood?"

"We have all night for—" He copied her hand wave between them. "But if something is on your mind, I want to settle it now, before it becomes a problem for us."

"It's not…" She ducked her head to avoid his gaze, and he angled her chin back up again.

"Look at me, Noelle. Talk to me. Let me in."

Taking a breath for courage, she admitted, "I was thinking how I should have fought harder to overcome my concerns about us when I had the chance. You were good to me, and I let worries about the future, clouded by my past, stand in the way."

He lifted an eyebrow. "What about the future?"

Here, she hesitated. After a taut moment of silence, she said, "Your family. Whether they'd accept me as more than a college girlfriend. If my own family couldn't love me, how could I think anyone else's would?"

"Noelle, sweetheart…" He drew her closer, held her firmly in his arms and kissed the top of her head. "My family would love you. Didn't my mom and dad welcome you today? And you've met one of my brothers and my cousin Kansas. Granted, Parker was teasing a bit about having caught us making out, but that was directed at me. Brother stuff."

She shook her head. "It's easy to be polite and kind in the short term, and a whole other matter to welcome someone…" she hesitated, almost said *different*, but went with "…*new* into their ranks. Especially someone like me who hurt you once and who never—"

He stopped her with a kiss. "If that is your concern, then I can ease your mind with conviction." He laced his fingers with hers and kissed her knuckles one at a time as he said, "My. Family. Will. Love. You."

She rested her forehead against his. "Easy enough for

you to say. Harder for me to believe considering my experiences with…rejection."

"Fine," he said. "You don't have to take my word for it. The proof is in the pudding, as they say. I deal in facts. Proof. Evidence. So, allow me to show you the truth."

"How?" she asked, narrowing a skeptical look on him.

"My mother's birthday party Sunday. You've been invited by more than one family member. Come with me and meet the family. *All* of the family. I think you'll see why I'm so sure after you've spent time with the whole motley crew for a while. Give them a chance. And if you're convinced, then give *us* a chance."

"I—I want to, but…can you afford to go to a family party with the investigation at this boiling point? With Scott out there—"

"The case takes priority, of course. But if we're not actively following a tip of a sighting or other time-sensitive leads, I can take a few hours off to toast my mother's health with the family. I'm only a phone call away if anything with the case changes. So…" Eli kissed her again, long and deep. "What do you say?"

She let out a sigh, feeling a bit of tension inside her release, as if by making the decision to move forward with getting to know Eli's family, she was taking the weight of a years-long uncertainty off her shoulders. "Okay. You win. I'll go with you Sunday."

"Good." Eli slid a leg up her calf and rolled on top of her. "Now that we've decided that…where were we?" He trailed his lips, his tongue along her throat. "Oh, yeah. I was about to rock you to your core, pretty lady."

He caught her giggle when he took her lips with his. When he moved on to nibble her shoulder, she teased,

"Bold talk, Mr. I-deal-in-facts. Where's your proof you can rock anything?"

And for the next several hours, he presented his very convincing case.

THE NEXT MORNING, Noelle woke, sore in places that hadn't been sore in thirteen years, but feeling a hopefulness and happiness she hadn't known in the same length of time. She rolled on her side and watched Eli sleeping in the light that seeped in from the window.

Light from the window? She furrowed her brow. If the sun was up, it had to be almost 9:00 a.m. She hadn't slept this late in months. And she and Eli had work to do on the investigation to find and bring in Scott Montgomery.

She was just debating whether to wake Eli now or let him sleep until she finished her shower, when his cell phone jangled on his nightstand.

Jolted awake, Eli squinted at the daylight and reached for his phone. "Yeah? I mean, Agent Colton. Oh yes. What can I do for you?"

Noelle shivered in the chilly bedroom and pulled the covers up to her chin as she listened to Eli's end of the conversation.

"Oh? Anything helpful? Really? Uh, yeah, that should work. No, it's no problem. Saturday or not, casework comes first. I'll be in shortly." Eli cut a glance to Noelle as he disconnected his call. "That was the lead investigator with the police department. As I asked, he's been working on the evidence recovery at Montgomery's house, and this morning they found a good bit he thinks will be helpful for the Fiancée Killer case. I'm meeting him at my office as soon as I can grab a shower." He shifted to face her and ran a hand down her bare back, sending delicious thrills spiraling inside her. "I hate to leave you by yourself, especially since we believe Scott is gunning for you. You can come with me if you want."

She toyed with a wisp of his hair that curled around his ear. She considered his offer but didn't want to be dependent on him for anything. Including his protection. Dependence led to disappointment and heartbreak. Despite her displeasure over his leaving, she mustered a smile. "I'll be fine. I've thought of a way to run some new analyses that will cross-reference the Fiancée Killer data with your aunt's murder. Do you think I could get access to the old case files from California?"

"Definitely. I'll make a call to the San Diego police and make an official request since Caroline's murder appears to be pertinent to our case. I'll have them copy you with any emails sent." Eli leaned in to give her a deep kiss, then gave her bottom a playful swat. "And now I have to get moving, before your perfect lips and hot little body tempt me to blow off responsibilities today in lieu of a day in bed with you."

A chill found her when he tossed back the covers and crossed the room. The cold had as much to do with the disappointment and the lonely void created when he removed his solid presence, his warmth and the shelter of his arms as it did the nip of the bedroom air. How quickly she'd returned to the place she'd known too briefly in college, where lying with Eli, wrapped in his arms, could make her feel safer and more complete than she'd ever known before.

Climbing from the bed, she found his bathrobe hanging on his closet door and tied it around her. She pushed the empty ache away, reminding herself of the hard work she'd done in the past decade. She'd focused on finding herself, learning to be comfortable in her independence and establishing a balance that wasn't dependent on anyone else's approval or recognition. The process had been slow but steady. In light of all the memories evoked by this trip north, seeing Eli and Aunt Jean and coming to grips with Allison's death, she realized just how far she'd actually come. She refused to let old hurts and ancient memories cause her to backslide.

She inhaled the tantalizing scent of Eli that clung to his bathrobe and let herself relish the intimacies they'd shared last night. Her feminine core tingled at the reminder of his body twined with hers, his hand and lips loving her, arousing her, waking a dormant part of her soul.

Noelle squared her shoulders and set the glow of their lovemaking aside. As enjoyable as the night had been, she had to put those tender feelings back in the box where she kept her treasured memories of Eli and prepare herself for her inevitable return to Seattle. Last night had been about closure for her. She and Eli could part as friends with one last precious memory of the sweetness of their shared passion. But she'd come too far, worked too hard to risk her fragile emotions to a fraught relationship with Eli.

She would help him catch the Fiancée Killer, bury Allison and return to her life in Seattle knowing she could put Alaska securely behind her once and for all.

ELI DIDN'T RETURN from his meeting with the local police investigator until that evening. Noelle had made herself a toasted cheese sandwich and tomato soup from a can in Eli's pantry and was just sitting down to eat when he hustled in from the cold, bringing the mid-November chill with him.

"Sorry I was gone so long. After I finished at the office, I stopped by the hospital to catch Asher up on what I've learned."

"Oh? And how is he?"

"Discharged, it turned out. So then I trekked by his house and found him surrounded by a gaggle of elderly neighbors who were feeding him up on casseroles and homemade sweets. I helped him shoo the well-meaning ladies away so he could rest and gave him the highlights of the new case information. When I left, he was starting an audiobook, grumbling about his doctor restricting his screentime, and enjoying the bounty of baked goods his neighbors had provided." Eli peeled off his coat and draped it over the back of a kitchen chair. "That smells good. I missed lunch, so I'm famished."

He started prowling the kitchen, and she waved him to her chair. "Eat mine. I'll fix more for me while you tell me what the police found in the wreckage of Scott's house. Anything useful for the case?"

Eli looked ready to reject her offered dinner, but hunger clearly won. He picked up half of the gooey cheese sandwich and took a big bite, groaning in satisfaction. "They definitely did."

Noelle tried to ignore how sensual Eli's enjoyment of the sandwich sounded as she dug in his pantry for another can of soup.

"Among the scattered and partially burned papers in Scott's destroyed home office," he said, "they found a file he'd made regarding my aunt's murder."

Noelle spun to face him, a can of minestrone soup in her hand. "Just as we thought. The similarities in the posing of the victims and manner of death weren't a coincidence."

"Seems not." He took another large bite and around the mouthful he said, "That's not all they found. Maps. Photographs of the locations where the bodies have been found. He'd made a plan where to leave his victims, it seems."

"Is there anything we can conclude from those locations?" she asked as she popped the top on the soup and dumped it in the same pan she'd used to heat the tomato soup. "Maybe my software program can predict where he might go next, and we can catch him red-handed."

"If only." He slurped a spoonful of soup, then cut a sharp glance at her. "Wait. Do you think your program *can* do that?" His eyes were bright with hope. "Predict future locations? If so, we can stake out those sites and wait for Montgomery to show up."

Her pulse pattered, and she was flooded by a desire to do anything she could to make Eli happy, to fulfill that look of anticipation and to be the answer to all his wants and desires. She swallowed past the sudden knot in her throat. "I haven't tried it yet, but I will tonight."

He rewarded her with a smile that melted everything feminine inside her. She was warm wax, eager to be molded to his liking, if only to receive that bright look of delight and affection for as long as possible. Or at least until she returned to Seattle.

That thought popped the fragile bubble of joy that had sidetracked her and mercilessly snatched her back to reality. Nothing had fundamentally changed in her situation or Eli's since she'd arrived in Shelby. They'd slept together, sure. And it had been as wonderful and moving as she remembered from college. But she was the same person, with the same difficult history and the same need to avoid further heartbreak. They still had separate lives in different states, and the same challenges of ethnicity and societal bias. She couldn't bear the thought of her relationship with Eli causing any tension or dissension between him and his family.

The sound of Eli scraping the bottom of his soup bowl roused her from her gloomy thoughts, and she pasted on a smile to camouflage her dejection. "I can fix more if you're still hungry."

He wiped his mouth on a napkin and rose to carry the dish to the sink. "Nah. Let's get back to work. I want to show you what the local detective gave me this morning. And I want to see what your software can do about forecasting where Montgomery might be going next."

Chapter Seventeen

Noelle and Eli spent most of the rest of Saturday trying new configurations and trials with her software…and getting nowhere. Eli's frequent calls to the Shelby PD for updates on possible sightings of Scott, any proof he was responsible for the break-in at the hostel and new evidence from the bombed house were equally unfruitful.

Whenever Eli displayed signs of his growing frustration with the case, Noelle did her best to ease the tension in his muscles with neck massages or by coaxing him to use yoga poses and breathing techniques to release his stress. By the time they tumbled into bed that evening, the therapeutic touches and collaborative deep breathing had worked them both into a state of arousal that they satisfied by making love late into the night.

Noelle spent Sunday with a twist of confused emotions in the pit of her stomach. The renewed passion between them had both refueled her affection for Eli and fed the fear that she'd lost control of her feelings. She was certain she'd set herself up for another devastating break from him.

Complicating this tempest inside her was the knowledge that she was going to be thrust into Eli's huge family and closest friends for his mother's party that evening. She'd toyed with faking a headache or other illness to keep her home, but Eli's eagerness for the family to meet her and vice versa was so palpable and endearing, she quashed her reluctance and mentally braced for the evening's event.

Noelle offered to drive separately in her rental car to the party—the easier to make a quick escape if she needed—but Eli convinced her to ride with him in his Jeep. "There's a forecast for snow to start about the time we leave the party, and I'm betting my Renegade can better handle winter conditions on the roads."

They stopped at a local bakery near Eli's house for their contribution to the family meal, where Noelle bought two loaves of freshly baked bread. Eli shopped next door at a deli, choosing wine and cheeses for his family and Asher's favorite pizza, which they dropped off at his partner's house on their way to the party.

"Give me the latest on the case," Asher asked, clearly bored out of his skull because of the concussion protocol that limited his entertainment options.

"Nothing you need to worry about. Concentrate on following doctor's orders and getting back to work in a couple weeks," Eli said.

Asher grumbled under his breath, especially when he heard they were headed to a Colton family party. "I'd kill to go with you. Colton gatherings are famously awesome, and all I have on my agenda tonight is staring at the old water spot on my ceiling and watching my toenails grow."

Eli clapped him on the shoulder as they headed for the door. "Sorry, pal. Maybe another time. Get well and get back to the office. That's your agenda right now. We need you."

Several minutes later, as Noelle and Eli drove through the winter-darkened outskirts of Shelby, Eli angled a look at Noelle. He placed a hand on her knee and said, "I do remember that you're an introvert, and I know parties like this are not comfortable for you."

She flashed him a weak smile, grateful for that recognition.

"If it gets too much, tell me, and we'll go." He returned his gaze to the road. "I would like to stay through dinner, though, if that's okay."

She covered his hand with hers, a mellow comfort filling her, knowing he had her back and recognized her personal parameters. "Thanks."

When he turned off the main road onto a narrow private lane, she steeled herself. She could handle a few hours with Eli's family, one way or another. She owed him that much.

Once Eli had parked on the long driveway, already full of vehicles indicating the party was in full swing, Noelle gathered the loaves of bread. Eli carried his sack with several bottles of wine and the selection of cheeses as they climbed from his Renegade.

He held her free hand tightly as they approached the front door of his parents' home. The windows of the large two-story home glowed with golden light in the dark Alaskan evening like welcoming beacons. Eli gave a perfunctory knock on the door but didn't wait for an answer before opening it and ushering her inside.

Just as well he hadn't waited, because the volume inside reminded Noelle of being at a sporting event. Cheerful voices and laughter competed with each other in the crowded living room, and music, ABBA if she wasn't mistaken, played over all the hullabaloo. Noelle smiled, deciding the seventies' musical group fit with the artistic and bohemian vibe she'd gotten from Sasha Colton earlier in the week.

Will Colton spotted them first and drew first Eli, then Noelle into a warm hug of welcome.

"I'm so glad you came with Eli, dear! Can I take your coat and purse? We're just throwing them all in the back bedroom, if you need it before the party breaks up." Will took the wine and cheese from Eli and flagged down a man of approximately his same age. "Ryan, grab that bag from Noelle and take it to the kitchen, will you, bro?"

Noelle could see the resemblance between the older men even before Will addressed the man as *bro*.

Eli shook the man's hand, saying, "How you doing, Uncle Ryan? Good to see you."

Noelle and Ryan exchanged smiles and simple greetings as she handed him the bread. As she shed her coat and handed it over, Eli asked his father, "Is Lakin here yet? I want Noelle to be sure to meet her."

Will twisted his mouth as he thought. "She is. I believe she was in the kitchen with Dove the last time I saw her. They were putting all the food on plates for folks to snack on."

"Thanks." Eli placed a hand at the small of Noelle's back and ushered her past a trio of men who seemed deep in discussion about a recent hockey game.

"Why do you want me to meet Lakin especially?" she asked.

"I want you to meet everyone, but I think we should start with Lakin. Just...trust me."

Before Noelle could say more, he guided her into a busy kitchen where savory aromas filled the air. Several women, including Eli's mother, bustled about and chatted joyfully.

"Eli!" Sasha cried with a wide smile. "My hands are a mess, or I'd hug you!" She held her hands up to demonstrate the dark sticky-looking *something* she was kneading with her hands.

"Happy birthday, Mom," Eli said as he made his way to his mother to kiss her cheek.

Noelle stayed close behind him and added her birthday greetings.

A young dark-haired woman—Inuit, Noelle guessed from her skin tone and beautiful bone structure—tried to squeeze past Eli, saying, "Tuck your butt in, Eli. I need to get by you."

Instead, he turned to block her path more fully and waved a hand from Noelle to the now-frowning woman. "Let me introduce you first. Lakin, this is Noelle Harris. Noelle, my sister Lakin."

Noelle blinked once, her only outward show of surprise. She kept a smile fixed on her face as she nodded to Lakin and offered a hand to shake while in her chest a wild fluttering started. *This* was Eli's sister?

The questions began to roll through her brain like scrolling credits at the end of a movie. She had to intentionally quiet the noise in her head and focus on what Lakin was saying or else embarrass herself with her inattention.

"—so much about you. Please make yourself at home."

"I've heard about you, as well," Noelle returned. That was true, although Eli had never mentioned he had an Inuit sister. A previous marriage for Will or Sasha? Adoption?

Just then Lakin waved her arm, signaling across the room to a light-skinned Black man. The target of Lakin's attention strode in through the back door with Parker, who announced, "The bonfire is ready! BYOM...bring your own marshmallows!"

"Troy, come here," Lakin called. "I want you to meet Eli's date."

Noelle was still processing the moniker of *Eli's date*, when Lakin tucked her arm through the Black man's and lifted a starry-eyed gaze to him. "Noelle, this is my fiancé, Troy Amos. Troy, do you remember Eli talking about his college girlfriend, Noelle?" With her hand, Lakin gestured to Noelle.

Troy's face lit. "I think I do, in fact. Wow, hi! Are you two back together?" He waved his index fingers between Eli and Noelle, his expression hopeful.

While Noelle fumbled, her mind spinning, Eli answered, "That's still to be determined."

Working to keep her smile in place while her mind and her gut spun, Noelle said, "I take it that means you've known Eli and the family for a long time."

"Since I was ten and Troy was eleven." Lakin leaned into Troy, and he hugged her close to his side. "Eli was already in college, but he talked about you so much when he came home for the holidays and summer, I felt like I'd met you. Everyone heard about Noelle!"

An odd buzzing filled Noelle's head. *Everyone heard about her...* But what had he told them?

"Lakin, honey, will you let everyone in the living room know we are ready to serve plates, buffet-style?" Sasha asked.

Lakin touched Noelle's arm as she headed off to do her mother's bidding. "It was great to meet you. I hope we'll get a chance to talk more later."

"I, uh…yes. I'd like that."

Noelle had questions for Lakin. Or Eli. No, it had to be Lakin. She had to have a firsthand account of what life had been like growing up in this white family, how the Coltons had reacted to her Black boyfriend. Only Lakin could give her the sort of personal insight she needed to weigh the true inclusiveness and acceptance of the Colton family.

And then it clicked. *This* was what Eli meant when he'd said he had to *show* her how he knew his family would love and accept her. Perhaps he knew it wouldn't be enough for him to say they had a racially integrated family. He knew Noelle would want to experience the dynamic, see firsthand how seamlessly Lakin and Troy fit in the Colton dynamic.

A shrill whistle silenced the clamoring crowd that had made its way into the kitchen. Will waved an arm, and in a booming voice, he said, "Before we eat, I just wanted to say a few words about how blessed our family is to have Sasha. She's been more than just my best friend and loving wife for all these many years. She's been a guiding hand, a safe place to fall, a nurturer and encourager, not just to me and our children, but to my brother's family and anyone else that crossed our threshold for our entire marriage. Darling Sasha, I wish you the happiest birthday and many more years of love and happiness. To Sasha!"

"To Sasha!" The family applauded and whistled, and Noelle felt a swell of tenderness in her soul, even though she barely knew the honoree. The affection the family had for their matriarch was clear. Noelle longed for that sort of bond, the sort of maternal relationship she'd never had with her own mother.

Once Will had the group quieted again, he said a prayer over the food and the family, and the serving began.

Sasha put a hand at Noelle's back, gently propelling her toward the front of the line, "Noelle, please don't hang back. Guests get priority."

Her cheeks heated, awkward with the attention she drew as she was escorted to the front of the line. Eli followed, and Parker called out, "Hey, Eli, save us some!"

"Maybe," Eli teased as he moved up to the line of serving dishes.

After filling her plate with an array of delicious-looking food, Noelle followed Eli to a folding table set up in a corner of the living room.

"We outgrew the dining room table for combined family meals years ago. We just keep adding portable tables and folding chairs as my cousins and siblings add plus-ones to the mix. When the weather's nice, we spill out on the lawn."

"A crowded table is the best kind of problem," a beautiful biracial woman said as she set her plate on the table across from Noelle. Extending her hand, the woman said, "Hi, I'm Hetty Amos, otherwise known as Troy's sister and Spence's better half."

Noelle shook her hand, glanced briefly to Eli. "Spence?"

"My cousin," Eli said, aiming his fork toward the food line. "That's him piling potato salad on his plate."

Eli's equally striking and muscular cousin joined them at the small table, and Noelle goggled. "The Colton family certainly got more than their share of handsome genes."

Hetty grinned. "Right?"

Conversation turned to Hetty's work as a pilot for RTA and Spence's as an adventure guide for the family business.

"Hetty and Spence were the ones who discovered the first victim of the Fiancée Killer," Eli said.

Noelle raised a startled look to the couple. "Oh, my! How horrible."

Hetty nodded. "It was definitely a disturbing discovery on what was a disaster of a trip this spring." She gave a little shudder. "Can we not talk about that while we're eating?"

Spence guided the topic to Noelle's career. While Noelle was sure Spence knew who she was and about her past relationship with Eli, he didn't dwell on it, which Noelle appreciated.

"If you're Troy's sister," Noelle said, mentally making the connections, "then you've known the Colton family for a long time, as well. Is that right?"

Hetty nodded and consulted Spence with a glance. "About fifteen years now, huh?"

"Sounds right." Spence stroked Hetty's cheek. "But it's hard to remember a time when our families weren't close. Troy and Lakin were sweethearts from the start."

Eli snorted. "Which is more than can be said for you two." He turned to Noelle. "These two were about as close as two bulldogs with one bone. Their love language was sniping at each other."

Noelle looked to Hetty for a denial, but the bush pilot shrugged. "It's true. Spence used to irritate the heck outta me." Her expression warmed as she leaned toward her fiancé for a quick kiss. "Then I got to know him better and saw how wonderful he actually was."

Over the next half hour, as the family members finished eating, they moved one by one to either clean up in the kitchen, head outside to the bonfire or move to different tables to chat with someone new.

When Noelle and Eli pushed back from the table, he touched her hand and hitched his head toward the back of the house. "Let's go see the bonfire. They won't serve Sasha's birthday cake until a bit later in the evening. It's a tradition from back when we were kids, and she was trying to teach us about delayed gratification. We couldn't open our Christmas presents until everyone was up and we'd all had a big breakfast together, either." Eli rolled his eyes, silently expressing his opinion of his parents' rule.

Noelle laughed, while privately envying that Eli had

had holiday traditions and big family breakfasts. Christmases for her, once Allison grew to age four or so, revolved around watching her sister tear into a pile of presents.

Allison opened toys, candy and extravagances, while Noelle received a fraction as many items—socks and underwear, toiletry items, the occasional used book or hand-me-down puzzle from Allison. The message had been clear. *Your gift is merely being allowed to live with the family and have basic provisions.* To Allison's credit, she had noticed and had shared her less-favorite candy with Noelle. The gesture had meant a lot to Noelle, giving her an indication of some camaraderie with her sister, no matter how small. Those small connections, scattered throughout their childhood and teen years, were why Noelle was in Alaska now. She was compelled to perform one last act of respect and kindness for her sister.

As they passed through the kitchen on the way outside, Noelle spotted Lakin at the sink washing pans and glasses. Noelle changed direction, telling Eli she'd join him after she'd helped with the cleanup.

"You don't have to clean up. You're our guest," he said, motioning again to the backyard where raucous laughter and conversation echoed in the winter night.

Noelle waved him out, grinning her reassurance. "I'll be out soon. I want to help, though. Shoo!"

He leaned in to kiss her cheek—an action that didn't go unnoticed by his mother or sister—then caught his mother's hand and dragged her to the door. "Mom, you should not be on the cleanup team. It's your birthday, for Pete's sake. Come out here and howl at the moon with me."

Once Eli and Sasha had disappeared outside, Noelle took up a position beside Lakin, armed with a towel, and began drying the pans. She worked in silence for a moment, dredging up the nerve to address the topic that had nagged her since meeting Lakin earlier that evening.

Eli had made his point about the diversity in the Colton family and the loving welcome they'd extended the Amos siblings from the earliest days of their acquaintance. But Noelle still had specific doubts and a burning curiosity that only Lakin could resolve. She cast a side glance to Eli's younger sister. "Lakin, can I ask you a question?"

"You mean two questions?" Lakin shot her a teasing grin. "Because you just asked one."

Noelle chuckled. "Two then." She curled her bottom lip in as she dried a pot and mulled how to word her question.

When she didn't ask anything for a full minute, Lakin smiled and said, "Yes, Eli is every bit as nice as he seems. He was a typical big brother, giving me guff at times, but he was protective and funny and good to me, too. He's a great guy."

Noelle blinked at Lakin and frowned. "No. I mean… yes, I agree. And that's all good to hear, but that's not…" She cleared her throat and blurted, "What was it like being adopted by the Coltons? Did you always feel accepted and loved and…like you were really part of the family?"

Lakin's face grew serious, and her brow furrowed. She turned off the water and rested her hands on the edge of the sink as she angled her body to face Noelle more fully, her entire focus on Noelle. "Yes. Absolutely. They adopted me when I was three, and I have never felt anything but loved and safe and included. I am every bit a part of the family in every way. I was never treated as anything but a full member of the Coltons. In fact, Mom and Dad went so far as to tell me I was extra special, because I was the youngest, their only girl, and because they *chose me*." Now her cheek twitched in amusement. "A fact they told me to keep as my special secret so that the boys weren't jealous. But I heard Mom telling the boys reasons why they were extra special when she'd tell them good night, too. Eli was the oldest and most responsible. Mitchell because he knew his own mind and had the courage to follow his own path. Parker because he had a wild energy and passion for the outdoors that made him an asset to the family business." She heaved a contented sigh, her eyes reflecting the same joy as her smile. "They're great parents, and I've never had one doubt they loved me."

Noelle forced a smile to her face for Lakin's sake, but despite her best efforts, tears burned her sinuses. Before she could rein in her tears, one bloomed and seeped through her lower lashes.

Lakin put a sudsy hand on Noelle's arm. "Hey, what's wrong? Oh my gosh. Did I say something I shouldn't have?"

Noelle dried her eyes quickly and took a breath to regain her composure. "It's nothing you said. I'm…so happy to know you were well loved."

Lakin paused. "Wait. Kansas told me tonight that you are the sister of one of the Fiancée Killer's victims. All the victims have been white."

Noelle pressed her mouth in a taut line and nodded. She hesitated only a moment before confessing, "I was adopted. My mileage, so to speak, with the Harris family varied from yours. After I left for college, I saw no reason to go back to Anchorage. The Harrises were never a real home for me."

Lakin's face crumpled in sympathy. "Oh, Noelle! I'm so sorry. Geez, and here I was gushing about how great the Coltons are to me." She wrinkled her nose in regret. "Forgive me."

Noelle shook her head vehemently. "No, you did nothing

wrong. I asked, after all, and I wanted the truth. I'm glad they accepted you. It bodes well for me, if—"

Lakin's face brightened. "If you and Eli get married?"

Noelle gasped so hard she choked. Coughed. Waving a hand and chuckling, she croaked out, "Whoa. Slow down. We're not even dating. I just meant if—" she picked up a glass and started drying it without meeting Lakin's eyes "—*if* we were to get back together."

Lakin threw her arms around Noelle and squealed softly. "Oh yes! I would love that! And I know it would make Eli so happy. He really mourned losing you when you broke up. I don't think he ever stopped loving you."

Noelle returned Lakin's hug before pulling away. "Don't say anything to anyone about that. Not that they aren't all thinking it already, but I still don't know what's going to happen with Eli. We have things to work out, and... I have a life in Seattle. I'm only supposed to be here to handle the final arrangements for Allison."

Lakin's shoulders drooped, and her smile fell. "I promise. But for what it's worth, my vote is for you and Eli to patch things up and let yourselves be happy at last." She pulled a shy grin, adding, "It's been pretty awesome for me and Troy."

Noelle gave Eli's sister a warm smile. "I can tell."

Lakin faced the sink again and handed Noelle the last dish. "I think that's all the dirties until we serve the cake. Let's get outside before all the marshmallows are gone. The guys tend to use them for projectiles rather than dessert, and the puffs disappear rather fast."

Sure enough, when Noelle and Lakin headed out to the bonfire, small white blobs were being hurled around the yard to the amusement of the men. Some were caught in mouths, others caught by hand and lobbed again, a few tossed in the fire to become gooey, blazing kindling.

Sasha tucked Noelle's arm under hers and gave her a withering look. "I apologize for these ludicrous shenanigans, dear. Some things, boys never outgrow."

Noelle watched Eli duck a marshmallow thrown by Parker. In a smooth follow-up motion, Eli returned a puff by underhand toss to Troy, who caught it ably in his mouth and, cheeks stuffed with the sugary treat, grinned broadly.

"No apology needed. I love it." Noelle tugged Eli's mother closer, savoring the maternal connection. "They're having fun. Making happy memories. What could be better than that?"

Eli spotted Noelle then and hurried over, wrapping her in a one-armed hug as they stood beside his mother.

"I'm just happy the predicted storm front held off long enough for us to have a bonfire. The forecast says we're in for possible whiteout conditions and up to a foot of snow later tonight," Sasha said. As if to echo her statement, a stiff breeze crossed the yard, making the flames dance and stretch sideways.

Noelle snuggled closer to Eli and pinched her coat closed at the throat.

After the bag of marshmallows was depleted, the family eased into quiet conversations around the bonfire. Eli arranged two lawn chairs beside Kansas's chair and tugged Noelle over.

"Any news on Scott's whereabouts yet?" Kansas asked Eli quietly as Noelle was settling in her chair.

"Not really. Workin' on it."

"Hey," Will said, snapping his fingers and pointing at Eli and Kansas. "You know the rule at family gatherings. No business talk. Family time is for relaxing."

"Aye, aye, Captain!" Eli called to his father and cast Kansas an amused look and shrugged. "Have you been to see Asher today?"

Kansas looked reluctant to answer but finally gave a quick nod. "What if I did? He's been discharged from the hospital for about thirty-six hours, and *someone* needed to be sure he was following his doctor's orders."

Eli scoffed. "You say that as if I haven't checked on him every day since the accident. I even took him a pizza tonight and shrimp salad from the Cove last night," Eli aimed a finger at Kansas, "which, I have it on good authority, you helped him eat after I left."

"Maybe I did. What of it?" Kansas said with a note of lighthearted challenge.

Noelle listened to the cousins' banter while casting her gaze around the circle of chairs. Only Kansas wasn't paired up with a significant other. The affection between the Colton couples, young and old, snuggling against the cold, made her ache for that kind of forever connection with Eli. The smiles and camaraderie between siblings and cousins tugged at her heart while also raking her soul with claws of longing. Did Eli have any idea how blessed he was to have such a large, loving family?

"You're awfully cozy with Asher considering your ongoing feuds at the office," Eli said, continuing to tease Kansas.

Kansas lifted a casually dismissive hand. "I'm cutting him a break while he's injured. When he's back on the job, being a pain in my backside, I'm sure our relationship will revert to normal."

Before Eli could reply, the jangling of his cell phone interrupted the peaceful evening and murmur of conversation. Noelle jolted, having become so relaxed and at ease, that the strident tones sent a ripple of alarm through her.

"Don't answer it!" someone called, while others groaned.

"No phones!" Will grumbled when Eli pulled out his phone to check the caller ID.

Sasha put a hand on his arm. "It's okay, honey," she said calmly. "Our boy has important work. He has to stay connected."

Eli's screen glowed brightly in the night-darkened yard, and Noelle held her breath, as if sensing the call was bad news. Hadn't most of the calls *she'd* answered lately been something ugly or troublesome?

Pressing the phone to his ear, Eli answered with, "Agent Colton here. What's happened?"

In the light from his phone, Noelle studied Eli's face and saw the swirl of a few fluffy snowflakes beginning to fall. He grunted as he listened, and his brow furrowed. With an angry huff, he lurched to his feet. He paced away from the fire, toward the house, where he could take the call in private.

Noelle and Kansas exchanged worried looks.

"This doesn't bode well," Noelle said quietly.

"Unless it does," Kansas said, a hopeful note in her voice. "Maybe they've caught him. Maybe they've got a confession or located his car or…" She grimaced as if knowing her optimism wasn't likely to pan out.

Noelle gnawed her bottom lip and watched the back door for signs of Eli returning. When he didn't for several minutes, her concern grew.

Kansas, too, seemed restless, and finally Eli's cousin stood and signaled to Noelle. "Come on. Let's go see what's up. I'm sure it's not nearly as bad as we're imagining."

The women hustled inside and found Eli at the kitchen

table, his head bowed and his phone set on speaker as he talked to a male caller. While Eli took notes on a scratch pad, the man on the line said, "We've alerted teams in all the nearby districts to keep an eye out. They have full descriptions of all the principals and for the car."

"Good. Send some uniforms to the area and have every business in a one-mile perimeter pull up their CCTV recordings for the time around the sighting—no, make that the last twenty-four hours." Eli paused and frowned. "Damn it, go back as much as five days on every camera in the area since that's when he disappeared. He may have been casing the region and targeting this woman."

Targeting this woman?

Noelle heard Kansas muffle a gasp, and her own stomach dropped. Bile filled her throat. Had another woman been killed? The grave expression on Eli's face said that was likely the case.

He angled a glance to find them standing at the end of the table and rubbed the back of his neck with his free hand. "Look, I should go. I need to get to my office and dig into the matter from there, watch the footage for myself."

"I should tell you," the man on the phone said, "we're keeping an eye on this storm front that's moving in. It's ugly and getting here faster than predicted. Towns to our west are already reporting high winds and heavy snow. Our search capabilities will be severely limited within hours."

Eli sighed and scrubbed his face with his palm. "Understood. Keep me posted. All right? Anything and everything you learn, no matter how trivial it seems."

"You got it." The man disconnected.

Sighing deeply, Eli raised a dark gaze to Kansas and Noelle. "That was Bobby Reynolds." Eli's eyes shifted to Noelle's as he added, "He's a senior officer at the Shelby PD."

Holding her breath, Noelle nodded for him to continue.

"Witnesses reported what appears to be a kidnapping in a key shopping district downtown about two hours ago. A man grabbed a woman off the street and shoved her in his car before racing away. They're gathering CCTV footage from cameras in the area, but the description of the man and the car the two witnesses gave fit Scott Montgomery."

"Which if we're right about him," Kansas said, her voice hoarse, "means he could be about to kill again. Another victim of the Fiancée Killer."

Eli's jaw hardened, and his blue eyes grew flinty. "Not on my watch. Not if I can stop him." He gathered up his scribbled notes and shoved his phone in his back pocket. "Kansas, will you let the family know that the bad weather is ahead of schedule and roads will start getting bad soon?"

His cousin nodded.

"And see that Noelle makes it home safely? I have to go in to headquarters."

Noelle raised a hand to halt Kansas's response. "Forget that. You made me a consultant on the case. I'm coming with you."

Kansas edged toward the door to the backyard. "I want to help, too. I'm sure the SAR team will be put on standby any minute. As soon as I let the family know the weather update and tell Will and Sasha we're leaving, I'll be right behind you."

Chapter Eighteen

Because of the distance the senior Coltons' home was from town and the first wave of snow sticking to the roads, Eli, Noelle and Kansas didn't arrive at the ABI offices until forty-five minutes later. When they reached Eli's office, the light was already on, and they heard the low muttering of a male voice.

Eli raised an arm, stopping the women from proceeding until he poked his head around the doorframe.

Asher sat at his desk, on the phone with someone, and looked up when Eli stepped into the room. Asher held up a finger, asking Eli to wait a minute.

When he didn't signal any danger to the women, Kansas and Noelle crowded forward to peer past him into the room. Kansas gave a discontented grunt when she spied Asher.

"What are you doing here?" she fussed the instant he disconnected his phone call.

"Last time I checked, I worked here," Asher said, narrowing his eyes. "Why are *you* here?"

"Why shouldn't I be? Within a few hours, I can bet my team will be called out for a search and rescue for the woman that was taken."

Asher shifted his gaze to Eli. "So you heard about the abduction then?"

Eli nodded. "I'll handle it. You should be home recovering. Until we know more about who the woman was and where the guy took her, it's all office work. I can manage that, especially with Noelle as my sounding board."

Asher's eyes widened. "She's a sounding board now, too?"

Eli huffed his pique. "She's been through the files as meticulously as we have at this point. She's smart, logical, good with analysis, and her software could prove valuable again." He squared his shoulders. "You got a problem with me including her?"

Asher raised both hands. "Not if you think she can help. I'm ready to nail this bastard once and for all."

"So…" Kansas strode over to Asher's desk and pinned a narrow-eyed look on him. "Since Eli has Noelle's help, you can go home and rest. The doctor told you to take it easy for at least a week before you returned to work."

"You're not my nurse, my mother or my conscience," Asher replied, his own tone firm and somewhat irritated. "I can help here, and I feel fine. I'm staying."

Eli chuckled. "It's good to see your relationship back in form. I got nervous when you two were all friendly and concerned for each other's well-being."

Both Asher and Kansas sent Eli churlish glares.

Noelle made a T with her hands, signaling a time-out, and cleared her throat. "Um, folks, we have a kidnapped woman to find before she's murdered. Can we focus on that now?"

Instantly the mood in the room shifted. Sobered.

"Of course," Eli said, settling behind his desk and waking his desktop. "Who were you on the phone with when we came in? Is there any new information?"

"Not much. Reynolds at SPD says they have the footage of a couple security cameras from nearby businesses in their possession with more in the works. They're sending it via encrypted email as we speak. Check your inbox."

Noelle pulled the guest chair in front of Eli's desk around beside him for a better view of his monitor. Kansas did the same at Asher's desk.

The subject of Asher's recuperation, Eli noted, had been tabled apparently. He was privately glad to have his partner's help in light of the new turn the case had taken.

When his new emails loaded, the message from the Shelby police department had arrived, and Eli clicked through to open the attached video. Holding his breath, he watched the low-quality images play out.

When the man in the video hit the woman in the head and her body went limp, he heard Noelle suck in a sharp breath. His reaction mirrored Noelle's. His gut tensed as they watched the man, whose jacket hood was up and obscuring most of his face, shove the woman in the passenger side of a blue sedan.

Leaning back in his chair, Eli ground his molars together before casting a glance to his partner. "Correct me if I'm wrong, but doesn't Scott own a blue Hyundai Sonata?"

Asher's returned glare was dark and angry. "He does."

"Well, that's what we expected, isn't it?" Noelle asked. "That the kidnapper was Scott?"

"Doesn't make it any easier to accept that a guy you worked with and trusted could have betrayed you, the office and the public he works for," Asher hissed in disgust. "And he could be responsible for such heinous crimes." He slammed a hand on his desk. "Damn him!"

Kansas gave an exaggerated shudder. "Ugh! The guy *flirted* with me! Thank God I had the sense not to date a coworker."

A ripple of ill ease spun through Eli. He recognized the feeling as the same whisper when he was on the verge of a breakthrough. This edgy feeling had haunted him for several days, telling him he had all but one piece of an important puzzle. When he fit it all together, he knew he wouldn't like the picture he discovered.

He growled his frustration and impatience under his breath. Yet another woman had been taken. The kidnapped woman's life was in danger, and he had to think harder, destroy any stumbling blocks that might have him shy away from the truth.

"Do we know the woman's identity yet?" Noelle asked.

Kansas pulled out her phone and tapped at the screen. "I'll check with my team and see if we have any new missing person reports."

"No name yet," Asher said, still studying and replaying the video of the abduction. "Witnesses describe the woman as Caucasian, medium height, long dark hair, slim and attractive."

Eli hit Replay on the security footage, leaning close again to see what details he could have missed. "Well, the video confirms the witnesses' description anyway. But it's not much to go on." When Noelle mumbled something under her breath that Eli missed, he cut a side look toward her. "What's that?"

She twisted her mouth, hesitating. "I said, 'I bet we can guess her eye color.'"

A chill raced through Eli, and he fisted his hands as he realized the truth of her assumption.

"How's that?" Asher asked, a frown denting his brow.

Eli scrubbed a hand over his face and met his partner's gaze. "It's something Noelle and I realized a couple days ago when analyzing the information in the case files about the victims. They all have blue eyes. Dark hair and blue eyes."

"Which is a somewhat rare combination, statistically speaking," Noelle added.

Kansas jerked upright. "Wait. All of us Coltons have dark hair and blue eyes. Well, except Lakin."

"Who was adopted," Eli reminded her. "And you're right. Every other Colton has blue eyes and dark hair." He paused and sighed. "Including our Aunt Caroline."

Asher's frown deepened. "The one who was murdered when you were a kid?"

Eli nodded. "Exactly."

Kansas threw up a hand. "Hold on. The guy that killed Aunt Caroline and our grandparents also killed himself at the scene. That case has been closed for decades."

"True. But Scott is a forensic specialist. And evidence from his house proves he had accessed the case files from Aunt Caroline's death. The Fiancée Killer is copying elements of the crime."

The color in Kansas's face drained away, and Asher divided a look between Eli and his cousin. "What elements is he copying? What exactly happened to your aunt? And why didn't you tell me about this link earlier?"

"Because you were—are—on medical leave. You're supposed to be resting, not working," Eli said. "Besides, when we first made the connection, I wasn't sure it would bear fruit." He groaned. "Or maybe I was praying it wouldn't."

Asher scowled darkly, and Kansas leaned toward Eli. "So tell us now. It's clearly important."

Over the next several minutes, Eli and Kansas filled

Asher in on the thirty-year-old murder and how the family had tried to put it behind them, not speak of it and move on when they relocated to Alaska.

"So the engagement ring, the pose, the victims' similar physical description, the manner of death… Scott's copying your aunt's murder. But why?" Asher asked.

"Because he's sick," Kansas said with a sneer.

"True. But the last couple of days, Noelle and I have been working a theory that these murders, everything Scott is doing—" Eli hesitated, knowing how it egotistical his idea would sound "—comes back to *me* somehow. He's mocking me or getting revenge or something."

Asher sat straighter, then winced, and rubbed his temple. "You? How? Why?"

Eli elaborated on the details of being at the scene when Caroline was found, the very specific physical description and pose of the new victims, and his position in charge of the investigation.

"But… Uncle Will was with you when you found Caroline," Kansas said. "Could your father be the focus of all this?"

Eli twisted his mouth and shook his head. "More recently, Noelle's brake line was slashed, and she wrecked her rental car on the highway just outside of town. Noelle—who I dated in college and have been spending lots of time with in the past two weeks. Scott knows I care about her. What better way to strike at me?"

Noelle added, "My hostel was ransacked while I was out on Friday, as well, and the hard copies of the Fiancée Killer case files were stolen. We don't have proof yet, because the thief was careful to stay out of view of security cameras, but Eli and I are working on the assumption it was Scott."

"So…" Eli spread his hands, palms up. "Because I find

it hard to believe any of this is coincidence, the facts seem to point to me."

Noelle cleared her throat. "Again, people, we're on the clock. A woman's life is at risk, and we have a storm closing in. Unless there's something about your aunt's murder that will help us track Scott, we need to change direction here. We have to find this woman…" she pointed to Eli's monitor "…before she becomes victim six."

Chapter Nineteen

Eli pushed his chair back and stood up. "She's right. Let's move to the conference room where we have the maps that lay out where the other bodies were found. We'll compare that with what we know about Scott and look for a pattern, see what we can figure out."

Asher nodded, then winced again as he tried to rise from his chair. Kansas gave him an I-told-you-so glare before offering a stabilizing arm to help him limp across the hall.

"I'm fine," Asher repeated through gritted teeth.

The foursome gathered around the conference table where Eli spread the map that he, Asher and the rest of the investigative team had marked and labeled over the past months. A second three-dimensional map reflecting the topography of the region and the few existing roads and trails hung on the wall.

"Okay, what do we know about Scott? Does he have any properties where he could be staying now that his house is kindling? Are his parents alive? Any siblings?" Eli asked, a sense of urgency pumping through his veins.

"He never talked about family that I remember," Asher said. "But he isn't someone I shared personal stories with."

He glanced at Kansas. "You were friendly with him. What can you tell us?"

Kansas scowled at Asher. "I was polite to him, but I didn't encourage him, if that's what you're implying."

"I wasn't implying anything," Asher tossed back. "Why so touchy?"

Kansas folded her arms over her chest. "Oh, I don't know. Maybe because you're suggesting I had a relationship with our coworker, who has kidnapped a woman and appears to be a serial killer?"

Asher raised his hands. "I only—"

Eli loosed a shrill whistle to stop the tense exchange. "This isn't getting us anywhere. Save the lovers, quarrel for when we're off the clock, huh?"

Asher and Kansas both jerked offended looks at Eli, which he dismissed as he leaned over the map again. Kansas turned her back to the table and stalked over to the wall map with a huff, while Asher drummed his fingers on the armrest of his chair.

Noelle stepped closer to Eli and pointed to the last spot where a body had been recovered. "Consider this—the last two bodies were both found close to Shelby. One here at the Two Bears River hiking trail and more recently one here in the lot behind Shelby Fish Cannery."

Kansas turned to look over her shoulder with an odd expression creasing her face, then returned her attention to the wall map, studying it more closely.

The niggling voice in Eli's head was shouting now. What was he missing?

"It stands to reason Scott will pick a place near Shelby again," Noelle said, "especially since he knows we're onto him and the roads upstate could be getting treacherous.

Statistically speaking, the crime scenes are—" Noelle fell silent, her brow furrowing as she leaned closer to the map, her gaze and her finger moving from one marked crime scene to another, muttering, "Lake Chahoogee… Muskee Glacier Pass…"

Eli's heart beat a double-time rhythm. "Noelle? What is it?"

Noelle spun around to face Kansas, who was still gaping at the topographical map. "Kansas, at the hospital earlier this week, you said you conducted rescues at Lake Chahoogee and Muskee Glacier Pass, didn't you?"

Eli pivoted his chair to study his cousin as his gut churned. Kansas nodded slowly, her attention still locked on the wall map, her complexion gone pale. She raised a shaking finger. "And Two Bears River and the lot behind the cannery."

Like a gong sounding, the message his brain had been whispering now shouted to him. He bit out a curse and plowed both hands through his hair.

"What?" Asher asked, then, his face blanching, he muttered the same curse word.

Kansas slumped against the wall, looking like she might collapse any second. She sent her troubled blue gaze from Eli to Asher and back again. "Please tell me this is just a very freaky and disturbing coincidence."

Noelle sat heavily in the nearest chair. "What is it you just said, Eli? There are no coincidences?"

"Yeah. That," Eli said hoarsely and lifted a troubled look to Noelle. "Remember the other day when I explained that a law enforcement investigator's job wasn't to build a case but to gather information and follow where the evidence leads?"

She nodded, her expression glum.

"I broke that rule, despite my best intentions. I got side-tracked, blinded by thinking this was about me. But…" Eli shifted his gaze to his cousin "…it looks like *you're* the link, Kansas. He's copying your aunt's murder and leaving the victims, all women who match your general description, at places you've been on rescues in recent months."

"But…why?" Kansas asked, her voice cracking. "Wh-why me?"

No one said anything for a moment, but finally Noelle answered quietly, "You said yourself he's flirted with you, and you've rebuffed his advances. Maybe his interest in you grew into an obsession. If he was already unstable and had within him the ability to murder without compunction, maybe he thought killing the women would snag your attention."

Kansas gaped at Noelle, then Asher…then clapped her hand to her mouth and raced from the conference room.

Asher started to rise, but Noelle lifted a hand. "Let me."

Once Noelle left the room, seeking Kansas, Eli pinned a hard glare on Asher. "If we're right about this, if Montgomery is doing this because of an obsession with Kansas, he could come after her next."

Asher's jaw clenched, and his eyes darkened with fury. "Over my dead body."

"And mine." Eli took a calming breath. He needed to weed out his own turbulent emotions and think clearly. "He could be hoping this latest kidnapping will trigger a search and rescue that will lead Kansas to him. Hell, now that he knows we're onto him, he could have been planning to snatch Kansas tonight. Thank God she's been with our family all day prepping for my mother's party."

"So we're agreed she needs twenty-four-hour protection until Montgomery is brought in?" Asher said, his jaw rigid.

Eli exhaled. "Good luck convincing her of that. She might be freaked out over this turn of events, but she's strong-willed and independent."

Asher only grunted.

Eli cast a glance to the map again. "Okay, so we have a better idea of Montgomery's motive and possible future target, but we still have to find the woman he took tonight—before it's too late."

Chapter Twenty

Knowing Kansas was likely the driving obsession behind Montgomery's heinous crimes, Eli attacked the investigation with renewed vigor. The perspective that the women's bodies had been left at sites where Kansas had participated in rescues gave them more geographic focus.

With Kansas's help, they began reconstructing a map of all her rescue work over the past three years. The possibilities were mind-boggling. Kansas went on dozens of rescues every year, both close to Shelby and far out into the hinterlands of the Alaskan wilderness.

"How on earth do we pin down where he's going?" Noelle moaned, the frustration in her tone matching the tension and urgency pulsing through Eli.

He stroked a hand over his mouth as he studied the well-marked map. "Will you enter all these sites and run cross-references and the like with your analytics software?"

"I will, but it's going to take some time to get it all entered, and my laptop is still at your place," she said.

From the corner of his eye, he caught the curious look Noelle's last comment roused from Asher. He didn't have time to address his partner's speculations about his relationship with Noelle.

"I can't help but wonder, though..." Noelle said. She paused, biting her fingernail while her brow dipped in thought.

"Go on," Eli said. "All brainstorms are valid."

"Now that he knows we're onto him, he might have guessed we put together the reason behind the previous crime scenes, the link to Kansas's search sites. And if he doesn't want to be caught, then wouldn't he break that pattern? Are we wasting time with the SAR locations?"

"You may be right on that point. If so, that would bring the possible locations Montgomery could have gone back to...anywhere in the world," Asher said, waving his arm at the map, his tone dark with frustration.

The foursome exchanged tired looks. It was already late, and their general lack of progress clearly ate at them all.

After an extended silence, during which Noelle's gaze remained fixed on the map, she suddenly blinked and jerked her head up. "Oh my gosh. I've been doing it, too— making assumptions based on small bits of information."

Eli cocked his head. "Explain."

"We've...well, I've been assuming he's traveling by car because of the kidnapping footage. But look at this map! This state! So few roads. So many lakes." She divided a look between Asher and Eli. "Does Scott have a pilot's license?"

Eli frowned but immediately rocked his chair forward, his mind picking up her train of thought. "Asher, can you send out notices to every bush pilot and plane-for-hire operation in a hundred-mile radius? If he was going anywhere too far afield, he'd have needed help getting there. Meanwhile, I'll contact the FAA and state licensing board to see if Scott has a pilot's license or owns a plane we didn't know about." Eli glanced at Noelle. "I'll take you back to my place, so you can start entering this new information and cross-referencing."

"What should I do?" Kansas asked.

Eli exchanged a look with Asher, then back to his cousin. "You need to stay safe. Don't go anywhere alone. If you think of anything Montgomery may have said to you about his favorite places to visit or a vacation home or a relative's house he inherited, let me know right away."

Kansas frowned. "That's not what I meant!"

But Eli didn't stick around to hear his cousin's complaint about wanting to be more involved in the investigation. He grabbed Noelle's hand and led her to the elevator and out to his car.

A heavier snow had begun to fall, and Eli bemoaned the fact that as the snow accumulation grew, it would affect road and flying conditions enough to hamper any pursuit of Montgomery. In his head, the countdown clock to find the latest kidnap victim clicked faster. *Please, Lord, don't let them be too late!*

As he drove through the night-darkened streets of Shelby, Noelle looked up the phone number for the Federal Aviation Administration's closest office and dialed the number. When she reached their after-hours emergency operator, she put Eli on speaker. Within a few minutes of giving his credentials and explaining the situation, Eli had reached the right person to look for any records regarding Scott Montgomery of Shelby, Alaska. The agent promised to do the required research and call him back.

They'd been at Eli's house for thirty minutes, beginning the process of Noelle's analysis of the SAR sites, when they had a return call from the FAA source.

Scott did, in fact, have a pilot's license and had registered a floatplane with the FAA five years ago. Since floatplanes typically fly under eighteen thousand feet and in low-traffic areas, flight plans weren't required, meaning Eli had no way of knowing if, when or where Scott might have flown tonight. Eli thanked the FAA official and disconnected, his thoughts splintering in new directions.

"If he has a plane at his disposal, where does he keep it?" Noelle asked. "The plane would have to be kept on a lake or river, right? While there are any number of places he could moor a plane here in Shelby, that water would have to be near a road, even if just a dirt track or logging road, in order to get the kidnapped woman to the plane without anyone seeing him. Once he gets wherever he's going, he'd need a body of water to land the plane, too." Frowning, she pinched her nose. "Which really doesn't help much. There are lakes and rivers all over Alaska and Western Canada."

Eli nodded, squeezing his eyes closed, replaying everything he could possibly remember ever discussing with Scott Montgomery. Had they talked about the activities and sport challenges that Rough Terrain Adventures took customers on? Had they ever talked about vacation rentals or family holidays or travel or—

Eli's heart tripped as a shadowy memory of a conversation long ago wafted through his brain like smoke from a distant fire. Hobbies. Fishing. A lake. Barely there, but...

"What if we—"

He held up a hand, signaling for Noelle to hold her thought. "Just a second, I'm trying to remember the name of a place..." He snapped his fingers repeatedly as he dragged his memory for the name of the lake that was alluding him. "Run a search for a lake… Starts with a *G* or *G-R*."

Noelle turned to her laptop, her hand poised over the keyboard as she waited for him to give her more information to narrow the search.

"Graybill? Grandiose? Grundy?" Eli said, trying out names and discarding them. "Montgomery told me once he liked to fish at a cabin. The cabin was on private property by a lake called…" Eli groaned and tapped his fist against his forehead. "Think, Colton!"

Using what little information she had, Noelle began searching databases and Alaskan maps. "Grouse Lake? Grant? Grayling?"

The name danced just beyond his grasp, and he waved Noelle silent again.

Gr—.Gr—.Gofer? Gross—

"Grossford!" He swung to face Noelle. "Look up Grossford Lake. See if anyone named Montgomery owns a property anywhere near there." Eli went to the duplicate map he had on his dining room table and searched for Grossford Lake.

He found the small remote lake roughly one hundred miles north-northwest of Shelby and tapped it with his finger just as Noelle announced, "Bingo. Public records show that a Harold J. Montgomery bought a fishing cabin there in 1986. Could that be his father? Grandfather?"

"Don't know," Eli said, his jaw tightening. "But I'm sure as hell going to find out."

Eli stared out his living room window in dismay as the snow streamed down harder by the minute. The panes rattled as gusts kicked higher, and the storm quickly worsened to whiteout conditions.

Moving up beside him, Noelle sent him a worried glance. "How are we supposed to mount a search in this weather? Assuming we can find a pilot willing to fly us to Grossford Lake, will the FAA even let us take off in this storm?"

"Unlikely. We can only hope the weather has stalled Montgomery's progress as well. But bad roads and unfriendly skies or not, the woman with him is in peril." He bit down on his back teeth, grinding out, "This waiting is unconscionable when we know her life is at risk."

"I agree, but what can we do? Heading out in this mess by land or air is far too dangerous. We're just as likely to get stranded as not. We aren't any help to the woman if we get our car stuck in a snowdrift or get ourselves and a pilot killed in a crash in the process of chasing Scott down."

"I know. It just sucks!" Eli grimaced, and Noelle wrapped a comforting arm around his waist.

After another moment of staring at the swirling blizzard, Noelle asked, "Didn't your cousin's girlfriend, Hetty, say she was a pilot for your family's adventures business?"

Eli gave her a side look. "She is. Why?"

"Any chance you could convince her to take us to Grossford Lake?"

He shrugged. "I'm sure she would, but she's grounded during this mess same as official state trooper pilots."

"But state troopers could be tied up with weather-related rescues, medical emergencies and the like long after the storm breaks. But if we're watching the weather maps, and she's ready to go the minute the weather is clear enough to get airborne…"

"She flies a seaplane. We'd be constrained by the amount of ice on the lakes, both here and at Grossford. If the lakes are frozen—"

Noelle groaned. "Right. Of course."

"But she's licensed for helicopters, too, and RTA has a contract with a local helicopter rental company. Question is, would they sign off on her taking up one of their birds under these conditions, even if most of the bad weather has passed."

"So we continue to sit here and *wait*?" Noelle's tone mirrored the impatience and anxiety that wrenched his insides in knots.

"I'm afraid so. We can keep watching the weather maps and getting reports from the state troopers on road conditions, but even if we can drive north and get closer to Grossford Lake, we'll still need a floatplane to get to the cabin."

Eli turned back to his coffee table where the large paper map had been unrolled, the curling corners anchored with books. He stabbed the map with a finger. "This doesn't show any private roads or logging trails around Grossford, and it's the most up-to-date GPS-verified map the Alaska State Troopers have."

Noelle used a hair band from her wrist to tie her hair back in a ponytail. "I'll make coffee." She paused and faced him again. "Unless you think conditions won't change before sunrise, and we should try to get some sleep now? Be rested and ready for what may be a long difficult day tomorrow?"

She'd posed it as a question, down to the rising inflection of her voice, but he knew her well enough to know it hadn't been an inquiry. She was right, as she so often was. Nothing could be done tonight, while snow piled up and the winds howled.

And when he looked at her, her face free of makeup, her hair back and her eyes bright, waiting for his response, Eli couldn't think of anything he wanted more than to hold Noelle in his arms.

Whether they slept or not… Well, that was another matter entirely.

Chapter Twenty-One

The howl of the wind and shaking shutters outside Eli's bedroom window kept Noelle awake long after Eli finally dropped off to sleep. With his arms around her, his slow steady breaths against her cheek, she cuddled close to him under layers of bedding.

Some undetermined time later, she roused to the nuzzle of lips on her ear, toes stoking her calf.

Not a bad way to be woken, she decided with a jaw-cracking yawn. She rolled closer to his solid warmth and muttered, "What time is it?"

"Don't know. Don't care. Still dark." Eli's voice was thick with sleep and…lust.

His hand slid down her back to cup her bottom and tug her closer to him. In response, she hooked a leg over his hip and raised her chin so he could drop kisses on her lips.

Like a match to kindling, one kiss set them both aflame. He opened his mouth to hers and their tongues clashed and parried. Her hands found the draw string of Eli's sleep pants and untied it, roamed inside and earned a moan of satisfaction and contentedness.

Her limbs tangling in the sheets and blankets, she wrapped herself around him, taking pleasure in his every touch, until—

Eli's cell phone rang.

The sound sliced through their heat and doused cold water on their passion, a reminder of the outside world and the serial killer still on the run. When Eli hesitated for a heartbeat, giving every indication he might ignore the call and finish what he'd started, Noelle pushed him away. "That's bound to be important. Answer it."

Resignation and agreement filled his face, and he snatched his cell phone from the bedside table. "Colton. What's happened?"

The response came through loud enough for Noelle to hear a male voice say, "We have an ID on the woman kidnapped last night from Shelby. Her name is Grace Galloway, and she works at Rise 'N Shine, a bakery downtown near where she was taken."

Noelle stilled, her chest clenching. Rise 'N Shine was the bakery where she and Eli bought the bread they'd taken to Sasha's party. She remembered a pretty young woman with dark hair and gray-green eyes working behind the counter. Not bright blue like the Coltons, but apparently close enough for Scott when targeting the rare coloring in the small town.

"Her roommate called the police worried about her when she didn't come home on time and the storm broke," the voice on Eli's cell continued. "When they showed the roommate the security footage of the abduction, she made a positive ID."

Noelle's stomach flipped, knowing they were among the last people to have seen Grace Galloway before the kidnapping. Could Scott have been following them? Could the bakery clerk have been victimized because she and Eli chose to shop there? Was the kidnapping a sick way for the serial killer to taunt them? Her gut soured. She squeezed handfuls of bedcovers in her fists.

Her ears buzzed so loudly with the surge of adrenaline in her blood that she missed part of Eli's call.

Eli rolled from the bed, throwing back his bedroom curtains, despite his dishabille. "How are the roads? What's the latest on the storm? The radar show more coming?" He pelted the man on the phone with questions without giving the caller a chance to answer. "Have there been any new sightings? A ransom call?"

Knowing she'd not be getting anymore sleep—or sex—this morning and that a long day of hunting Scott Montgomery and hoping to rescue Grace Galloway had begun, Noelle crawled from the bed and headed for the shower.

She was done bathing by the time Eli stumbled into the bathroom, dropped a kiss on her lips and took over the shower stall. "Grab some breakfast and put some warm clothes on. I need to be at RTA in thirty minutes."

Rather than question him about the call, she got busy dressing, drying her hair and finding food in his kitchen with enough protein to stick to their ribs for several hours. Who knew when they'd get a chance to eat again?

Twenty-one minutes later, they were headed down the freshly plowed highway in Eli's Jeep, headed to the main office of his family's outdoor adventure company, Rough Terrain Adventures. Eli ate a protein granola bar as he drove. Noelle had stashed extras in her coat pockets for later. Based on what Eli had told her of his update from the state troopers, today could be a long, tense day...

The storm had quieted, leaving significant accumulation across the southernmost part of the state. Snowplows were busy clearing roads and landing strips, and lakes needed for seaplanes were being assessed for ice.

"No sign of Scott or Grace since the surveillance video," Eli said, giving her a rundown of his call, "but his car was found abandoned at a marina where both seaplanes and fishing boats are moored. We're working on the assumption that he got out ahead of the worst of the storm and could be almost anywhere upstate. State troopers are working a number of angles and sending searchers to several remote lakes, moving the search outward in an increasingly larger radius of Shelby."

"And you?" she asked, watching him stuff half of a snack bar in his mouth at once.

He chewed, swallowed. "I've arranged with Hetty to take me to Grossford Lake."

Dread slithered down her back. "Alone? What about backup?"

He cut a glance to her. "This storm has left law enforcement rather shorthanded and overstretched. And Asher can't—"

"Then take me."

Eli frowned and did a double take. "What! No. Hell no!"

Noelle grunted her affront. "Excuse me?"

His lips compressed for a moment as he exhaled heavily, his nostrils flaring. "Pardon my language, but I can't allow that."

Noelle angled her body toward him, tugging at her seat belt when it cut into her neck. "Why not? Hetty will be with the plane, and it only makes sense that you'll need someone to watch your back, be an extra set of hands, help with—"

"I don't want you in harm's way, okay?"

"But you're putting Hetty in harm's way. How is that different?" She folded her arms over her chest, challenging him with a hard stare.

"Because she…" Eli fumbled. He scowled and started

again. "You're not trained for this sort of thing. Can you even shoot a gun?"

Noelle huffed a humorless laugh. "I'm not saying I have to play cop and charge in with guns firing. I just don't want to be sidelined. I can be an extra set of eyes and hands in case they're needed."

The discussion continued until they reached RTA and found Hetty waiting.

Overhearing the ongoing disagreement, Hetty cleared her throat. "I know you didn't ask for my opinion, but I'm going to give it anyway. I, for one, would feel better having Noelle go with us. You may remember, I was in a bad position not long ago when extra help would have been welcome. You can't over plan going into an unknown situation like this, and I'd feel more comfortable if I weren't your only plan B."

Eli's mouth opened and closed as if trying to form a counterargument and falling short. He scrubbed a hand through his hair and divided a disgruntled look between the women. "Look, we don't have time to stand here and debate this any longer. We're already a day behind Scott, thanks to the storm." He pinned a stern look on Noelle. "You can go, *but…*" he aimed a warning finger at her "… you stay with Hetty in the plane. No heroics or putting yourself in the mix. I don't want you—"

Noelle took hold of the finger pointed at her and pushed it down. "Fine. No heroics. Can we go now?"

Hetty muffled a chuckle as she shrugged into her coat and marched toward the door. "Shall we ride together in your Jeep to the dock?"

THANKS TO A combination of high winds churning up the lake, a stint of warmer weather earlier in the week and overnight temperatures that stayed close to the freezing point, little ice had formed on the lake where Hetty moored the RTA seaplane. The lucky break meant they had little trouble with takeoff, but Hetty warned them conditions might not be as good at Grossford Lake. "No guarantees whether I'll be able to land."

Eli didn't like the news, but he knew Hetty was right. He sat in the copilot's seat, a headset allowing him to talk to Hetty and Noelle over the seaplane's engine. He gave Hetty a grim nod and peered through the windshield at the snowy landscape below them. "How long will it take to get to Grossford Lake?"

Hetty twisted her lips as she consulted her flight equipment. "Maybe an hour?"

Eli bounced his heel restlessly and nodded. "Okay."

As they traveled north, Hetty kept him updated on her reading of the conditions below. "So far so good. There is some ice at the edge of the lakes, but the sun is catching ripples, indicating movement on the water." She turned to look at him. "But also surface wind."

"Can we land?" he asked, cutting to the chase.

She hesitated but finally nodded. "I'll do my best. Grossford Lake is just up there." Hetty pointed out an area just to their left, beyond a low mountain.

As the blue-gray waters of the small lake came into view, Eli reached a hand behind him, casting Noelle a satisfied glance. "I see a floatplane tied up at a dock on the east shore. I think we've found him."

Chapter Twenty-Two

Noelle took Eli's hand and squeezed it, knowing that finding Scott was only the beginning. They had to bring him in…and pray he hadn't already murdered Grace Galloway.

"Hang on," Hetty said through the headset. "The winds are tricky. I'll do my best to set us down gently, but be ready for bumps and swoops."

Noelle swallowed hard and clutched Eli's fingers with one hand while her other grabbed the edge of the seat. She kept her gaze on the small dock until a cabin came into view, nestled in a copse of winter-bare trees and lodgepole pines. A thin line of smoke rose from the stone chimney, testifying to an inhabitant. When she pointed out this detail to Eli, he nodded, his mouth in a grim line.

"Remember, I want you to stay in the plane with Hetty. I don't want you anywhere near Montgomery."

Noelle lifted her chin. "Well, I don't want *you* anywhere near him, either, but here we are. I won't take unnecessary risks, but neither will I sit on my hands if a situation arises where you need help."

Eli frowned. "Our deal was you stay with the plane. Period."

"I agreed to no heroics, not staying on the plane."

Eli opened his mouth to argue, just as the plane dipped and lurched to the right. He braced a hand against the side door and cast a glance out the windshield, as did Noelle. They were hovering above the water, and Hetty was working hard to level the wings as they touched down on the glassy lake.

Once they were on the water, Hetty made a careful turn and pulled up to the dock opposite the floatplane that was already tied up.

Noelle ducked her head to better view the cabin, watching for further signs of life.

In the confines of the copilot's seat, Eli withdrew his sidearm and readied it. When he lifted his eyes to Noelle again, his gaze was hard and unrelenting. "Stay. Here." Turning to Hetty, he said, "Can you keep the engine on, ready to take off again quickly?"

She checked her fuel gauge. "I think so."

"And radio back to base for support. I need *armed* backup—" he gave Noelle a pointed look "—from whatever law enforcement agency can get here fastest."

Hetty nodded and put a hand on his arm. "Be careful. Your family will never forgive me for bringing you here if you get hurt."

Eli flashed a lopsided but clearly uneasy grin. "Careful is always the plan."

Noelle gritted her back teeth, choking back tears of fear and frustration. She did not like being told what to do, even if she knew why Eli had ordered her to stay with Hetty and the plane. But the directive chafed. She wanted to be useful, wanted to play a more active role in having Eli's back and wanted to decide for herself what level of risk she took to help bring Scott in.

"Eli!" she called, whipping off her headset as he climbed out of the plane and made the leap to the dock.

He turned back, pressing a finger to his mouth to signal for quiet.

Hetty chuckled as she opened her door, saying softly, "As if he didn't already hear us fly in and pull up here."

Noelle had been thinking the same thing, that Scott had to have been alerted and was now watching Eli from the cabin, but she said nothing. Eli had to be aware of as much himself.

Hetty climbed out, staying low as she looped ropes and straps to the dock that would keep the plane from drifting.

Noelle divided her attention, half of the time scanning the cabin for movement and the rest following Eli's progress. He moved quickly, his weapon raised as he hustled down the dock and onto shore. Shoulders hunched, he darted to the nearest tree—and barely reached the hardwood's cover before the first shot blasted from the cabin.

Noelle clamped a hand to her mouth to silence her scream.

Hetty scrambled back inside the plane, hissing, "Get down!"

She slumped lower, but Noelle kept her head high enough to keep Eli in her sights. If anything changed the current dynamic in Scott's favor, Noelle intended to race to Eli's aid, his directive be damned.

BARK SPLINTERED FROM an old-growth tree as Eli flung himself behind the wide trunk. His adrenaline pumping, he took a beat to catch his breath before he carefully turned toward the cabin without allowing any part of his body to protrude.

How many weapons did Montgomery have in the cabin?

And how good of a shot was the forensic scientist? Eli had taken top honors at the academy firing range, but Scott had the advantages of better protection and clearer line of sight.

After a moment, Eli pulled a small mirror from his coat pocket, the one he kept handy for signaling rescuers if he ever got stranded in a remote area. He angled the mirror to check the cabin windows. One of the windows nearest him was cracked open, and he spotted the dark shadow of a body standing just to the left side. The weak sun that leaked through the cloud cover glinted off the metal of a rifle barrel in the narrow window gap.

"It's over, Scott!" he shouted, knowing Montgomery could hear him through the window. "Lay down the rifle and come out unarmed, hands up. I don't want any more bloodshed." When he got no reply, he added, "If you surrender without resisting, it will go easier for you at trial. We've got you dead to rights, and this can only end one of two ways for you. Prison or the cemetery. Your choice."

"I'll take option C, thanks," Scott shouted back. "I kill *you* and walk out of here to live another day."

Eli gritted his teeth, remembering how his colleague, a man he had trusted, had rigged a bomb for him and Asher. "You already tried that once, and it didn't work." He considered what else he should say, how best to win Montgomery's cooperation. Antagonizing him would put Scott's back up, but the man was a scientist. Would logic work?

"Scott, listen…it may just be me here now, but a whole SWAT team is on its way." At least he prayed they were, storm conditions and workload notwithstanding. "You'll soon be outnumbered."

"Maybe soon, but not yet," Montgomery called back. "Right now, it's just you and me. I like those odds, and I'm playing to win."

NOELLE PEERED OVER the edge of the back seat, Eli still in her view. The shooting had stopped, and Eli was in a verbal exchange with Scott.

"What are they saying?" she asked Hetty.

"I don't know. My focus has been on trying to raise someone on the radio and call in some backup. Nobody's responding."

Noelle's heart scampered at the notion that any assistance Hetty might alert could arrive too late to help. Knowing she could do nothing to help Hetty with the radio, Noelle retrained her focus on Eli and Scott. A compelling need to know what was transpiring, what direction the standoff was going swamped her. How could she be of any use to Eli if she stayed huddled in the back seat of Hetty's plane like a lump of useless cargo?

While Hetty continued to appeal for backup, changing the radio frequency and repeating her handle and location, Noelle sucked in a lungful of courage and cracked the passenger door open. Climbing awkwardly from the back seat and earning a panicked frown and vigorous head shake from Hetty, she wiggled her way out to crouch on the dock beside the seaplane.

Noelle peered under the belly of the aircraft and decided she'd get a better view from nearer the nose and propeller. Staying as hidden as she could behind the landing gear and fuselage, she perked her ears over the hum of the engine to hear what was transpiring on shore.

"We can end this now, without further bloodshed, yours, mine or Grace's," Eli shouted. He paused, and in the lull, Noelle strained to listen for a reply. After a few seconds, Eli continued, "Yes, we know you have another woman in there with you. We know her name, and we want her released unharmed. Let's start with that as a goodwill gesture."

"Counteroffer," Scott shouted. "I trade you this woman for Kansas."

Noelle's gut roiled. So they'd been right about what, or rather who, was at the heart of Scott's crime spree. Poor Kansas. Noelle could only imagine how she'd feel if a sociopath had killed innocent women because of an obsession with *her*.

She thought back to the night at the ABI offices when they'd realized the connection. Noelle had tried to comfort and support Kansas in the ladies' room after Eli's cousin had fled the conference room in horror. Kansas had been pale and shaking, emptying her stomach in one of the ladies' room stalls. And though her disgust and dismay over the twist in the case remained as shadows in her eyes, Kansas had regained her composure in short order. Kansas, who faced difficult circumstances, rough terrain and occasionally gruesome discoveries on the job, was a model of strength and courage to Noelle.

Mustering some of that same bravery for herself, Noelle mentally searched for a way to gain Eli the upper hand. Could she create a distraction? Find him access to the cabin from another direction? Provide him valuable time for the support teams to get here?

She saw movement from Eli's post behind the large tree and peeked between the propeller blades to see what was happening. His gaze was on her, his mouth scowling darkly as he waved a hand, signaling for her to get back inside the floatplane.

Before Noelle could either signal back a refusal or follow his direction, Scott fired a shot from the cabin. The bullet carved a hole in the dock a few feet from where Noelle stood.

Then another even closer.

Eli returned fire, and Noelle plastered herself closer to the plane, adrenaline making her head spin.

"Noelle!" Hetty shouted, jolting her from her shock. "Get away from the propellers! I have to get the plane out of range!"

Noelle gaped, scuttling closer to Hetty. "You're leaving!"

"I have to! This plane will be of no use to us if he shoots the engine or punctures a float and sinks it!" Even as she shouted her reply to Noelle, Hetty revved the engine and restarted the propellers. She tossed a flare gun out onto the dock. "Use this to signal when it's safe to return. Now, untie me!"

"But—"

"Untie me! I have to protect the plane. I can't risk him hitting the gas tank or other parts critical to getting us out of here. I'll be back when I get the all clear."

Another shot hit the slushy water at the edge of the lake, sending up a spray of ice and pebbles. Noelle had no time to debate with Hetty. She had to trust that the pilot knew what she was doing. Staying crouched low, Noelle pulled up the ropes securing the aircraft, and immediately Hetty had the plane in reverse, backing into the open water.

Noelle scooped up the flare gun and stuck it in her coat pocket, then darted to the far side of the dock, next to Scott's plane as Hetty left. Her stomach rolled as she re-assessed her situation. The cold that washed through her had nothing to do with the weather and everything to do with how exposed she felt, how drastically the situation had changed and how furious she knew Eli would be with her for disregarding his directions. But then a new thought occurred to her.

Parts critical to getting us out of here...

If she could disable Scott's plane in some way, keep

him from escaping, she could buy the time Eli needed for backup to arrive. Huddling close to Scott's floatplane, she dug into her limited knowledge of aeronautics and the physics of airplane design. Jamming the propeller or rudder? Puncturing his gas tank? She looked about for something heavy and sharp enough to pierce the gas tank. A rock? Scrap metal? A tool? What if—

Behind her, she heard a shout, then a woman's panicked cries. She spun to find Scott coming out of the cabin with a dark-haired woman in front of him and a handgun to his hostage's temple.

ELI'S ATTEMPT TO stay calm and focus wavered when Scott started firing near the plane, where Hetty and Noelle were waiting. He'd believed Hetty's plane was the safest place for them, but now—

His composure dipped further when Hetty pulled the seaplane away from the dock and disappeared from the cove. He gnashed his teeth and let his shoulders drop in frustration. He'd wanted her standing by, ready to fly them off in an instant if needed. Yet when he considered Hetty's actions more practically, he realized she'd made the right move, protecting herself, Noelle and the plane.

Then he noticed a figure scurrying next to Montgomery's aircraft. *Noelle.* His heart added a beat, and he muttered a foul word. She hadn't gotten back in the plane before Hetty left? Why hadn't she stayed safe like he'd asked her, *told her* to?

But when had Noelle ever been one to follow someone else's wishes when she believed she had a better plan for her life? Certainly not when he'd wanted to continue their relationship after college. He set aside the pang of disappointment tinged with bitterness. Now was not the time to dwell on past hurts.

As if to prove Eli's last thought true, Montgomery shoved through the front door of the cabin with his hostage in front of him, a human shield. The woman's eyes were wide with fear, and Scott had a gun pointed at her head.

"Scott, damn it, man! Don't do this! Do you really think killing Grace or anyone else is going to win Kansas's heart?" Eli shouted.

Scott hesitated, glaring in his direction. "Maybe winning her affection is no longer my goal. We'll just see what happens once I have Kansas to myself, without any interference from you or Asher!"

"Let Grace go," Eli returned. "Any negotiation concerning Kansas starts with you letting your hostage go. She's an innocent in this. Can't you see clear to release her to me?"

Scott jerked Grace closer, making the woman whimper her fear. "No deal."

Eli growled his frustration. Where was his backup? Surely Hetty had reached *someone* before she moved the plane out of danger. He turned his attention briefly to the dock where he'd last seen Noelle.

She'd moved off the dock to the edge of the lake where she was scrounging around on the ground…for a rock? Did she plan to defend herself with a stone?

Eli took a breath to restore his control over his emotions. He had to stay focused. Not act rashly… "Scott, do the right thing," he said, mentally searching for an argument or tactic that would change the mind of a man who'd already acted without compunction in murdering five women.

Instead of complying, Scott dragged Grace across the snowy yard toward the lake. Toward his plane. Toward Noelle.

Eli pursued, knowing he couldn't fire on Scott without risking Grace's life. Or hitting Noelle. Damn it! Where was Hetty? How did he signal her to return?

He needed a plan. And fast. Or Scott would get away.

NOELLE FOUND A rock the size of her hand with a narrow end she thought might work to puncture the gas tank or a pontoon on Scott's plane. Glancing back to shore, she saw Scott and his hostage, her hands bound behind her, staggering through the snow, coming closer. Her heart beat triple time as she hurried back to the moored plane and smashed her rock on the pontoon as hard as she could. The reverberation of the strike sent painful judders through her freezing hand and up her arm. She swung again and made a dent.

"Hey!" Scott's angry voice rang across the frozen landscape. "Get the hell away from my plane!"

She angled her gaze to see him shift the aim of his weapon from Grace to her. She realized she was exposed, and her chest tightened.

A shot rang through the winter stillness, and she heard the ping of the bullet hitting the plane.

Scott clearly heard it, too, and realized his mistake. He cursed a blue streak and moved faster, all but carrying Grace as he hustled to the dock to rescue his getaway vehicle from Noelle's tampering.

She darted around to the far side of the aircraft, banking on the idea that Scott wouldn't shoot at her if it risked damaging his plane. Tucked behind the plane, she continued smashing the rock against the hull, anywhere she thought she could inflict enough damage to hinder its ability to get airborne.

When she felt the vibrations of heavy footfalls on the dock, she didn't have to look to know her time was up.

Scott was almost upon her. Soon he'd be able to kill her at point-blank range. Her gut swooped, and she choked back a moan of fear.

She'd drawn Scott's attention away from Eli, but now what did she do?

ELI SET OFF, retracing his steps in the snow as he raced after Montgomery. He weighed his options rapid-fire, needing to choose a plan of action. If he could catch up to Scott, could he tackle his opponent and free Grace? Or would that move cost Grace her life? The one thing he knew for certain was that he couldn't stand by and let Scott and his hostage escape. He had to find a way to subdue Scott, while prioritizing the safety of Grace and Noelle.

And the nearer the serial killer got to Noelle and the floatplane, the more both of those goals dimmed. Fueled by adrenaline, Eli pushed his legs to run faster.

AS SCOTT DREW CLOSER, Noelle backed toward the far end of the dock. She had nowhere to hide…except in the icy water under the dock. But could she do it? Could she make herself climb into the freezing lake? It wasn't a perfect solution, but it was better than staying here, waiting for Scott to shoot her.

Hearing a loud cry, Noelle shifted her attention to Grace Galloway. The woman had fallen, and Scott was struggling to haul her back to her feet.

"Get up!" Scott shouted cruelly to Grace, yanking her arm.

But the woman, whose hands were bound behind her, wobbled, her legs not supporting her.

Raising his gaze, Scott clearly spotted Eli's rapid approach and made a decision. In the next instant, Scott planted a foot in his struggling hostage's backside and shoved her into the icy water.

Hands tied, Grace sank under the surface, and Noelle gasped her horror. Without her hands free, how did Grace swim or tread water? How did the woman get out before her body shut down from the dangerous cold?

Where earlier Noelle had hesitated to go into the icy water to save herself, now her choice was clear. She charged to the edge of the dock, pausing only long enough to take her shoes off and pull the flare gun from her pocket. She fired one flare in the air, and seeing Scott glance her way, she fired the second in his general direction. While he dodged the sizzling rocket, she leaped into the water.

WHEN GRACE FELL, Eli gained ground on Scott. He was nearly on his prey when Scott dumped Grace into the lake. Eli sucked in a sharp breath, as if he were the one dunked in the icy drink.

He veered toward the side of the dock where Grace had sunk beneath the surface, mentally bracing to go in after the woman, when he heard the crack and sizzle of a flare firing. He jumped out of the way as one of the flares zipped close to him. Montgomery, too, had to scuttle out of the way, but he quickly recovered and, jerking free the straps securing his aircraft, he dashed toward the cockpit of his plane.

When Noelle jumped in the water near Grace, Eli's heart stopped for a moment. A strong tug pulled him toward the lake, demanding he go in after both women. But Scott was getting away.

Noelle's head broke the surface, and she swam closer to the drowning woman.

"Noelle!" Eli shouted, toeing off his boot, readying to dive in.

"Go! S-stop him!" Noelle shouted back, sputtering from the icy lake water.

With one boot on, Eli raced toward the seaplane. He fired at the cockpit, then dropped to his stomach when Scott returned fire through the open cockpit door. From his prone position, Eli squeezed off two more shots as the propeller of the small plane started turning. The engine revved, and the plane moved slowly away from the dock.

Gritting his teeth, Eli sprang to his feet. He aimed for the gas tank and fired again. A small stream of fuel started leaking from the bullet hole. But that wasn't enough to stop Scott or the floatplane's departure.

Without stopping to debate his choice, Eli ran to the edge of the dock and leaped onto the closest pontoon, grabbing a stabilizing bar connected to the wing.

Montgomery, obviously having felt the jolt as Eli landed on the plane, aimed another shot in Eli's direction.

Eli ducked, dropping to a crouch and losing his grip on his gun as he fought for his grip on the slippery bar. The floatplane bobbed and waggled as Montgomery accelerated across the lake, preparing to take off.

Eli's unbooted foot slipped, and again, he struggled to cling to the plane and stay on the float. How fast would the fuel tank empty? How far could Scott get before he ran out of gas?

And how the hell did he get inside the passenger door without Montgomery shooting him? Eli grimaced as icy cold spray, kicked up by the pontoon, hit his face. The changing sounds of the engine told Eli Scott was nearly ready to lift off.

Eli tightened his grip. But as the aircraft lifted from the lake, Scott dipped his passenger-side wing once, then again, clearly trying to shake Eli off. The third time he dipped the wing, Eli's foot slipped again, and he came perilously close to sliding off the pontoon.

Eli had a choice to make. Cling on and risk his life in one reckless attempt to get in the plane with Scott and stop him…or jump off before their elevation made such a feat a fatal drop.

With a sinking sensation in his gut, Eli knew his only real choice was to let Montgomery get away and save his own life in order to fight another day. Shouting a blistering word of frustration, Eli leaped from the float.

His arms windmilled, and he arched his back, trying not to pitch forward. He lifted his arms over his head as he reached the lake, making his body as pencillike as possible as he pierced the surface.

The icy cold hit him like a sledgehammer, and he mentally shifted into survival mode. He had to swim to shore, get out of this frigid water before hypothermia claimed him.

Chapter Twenty-Three

Noelle gasped for air as the icy lake stole her breath. A thousand needles pricked her as she kicked her legs, struggling with the weight of her saturated coat and clothes. She forced herself not to think about how painful the cold water was or what was happening with Eli and Scott. She had to focus instead on reaching Grace. The sooner she got Grace out of the lake, the sooner they could both get warm and dry.

Forcibly shutting out the drone of the seaplane's engine, she goggled at how hard it was to move in the freezing water. Her limbs were leaden. She seemed to be swimming through sludge. With numb fingers, she tugged at her zipper and peeled off her coat. Once free of the encumbering weight, she kicked her feet and stroked her arms as best she could to reach Grace. The panicked woman's eyes found Noelle's as Grace sank under the surface again.

Noelle slid her arm under Grace's and kicked harder, struggling under the burden of Grace's weight dragging them both down.

Noelle was finding it harder and harder to breathe, the icy chill sapping her energy. *Just get her to shore...*

Turning her head toward land, Noelle estimated the distance to be no more than fifty feet. As she swam, increasingly more of a flail than a productive stroke, she began to realize the distance might as well have been a mile. She wasn't making fast enough progress, and both she and Grace were becoming still and stiff as the cold lake chilled their cores.

Fight. She heard Eli's voice in her head as if he were standing on shore shouting to her. *Don't quit. Survive. Live for me.*

The pain that wrenched inside her now came from a longing for a future with Eli. Here, splashing helplessly in this freezing Alaskan lake, the yearning crystalized for her. She'd wasted years on foolish fears. Eli was nothing like her mother and father. Sasha's party had demonstrated that Eli's family was the complete opposite of the one that had rejected her. Pushing him away had been the biggest mistake of her life and had caused her more pain than it had spared her.

Regret and frustration churned inside her. But rather than draining her, her new understanding mobilized her. She clenched her teeth, determined not to fail Eli again. Not to fail Grace, or herself, in this moment. No matter the pain in her arms and legs, no matter the effort, she *would* get out of that water and bring Grace with her.

Grunting with the strain, she hauled Grace up until the other woman's head was above water and shouted, "Kick, Grace! With everything you have, kick!"

The woman's feeble effort was enough to keep Grace's head up as Noelle rolled to her side and did the best side-stroke she could under the circumstances. But they were moving, drifting closer to shore. Slowly, inch by inch.

ELI WAS FAR from shore, and every kick as he tried to swim to shore told him he'd wrenched his ankle when he hit the water. The numbing cold stung so fiercely he found it hard to draw air in his lungs, but he kept moving, kept stroking his arms toward land.

When a droning sound reached his ears, he checked the sky for Scott's plane. Had the bastard circled around to come back and shoot him? Instead, the low rumble was at ground level.

Eli blinked as he attempted to wipe icy water from his eyes. *Hetty! Thank heavens!*

Hetty pulled alongside him and tossed him a line to grab. With her help, he climbed from the water onto the float-plane, then moved stiffly onto the copilot's seat.

"Kinda cold today for swimming, isn't it, Eli?" Hetty quipped.

"Much, much too c-cold," he replied, his teeth starting to chatter.

"I saw the flare and was on my way back to pick you up when I saw your acrobatics…or whatever you call that derring-do you just performed." Hetty sent him a worried look as she drove the plane back toward the cabin.

Eli squeezed his eyes shut and shook his head. "I call it a failure. Montgomery got away."

He heard Hetty grunt. "You're lucky to be alive! I call that a success. I've radioed local authorities and given our location—Montgomery's location and aircraft ID number—to the ABI. At last report, a team from Fairbanks is thirty minutes out."

"Good." He returned his gaze out the window, his body shivering and his nerves strung tight as he strained to see ahead of them. "Can we go any faster?"

He'd left Noelle in the water to rescue Grace by herself. But as he learned himself moments ago, the frigid lake could hamper normal capabilities surprisingly fast. When they finally reached the dock by Scott's cabin, he found Noelle and Grace mostly back on shore but still lying in shallow, ice-crusted water.

He stumbled out of the floatplane as soon as it was near enough the dock for him to make the leap. When his foot landed, a sharp pain in his ankle reminded him he'd not survived his drop into the lake unscathed. But an ankle ache was not going to stop him from getting Noelle and Grace inside the cabin to warm up.

Once Hetty secured her plane, she was right behind him, racing down the dock to wade into the shallows.

Noelle raised her beautiful brown eyes to him as he approached, and, her chin quivering with cold, she stuttered, "S-Scott-t-t?"

He squatted beside her, shaking his head. "He got away." He hooked his arms under hers. "Can you stand?"

"T-t-try."

Working together, Eli and Hetty dragged, supported and carried the women into Scott's cabin.

A fire still smoldered in the grate, and though his hands were shaking from his own hypothermia, Eli fed the embers and stoked a blaze. Glancing at Hetty, who was helping the women strip out of their wet clothes, he called, "See if you can find anything hot for them to drink."

He shucked his own wet coat and shirt as he turned up the cabin thermostat and went in search of blankets, towels and dry clothes. He found enough of the first two, but no clothes. Scott hadn't prepared for his trip north, clearly. But the cabin had a washer and dryer, and while Eli, Noelle and Grace wrapped themselves in blankets, Hetty started a load of wet clothes in the drier.

As they huddled by the fireplace, catching their breath and towel drying their hair, Grace burst into tears.

Hetty, the most mobile of the group, hurried to put an arm around the frightened woman. "Hey, you're safe now. You're going to be okay."

"H-he said h-he was going to k-kill me. He was w-waiting for someone named K-Kansas." Grace swiped her face with a cold-reddened hand. "Someone h-has to warn h-her! K-Kansas…"

Hetty sent Eli a wide-eyed look of horror.

Eli gave the trembling woman a nod. "We know. Kansas knows." He paused as a shudder raced through him. "That rat bastard won't get anywhere near her if I have anything to say about it."

"How d-do we find him now?" Noelle asked, her voice thin as she shivered. "It seems un-l-likely he'll come back h-here now that he knows w-we know about it."

"His fuel tank was leaking fuel. He'll have to land somewhere soon." Eli looked to Hetty. "Any guesses how far he could make it?"

Hetty gave him a withering frown. "Hardly. Too many unknown factors. How much fuel did he have to start with? How fast is the fuel leaking? What sort of tailwinds or headwinds will he encounter? Did he—?"

"Okay," Eli said lifting a hand. "I get it." He scrubbed a hand over his head, mussing his hair. "Damn it! We were so close to bringing him in!"

Noelle ducked her head. "It's m-my fault he got away. Isn't it?"

Eli's pulse jolted, and he cut a sharp look toward her. "What?"

"No!" Hetty said. "Don't you dare take this on yourself."

"If I had stayed in the plane like Eli wanted—"

"You wouldn't have been there to save Grace from the lake," Eli finished for her.

Grace nodded, her movements still stiff and choppy as she sniffled. "You s-saved my life. You *all* did. Th-thank you so m-m—" The young woman dissolved in sobs again, and Hetty rubbed her back.

Noelle wouldn't meet his eyes, and Eli said, "Hey. No-elle, look at me."

She angled a dubious look at him. "I thought I could do more to help. I wanted to stall him…or distract him…or—"

Eli moved to squat right in front of her, his ankle protesting. But Noelle mattered more than the throb in his ankle. In a low voice meant only for her, he said, "Listen to me. If you'd stayed in the plane, Scott would still have used Grace as a human shield. I still wouldn't have had a clear shot of him. He would still have gotten to his plane. He might have still pushed Grace in the water, or he might have taken her with him. We don't know. But what you did, tampering with his plane, distracted him enough that I got close enough to at least make an effort to stop him." He pressed his lips in a frown of frustration at the reminder of Montgomery's escape. "If you'd been at the other end of the lake with Hetty, though, you couldn't have gone in after Grace."

"But you would have," she said, correctly. "You'd already started to."

He sighed, scowling as he acknowledged a hard truth. "And either way, Scott still escapes. So you—"

"I was still too stubborn," she said, her voice stronger now as she cut him off. Tears bloomed in her eyes. "I was too determined to do things my way, thinking I somehow knew better. But I was wrong. Again. Like I was in college. I should have listened to you. I—I should have trusted you more!"

Eli flinched. "In college? What are you saying?"

She drew a long, slow breath and cupped his face with hands that were at the same time freezing cold and a balm to his heart. "I'm saying I made a mistake. I should never have left you. Should never have shut you out."

Eli furrowed his brow, startled by her change of topic. His pulse pounded so loud in his ears, he could barely hear his own voice asking, "A mistake?"

When the women's heads all lifted, their gazes darting toward the cabin door, Eli realized the thrum in his ears had drowned out another noise. Someone was outside the cabin.

Chapter Twenty-Four

Noelle heaved a huge sigh of relief when the men outside the cabin identified themselves as from the state trooper detachment from the Fairbanks office. A medic with the responders checked her, Grace and Eli, and though they all would need further treatment and checks once they arrived at the hospital in Fairbanks, they were all doing remarkably well under the circumstances.

Grace was showing signs of shock. Eli had a sprained ankle. And Noelle had a huge case of guilt, despite Eli's attempts to assuage her regrets. She needed time to process her feelings and talk to Eli alone, and neither looked likely to happen soon.

Eli stayed behind, returning to Grossford Lake to take charge of the state troopers as they continued the search for Scott. Noelle, having signed a waiver refusing further medical treatment once she'd gotten warm and dry, accompanied Hetty back to Shelby.

Having gotten snippets of information about what had transpired at Grossford Lake, a large representation of Coltons, plus Asher, awaited Noelle and Hetty at the RTA offices.

Kansas was among the first to rush to Noelle and wrap

her in a hug. "Good grief, Noelle! You don't do things by half measures, do you? I'm not sure how you translated 'case consultant' to mean 'risk your life saving a hostage,' but kudos to you for your bravery!"

Noelle flashed a sheepish grin. "I'm not sure how you translated 'foolish stubbornness' to mean 'bravery.' But, no, I'm not known for holding back. I'm headstrong to a fault, and…" she choked as a bubble of emotion rose in her throat "…and Eli has paid the price of that stubbornness and fear for too long."

Kansas took her by the arm to pull her away from the clamoring family. "Hey, are you okay? What does 'Eli's paid the price' mean?"

"I saw it so clearly today, everything I'd been trying to hide from, but I'd only been hurting myself and Eli instead." She sucked in a deep breath, not wanting to cry in front of Kansas and the other Coltons.

"Noelle?" Sasha said, stepping over from where she'd been clustered with Troy and Lakin, listening to Hetty recount their day. "I promise I wasn't intentionally eavesdropping, but did you say Eli was hurt? Is that why he's not with you?"

Noelle mustered a smile to calm Eli's mother. "He's fine. Well, mostly. A twisted ankle." She summarized how Eli had stayed with the phalanx of state troopers and local searchers to hunt Scott, and Sasha shook her head.

"Lord, protect my young man," Eli's mother said under her breath before meeting Noelle's gaze squarely. "And you… Noelle, dear, you look worn out. Can I get you anything? Food? Coffee? A quiet room with a pillow and blanket?"

Noelle chuckled, even as moisture filled her eyes. "All of the above. And…the last thirteen years back to do over again the right way?"

Sasha squared her shoulders and took hold of Noelle's hands. "Oh, my dearest. I wish I could do that for you. But the important thing is, whatever you wish you could change about the past can still be a lesson for today. Go forward living the way you want the next thirteen years to unfold, whatever that involves. Forgive whoever needs forgiving. Love whoever needs loving. Change whatever needs changing."

Noelle, her throat too tight with unshed tears to speak, nodded hard. She flung herself into Sasha's arms and clung to the woman who'd been a better mother to her in a few days than her birth and adoptive mothers had been her whole life. And in the woman's comforting arms, she felt optimistic about the future for the first time in far, far too long.

NOELLE DIDN'T HEAR from Eli that night or for most of the next two days. She rattled around his empty house, feeling like an intruder. She began to worry that something had gone awry with the hunt for Montgomery—or her relationship with Eli—that the Coltons were keeping from her.

She'd checked in with Kansas, Sasha and Asher on a regular basis over the last fifty-six hours and was assured Eli was fine, just busy upstate with the search. Noelle wasn't convinced that was all there was behind his ghosting her. Was he staying away, knowing she was in his house?

She thought about the grim expression he'd worn in Scott's cabin as they'd warmed themselves by the fire. Hetty had tried to absolve Noelle of any fault for the way things had unfolded. But she couldn't help but feel a dark, angry vibe from Eli.

She was sure he blamed her for Scott's escape, no matter how he'd dismissed her explanations. The dour slash of his mouth as he contemplated Scott's getaway hadn't eased for a moment. Even her admission of wrong regarding their past had yielded a heavily lined brow and a querulous expression.

Was she too late in recognizing the error of her ways? The notion sat heavily on her chest. Not even Sasha's and Kansas's reassurances could lift her from the funk that hung over her, waiting for Eli's return to Shelby and time alone with him to make amends.

During the same two-plus dreary days, however, she *did* hear from both the interim coroner appointed to take Scott's place and the funeral home director. Both men reported to her that Allison's body had finally been released for burial. The funeral could be held in the next day or two. Afterward, Noelle would have no excuse not to go home to Seattle.

Though she'd finally have closure on that front, she longed for the chance to talk with Eli and set things right with him.

When she still hadn't heard from Eli by the evening of the second full day back in Shelby, she packed her few belongings and moved to a small motel room near her former hostel. Noelle had heard from Sasha that Eli had returned to Shelby just hours after she'd vacated his house, but he'd continued his radio silence. Telling, Noelle decided.

The next day, the day of the funeral, she donned the dress she'd packed more than two weeks earlier, thinking she'd only be in Shelby for a couple of days, and prepared her suitcase to leave. As she checked out of the motel, she put her bag in the rental car, ready to drive to the Anchorage airport that afternoon after the funeral. She'd booked a seat for the red-eye back to Seattle for that evening.

Holding her head high and bracing for the likelihood

of another confrontation with Aunt Jean and Uncle Clyde, Noelle drove to the small church where she'd arranged the funeral service. When she arrived, she was stunned to see a large number of vehicles in the church parking lot. She dismissed her surprise, reminding herself Allison likely had many friends, and the funeral home had printed the funeral announcement in the Anchorage paper.

Taking a deep breath and smoothing her skirt, she made her way into the church's chapel, where her second surprise of the day awaited her.

The crowd assembled for Allison's funeral was overwhelmingly comprised of Coltons. She blinked as her gaze drifted from face to face—Lakin, Troy, Mitchell, Dove, Kansas, Parker, Sasha and Will—and on and on. Row after row. A show of family support unlike anything she could have ever imagined. Even Asher had come. Her eyes filled with tears, and a bittersweet stab of longing pierced her chest. Because the one face missing was Eli's.

In the front row, Kansas waved to her, indicating the empty seat she'd saved for Noelle. Walking numbly to the pew, she glanced at the coffin, draped with a simple but lovely flower arrangement. *Oh, Allison! I'm so sorry for what you suffered because of Scott.*

Noelle sat beside Eli's cousin and dabbed at her damp cheeks and runny nose with her gloved hand.

Kansas pulled several tissues from a box printed with the funeral home's logo and handed them to her. "We wanted you to know you're not alone today. We care about you."

"Thank you. You can't possibly know what this means to me." Noelle forced a tremulous smile, belatedly realizing how difficult it must be for Kansas to be there, knowing Scott had killed his victims due to his twisted obsession with her. One more reason to respect and admire Kansas.

As they settled in for the service, Kansas put a reassuring arm around Noelle and gave her shoulder a squeeze. The warbly music of a small electric organ played, signaling the start of the service, and the minister walked out from a door beside the choir loft.

"Dearly beloved, thank you all for joining us today as we remember Allison—"

The door at the back of the chapel thunked as a late arrival entered. Noelle was blowing her nose and gathering her composure when the latecomer settled into the seat beside her. She glanced up, and her heart jolted.

Eli.

The minister continued, but Noelle only half heard the words spoken as she studied the man sitting beside her. He gave her a tepid smile, before facing the pulpit, more evidence of his pique with her, and she worked to hide her disappointment.

He smelled good. Of pine and ocean and frosty air, as if the very essence of Alaska had been bottled just for him. His cheeks showed raw spots where he'd clearly just shaved and nicked himself, and his hair was still damp from a shower. He wore a well-tailored dark blue suit that fit him perfectly and emphasized his broad shoulders and lean physique.

But for all his fine features, she saw signs of fatigue and worry and wear. His eyes were shot with red, as if he hadn't slept. Tiny lines radiated from the corners of his mouth and smudges of blue-black shadowed beneath his eyes. His lips were chapped and peeling, and his cheeks and nose bore witness to time in the winter sun and bracing wind. Most telling to her was the sag of his posture. He seemed beaten down. Worn out. Defeated. And her heart ached for him.

Turning her attention back to the service, Noelle restlessly twisted the clean tissue in her hands...until Eli's hand covered hers. He laced his fingers with hers. Squeezed. Noelle cut a quick look to him, and with his face inscrutable, he gave her a small nod.

She held tight to his hand, her heart breaking, as the minister said a prayer, eulogized Allison and led the congregation in a closing hymn. When the funeral director motioned for Noelle to follow the casket out as it was wheeled to the waiting hearse, she refused to let go of Eli's hand. Instead she tugged him from his seat. Snagging both his coat and hers from the pew, he fell in step next to her.

Once outside, while the casket was loaded for the drive to the cemetery, Eli helped her into her coat, then wrapped Noelle in his embrace.

"Can we talk later, after the burial?" he whispered and kissed the top of her head.

"I—I don't know."

He backed out of the hug and gave her a puzzled look.

She dropped her gaze to the ground. "I'm leaving town right after the burial. I fly out of Anchorage at six."

"You're leaving...*today*?" He took a step back as if punched in the gut. "But..."

"I thought it was best if I—"

"Best for who?" he said bitterly, his volume loud enough to attract the attention of the funeral home staff. "I thought we'd gotten past this...this delusion of yours that you were somehow better off alone! Do my wishes not count for anything?"

She looked up at him, her brow pinched. "Of course they do! That's why I made a reservation to go home! To get out of your way!"

He huffed loudly and tugged her by her arm to stand away from the crowd of mourners emerging from the church. Melting snow crunched under their feet as they crossed the churchyard. When he stopped and faced her, irritation and—was it panic? desperation?—lit his bright blue eyes. "Tell me, please, what I have done or said that makes you think for *one second* that I don't want you here?"

She lifted her chin, battling back the sting of tears and flurry of self-doubt. "It's not what you said so much as what you haven't. For the last three days! I've been worried sick about you, and if not for reports from your family, I'd have gone nuts thinking you could be hurt or…or d-dead! Why haven't you answered any of my texts or calls?"

He groaned and chuckled without mirth. "Oh, Noelle. You have been gone from here a long time, haven't you?" He cupped her chin and stared deep into her eyes. "One, this is Alaska, not Seattle."

"Meaning?"

"Cell reception is sketchy at the best of times, and in the part of the state where I've been the past three days, it's nonexistent."

Her mouth tightened. "But you talked to your family."

"I reached Kansas through the SAR and ABI satellite phones and shortwave radios, and she relayed messages to my mother and the others as I asked."

Noelle blinked, lowered her gaze, though his palm still gripped her chin. "Oh."

"Oh," he repeated. "Second, I've been *a little* busy tracking Scott the last few days." He arched an eyebrow to highlight his understatement. "I've had *maybe* seven hours of sleep in the last sixty, and the only reason I'm here in Shelby instead of up north still looking for Montgomery is I was determined to be here for you when you buried Allison."

Eli's face blurred as tears puddled in her eyes. She tried

to choke down the tears, but the constriction in her throat made swallowing difficult and talking impossible.

"So, let's try this again. Why are you leaving?"

She opened her mouth, struggling to make some sound, but before she could, he added, "And don't go with the easy answer. Don't tell me you have a job and a house in Seattle. I want the truth. The real truth. Why are you *really* leaving?"

Pain slashed deep to her core, because she knew the answer. Fear. She'd thought she'd moved past feeling scared about giving Eli her whole heart and trust. Yet the minute he didn't—couldn't—answer her texts, she let the doubts creep back in.

Love and trust have to be unconditional.

Sasha's words from last week sounded in her head like a gong. What was she doing? She couldn't run away again, couldn't shut Eli out of her life and hide like she had thirteen years ago. If the past weeks had showed her anything, they'd proven her fears had been unwarranted. Eli's love had remained true. His family had proven warm, accepting and supportive. Hadn't they all showed up for her today to love her through her grief?

"Ms. Harris, we're ready to go when you are," the funeral director called to her.

Eli's eyes narrowed on her. She hadn't given him an answer yet. But he deserved more than an answer. He deserved a demonstration of her love and full commitment.

She did a quick mental calculation, then turned to the funeral director. "Please go ahead. I'll meet you at the cemetery in a little while."

The man gave a nod and turned to go.

Eli was frowning when she faced him again. "Come with me. Please." She started back across the churchyard, but Eli didn't. She turned back and found him scowling, clearly unhappy with her lack of response. "Please," she repeated, and he trudged toward her, then followed her back to the church steps.

Eli's family was filing out of the church and heading to their respective cars. Feeling a confidence and rightness that kicked up her pulse, she waved her hands over her head and shouted, "Excuse me! Can I ask that you all reassemble inside for a moment?"

Turning back to Eli, she said, "I'll be with you shortly. Have everyone take a seat again."

"Noelle, what's going on? What about the burial?"

"We'll go. Soon. I just need a moment..." She waved him inside, then hurried to the edge of the parking lot where she pulled out her phone and checked for a signal.

ELI GRITTED HIS back teeth as he moved back into the church and sat in the front pew where he'd been for the funeral. What was Noelle's plan? Why couldn't she just give him a straight answer? If she was leaving him again, this time he *would* have the truth from her. *If* she was leaving him? He snorted and balled his hands in his lap. Hadn't she just confirmed that she was flying out of Anchorage tonight? Once again, he'd let himself fall for her only to have the rug jerked out from under him.

He could only blame himself this time. How did the saying go? *Fool me once...*

"Do you know what this is about?" Parker asked as he settled in the pew next to Eli.

"No," he answered tightly, not bothering to hide his frustration or disappointment in his tone.

The church door thumped shut, and his family fell silent as Noelle marched to the front and stood before them with her shoulders back and her chin high. Despite her body language, Eli read anxiety in her gaze as she cast her eyes toward him.

"Thank you for staying just a few moments longer. I need to be going soon to the cemetery, but first... I wanted you all here to be witnesses... I mean, I wanted you all to share..." She buzzed her lips in exasperation. "I'm already blowing this. Eli, will you come up here?"

He glanced to Parker, looking for confirmation he'd heard Noelle correctly. His brother waved a hand, motioning he should go.

Fatigue and achy muscles dragged at him as he joined Noelle at the chancel railing.

She took a deep breath and said in full voice, "As I look around this little church, full of family and friends and flowers, I can't help but think it would be a nice place to have a wedding."

A murmur rippled from the pews. Eli tipped his head and fixed a curious look on Noelle. Had he heard her correctly? Suddenly blood was pumping through him so hard and fast he could barely hear her over the whoosh in his ears.

"Eli, I have no excuse for the heartache I've caused you these last many years. Nothing I can do will erase that hurt. The choices I made after graduation are my biggest regret."

He opened his mouth to reply, to tell her she was forgiven, but she placed her fingers over his mouth, adding, "But... I'm not finished."

A few chuckles from his family twittered in the sanctuary.

"I'm asking you for the opportunity to go forward with a clean slate." Noelle swallowed hard. "I'm asking you for a second chance, and...and I don't take my request lightly or without offering you long overdue assurances. Today, in front of your family, I'm pledging you my full, unconditional love and trust." Noelle cut a quick glance to the pews, and Eli followed her gaze to his mother, who beamed and nodded.

Noelle cleared her throat. "I want to spend the rest of my life making it up to you and showing you how deeply I love you."

Eli's body grew still, and he dared not breathe for fear he was dreaming.

She took both of his hands in hers and got on one knee. "Eli Colton, I want to come back to this church in a few months and marry you. Will you be my husband?"

He sucked in a gasp—or maybe the sharp sound of an inhale came from his family. He couldn't be sure, because he was numb. Dreaming. So damn tired he was hallucinating.

Except Noelle was down on one knee. Looking up at him with wet eyes and a hopeful expression.

After some awkward amount of time, Parker stepped up beside him and poked him in the ribs. "This is the part where you say yes."

Eli exhaled and pulled Noelle to her feet. He felt the prick of tears sting his eyes as he framed her face with his hands and kissed her soundly. "Hell yes, sweetheart. Absolutely, yes."

Epilogue

One week later
Thanksgiving

Eli sat back in his chair and put his hands on his stomach with a happy groan. "My compliments to the cooks, one and all. Everything was delicious!"

"Hear, hear!" Troy said, lifting a glass and leaning over to give Lakin a kiss on her cheek.

Noelle chuckled and said, "This is the first Thanksgiving I've celebrated in about four years, since my friend Emma moved out of state, and I think I made up for it in one sitting."

"Not so fast! We still have pies," Eli's Aunt Abby said, rising from her chair across the room at another table and waving Spence and Parker back to their chairs.

"What if we save the pies for later and have them with coffee this evening once we've…well, digested for a while?" Will asked.

"Yeah," Eli replied, "what Dad said."

A round of voices in agreement lifted from one end of Will and Sasha's home to the other. The scrape of chairs followed as people began to depart the tables for other activities.

Aunt Abby stood at her place and called to the family. "Hey, hey, hey! Where are you going? We may be saving pie for later, but after the past year we've had, both the good and the bad, I feel it is more incumbent upon us than ever today, this Thanksgiving, to give our thanks for our blessings."

Sasha stood as well. "I agree."

The Colton siblings and cousin exchanged glances. Nobody seemed prepared to defy the matriarchs on what, in past years, had seemed a somewhat cheesy tradition. This year, Eli and his siblings, cousins and significant others shared glances and nods that affirmed they were eager to share their gratitude with the group. One by one, the younger Coltons and their partners sat back down.

"I'll start," Mitchell said, his posture and booming voice reflecting his comfort speaking to a courtroom. He stood and beamed at Dove, who was at the table beside him. "First and foremost, I'm thankful for Dove and the life we have together."

The family clinked their forks and applauded in support and agreement.

"And I'm thankful for you, love," Dove replied.

Troy shot to his feet. "I'm grateful that Lakin is officially my girl and that we're planning our wedding."

More cheers erupted, but Troy held up a hand. "And… I'm thankful the renovations on Suite Home are back on track after the delays the snowstorm caused."

"Ditto!" Lakin said with gusto as she stood and lifted her glass. "And of course for you." She gave Troy a kiss and sat again.

Across the table from Noelle and Eli, Kansas stood, and she took a deep breath as she glanced from one face to another. "I'm grateful for my family, every last wild and wonderful one of you. And I'm grateful that Eli is back safely from looking for Scott Montgomery and that Grace Galloway is alive and well." Her voice cracked, and Eli saw the strain Kansas had been under these last few weeks in the creases around her eyes.

As Kansas sat back down, the family clapped and voiced their agreement in a more subdued manner. Abby placed a hand on her daughter's shoulder and spoke softly to her. Kansas offered her mother a wan smile.

Spence rose to offer his gratitude, but the discussion faded to background noise as Eli leaned across the table to say quietly to Kansas, "Thanks for that."

"I meant it," Kansas replied. "I don't know what I'd do if I lost you or A—" She cut her words short and frowned. "I feel bad enough that Scott is doing all of this because of me."

"No." Eli reached across the table to take his cousin's hand. "*None* of this is because of you. One hundred percent of the blame is on Scott's head. Do you hear me?"

Kansas sighed but finally nodded. "I hear you."

"And hear this, too," he said, squeezing her fingers before letting go. "I promise you, if it is the last thing I do, I will see that Scott Montgomery is caught and that he pays for his crimes." He glanced to Noelle, who was listening to the exchange. "I promise you both. This isn't over. Asher and I will get that bastard, and he will pay."

When Noelle winced, Eli tipped his head. "What?"

"I only just got you back. When Scott was shooting at us, I was more scared of losing you than getting hurt myself. I just…don't want you in the line of fire again."

Eli stroked a hand down Noelle's face and pressed his forehead against hers. "I'll be careful. I swear."

"Eli? If we can drag you away from your lovely lady

for a minute," Parker called across the room, "I think it's your turn."

Eli leaned back, moved his napkin from his lap to his plate and pushed his chair back.

Before he could stand, Noelle rose to her feet. "I'd like to go next if you don't mind. Because I have to tell you all how much I appreciate—no, that's not a strong enough word—how much I treasure all of you. You have welcomed me to this family in such a warm and loving way. I've never had this. Family support. Inclusion. Acceptance. Love. And… to gain a family like yours in addition to finally being with the man who stole my heart years ago—" Noelle paused and chuckled. "I've won the love lottery. That's how it feels. So thank you all, so much for letting me be part of your big, incredible family."

A boisterous cheer rang from the ceiling and walls, but before she took her seat, Noelle added, "And I am most thankful this year for Eli and for second chances." She bent to give him a deep kiss on the lips, whispering, "I love you so much."

"The feeling is mutual, sweetheart. You are worth the wait."

Scott Montgomery lay on his lumpy air mattress, his flashlight his only illumination in the Alaskan wilderness. He shone the beam on the only picture of Kansas he'd salvaged before he'd blown up his house. It was his favorite shot, one he'd taken with a high-power lens on his camera. She was completely at ease in her home, unaware that he was watching from a few blocks away. He'd had to cut down a couple bushes and some branches to have a clear line of sight, but it had been worth it.

He'd seen so many candid moments of Kansas's life

through the years through that window. Mornings in her nightgown, evenings when she ate dinner alone, weekends as she practiced yoga, even times she clearly thought no one could see her as she danced and sang with music he couldn't hear. Her uninhibited moments, when she was most vulnerable, were the ones that stoked the fire in him. Catching a glimpse of unguarded moments...

Planting a microphone in her house should be next on his agenda. First, he had to lie low for a few more days, allow his trail to go cold, before he resumed his observations of Kansas and found a new way to get her alone. Once he had her alone, under his power, in his control, he could win her over.

He clicked off the flashlight and allowed his senses to focus on the sounds and scents just outside his makeshift shelter. This would be his last night shivering in the cold, he promised himself.

One week ago, he'd watched from a vantage point on the next mountain ridge the moment the state troopers had found his abandoned plane. They'd swarmed over it like ants on dropped bread crusts at a picnic, Eli among them. After that, Scott had hidden in the frozen hinterland, staying one step ahead of search teams for long, miserable hours.

But tomorrow, he'd steal a car or a floatplane and go somewhere well outside Eli Colton's and Asher Rafferty's purview. His beard had filled in, changing his appearance at least a little. He hadn't maintained his anonymity as the Fiancée Killer for three years without having some skill for staying hidden up his proverbial sleeve. Then, in a week or so, he would shift his plans into the final stage of execution.

But not yet. He'd give the authorities a little time to realize he'd truly gotten away, let them relax their vigilance...

Then he'd step up his plans to bring Kansas to heel. Enough of her baseless rejection. They belonged together. He'd lied for her. Waited for her. Killed for her. The time had almost come. Soon Kansas would be his.

Very soon.

* * * * *

COMING SOON!

We really hope you enjoyed reading this book.
If you're looking for more romance
be sure to head to the shops when
new books are available on

Thursday 18th December

To see which titles are coming soon, please visit
millsandboon.co.uk/nextmonth

MILLS & BOON

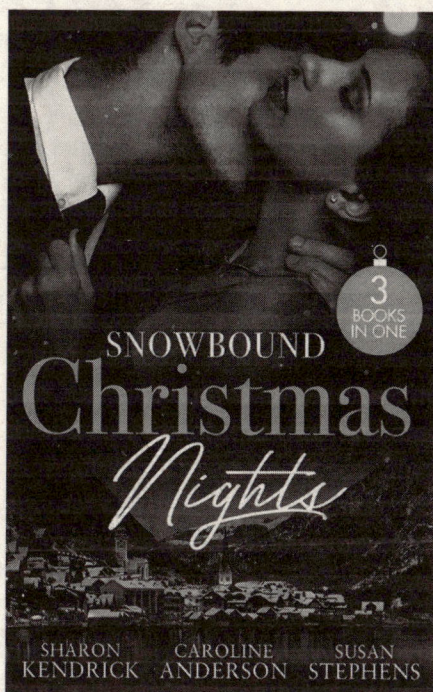

LET'S TALK

Romance

For exclusive extracts, competitions and special offers, find us online:

- **f** MillsandBoon
- **X** @MillsandBoon
- **O** @MillsandBoonUK
- **♪** @MillsandBoonUK

Get in touch on 01413 063 232

For all the latest titles coming soon, visit
millsandboon.co.uk/nextmonth